WILD EMBERS

IVY KING

HEARTLEAF PUBLISHING LLC

Wild Embers
Published by Heartleaf Publishing LLC

Editing by Sav Dee - Flor and Forma Editing
Cover Design by Mayonaka Designs

Formatted with Vellum

To the souls who love and mirror my own -
dance in your wild embers

PLAYLIST

Falling by Trevor Daniel
Last Night by Morgan Wallen
Play with Fire (feat. Yacht Money) by Sam Tinnesz
Cravin' by Stileto & Kendyle Paige
The Man Comes Around by Johnny Cash
Wild Horses by Bishop Briggs
Erupt by Stileto & AViVA
What I Want by Morgan Wallen & Tate McRae
July by Noah Cyrus & Leon Bridges
1950 by King Princess
Therefore I Am by Billie Eilish

TROPES & CONTENT WARNINGS

Tropes: why choose, suspense, age gap, dad's best friends, cowboy romance, morally gray characters, dark romance, return to hometown, romantic suspense

Content Warnings:
Animal abuse/injury (not explicitly described)
Arson
Child Abuse and Molestation (implied/off page)
Death by Suicide (not on page, briefly recapped)
Emotional Abuse (not by main characters)
Graphic Descriptions & Scenes
Injured Animals (no animals were killed fictionally or otherwise in the production of this story)
Murder
Nightmares
PTSD & Flashbacks
Sexual Abuse (implied/off page)
Stalking (the morally gray kind and the bad kind)
Suicidal Thoughts (no attempt)

Torture
Violence

*Please keep in mind that this book contains MF, MFM, MMF, and MMFM

PROLOGUE

BLAKE – 7 YEARS OLD

I keep my mouth clamped as I wait for Daddy to come back. He left my room in a huff with Walker, Levi, and Santigo, Daddy's best friends.

They were all talking really loud. Levi sounded scared. Santi sounded mad. Walker was yelling.

It hurt my ears. I'm glad they left. But now I'm home alone because Mama's at work tonight.

I don't like being alone when it's dark outside.

Throwing my fluffy purple blanket over my head, I hide. My breath makes it hot, but no one can get to me here.

The creak of the front door makes me bring my legs to my chest and wrap my arms around them. Footsteps thump down the hallway, and I bury my face in my knees.

Daddy's back. But I don't want him in my room.

Squeezing my eyes shut, light from the hallway brightens my room.

"Blake?"

That's not Daddy.

Ripping the blanket off my head, my hair falls on my face, but I know who it is. I know that voice.

Walker stands in the doorway. Levi and Santi are right behind him. Levi looks like he might cry. Santi won't look at me.

"Walk?" I push the strands away. "Where's Daddy?"

"He'll be back later." Walker comes in, sitting on the edge of my bed.

Levi kneels on the floor in front of me. Santi quietly closes the bedroom door before leaning against it with his arms folded.

They look sad.

Walker keeps rubbing his hands together. Levi keeps swallowing hard. Santi's jaw looks funny, like he's biting his teeth together.

Why are they sad? Did Daddy say something mean?

I feel my mouth frown. "He left?"

Why would Daddy leave me?

"Don't worry about it." Walker shakes his head.

"Do you know when he's coming back?" I ask again, moving my legs so I'm sitting crisscross.

Walker sighs. "I'm not sure."

My shoulders feel heavy. "Do you think it's safe to get Mr. Bear?"

"Where is Mr. Bear?"

I look down at my lap. "He's hiding under my bed."

Levi reaches beneath the bed. "Found him." He dusts Mr. Bear off before carefully placing him in my lap.

I hug him close to my heart. "Thank you."

Walker tilts his head. "Blake, why was Mr. Bear under the bed?"

I don't want Walker to be mad. I don't like it when grown-ups are mad. "I'm sorry if I made you upset. I'm being good to him, I promise. You, Santi, and Levi gave him to me, and I love him."

Walker shakes his head. "I'm not upset, and I know Santigo and Levi wouldn't be either. I just want to know why Mr. Bear was hiding."

My throat feels tight as I answer, "He's afraid."

"Of what? You can tell me."

I roll my lips and confess, "Daddy."

Nobody says anything. When I look up, Santi's hand covers his mouth.

Mr. Bear doesn't like Daddy. It's my biggest secret, and I've never told anyone before.

Walker still looks sad as he says, "He doesn't have to be afraid of him anymore."

Levi sets his hand next to mine in the bed. "Neither do you."

Santi moves closer to my bed and kneels beside Levi. "We're going to keep you safe."

Blake, 23 Years Later

A VOICE over the intercom thrums. "Delta flight twenty-three fifty-one to Jackson Hole has been delayed."

Of course, my flight's delayed. Just my damn luck.

This is what I get for traveling at the last minute. But I didn't have a choice.

I packed so fast that I'm not sure I grabbed enough underwear, or if I brought the right clothes for where I'm going.

The only thing keeping my eyes open is the crappy hot coffee in my hand. The LED lights and the rumble of my fellow travelers are too much for my brain after a night of no sleep.

Sitting in the uncomfortable airport seat, I pull out my phone and read the texts I received from an anonymous sender.

Unknown: You left Evergreen Falls behind, but Evergreen Falls didn't forget you.

Unknown: When's the last time you checked on your mom, Walker Maddox, Levi Harding, or Santigo Ramirez?

> Unknown: If you don't return, you won't like what happens next. And I don't recommend sharing this with anyone.

Rubbing my eyes, I smear the makeup I haven't taken off from the day before. I tried replying to the texts, but I kept getting an error message.

Whoever this person is, they knew just what to say to get me to go back to the one place I swore I'd never step foot in again.

Home.

CHAPTER 1

BLAKE

My shoulders shake as I rub my arms, hoping to get some feeling back in my frozen limbs. The bitter morning chill bites at my skin as I sit in my rented Jeep Wrangler, inconspicuously parked in the Riverbend Trailer Park. My thick parka does little to keep me warm, and my eyes fight to remain open after a long night of surveillance. The engine of my car struggles as the heater works overtime to keep the frost out.

Across the trailer park, a dog barks at the late morning haze, and a generator hums to keep the lights on. A rusted wind chime clinks somewhere nearby, the sound drifting on the icy breeze. Thin columns of smoke sail from trailer chimneys, disappearing into the gray Wyoming sky.

Outside, the roads are thick with ice, and there's a layer of snow over everything else. The clouds block the sun, turning the world a shade of gray.

Another cheery winter day in Evergreen Falls, Wyoming.

My arrival went exactly as planned.

Unnoticed.

But that's the only thing that's gone right since I got here.

My plan to decipher the not-so-cryptic messages and find the perpetrator has gone nowhere. Either I haven't watched enough true crime, or I have seriously overestimated my skills.

Reaching into the passenger seat, I grab my sketchbook and charcoal pencils. This is the only thing that has kept me sane—sketching. It's not my oil paint and brushes, but it will suffice.

We used to live in a small neighborhood on Mill Creek Drive—long driveways, picket fences, and green lawns. After Daddy died, Mama moved us into this trailer. I thought Mama and I would lean on each other, but she chose the bottle instead.

I quickly outline the small home and begin adding the details.

There's the dent next to the door where Mama hit the trailer with her car when she drove home drunk one night while I was in high school.

The rusted metal siding that has gotten worse in the last twelve years.

The curtain-covered windows that Mama never let me open because the sunlight was too much for her eyes when she was hungover.

Once I've added shading, I write in the top left corner, "Monday morning, River Bend Trailer Park."

I'm not sure which home I hated more. The dirty trailer or the nice house on the cul-de-sac.

Both contain memories I've tried to forget.

As I set my sketchbook aside, the trailer door opens and out walks Mama.

The bags under her eyes are heavier than they used to be. Her ivory skin looks as if it hasn't seen the sun in years. Her almond-brown hair has become brittle. Her clothes look as if they don't keep her warm at all.

She hops into Daddy's old pickup. The engine sputters before catching, then she eases the truck onto the road.

Right on schedule.

Her routine hasn't changed. Every other day or so at this time, she drives to Fall River Market to buy a plastic bottle of cheap whiskey. Occasionally, she buys herself a few grocery items, but it's not the food that she runs out of first.

At least I now know where the money that I send her every month is going, but I hope I'm wrong.

Passing Evergreen Supply and Timberline Bar, Mama steers her vehicle into the grocery store parking lot as I trail a short distance behind her.

Tired of the banal routine, I continue down the empty road toward the outskirts of town where Moose Gap Lodge, my motel, is located.

I need a shower, a warm blanket, and a nap. Not in that particular order.

I'm only a minute from Moose Gap Lodge when something bright and red dances in the distance outside my driver's side window.

Slamming on my brakes, my Jeep slides to a bumpy stop on the slick ice. When I turn toward the crimson shape, I squint. It's so far away in a barren field that it's barely a few inches tall, but my mind immediately knows what that is.

Fire.

This isn't right.

It's too early in the year for this to be a farmer burning their field.

I make a sharp turn onto a dirt road, speeding toward the flames.

Not my smartest move, but this is the first suspicious thing that's happened since I got here.

As I get closer, the pyre gets bigger. I'm less than thirty yards away when I'm finally able to make out a figure in the fire.

A *human* figure.

Shit.

Throwing the gear into park, I don't even take time to turn off the engine. My stomach contracts into a tight ball when I realize the person in the fire is draped on a cross like a scarecrow.

And they aren't moving.

I grab handfuls of snow and rush them over to the base of the stake. As I drop the snow in an attempt to douse the flames, my face turns pink from the heat.

Repeating the method multiple times barely makes a dent.

I pant heavily, the cold creating its own type of burn in my lungs. A bead of sweat trickles from my hairline down the side of my face from exertion. My gloves are wet from the snow, causing my fingers to throb.

Defeat and exhaustion weigh on my shoulders.

Who did this? Who is in the fire? And why?

The piercing shriek of sirens has me turning my head toward the sound as a large truck turns onto the dirt path I used a few minutes ago. The flashing red and blue lights on top of the cab hurt my already tired eyes.

When the truck slams on the brakes, stopping next to my Jeep, I'm able to make out a word on the side in big bold letters.

SHERIFF.

My racing heart stills.

The cab door opens, and out hops someone I haven't laid eyes on in twelve years.

A man who has always been closed off to me.

The last person I wanted to see.

His tanned wool coat hangs open despite the cold, revealing a charcoal Henley stretched across his broad shoulders and muscled chest. Faded jeans disappear into weathered boots that have seen more Wyoming winters than most people.

His dark hair is almost a little too long, his jaw perpetually covered in stubble. He's all sharp angles and hard lines.

There's something about the way he carries himself—steady, controlled, unmovable. He's intimidating without trying to be.

He's the type of man that parents warn their daughters to stay away from.

Walker Maddox.

And he looks pissed to see me.

CHAPTER 2

WALKER

Taking one last drag from the cigarette between my fingers, I drop it on the asphalt of the Main Street Diner parking lot and step on it with my boot. I release the heavy smoke from my lungs along with the sweet burn.

The burn makes me feel. It cuts through the numbness in my chest where nothing else can.

Not freezing air.

Not a quick romp in a bar bathroom.

Not the crack of a bullet leaving the barrel of my gun.

I feel nothing.

Hopping inside my Dodge Ram, I look down at the sheriff's badge I left in the cup holder. It's more than just a piece of metal.

It's both my chain and my freedom.

When I was first elected for this job, I didn't realize what would be asked of me—what I would have to compromise to keep the people of Evergreen Falls safe.

A static voice comes through my department radio on the dashboard. "Walk, you there?"

The sigh that leaves me carries the weight of things I don't want to think about.

"Walk, pick up the damn receiver," Jolene commands.

Jolene Thatcher has been with the police department longer than I have. That woman would just as soon smack me upside the head as she would bake me a batch of chocolate chip cookies.

I do as she says and answer. "I'm here."

"A 911 call just came in. A man said he saw a fire in a field off County Road 15."

My mind goes over the map of the town. "Isn't that Taylor Morrison's land?"

"Sure is," Jolene confirms.

Not wanting to move my body just yet, I respond, "Have Tessa and Ridge check it out."

"They're over at the Dixon Ranch, remember? Investigating his missing cattle," she reminds me.

"Alright. I'll head out there and see what's what." I return my radio to the stand and head toward the west end of town.

I haven't even reached Morrison's property line when I spot a pillar of black smoke in the sky, growing too quickly.

I step on the gas and flip on my emergency lights and siren. Snagging my receiver, I radio to Jolene, "Send the fire department out this way." My eyes glance to the right, finding what I'm looking for. "Mile marker one twenty-five."

"On it," she replies.

Dropping the radio, I make a sharp left turn onto a gravel road, snow mixed with dirt kicking up in my wake. The fire seems to be somewhat contained by the surrounding snow. A good thing considering all the trees less than a hundred yards away.

I watch as someone stands in front of the building fire, and my mouth tightens into a line.

It looks like this may turn out to be an open-and-shut case. Criminals truly are among the dumbest people. Only a dimwitted jackass would stick around at the scene of their own crime.

I come to a stop next to a deep green Jeep Wrangler. Jumping down from the cab, I head straight for the culprit.

"What the hell do you think you're doing?" I bark.

The person—No, woman—spins to face me, and I'd swear on every single bullet in my gun that all the air in my lungs evaporates, stopping me just a foot away from her. I feel like I've been kicked in the ribs with steel-toed boots.

There's no mistaking who this woman is.

Blake Jennings.

The last time I saw her, she told me to go to hell, then drove off in her beat-up Chevy. She left town right then and there. That was the day after she graduated from high school.

She looks nothing like she did that day.

Her onyx hair is shorter, her hips are fuller, and her eyes are sharper. Her hair catches the sunlight like dark silk, and her eyes are an inferno of spirit.

I want to run my hands over every curve of her body.

My dick twitches in my Wrangler jeans, and a small spark of something light—lighter than I've felt in decades—ignites in my chest.

Nope. Not her and not here.

"I was trying to put it out!" Blake lashes back, throwing her hands up in the air, then the fury in her deep cedar eyes dims. "I was trying to save him."

Him?

I finally look past the curvy distraction in front of me and peer into the fire. A man with his arms draped over the T of a cross is burned to a crisp.

Did she do this?

My eyes narrow on Blake. "You just so happen to show up in Evergreen Falls at the exact moment that this happens?" I gesture toward the flames.

"You're blaming me? I was trying to help." She takes a step forward, closing the distance between us, and pokes me in the chest. "You should be thanking me."

The top of her head is perfectly level with my chin. She's at just the right height that if I wanted to, I could...

Not. Her.

What is this woman doing to me? First, I completely ignore the crime scene, and now I can't stop thinking with my dick.

I don't need this right now.

She has to go.

Retrieving my handcuffs from my belt, I grab her arm and turn her around. "Blake Jennings, you're being detained for suspicious activity."

"You're arresting me?" She shouts.

I secure the cuffs around her wrists and guide her to my truck. "Detaining. There's a difference."

Blake's sass doesn't stop, not that I expected it to. She's never known how to bite her tongue. "Is this your way of welcoming me back? Twelve years, and you slap on the cuffs? If I had waited fifteen, what does that get me? A night in lockup?"

I hesitate briefly when we reach the cab doors. Do I place her in the back like I would any other suspect, or do I let her ride shotgun?

The real question is, do I actually think she could've done this?

That answer is easy.

No.

Changing direction, we round the hood, and I open the passenger-side door. "Watch your head."

She slides into the seat smoothly. "I haven't been in the city *that* long. I know how to get into a goddamn truck, Walk."

Her use of my nickname is doing things to me that I can't admit to right now.

I reach over her, turning up the heat to warm her and catch a whiff of her amber and vanilla scent.

Another spark of light. Another feeling I don't need or want.

I back out of the truck, putting some much-needed distance between us.

"Don't move."

Blake's expression of outrage is almost comical. "Where the hell am I going to go?"

I don't answer her and slam the door shut, kidding myself into thinking I've severed this new connection.

Fuck. This woman is not what I need right now.

IT DIDN'T TAKE MUCH for the firefighters to extinguish the flames. They arrived quickly and had everything under control in minutes.

My boots crunch on the icy snow as I walk the scene. There isn't a point in tracking my footsteps. The fire department was all over the place, contaminating the evidence.

The camera's shutter clicks as one of my deputies, Tessa, a hardworking woman with fiery red hair, documents what evidence we can make sense of.

Tessa McCreedy has been one of my deputies for almost as long as I've held this position. She's a capable woman and a skilled interrogator.

I stare up at the charred remains in front of me. I've seen many dead bodies in my time, but it never gets easier. Innocent people don't deserve to die.

A sweet yet chemical aroma invades my senses. "You smell that?"

Tessa angles her head and sniffs. "Gasoline?"

"Yeah," I confirm. "Killer must've used it as an accelerant."

"Could the killer be our arsonist who's been terrorizing the town for the last few months?" Tessa speculates.

Shaking my head, I respond, "I don't think so. Arsonists rarely cross over into murder. They want fire, not blood."

"When's Levi supposed to arrive?" Tessa asks from her crouched position at the base of the cross.

"He's on a farm call. He'll get here when he gets here," I answer.

Ridge Talbot, my other deputy, green as a young sprout, approaches. "The fire department is about done loading up their equipment, then they'll be out of here. It's taking them a little longer than usual because they're down a man."

That gets my attention. "Who? Everyone okay?"

Ridge nods. "They said Derek Holt didn't show up for his shift today, but not to worry. Apparently, it's happened a few times."

"Let's still do a wellness check," I instruct.

"I'll do that after we're done here," Ridge says.

Placing my hands on my hips just above my belt, I respond, "Thanks. Start a canvas. There's got to be a witness out there."

"Well..." Ridge trails off as his head turns in the direction of my truck, his eyes a little too eager.

I grit my teeth. "Not her."

I know we need to question Blake, but I can't bring myself to do it, and I sure as hell don't want Ridge questioning her.

"Sheriff?" Tessa gives me a questioning look.

"I'll do it." My jaw works back and forth. "Ridge, work on ID'ing the body."

Trudging over to my truck, I move as if I'm walking to my death, which I might as well be. Blake has always been a terror if she wanted to be, and I know she isn't going to be happy about me cuffing and locking her in my truck.

However, I have a job to do. That needs to come first.

As I approach the passenger window, Blake looks at me with narrowed eyes. Opening the door, I'm hit with a burst of hot air. I rest my hand on the top of the cab and lean my arm on the door frame.

"Miss Jennings—"

Blake scoffs. "Miss? Walk, you've known me my whole life. Just call me Blake."

"*Miss Jennings*," I repeat, "what were you doing out here?"

"I was on my way to Moose Gap Lodge," she answers with a tight, fake smile.

I nod my head. "Why not stay at Silver Pine Resort? They finished the hotel and have been taking bookings for a few weeks before their grand opening."

Blake rolls her eyes like the answer is obvious. "Because Moose Gap is cheaper."

She's got me there. It costs more than I make in a week to stay just a couple of nights.

Silver Pine is a ski resort in the making. Neil Redford purchased the land six months ago and has been working nonstop to get the resort up and running. Once the zoning for the land changed, Neil jumped on the deal, and it's been full steam ahead since. Tourism has been good for the town, but not for crime.

Continuing with the interview, I question, "What brings you to Evergreen Falls?"

Her face turns more controlled. "Personal business."

"And that would be," I prompt her.

"None of *your* business," she snaps back.

Her sass has all my blood rushing south, and I don't like it. Blake is the daughter of my best friend.

Well, my *former* best friend.

Landon died when Blake was young, when I was still just a deputy in the sheriff's department.

Regardless of Landon being alive or not, I should not be reacting to Blake Jennings this way.

"Why didn't you call 911 when you saw the fire?"

Blake shrugs a shoulder, turning to stare out the windshield. "It didn't occur to me."

My tone sharpens, and my volume rises a pitch. "It didn't occur to you to call emergency services when you saw a man burning in the middle of a field that's surrounded by trees? Dry trees. You could've been hurt, the fire could've gotten out of control."

Blake's face snaps back to me. "No. It didn't occur to me."

She's lying.

"Why not?"

Blake squares her shoulders. "I don't know."

Heat creeps up the back of my neck. "That's not an answer, Baby Girl."

Did I just call her Baby Girl?

"I didn't think it was necessary." Blake's breathing increases.

"That answer keeps you on the suspect list. Try again." My hand on my truck tightens. I'm sure if it were possible, I'd leave behind a handprint on the metal.

"I didn't want you to know that I'm here," Blake shouts, and my chest tightens. She deflates and falls back into the seat. "Besides, it's not like there was much anyone could do."

Blake's confession lands like a punch to my chest.

Ignoring the feeling, I focus on her second statement and tilt my head. "What do you mean?"

She stares down at her lap as she responds. "The fire started when I was driving by. I immediately turned onto the property and came over to help. He wasn't moving when I got here. I think he was already dead."

Whoever did this is a cold-hearted killer. That much I know. Even a normal person in their most irate state doesn't set someone—dead or alive—on fire.

"Could you see who the person was? Did you see anyone fleeing when you drove up? A person on foot or a vehicle?"

Blake shakes her head. "No. The flames were too thick, and there wasn't a soul in sight when I arrived."

I don't like seeing her like this.

Weary.

It makes me want to reach out, run my hands through her hair, and wrap her up in my arms. It makes me want to keep her safe in a way that's more than just protecting my friend's daughter like we did all those years before.

I want to hold her like she's mine.

I can't do that, let alone *want* that.

Placing my hand on her back, I urge her to lean forward to remove her cuffs, only to find that they're already off.

Blake sits back up, grabbing my wrist and placing the metal bracelets in my hand. "Got tired of waiting."

My mouth hangs open. "How—"

Blake pulls out a standard handcuff key from the back pocket of her jeans. "Always be prepared. That's my motto."

I pluck the key out of her hands. "No, that's the Boy Scouts."

Blake shrugs. "No bother. I have more of those anyway." She drops her hands on her thighs—her thick, gorgeous thighs, and her optimism restores. "Can I have my car keys back so I can leave? I had a long night, and I'm starving."

I know she didn't do this. I'm confident in that, but I can't seem to hand over the keys to her Jeep.

Shaking my head, I answer, "Sit tight. I'm going to need you to stick around for a bit in case I have more questions."

Her perfect plump lip curls. "You, son of a—"

Stepping back, I swing the door shut and slide her keys into my pocket, cutting off her colorful epithet.

"Hey, Walk! I think we got something over here," Tessa shouts, waving at me.

Heading for them, I realize that Ridge is on his hands and knees with Tessa standing on his back, bringing her face to face with the victim. I stop by Ridge's head and cross my arms.

"Newbie's gotta pay his dues," Tessa says, answering my question before I can ask. With the victim's mouth open, she peers inside and slides on a pair of gloves. "There's something lodged in his throat."

Ridge cranes his neck to get a peek up at Tessa. "Are you really going to put your hand in there?"

"How else are we supposed to find out what it is?" Tessa snarks back as she reaches in.

"The M.E.," Ridge returns.

"That'll take too long," I respond for Tessa.

"Got it," Tessa informs us, removing her hand from the crisp body. "It's a piece of paper with part of a logo on it."

I pull an evidence bag out of my pocket and open it. Tessa drops the paper in the clear plastic, and I seal it up. Narrowing my eyes, I take a closer look and recognize the image immediately.

"Make a call to—" I'm cut off by the sound of an engine turning over.

My head snaps up, and I spot Blake behind the wheel of her Jeep. Shoving the evidence bag toward Tessa, I search my coat for her keys but come up empty. I pump my arms and legs, running straight for her, even though I know I won't get to the car in time.

Throwing her shifter into gear, Blake rolls down her window and blows me a kiss as she turns her car around. "It was nice seeing you, Walk!"

Wheels kick up snow in their wake as the car speeds toward the road, making a right to head into town.

You're going to pay for that stunt, Baby Girl.

CHAPTER 3

BLAKE

Eyeing Walker in my rearview mirror, I smirk. He's standing there as the snow clings to his shoulders and the brim of his hat. The cold paints his cheeks red, but the rouge could be from the fact that I didn't do as he wanted me to.

As usual.

Seeing him, all the feelings I had the day I left came rushing back. I tried to kiss him, and he turned me away. Embarrassed, I exploded and said things I didn't mean.

I thought distance and time would have helped me build up a tolerance to the man, but that tolerance threw itself into the fire when I laid eyes on Walker again. I wanted to run my hands over his broad shoulders, wrap myself in his thick arms, and bask in the way his eyes see me—truly see *me*.

Another glance and Walker's sharp gaze let me know that he's *not* happy. I'd feel bad if he hadn't handcuffed me like I was some sort of criminal.

I'm always down for a good time, but I imagined Walker using handcuffs for a whole different reason. And arresting me, or detaining me as he likes to call it, is not what I thought would happen when I finally saw him again. In all honesty, I wasn't ready to see Walker.

Maybe that's my real reason for not wanting to come clean with him. I'm not actually ready to see any of them.

The men I've been head over heels for since I was a child.

Over the last couple of weeks, I've been telling myself that it was just a childhood crush and that I'd feel differently when I finally came face-to-face with them again.

But if how I'm feeling right now is any indication, my childhood crush has turned into an adult infatuation.

Sighing, I slouch into my seat.

Oh well.

With my anonymity out the window, I decide I no longer need to stay away from the food establishment that I've been dreaming of for the last decade.

Main Street Diner.

Pulling into the parking lot, I find the last available spot and make my way inside. As expected, the place is packed. Martha and Gus McCall's cooking has never failed to satisfy the masses.

Heat rolls over me the second I step inside. The smell of bacon grease, maple syrup, and fresh coffee wraps around me like a blanket. Every booth is filled with familiar and unfamiliar faces alike, conversations blending beneath the clatter of silverware.

I spot the last available table in the corner, covered in worn laminate. Sitting in the booth, I take a quick glance over the menu and note that not a single item has changed. A group of men dressed in work clothes chatters at the bar, sitting on their mismatched stools. Friends and family occupy the remaining tables, enjoying their meals.

The scent of bacon grease, coffee, and maple syrup hangs in the air. Evergreen Falls High School memorabilia covers one wall beside a collection of framed photographs showcasing rodeo champions and the Rocky Mountains. The vinyl booths have been patched so many times that no two seats are quite the same shade of red.

An oversized mug is set in front of me, and the waitress immediately fills it with coffee. "What can I get you, sweetheart?" she asks without looking in my direction and pulls out a pad and pen for my order.

A smile tugs at the corner of my lips as I peer up at Martha's heart-shaped face. She looks exactly the same. Expressive eyes, a tender smile, and a button nose. Her style hasn't changed either. Flannel and denim—a common choice in this town.

It's about lunchtime, but I have a craving for my favorite. "French toast, extra crispy, and can you put the butter between the slices instead of on top?"

Martha stops scribbling, finally looks at me, and beams. Her hands find my own and pull me from the booth, wrapping me in a warm hug. "Well, I'll be. Blake Jennings. What're you doing back here? Last I saw you, you were hightailing it out of dodge."

Three heads immediately turn.

Small towns never let a secret stay a secret for long.

Martha doesn't give me time to answer her question as she pulls back and turns her head toward the kitchen. "Gus!"

"What?" a gruff voice shouts back, gaining the attention of a few customers.

"Look who's here!"

A tall, broad-shouldered man steps out from the kitchen behind the counter, rubbing his hands on a dish towel. His white shirt and light-wash jeans are spotted with grease stains. The smattering of gray hair on the sides of his head is the only indication that time has passed.

His expression brightens, and the corner of his mouth curves upward. "Are my eyes working, or is that Blake Jennings?"

Martha releases me, passing me to Gus, who greets me the same way. The smell of bacon radiates from his clothes as I bury my face in his shoulder.

Gus lets me go but keeps his hands on my shoulders. "It's good to see you, Squirt."

His smile causes a warmth to spread through my chest.

"Get the girls some food. We need to feed her so well that she doesn't leave again," Martha directs to her husband.

A pang of guilt stabs at me. Once I figure things out, I'm gone. This town has too many ghosts for me to stick around.

"French toast?" he questions.

"French toast," Martha confirms as she leads me back to my seat and sits across from me. "I should be cross with you. No calls, no letters. I thought I'd never see you again."

"I know. I'm sorry. I just couldn't..." My throat closes up as I try to explain. I've never been able to say out loud exactly what made me leave.

It's too much. Too heavy.

Martha envelopes my hand in both of hers. "I understand. We all have things we'd rather stay buried. You don't have to tell me why you left. You don't even have to tell me why you came back. I'm just happy you're here."

"Thank you," I return with a half-smile.

Martha and Gus have always been good to me. When I was little, before Daddy passed, Mama worked here. And when she chose to drown her sorrows instead of going to work, Martha had to let Mama go, but that didn't stop Martha and Gus from making sure I was fed. If it weren't for them, I'm not sure I would have survived.

Patting my hand, Martha rises to her feet. "I'm going to go check on your food. Anything else I can get you? A milkshake?"

"No, thank you."

Before heading for the kitchen, Martha looks me over like she can't believe I'm actually here.

That makes two of us.

Sighing, I rub my eyes and take a sip of my coffee. Scanning the diner, I pray that our reunion didn't draw too much unwanted attention. Just because I've given up on being incognito doesn't mean I want a parade of greetings.

My gaze meets a pair of steel-gray eyes, intent on mine. My

heart practically skips a beat as I recognize another of Dad's best friends.

Grant Calloway.

Another man I was never supposed to want.

He bought me a bike the Christmas after Daddy died because Mama sold mine. I always loved his military haircut and the dimples he gets when he flashes a genuine smile.

I lift my hand to wave and say hello, but he slides his chair back abruptly, causing me to flinch at the grating sound. His mouth thins to a firm line, and the veins in his neck pop out livid corrugations.

Grant tosses some cash on the table next to his half-eaten sandwich and glass of pop and storms out of the diner, the door shutting vehemently behind him.

Closing my mouth after I realize it's open, I feel heat creep up the back of my neck and darken my ears. I try not to look around again, but I can't help but want to make sure no one else noticed Grant's reaction.

Still, too many people are eyeing me, but one stands out among the rest.

You've got to be kidding me.

She tosses her thick copper hair over one shoulder, snagging her designer purse and beelining straight for me. Her sharp eyes attempt to pierce me like she's trying to wear me down before her words have a chance to punch me in the gut.

Fortunately, I built up a tolerance to her bullshit a long time ago.

Standing over me, she sports a cold smile. "Well, if it isn't Evergreen Falls' trashiest runaway. What brings you back here, Blake?"

I return her fake sentiments. "Victoria Wood. How are you?"

She brandishes her left hand, flashing me a huge diamond and gold band on her ring finger. "It's Reynolds. Bridger and I tied the knot. He's the mayor now."

Head cheerleader and star football player. The mean girl and the asshole. A match made in heaven.

"Good for you," I half-heartedly congratulate her.

Victoria's smile gets tighter as she squints her eyes. "How long are you in town for?"

I shrug. "However long is needed."

Her voice is soft, but her words are anything but. "Evergreen Falls doesn't need more trash, so feel free to leave at any time." Her eyes drift over my clothing, and she sneers as if it's the most offensive thing she's ever seen.

I match my tone to hers. "And they don't need a bitch either, yet here you are."

Victoria finally drops her phony pleasantries. "Same old Blake."

"Same old Victoria."

Her eyes narrow. "Just stay away from my man."

The delusions of this woman never cease to amaze me. Bridger was the typical rich kid and acted like he was too good for me until one night when he drunkenly decided that no means yes. I ended up breaking his arm, and he told everyone I wanted it.

As if I'd travel thousands of miles just to see the man who tried to assault me.

I scoff. "That won't be a problem. Never was."

Victoria turns her nose up at me and stomps away, shoving open the diner door and leaving.

And now that I've given the whole place a show, all eyes are on me.

Now that's more like the welcome home I was expecting.

CHAPTER 4

SANTIAGO

The sound of a desperate man's screams echo in the old cabin as the flesh on his shoulder sizzles under my hot iron. When I pull back, he drops his head forward. The only thing keeping him upright is the rope tying him to the support column in the center of the main room. The air smells of burnt flesh, cold ash, and weathered pine.

He pants, on the verge of vomiting, as he begs, "Please, please. I've told you everything."

My boots crush the bits of hay as I circle his pathetic form. I note the burns covering every exposed inch of flesh. Each in the shape of a star with the letters "FS" in the center. "You see, Evan, I'm not so sure I believe you."

Evan Lockhart begins to silently sob.

Weak daylight filters through the grime-coated windows, casting long shadows across the warped floorboards. A freezing draft slips through the cracks in the walls and rattles the loose panes of glass, but it does nothing to cool the sweat dripping down Evan's face.

The stone fireplace looms behind him, cold and blackened with soot as dust hangs in the air.

We've been at this for hours. I'm exhausted, but I'm not giving up until I'm certain that he's given me every last detail.

I crouch down and unholster my revolver. Pressing the barrel under his chin, I tilt his head so he can look me in the eye.

"Where are the rest?" I ask again with a growl.

Lockhart's shoulders shake as his cries become more audible. "I s—swear, there isn't anymore."

I study his face, searching for the lie.

Blood slowly drips from his nose. His right eye is practically swollen shut. His lips quiver as I click the hammer of my gun, toying with him.

"*Creo en ti*," I reply, rising to my full height. *I believe you.*

Lockhart's shoulders drop in relief.

I raise the revolver again, aiming it between his eyes. "But that doesn't mean you get to live."

"Wait! No—"

Squeezing the trigger, the pop of the bullet exiting the chamber rings in my ears.

Checking the time, I realize why I'm ready to fall asleep standing.

Nine hours? Damn. The high school teacher lasted a lot longer than I thought he would.

My phone vibrates in my hand.

Walker: Are you done yet? We have a problem.

Me: Just finished. What's up?

Walker: Clean up, then meet me at the edge of Taylor Morrison's land.

Me: What happened?

Walker: Just get here.

Damn *gruñón*.

Shoving my phone into my pocket, I groan as my stomach rumbles.

Lunch then Walker.

KILLING the engine of my truck, I stretch my neck side to side before heading into Main Street Diner.

If it wasn't for Javier, my right-hand man at Falling Sky Ranch, I'd be dead on my feet. I gave him a call and let him know there was a mess to get rid of in the old barn on the edge of my property, and that was it. Javier doesn't ask questions. He's been with Falling Sky since my father ran it.

Entering the diner, I note the peeling teal paint and the shelves covered in mismatched mugs. The tightness in my chest eases a fraction just by being here.

The usual lunch rush crowds every single table, so I head to the counter to place my order. With Silver Pine located just up the road, we get a lot of tourists.

As I weave between occupied seats across the worn linoleum, I inhale the hunger-inducing aroma of burgers and fries.

"Hey, Martha," I greet the owner as she taps away at the register screen. I rest an elbow on the short counter, leaning on my side and facing the rest of the diner.

She flashes me a tender smile. "Hey, Santi. The usual?"

I nod. "To go, please."

By my elbow on the counter are various fliers and ads printed on neon paper. The one for the grand opening of Silver Pine catches my eye.

I know business like this is good for the town. It creates jobs, boosts the local economy, and all that. But Walker has been on edge since he found out about Neil's plans for the tourist attraction. He says that crime will spike, and while I prefer not to borrow tomorrow's worries, he's not wrong.

Scanning the crowd of tourists and locals, my attention stops. I can't see her face, but something about her has me ensnared. I'm not sure I can even name what it is. Maybe it's the slope of her neck or the way her ample hips taunt me.

Whatever it is, I can't look away.

Something about her draws me in. It's like she's my center of gravity.

She's so focused on the notebook in her hand, I'd be surprised if she even noticed the grumpy toddler flinging his food at the table beside her.

I smirk to myself and inform Martha, "Actually. I'll be over there." I nod my head in the captivating woman's direction. I'm not sure if Martha hears my change of plans, but I don't wait to find out.

The woman's rust colored sweater hangs off one shoulder, the knit thick. A long silver necklace disappears beneath the fabric, and dark jeans hug her hips before tucking into a pair of brown boots.

Approaching her table, I stop by her side. I clear my throat and ask, "Mind if I join you?"

When she looks up at me from under her long, thick lashes, I feel my cock harden in my jeans. The sight in front of me is one I want to recreate later, but with a lot less clothing.

The sharp lines of her cheekbones and jaw are contrasted by the smoothness of her honey skin.

"Santi?"

The use of my nickname causes me to blink rapidly, and it finally clicks who is sitting in front of me. "Blake?"

I should hesitate. I should run to the nearest church and confess my sins. But my feet won't move. Something about this feels right. I feel it in my gut, and my gut has never steered me wrong.

Blake tries to hide her perusal of my body but ultimately fails. "Yes, please, sit with me." She gestures to the seat across from her.

Bending my knees, I move to sit on the bench with her, and she slides over to make room.

Shutting her notebook, she snorts. "A little forward, don't you think?"

Angling my body toward her, I rest my arm along the back of the booth. "Me? Forward? What gave you that idea?" My words claim innocence, but the smirk I'm flaunting conveys the opposite.

I feel like my conscience should be urging me away, but it remains silent. In fact, it's cheering me on.

"You're trouble incarnate, aren't you?" she surmises as she tries to stave off a smile.

Placing my hand on my chest, I contest, "I'm an angel."

Blake chuckles into her mug as she sips the dark coffee.

Unprompted, I hold my hand out, palm up. She eyes me curiously but still places her hand in mine. A soothing sensation spreads through my body at the contact. It's a shock to my system, but one that I embrace eagerly.

I bring the back of her hand to my lips and place a kiss on her delicate skin. Her gasp is barely above a whisper, and a cute blush rises in her cheeks.

I lower her hand, but don't let go. "It's nice to see you, Blake.

"You, too," she breathes out.

"So, tell me. What brings you back to Evergreen Falls?"

She shifts in her seat and drops eye contact. "Business," she answers.

Well, that's a flat-out lie, and clearly not a topic of discussion that she's comfortable with. But I'll get the truth out of her soon enough.

For now, I'll try something easier. "What have you been up to?"

"Oh, you know. This and that," she answers with a shrug.

I raise my brows and smirk. "How intriguing." My eyes wander to the side and catch the notebook she was concentrating on before. "What's that?" Leaning past her, I reach for it.

"Oh, it's nothing," she claims as she scrambles to get it away from me.

I tighten my hold on her one hand and look down at the drawing in my other. It's a sketch depicting a fire in the snow, and it's highly detailed.

"Blake, this is really good." Using my free hand, I set the notebook down on the table and turn the page. "Have you always been into art? How did I not know that about you?" Blake's cheeks turn pink as she chews on her bottom lip. On the new page, I catch a quick glimpse of what looks to be me, Levi, and Walker. "Why did you—"

The drawing is snatched away. "That's enough of show and tell."

"Do you draw me often?"

Blake rolls her eyes. "Next subject."

Definitely circling back to this later.

"So...Where have you been?"

"Here and there." Blake won't look me in the eyes.

I shake my head. "Nah. You don't get to be vague with that one."

She sighs. "New York."

My eyes widen. "What? What took you there?"

She finally gives me those beautiful brown eyes. Clearly avoiding my question, she asks, "What about you?" Blake sets her elbow on the table and rests her hand on her fist.

I don't like her evasiveness, but I'll let her have her privacy for now. She shouldn't get used to it, though. I want to know everything about this woman.

Intimately.

I tip my hat. "Still running Falling Sky Ranch."

She nods. "Still love it?"

"Always. I was born and raised in a saddle."

"Ooo. A true cowboy," she teases. "My Mama always warned me about cowboys."

"Hey, *no todos somos iguales*," I say with a wink. *We're not all that bad.*

Blake makes a face, conveying her doubt teasingly.

I won't let her brush me off so easily.

"What's wrong with *vaqueros*?"

She holds up two fingers. "There are two types. The players and the statues. The players are the ones who promise you the world but only deliver regret and a half-assed orgasm. The statues are the ones who draw you in, but their hearts remain cold and closed. I wonder, Santiago," She lifts her hand and flicks the brim of my hat, "which type are you?"

Leaning in close, I eye her lips, then look back up at her alluring brown eyes. Lowering my voice, I ask, "You want to find out?"

She opens her mouth to respond, but our connection is interrupted by a brown paper bag dropping on the table in front of us. Peering over my shoulder, I find an unhappy Martha.

"Leave the girl alone, Santiago," she commands as her eyes glare at Blake's hand in mine.

"It's okay, Martha," Blake interjects. "Santiago was just making sure I feel the Evergreen Falls neighborly love." Her explanation is said in a playful tone.

"Your food's ready. Time to go." Martha grabs the elbow of my shirt and pulls. I follow her direction and stand, even though a small woman like Martha wouldn't ever be able to make me move.

I'm not a boulder or anything, but I've worked on the ranch my whole life. It's the kind of work that builds strength.

Blake squeezes my hand before she lets go. "Thanks for the company," she says as she looks me up and down one more time.

"I'll see you soon, *Mi Cielo*," I promise.

Martha shoves the bag of food into my hands and steers me to the exit.

Climbing into my truck, I peer through the large window at the front of the diner and watch Blake and Martha deep in conversation—hopefully, about me.

The tension surrounding Blake is so thick I could bathe in it. That kind of conflict usually wards people away, but not me.

I want to dive into the deep end and discover all her secrets.

I'm not the type of man to get attached, which, I'm sure, is why Martha was determined to get me away from Blake.

But something's different with Blake.

She has immediately become my obsession.

And I won't take no for an answer.

CHAPTER 5

LEVI

Mixing the blue putty with a tongue depressor, I look across the sterile room toward the white cardboard box—a box that is way too light on evidence.

Finding out who did this is not going to be easy.

The refrigeration unit hums steadily in the background, and condensation gathers along the metal walls of the cold storage room. The stench of charred flesh invades my senses, despite the surgical mask covering my nose and mouth, as I transfer the putty to the tray for dental impressions.

Most veterinarians don't spend their afternoons taking dental impressions from murder victims.

Then again, most veterinarians don't live in Evergreen Falls.

Normally, Dr. Marcus Adler would be the one to do this, but his office down in Jackson doesn't have the cold storage space for this body. That doesn't happen often, but when it does, my clinic, Northfork Veterinary, is used.

I'm the first on scene anyway, so it makes sense.

I told Doc that I'd take care of the evidence gathering so he'd have one less thing to do when he got here. I didn't disclose that my generosity is also because I don't need him sticking around longer than necessary and putting his nose where it doesn't belong.

I can't have him poking around my cremator.

After taking the dental impressions to ID the body, I move through the motions. This isn't the first dead body that I've had to work on. I know the routine.

I'm more than happy to help out when and where I can. Northfork Veterinary Clinic isn't too much to look at from the outside, but it's mine. Every exam room, kennel, and cabinet is arranged where and how I want them.

There's a reception when people walk in. I haven't had an actual receptionist in years, but I keep the desk out there anyway. Past that is a hallway that leads to two exam rooms, my office, a break room, and a cold storage room. At the end of the hallway, a door leads to a room filled with rows of kennels that stretch through the back half of the clinic.

Corpses don't scare me. They haven't since I was fourteen years old.

The bell above the front door of the clinic rings.

"Hello? Anyone here? I need help!"

My head turns toward the urgent voice coming from the reception area. Striding in that direction, I rip off my mask and disposable gown and toss them in the trash.

Silently, I curse myself for giving my assistant, Abbott, the day off.

The familiar sounds of the clinic greet me as I step into the hallway. A dog barks somewhere in the kennels as a cat yowls its displeasure from another exam room. The steady hum of the HVAC system rattles through the ceiling vents.

The reception area looks normal. Sunlight filters through the front windows, illuminating floating dust above the tiled floors. A row of mismatched chairs lines one wall beneath framed photographs of local pets and livestock.

Only one thing is out of place.

A woman momentarily strikes me speechless—a foreign feeling. Regardless of how hard I try, I'm mute.

She looks exhausted. Windburn colors her cheeks, and her hair is tangled from the Wyoming winter.

But she's still the most beautiful thing I've seen all day.

Her smooth caramel skin glows in the dismal lighting. Her shoulder-length waves are slightly disheveled, but I want to run my fingers through them. The rouge in her cheeks has me wanting to make her blush for a whole different reason.

"Oh, thank God, Levi," she breathes out and rushes toward me. "Can you help him?"

Snapping out of my stupor, I finally notice that this isn't some random woman.

It's Blake Jennings.

She's carrying something in her arms, wrapped in fabric. A paw sticks out from the bundle.

Peering down, I find the broad head and blocky jaw of a blue pit bull. His steel-gray coat is dulled beneath dirt and dried blood, interrupted only by a white blaze stretching across his chest. One ear folds forward while the other struggles to stay upright, giving him an almost lopsided look that would be endearing under different circumstances. Sad amber eyes meet mine, glazed with pain but still alert enough to follow every movement.

The emergency switch in my brain flips on.

"This way," I direct as I spin on my heel and head for the exam room. Blake follows me inside, I point to the table, and quickly wash my hands at the sink. "Set him there."

Slipping on a pair of gloves, I turn back to them. She's kneeling on the tiled floor next to the dog, whispering as she pets his face.

Moving to the other side, I remove the cloth from the dog and see what I didn't before.

Blood.

As I assess his injuries and gather supplies, I ask, "What happened?"

Blake watches me as I get to work. "I'm not sure. I found him like this on the side of the highway."

I nod. "He was probably hit by a car and left for dead. Happens often enough."

He's losing too much blood.

"I need you to apply pressure to his front leg to stop the bleeding," I instruct. Out of the corner of my eye, I see her jump into motion.

As I reach for his injured leg, he doesn't growl or snap. He only lets out a quiet whine before looking toward Blake, as if asking her whether he should trust me.

I get lost in the process of patching the canine back together.

The more I examine him, the more convinced I become that he's almost entirely pit bull. Broad chest. Thick neck. Powerful shoulders. If he were healthy, he'd probably tip the scales somewhere around sixty pounds of solid muscle.

I'm not sure how much time passes when I finally step back from the table. There isn't much more I can do at the moment. Exhausted, I sigh. The bleeding has stopped, he's sedated, and he's hooked up to an IV.

"Is he going to be okay?" she whispers.

Nodding my head, I look over him again. "The next few days will be telling, but he's a fighter."

"So...Do Walk and Santi know—" I begin as I turn to her, but the words get trapped in my throat. I can't help but allow my mouth to hang open as I stare at her. Her jeans are molded perfectly to her hips, but it's the lack of clothing on top that has me stuttering.

Her breasts look ready to spill out of the thin, lacy fabric covering them. I watch as her nipples harden under my gaze. My eyes wander down her frame, and I feel my cock harden.

I want to devour this woman. I want to run my tongue over her silky bronze skin. Even just once, so I can live with the memory of her taste.

"Oh my God!" she shouts, snapping out of the spell she

unknowingly put me under. Her arms cross, covering her chest, and her cheeks pinken. "Don't look!"

"I didn't see anything."

A lie so bold that I'm sure if I didn't already have a one-way ticket to hell, it would buy me one. There's no way I'll ever forget that image. I never want to.

Hiding my smile, I turn and give her my back. "Where did your shirt go?"

"I used it to stop the bleeding, like you asked me to."

"I didn't ask you to use your clothes," I respond with a little too much sarcasm, but I'm having too much fun rubbing salt into her wounded pride.

"What else was I supposed to use?" she asks indignantly.

"There are towels in the cabinet behind you." I point my finger over my shoulder.

"How was I supposed to know that?"

"I figured you'd look around," I retort.

She raises her voice. "I didn't think there was time."

Deciding to fix the situation, I turn, sliding my scrub top off over my head.

She squeaks. "What are you doing?"

Pointing to the table, I answer, "Your coat and shirt are ruined."

Blake's arms are still wrapped around her chest. "So your idea is to take off your clothes too? Even the playing field?"

I give her a lop-sided smile and hold out my shirt. "For you to wear."

She blinks. "Oh." Grabbing my shirt, she steps closer. "Thank you."

I take another step. The shirt I handed over is the only thing preventing me from feeling her skin against mine.

I shouldn't want her. Not Blake Jennings. Not Landon's daughter.

She left Evergreen Falls a girl and returned a woman.

The longer I stare into her eyes, the faster my will dissolves.

She closes the gap between us, her chest pressing against mine as her breathing increases. Her eyes leave mine for a brief moment, dropping to my lips.

Fuck.

She wants this too.

"Don't look at me like that, Blake," I warn her.

"Why not?" Her voice is barely a whisper. She places her hand just over my heart.

Leaning down, my lips brush against hers as I say, "Because it makes me want to—"

A voice clears from the doorway. "Am I interrupting something?" Santiago stands at the door to the exam room with a huge smile on his face. All that's missing is the popcorn in his hands.

Blake jumps back. "Nope!" She slips the shirt on, covering herself up. "Thank you again, Levi. I'll check on the dog later." She moves to leave, but I stop her, grabbing her arm.

"Let me give you a jacket so you don't freeze out there," I insist.

"No need," she brushes me off. "The shirt was more than enough. I have another coat in my motel room anyway."

"Then at least let me give you my number." I run over to the cabinets and retrieve a business card, placing it in her hand. "Call me. I'd love to catch up."

"Will do," she says with a small smile. "It was nice seeing you, Levi. You too, Santi," Blake adds as she slips past Santiago and out of the clinic.

"Very smooth," Santiago jests as I move to stand next to him. We both stare at the clinic door, as if hoping Blake will come back.

I nudge him with my elbow. "Did you know she was back in town?"

"I saw her yesterday at Main Street Diner," Santiago answers simply.

"Shit," I return, shaking my head. "Does Walk know?"

Santiago shrugs a shoulder. "I'm not sure."

"We should tell him." I rub my hand over my face, already exhausted from the conversation to come.

Santiago grabs my shoulder, turning me to face him. "We will, but first…"

He grabs my face, bringing his mouth to mine as he backs me up against the doorframe. My hands find his waist, pulling him in closer. Our lips move together in a motion we've done together hundreds of times. Santiago's hat falls off his head as he leans into me further. My tongue swipes into his mouth, tasting him.

When Santiago comes up for air, I ask, "What was that for?"

"I saw the way you were looking at her."

I pull my head back a few more inches. "So? You were, too."

Angling his head, Santiago replies, "I'm saying that we should probably talk about it."

I don't know why, but I'm not ready.

Santiago has been my best friend for as long as I can remember. We were barely adults when we discovered that we wanted to explore more than friendship, but we also realized we were okay with having relationships and intimacy outside of the two of us.

Not wanting to talk about Blake with him doesn't make sense to me. Then again, I'm not ready to face the facts about how I just felt about Blake to myself either.

Stepping to the side and breaking Santiago's hold, I reach for my cell phone on the counter. "Let's call Walk. I need to give him an update on the dead body in the other room anyway."

Santiago is leaning against the sink as I finish up collecting evidence when Walker finally arrives.

"What do you have for me?" Walker asks, stopping on the other side of the metal slab from where I stand.

Santiago jumps in before I can answer. "First things first, Blake is back."

Walker purses his lips, and his brows scrunch together. "Blake who?"

His expression feels too practiced.

What's with the act?

Santiago's head rears back in disbelief. "What do you mean, 'Blake who?' Do you know another Blake?" He rises from his perch and moves to stand at the head of the slab.

"Blake Shelton." Walker shrugs.

Santiago scoffs. "When has Blake Shelton ever been to Evergreen Falls?" When Walker doesn't have a retort, Santiago quips, "That's what I thought."

He knows exactly which Blake we're talking about. Normally, I'm a patient man, but we don't have time for whatever has him acting like this.

"Blake Jennings, you jackass," I deadpan.

Walker doesn't look the least bit surprised.

"You already knew," I accuse him. When he doesn't deny it, I know I'm right. "Why didn't you say anything?"

Walker fidgets with the radio on his belt as he confesses, "She may have been the first on the scene."

I don't like the way he said that. The insinuation is almost offensive.

"She didn't do it," I blurt out.

"I know that," Walker snaps back. "But you have to admit it's suspicious that she shows up the same time Evergreen Falls has its first murder since the Bride Butcher."

"It could be a coincidence," I challenge.

Walker crosses his arms. "I don't believe in coincidences."

Honestly, I don't think it's a coincidence either, but I know she's not involved. If anything, trouble followed Blake back to Evergreen Falls.

Santiago rubs a hand down his face as he sighs. "I got a peek at her sketchbook."

I give him a confused look. "Okay. And?"

"There was a sketch of the three of us." Santiago divulges the information like it's no big deal. "It was really good too."

"What does the quality of the drawing have to do with anything?" Walker bites.

Santiago squares his jaw, his annoyance apparent. "I think she's an artist. As in on her resume, it probably says, 'skilled as fuck with charcoal.'"

Disregarding their spat, I get back to the important question. "Are you saying that she's been stalking us? For how long?"

"She's been *watching* us," Santiago corrects. "And I don't know how long. The drawing looked like we were outside the station."

Walker rubs his hand over the facial hair on his chin. "I need to figure out what brought her back."

"*We* need to figure it out, and we will," Santiago amends for Walker as he gestures to all three of us. "*Together.*"

"We'll see," Walker says. Before Santiago can argue, Walker asks, "How did it go with Evan Lockhart?"

Santiago's eyes light up. He likes getting information out of people. It's like a game to him. The more they hold out, the more excited he gets, and judging by his reaction, the teacher showed Santiago a real good time.

"The sick fuck gave me all the images. I anonymously emailed them to the FBI yesterday. They'll be able to find all the teenage girls in them and get them the help they need. Then Javi cleaned the barn."

We caught Lockhart preying on his students. He'd give them a bad grade, then offer them a way to make it up. Four days ago, Lockhart's garage caught fire. After the initial fire was put out, Walker and some patrol officers secured his house. They wanted to make sure no one was hurt in the home and that there weren't any other threats. Walker realized the teacher wasn't home, but his stash of images was out in the open. And that was that.

When someone threatens our town, we don't forgive. Forgiveness is for God, and I ain't him.

"Did you find out if he was working with anyone else?" Walker raises a brow.

Santiago's smile is vicious. "I got a name."

"Good." Walker nods.

A switch in my mind flips. The urge to drag the person attached to the name to Santiago's barn and beat them bloody rides me. It's an itch that I can't ignore for long, but patience has become second nature to me. I know that once everything falls into place, I'll be able to let the animal inside me free.

Clearing my throat, I begin, "Now that that's settled." I remove the sheet from the corpse's face. "I have a positive ID on our barbecued body."

"Way to bury the lead," Walker snarks. "Who is it?"

"Derek Holt," I answer.

Walker looks down at the charred man. "The hell? How did you get an ID so fast?"

I retrieve an evidence bag from the box and hand it to Walker. "His accountability tag was in his pocket."

Walker examines the burnt stainless steel, squinting at the inscription on the metal.

Derek Holt

Evergreen Falls Fire Dept

"Adler will need to confirm with dental records for an official identification, but I'd be surprised if his results indicate this is someone else," I add.

"Who would want him dead?" Santiago wonders out loud.

"That's for the police to figure out." Walker's words insinuate that Santiago and I aren't allowed anywhere near the investigation.

"You deputized us last year," Santiago argues. "Plus, you don't need Emmett at the Evergreen Gazette making things worse."

"Emmett is the least of my concerns. Whoever the killer is, he means business. He's sick and cruel. I don't need you two putting yourselves in his crosshairs." Walker points at us, emphasizing his position on the matter.

"Too bad," I retort.

"I have two deputies at the station," Walker returns.

"Yeah, but with the increase in tourism, you could use our help, and you know it."

"Don't you have a ranch to run?" Walker shoots at Santiago then turns to me. "And you have the clinic."

"Abbott is more than capable," I debate.

"Javier can handle the ranch hands for a bit." Santiago waves his hand like handing off the responsibilities of running a ranch isn't a big deal.

"We're going to do this whether you like it or not." I widen my stance like I'm preparing for Walker to charge at me like a bull.

Walker's nostrils flare as he exhales a frustrated breath. He turns his head away an swears, "Fuck."

That's all the permission Santiago and I need.

Santiago perks up with an idea. "Can we add a deputy decal to the side of my truck?"

I snort. "No one wants your lame ass GMC associated with Evergreen Falls PD."

"You're just jealous that I had to pull your Chevy out of the snow last week," Santiago taunts back.

I hate that I had to call him for help, but my truck slid into a small ditch when I was leaving the Dixon ranch, and I couldn't get out.

Walker massages his temples. "I'm leaving before you two give me an even bigger headache." His boots click on the tile as he leaves the clinic.

"Don't worry. We'll look into what brought Blake back after we question Derek's friends and family," Santiago hollers the information at Walker's back.

"Don't make me regret this," Walker returns over his shoulder.

I'd like to think that he won't, but in all honesty, he probably will.

Oh well. Too bad for him.

Now that that's settled, I have a reason to spend time with the woman who has effortlessly become my addiction.

CHAPTER 6

BLAKE

The life of a small-town sheriff is boring. Absolute snooze fest. And I would know because I've been following Walker around for the last couple of days.

A few cows who escaped their corral were walking down the highway.

A bit of graffiti on the side of Harold Whitcombe's horse trailer.

A moose on the football field at the high school.

Nothing that would indicate someone is lurking in the dark, waiting for an opportunity to send Walker to the grave.

Condensation fogs the corners of my windshield, forcing me to wipe away a clear spot every few minutes. The pencil feels stiff between my gloved fingers, refusing to glide across the paper the way it normally does.

Sitting in my warm car, I attempt to finish my sketch of Walker placing Arthur in the back seat of his truck.

The old man was stumbling around the center of town. His lack of balance and inability to put together a full sentence were more than enough for Walker to arrest him for public intoxication, but Walker, being the man he is, is taking Arthur to the drunk tank at the station.

Or at least I hope that's the case.

Walker can be cold as hell, but he's not a hard ass.

Evergreen Falls Police Department isn't much to look at. The one-story brick building sits on the corner of Main Street beneath an old wooden sign with faded gold lettering. Snowbanks line the edge of the parking lot where a handful of sheriff's trucks and well-used pickups are parked crookedly between the white lines.

From my hidden spot across the street, I watch as Walker escorts Arthur inside. He'll probably be in there for a while.

My attention shifts to my phone in the cupholder as it buzzes, alerting me to a new text. I can't stop my lips from curving into a smile. I couldn't stop them if I wanted to.

I should be horrified that he texted me at all, but the picture of a happy dog is distracting.

Levi: He's recovering quickly. When do you want to pick him up?

Me: How did you get this number?

Levi: Not important.

Levi: If you don't take him, then he has to go to the pound, and they'll probably put him down.

Me: You're manipulating me. You know I would never let that happen.

Levi: Maybe...What if I just wanted to see you again? You can keep your clothes on this time.

Me: You're lucky I was planning on keeping him anyway. You can see me when I pick him up.

Levi: He'll be ready at the end of the week.

Levi: What would I need to do if I want to see you before then?

First, Santiago shamelessly flirts with me, and now Levi. This could just be a game to them—their only source of entertainment in this isolated small town. Or maybe all of this is completely innocent. I'm an adult, and now they're treating me like one.

Finally.

I get why they didn't do this when I was eighteen. I was legal, but still just a kid.

Even if this is just some innocent fun, I'll take it. I'll treasure their words and these memories when I leave here.

If only Walker were on the same page...

But seeing them all again makes me forget—forget the bad and horrifying memories.

Santiago's long hair, disarming smile, and deep brown eyes, paired with his dimples, make him look like he belongs in both a country song and a cautionary tale at the same time. His skin looks as if God himself mixed the most precious dark honey hues together and painted them on.

Levi's strong, unshaven jaw and ocean blue eyes make him appear as if he walked right out of a high-fashion magazine. The way his chiseled muscles naturally flex as he moves is mouthwatering. Scrubs have never looked so sexy to me.

Walker's perpetually stoic expression makes him seem unapproachable—beautiful but unapproachable. And when he softens, his sly smirk is downright panty-dropping.

Describing them as "tall, dark, and handsome" is not even close to being accurate.

My soul just about leaves my body when there's tapping on my driver's side window. My phone flies out of my hands, landing somewhere in the car.

Gripping a freshly sharpened pencil in my hand, I turn to my left. My stomach sinks when I see a very unhappy man glaring at me like I'm the most disgusting thing he's ever seen.

Walker's distaste for my presence shouldn't hurt. It reminds me of the same hurt I felt when he rejected me as a teenager all those years ago, but I gathered my pride just like any other eighteen-year-old and moved on. I'll have to manage and do the same thing now.

In reality, I know I never completely moved on from his dismissal of me.

Maybe no one ever truly moves on from their first crush. If

that's true, then I need to figure out a way to lock my heart behind reinforced steel. If I don't, then I may not survive my time in Evergreen Falls.

"Roll down the window, Blake." Walker's voice is dulled by the glass separating us, but his impatience comes through loud and clear.

Doing as he says, I don my armor and bat my lashes. "What seems to be the problem, Officer?"

"Don't do that." His brows lower.

I shrug a shoulder, and my voice comes out a bit higher than I intend. "Do what?"

"Play dumb." Walker sighs. His frustration is evident, but that only encourages me more.

Giving him a fake frown, I retort, "I don't play games. It's not fun when I win all the time."

"Blake," he responds curtly as he places his hands on the window.

"Glad to see you haven't forgotten my name," I emphasize my sarcasm by patting one of his hands.

His shoulders drop a fraction as sincerity enters his tone. "I could never forget you."

I'm speechless. His candor is throwing me off balance. Once upon a time, I would've killed to have him look at me like this—like I'm important to him.

Walker's tone goes hard again. "Why have you been following me?"

Shit. I thought I was being discreet. I can't believe he's known this whole time.

But...why not say anything until now?

Frowning again, I answer, "I don't know what you're talking about."

"Then what's that?" Walker nods, pointing over my shoulder and leaning down to rest his forearms on my car.

I turn my head and find my sketchbook wide open on the

passenger seat. The drawing of him and the town drunk is on full display. Scrambling to close it, I respond, "Nothing."

Walker quirks a brow and smirks. "That's not me?"

"No. You think I have nothing better to do than follow you around?" Facing him, the rest of my argument dies in my throat. His face is inches from mine. I can feel the heat from his breath. It smells of a mix of cigarette smoke and peppermint.

"Tell me why," he commands, and his breathing picks up.

Is he just as affected as I am?

My eyes drop to his lips, and he notices. I should be embarrassed, but with the possibility of a kiss so close, I can't force myself to give a damn.

"Maybe I just miss you," I admit.

It's a half-truth, but he doesn't need to know that.

And evidently that was the wrong thing to say. Walker's mouth hardens, and he stands to his full height.

"Stop it," he barks, and his knuckles turn white as he grips my windowsill. "I don't know what you're up to, but I promise you, I will find out."

I nod my head and chastise him a bit more. "Sure, you will. Big, strong Sheriff Walker Maddox. Nothing gets past him."

He slams his hands down, causing a loud boom to ring out. I'm not sure how, but I don't flinch. Maybe it's because I know he'd never hurt me.

"I don't have time for your childish games. I have a job to do, and you following me around is keeping me from doing that job," he seethes. "Whatever delusion you're under, let it go. Stop following me and go back to the life you built far away from here."

Walker pushes off my car door and stomps away. He heads straight for his truck, hops in, and speeds away.

My chest feels tight as I feel tears line my eyes, but I will them to stay put.

Maybe I should just tell him. Rip off the band-aid. But at this point, would he even believe me?

Resigning myself to my mission once again, I shift into drive and steer my car in the opposite direction of Walker.

I wish I could say, "fuck this," and get the hell out of here, but I can't leave any of them to face the threat on their own—a threat they don't even know exists.

STARING at the off-white rusted metal door, I lift my fist for the fifth time and lower it once more. I'm not sure how long I've been standing here, but a good indicator is the loss of feeling in my fingers.

You can do this, Blake.

Taking a deep breath, I finally knock. Footsteps thud on the other side, and the metallic latch clicks. The hinges creak as a withered face comes into view.

She removes the cigarette from her mouth and expels the smoke from her lungs in my face. I hold my breath as I wait for the smoke to disperse.

This close, I can see the new wrinkles all over her face. Her skin looks thin and lifeless. The pink undertone she used to have isn't there anymore.

"Hi, Mama," I say, interrupting the silence.

"What do you want?" Her expression remains empty as she takes another puff.

Is that all she has to say? I'm her only child, and we haven't seen each other in years, let alone spoken.

"What?" Mama's disinterest is like a slap to the face.

"I don't have any money," she says.

I keep the hurt off my expression. "That's not why I'm here."

She rolls her eyes and walks back inside, leaving the door open. Assuming it's the only invitation I'll get, I follow.

The moment I step over the threshold, the smell hits me.

Cigarette smoke mixed with stale whiskey and dust.

Underneath lingers a faint scent of something floral, reminding me that Mama once tried to make this place feel like home.

But that didn't last.

The front door opens directly into a cramped kitchen. Yellow linoleum stretches beneath my snow boots, the pattern worn thin in places people have walked over often. To the right, the kitchen gives way to a small living room, and to the left, a narrow hallway leads toward the bathroom and two bedrooms.

Just like the outside, not much has changed in here. The recliner is different, but everything else is the same.

A floral couch that should've been replaced years ago sags in the middle. An afghan blanket is draped over one armrest. The recliner sits near one end of the couch, and the TV remains at the other end.

The only difference is that everything is more worn down.

The TV has a small crack in the corner of the screen, the couch fabric is frayed in random spots, and the carpet has a black path from the edge of the tile to Mama's chair that has a mote of glass bottles and other trash. The coffee table in the center of the room is cluttered with remotes, pill bottles, unopened mail, and water rings from forgotten drinks.

There's a pile of dishes in the sink that looks like they haven't been touched for months. Maybe longer. The laminate countertops are scratched and faded. One cabinet hangs slightly crooked on its hinges. The refrigerator hums loudly in the silence, covered in old magnets and fast-food coupons.

I shuffle in closer, leaning my hip on the dirty linoleum counter. "How are you doing?"

Mama grunts.

The bags under her eyes and the grease in her hair alarm me. "When's the last time you ate?"

This wouldn't be the first time she chose indulgences over taking care of herself. I can't count the number of times I had to remind her to eat and shower. But I hoped that without me here, she would see the need and take care of herself.

I guess I was wrong.

"What do you care?" she snaps without taking her eyes off the screen.

"I care, Mama." I sigh and push off the counter. Opening the fridge, I note the abundance of beer and the lack of anything of sustenance. Brown bananas, a jar of pickles, and a ketchup bottle. I try not to cringe. "You need groceries."

"If you're here to judge me, there's the door." Her gaze still on the TV, she points to the door.

Shutting the refrigerator, I move back into the living room with my arms crossed. "Please tell me you're doing more than just buying booze with the money I send you every month."

She snorts. "Is that where the money comes from?"

Dropping my arms, an invisible weight settles on my shoulders. "Where did you think it came from?"

She shrugs, putting out her cigarette on the ashtray next to her. "Never bothered to ask."

Pressing the power button on the TV, I stand in front of the screen.

"Hey!" She shouts as she sits up in her chair.

"Come on, Mama. How about I cook you some dinner while you take a shower?" I reach for her hand, but she swats it away.

"No."

The weight increases, pushing my shoulders down further. "I'm just trying to help."

Mama glares at me. Something she's done countless times before. I know what comes next. I'm ready for it. But her words are like a knife, cutting open a wound I thought healed long ago. "You're nothing but a burden. A worthless, good-for-nothing burden."

I swallow. "You don't mean that."

She sharpens her weapon, aiming with precision and accuracy.

"You always have been. You drove away everything good in my life, like your father. You do nothing but take."

Widening my stance, I place my hands on my hips. "I didn't drive him away. He was depressed, and he only saw one way out."

Mama pounds her fists on the armrests. "Bullshit! You're the reason! It's always because of you!"

"Please, just let me—"

"I don't want your charity." Even though she's sitting and I'm standing, she's still able to look down her nose at me like I'm gum on the bottom of her boot. "Get out! Leave!" She gestures to the door again, and this time, I don't argue.

But I stop in the kitchen and find a pen and paper. I jot down ten digits and hand them to her.

"Here's my number. I'll be in town for a bit. Call me if you need anything."

She snatches the paper and crumbles it, adding it to the trash pile on the floor. "Don't hold your breath."

As I walk out, I hear her click the TV back on, and the voices of daytime soap actors fill the trailer.

Walking to my car, I can't even feel the snowflakes landing on my face. The tears finally fall, and I let them.

I shouldn't have come back.

I've never had a place in Evergreen Falls and never will.

CHAPTER 7

BLAKE

My boots stomp across the floor as a sad country song about a cowboy who loses everything drifts around me.

Cliché, but I'd expect nothing else at Timberline Bar on a Tuesday night.

Pine paneling covers the walls, darkened with age and decades of cigarette smoke. A collection of antlers and old hunting photographs hangs crookedly above booths lining one of the walls. The floor creaks under my boots as a waitress weaves through the room carrying a tray of drinks, burgers, and fries.

Behind the bar, rows of liquor bottles glow beneath the strings of warm white lights. Pool balls crack together from somewhere near the back, followed by a chorus of cheers and groans. The scent of grease, beer, and wood polish hangs in the air—a scent that is unique to Timberline.

Casually taking a seat at the bar, I rest my elbows on the deep wood counter, intertwine my fingers, and wait for the bartender. The deep wooden bar is marred by thousands of tiny scratches collected over generations of bad decisions. Sharp light from neon signs would normally annoy me, but I ignore them.

I don't remember consciously deciding to come here, but after leaving Mama's, all I knew was that I needed a drink and didn't want to do it alone. So here I sit on a high-top stool, waiting to numb the ache inside me.

The bar isn't so full that it's overstimulating. There are just enough people that I can blend in and allow their chatter to tune out the voice of self-loathing in my head.

Ranchers fresh off work occupy a handful of tables. A couple sits in one of the corner booths, sharing a basket of deep-fried food. Two men argue over a game on the television mounted above the pool tables.

Nobody pays me much attention, and that's exactly how I like it.

Near the back of the room, Bridger Reynolds occupies the largest booth despite only having one other person with him. Tailored wool peacoat draped across the seat beside him, expensive watch flashing whenever he gestures, he somehow manages to look overdressed in a place built for denim and mud. Even seated, he carries himself as if the room belongs to him.

People stop to shake his hand as they pass. Others simply nod and keep walking.

The mayor accepts both with the same practiced smile—the kind politicians perfect after years of pretending to like everyone.

I quickly look away before he notices me.

One run-in with the Reynolds family this week is more than enough.

The scrape of polished boots against the floor pulls my attention toward the end of the bar.

Well. Speak of the devil.

Bridger Reynolds strolls over with the easy confidence of a man who's never been told no. A charcoal sport coat sits over a crisp button-down, and his expensive leather boots look as though they've never stepped in actual mud. His blond hair is neatly combed back, not a strand out of place.

He smiles. It's the kind of smile politicians wear. Practiced and empty.

"Blake Jennings."

"Mayor Reynolds."

His mouth twitches. "You don't have to call me Mayor."

"I know." I take another sip of my drink, hoping he'll go away.

He leans one elbow against the bar. "Word travels fast around here."

"So I've noticed."

"I heard you were staying awhile." He smirks.

"I heard you got elected."

His smile widens just enough to look smug. "The town thought I was the right man for the job."

I nod my head unenthusiastically. "I'm sure they did."

His eyes sweep over me. Not lingering long enough to be obvious, but long enough for me to notice.

"You look different."

I give him an annoyed smile. "I got older."

He chuckles. "I suppose we all did."

I take another sip of my drink.

"So," he starts, "what brings you back?"

I shrug. "Family."

His expression becomes unreadable. "Dangerous reason."

Something about the way he says it makes me pause. "What do you mean?"

He taps two fingers against the bar. "Some ghosts are better left buried."

Before I can ask what that's supposed to mean, he pushes away from the counter. "Enjoy your drink."

He starts to walk away, then stops over his shoulder. "If you need anything while you're in Evergreen Falls," his smile returns, "the mayor's office is always open."

I watch him disappear toward the back of the bar. The offer sounds polite, but it doesn't feel that way.

"Blake Jennings," a voice on the opposite side of the counter snaps me out of my head. "Heard you were back in town."

I look up and find a man with his hands spread wide and resting on the bar. His dark hair is a stark contrast to his alabaster skin, but his smirk and warm eyes let me know I'm in good company.

Tilting my head, I give him a half smile. "How's it going, Wes?"

"Can't complain," he shrugs and slings a rag over his shoulder. "What can I get you?"

I ramble off the first drink that comes to my mind. "Jack and Coke. Make it a double, please."

"Can I see some ID?" he asks.

Raising my brows, I tease him. "I'm not sure if I should take that as a compliment or if I should be worried that you're forgetting things in your old age."

He plays at being offended. "Old age? I'm only in my forties." Wes sobers his expression. "You know I have to ask."

In my teenage years, I snuck in here more than once, but Wes always caught me.

"Yeah, yeah," I return as I fish my license out of my purse and hand it over. He takes a quick peek and returns it to me.

As he makes my drink, he questions, "What have you been up to?"

Glancing down at my hands, I reply, "Oh, you know. This and that. What about you?"

"Well, Gary wanted to retire and travel the country in an RV with his wife, so I bought Timberline from him."

"Why am I not surprised?" I shake my head at him. "I'm happy for you."

"Thanks," he says as he slides me a short glass. "Holler at me if you need anything else."

"Will do." I nod.

Wes taps the bar, then walks to the other end of the bar toward a group of men waving him down.

Staring down at the brown carbonated drink, I tilt my head

back and down it like a shot. The sugar in the Coke does little to mask the steely bite of the alcohol.

I don't know why I ordered whiskey. I don't even like whiskey.

Walker's and Mama's words play on an endless loop in my mind, poking at an insecurity that I've gotten good at hiding.

Problem. Inconvenience. Overlooked. Worthless.

That's me.

Rubbing my temples, I push the thought away. I can ruminate over the nuances of my childhood some other time. Preferably, when I'm back in New York.

"Wes, another drink, please," I request as he walks by. "But something with gin this time. Surprise me."

He nods and quickly hands me another glass.

Turning on my seat, I scan the rest of the bar and sip on my new drink. The low light illuminates just enough for me to see, but not enough to make out specific details.

Everything is in the same place.

The dart boards, worn billiard tables, and scattered seating. The wall of pictures of famous people who have stopped in for a quick drink. Even the random sets of antlers.

It's almost like walking into a time capsule, but the view makes me smile.

"Jelly Bean!"

My head jerks to the side in shock. Turning to the voice, a wave of confusion stirs inside. The same gray eyes from the other day are playful rather than full of unexpected malice. Then again, after the way Grant looked at me at the diner, I could claim the gaiety is unexpected.

While I'm still trying to decide how to react, Grant plops down on the stool next to mine with a half-empty beer in hand. "Don't tell me you've forgotten me already, Jelly Bean." His lop-sided smile puts me at ease.

"I could never forget you, Grant," I finally reply as I gently shove his shoulder. "But maybe we could forget that nickname."

"I don't see that happening any time soon." Grant finishes off his beer, setting the glass on the bar top. "It's good to see you."

Deciding I'm not going to beat around the bush, I just go for it. "You didn't seem so happy the other day at Main Street Diner."

Grant tips his head from side to side. "I had a migraine." I start to say something else, but he doesn't let me get a word in. "I'm really happy you're back," he declares, lowering his voice and leaning in closer as his words slightly slur together.

"I—"

Grant's eyes slide past me and narrow. He rises to his feet and engulfs me in a hug. I feel him kiss the top of my head, then he pulls back. "I'd better get going. See you around, Jelly Bean."

He trudges away, grabs his jacket by the door, and leaves.

I sit there for a moment, confused as hell. Grant and I always had easy conversations. I never confided anything of great importance in him, but that entire interaction was awkward. And I don't know why.

Maybe I really am what Mama says I am, but to more than just her…

Burden.

My smile falters.

Good-for-nothing.

My vision blurs.

Worthless.

My chest aches.

"Something wrong, *mi Cielo?*"

Shaking off my rumination, I blink away the fog and find exactly what I need right in front of me—a distraction. A very sexy distraction.

"Santi, hi!"

I'll wait until later to analyze how he pulled me out of my head with just a few words and that smile. But I'll let myself admire his ivory cowboy hat and those nice-fitting jeans.

I swear, Santiago looks like he was born in the saddle. His dark hair brushes the collar of his shirt beneath the brim of his cowboy hat, and his skin carries the warm bronze of a man who spends more time beneath the Wyoming sun than indoors.

"I was hoping I would run into you again," he admits as he sits on the seat next to me.

I turn on the stool to face him. "Oh, yeah? Why's that? Checking on your best friend's daughter?"

"Not quite." Santiago tenses for a moment as his eyes harden, but the intensity quickly dissipates. "We never got to finish our conversation."

Strange but okay...

"No need. I know what type of *vaquero* you are." I spin on my stool again, giving him my profile.

Santiago grabs my seat and turns me back toward him. "I feel like I'm supposed to challenge you to a duel or something for insulting my way of life."

I scoff and let sarcasm seep through my words. "What is this? The wild west? Is your ego that delicate?"

"No, but I don't want this to end." He hops up, grabbing my hand. "How about a game of darts?"

This is definitely the distraction I need right now.

"You're on, player." I jump off my stool just like he did and let him lead me across the bar to the dart board in the back corner. I ignore the stares from the nosy townsfolk as we go. "You do know that Levi taught me darts when I was twelve, right?"

Retrieving the six darts when we get to the board, Santiago hands me three and keeps the other three for himself.

I'm not sure if he saw the curious looks, but if he did, he's brushing them off well.

He leans down, whispering in my ear, "Who do you think taught him?"

Shit.

I don't want to lose, but I don't think I'm actually upset about this. Teenage Blake is jumping up and down for this one-on-one time with Santiago Ramirez.

Not to mention the flirting.

I could be making it all up in my head, but I'll let myself live in this fantasy a little longer.

"Ladies first," Santiago offers with a smile.

"Don't mind if I do," I return. Getting into position, I hold up the first dart and aim. I keep my eyes on the target and prepare to let the dart fly.

But before I can, a pair of hands land on my hips, and I'm pulled back into a firm body. My nose is filled with notes of oakmoss and leather, and I feel my heart race in the best way.

"You're doing it wrong." Santiago's lips brush the shell of my ear, and my core begins to ache.

Dear God. I don't want this to end. Even if it's just for tonight, I'll take it.

Allowing myself to lean back into his body, I reply, "I was doing it just fine." My rebuttal comes out more husky than I mean for it to.

Santigo's tongue lightly traces the tip of my ear. "Why settle for fine when you can have it so much better?"

My panties flood with need. Trying to come up with something to say back is like running through knee-deep mud.

"I—Um—I—" Clarity hits me like a ton of bricks. Pushing off of him, I spin and point a finger. "Santiago Ramirez, are you teasing me so I mess up?"

He shrugs. "Sounds like something I'd do, but" he tilts his head to the side, "no."

"I don't know if I believe you." Spinning on my heel, I quickly aim and release the dart, hitting the board right in the middle.

"How about we make this more interesting?"

Turn back to face him, I place my hands on my hips and size him up. "You're right. Your pride isn't a high enough price." I purse my lips and see my opportunity. "I win, you teach me how to ride."

Santiago's eyes widen. "A cowboy?"

If I had a drink in my mouth, I'd spit it out all over Santigo. "A horse," I correct him.

"You're born and raised in Wyoming and don't know how—" Santiago starts, but I cut him off with a look. "Fine. Deal." Santiago holds his hand out to me and I take it. We shake, but before I can let go, he pulls me close. Leaning down, his mouth is close to mine. "But when I win, you owe me a kiss."

The lack of space between us has my brain going all fuzzy. "Just a kiss?" I breathe out.

"If I ask for anymore, I could be arrested for solicitation," Santiago jokes.

I smile up at him. "You're on."

A few minutes later I'm close to winning, and Santiago suggests, "Best two out of three?"

"Not a chance." I shove his shoulder teasingly, and a thought occurs to me. "What if I want to cash in for both?"

Santiago's brows lower. "Both?"

"Your prize and mine," I clarify as my stomach flutters with nervous energy. Normally, I don't have a problem being bold, but this is different. This is Santiago. I've dreamed of something like this since I was a girl. Rejection from him will land differently.

Santiago's hands find my waist, and he pulls me into his body. "I won't complain."

I swallow, gathering more courage to push further. "And what if I want more than a kiss?"

"How much more?" His brows furrow adorably.

He really doesn't know what I'm trying to say. Time to let Bold Blake out to play.

My mouth curves into a mischievous half smile, and Santigo's expression becomes more confused. I reach up, grabbing the top of his hat and snagging it from his head. Taking a few steps backward, I place his hat on my head.

Santiago, with his mussed waves, stares at me like he can't believe what I just did, so I push a little more. "What's the saying? 'Save a horse, ride a cowboy?'"

"You don't know what you're doing, Blake Jennings." It's like he's warning me, but his red flag looks to be a lovely shade of green.

"You forget. I grew up here. I know exactly what I'm doing." Returning to the position he had me in before, I angle my head so he can look me in the eyes and know I mean what I say. "I know what I want. And I want you." Raising up on my toes, I place my lips in a gentle kiss on his jaw. "Take me home, cowboy. Show me what kind of *vaquero* you really are."

"No sabes en lo que te metiste," he growls. *You have no idea what you just signed yourself up for.*

Santiago spins me around and ushers me to the exit, grabbing our jackets along the way. He leads me to the passenger side of his Ford and crowds me up against the door.

He tilts his hat back on my head, enabling me to see him more clearly. In the next moment, his lips are on mine, and it's my turn to stand there in disbelief. He rests his forearm on his truck next to my head, and his other hand goes straight to my ass. He urges my hips forward, allowing me to feel his hard length.

After a couple blinks, I fall in. My fingers dive into his hair. I give his strands a small tug, and the growl he places on my lips has my panties soaking. I open my mouth, inviting him and he takes the offer eagerly.

Holy shit.

I'm kissing my dad's best friend.

And I don't want to stop.

His tongue slides along mine, the sensation increasing my need. A whimper escapes me, and I feel him smirk.

A shiver races up my spine, and he pulls back.

"Cold?" he asks.

"A little," I admit breathlessly.

Santiago wraps an arm around my waist, moving me to the side so he can open the door. "Get in," he directs with a nod of his head.

The man has literally kissed me speechless, so all I can do is step up and place my ass in the seat. He reaches in over me, fastening my seat belt—something I could easily do myself, but again, I'm fucking speechless.

"Get ready, *mi Cielo*. When we get to my house, I'm not holding back. You're going to find out exactly the type of *vaquero* I am." He steps back, shutting the door and moving to the driver's side.

Fuck.

My pussy is practically doing the jig, but my heart is frozen. I didn't think far enough ahead.

What if he regrets this tomorrow?

I won't, but if he does, I won't survive the heartache.

CHAPTER 8

SANTIAGO

When I saw Blake talking to Grant Calloway at Timberline, I just about ripped him limb from limb. There are only two men that I'm okay with Blake talking to, and Grant isn't one of them.

He finally felt my stare, and when he looked at me, I let my face do the talking. And my face said that I'd burn his body and bury the corpse if he didn't walk away right then.

Wisely, he left.

I was going to leave Blake alone, give her some space. But then, of their own accord, my feet took me right to her. I didn't think it'd lead to this. I mean, there's always hoping, but hope doesn't mean it'll happen.

As I drive down the dark road toward Falling Sky, I send up a silent thank you to my lucky stars.

Evergreen Falls is nearly asleep. Warm porch lights glow from scattered homes, and smoke curls from chimneys into the ink-black sky. Fresh snow blankets the pastures on either side of the road, reflecting just enough moonlight to make the landscape shimmer. The only sounds are the steady hum of my truck and the occasional crunch of tires over packed snow.

As my house comes into view, the porch lights burn amber against the dark night, reflecting off the snow. The house doesn't look the same way it did when I was a kid because of the remodel I did when I took over the ranch after my father. But it's still the place I lay my head every night.

It's home.

She watches the ranches roll past with the kind of quiet wonder that tells me she's imagining what it's like to live here.

I don't usually bring women here. This is my space.

But it feels right to bring Blake.

Somewhere along the drive, she gave me my hat back.

She tucks a loose strand of dark hair behind one ear before settling deeper into the passenger seat. Her oversized olive-green cardigan nearly swallows her, falling open just enough to reveal a cream knit sweater beneath it. A long pendant necklace rests against the fabric, swaying gently every time we hit a bump in the road.

When I park my truck in the driveway on the side of the house, Blake's hand lands on my thigh, and my skin burns with desire at her touch.

My cock hardens in my jeans, ready to explode.

Just one simple touch, and I'm on the verge of coming in my pants.

Blake leans across the center console, lowering her voice to a tone that makes my inner caveman pound on his chest. "You going to sweep me off my feet?"

This woman is going to be my undoing.

"Stay right there." I step out into the crisp night air, circle around the truck, and open her door. Before she has a chance to protest, I slip one arm behind her knees and the other around her back.

She lets out a surprised laugh as I lift her into my arms. "You weren't joking."

"Never."

Her arms slide around my neck, and she looks at me with that same bright smile she's worn all evening.

The porch light catches the snowflakes tangled in her hair, making them sparkle like tiny stars.

I don't think I've ever seen anything more beautiful.

The walk to the front door feels like an eternity as Blake's mouth moves up and down the column of my neck.

Sucking, kissing, licking, biting.

I'm barely inside the door and kick it closed when her mouth reaches my ear. "I need you now," she pants.

I'm frozen in the entry as a groan rumbles through my chest. "I'm trying to be a gentleman and at least get you to my bed before I dirty you up."

Blake hops down from my arms, the look in her eye almost has me nervous. She steps backward, kicking off her shoes one at a time. "I didn't ask for the gentleman tonight."

Her hands go to the top of her pants and push them down her legs—her legs, sexy legs. My eyes travel her body, starting at her toes and up the inside of her leg. I stop at the juncture of her thighs, her core barely covered by a small strip of black fabric.

The hardness in my jeans throbs.

I follow her lead, slipping off my boots.

"I went home with the cowboy." Blake reaches for the hem of her top, ripping it over her head and revealing a heathered gray bra. "Give me the *vaquero*."

She spins on her heel, dashing for the living room, and I get the perfect view of her ass. That thin black thong slips between her round cheeks.

"Fuck me." I bite my fist to keep myself in check.

This is Blake.

Blake Jennings.

She's not just any other hook-up.

Despite my self-control, I find myself chasing after her, unbuttoning my jeans as I go.

She stops in the middle of the living room, spinning to face me. Her eyes widen, not expecting me to be right on her tail.

I pick her up, stride to the couch, and sit, placing her on my lap.

Her legs automatically fall to either side of my thighs, straddling me.

Blake's hands go to the front of my shirt, unfastening the buttons. "Now what?" Once she's done, she pushes the flannel fabric down my arms, running her hands over my chest.

Removing my hat, I place it on her head. "Now, I take you for a ride."

She whimpers. I doubt she's aware that she's rubbing her center all over the front of my pants.

I slip my hand under the fabric of her thong at her hip and yank. I gather her ruined panties and stuff them in my pocket.

She quirks a brow. "Souvenir?"

"More like a memory."

Her eyes widen imperceptibly, but I catch it.

Before I can ask, her hands are in my hair as she angles my head for a deep kiss. Her tongue invades my mouth, tasting me with fervor.

My hips thrust up, applying pressure in just the right spot for both of us. My hands slide up her thighs to her hips. Blake sighs into my mouth. My hands continue to roam until I reach the clasp of her bra.

Blake pulls back just enough to say, "Take it off."

I don't wait for further permission. The tension in her bra releases. Blake sits up, sliding the straps down her arms, allowing me to take in the view of her tits.

And damn, they're perfect.

I cup them in my hands and swipe my thumb over her nipples, back and forth, causing them to tighten into a stiff peak.

Blake throws her head back in pleasure and moans.

"More," she begs.

She'll soon learn that she never needs to beg with me.

Lifting one breast, I lean forward and wrap my lips around the tip and suck, flicking my tongue. Blake's hands grip my upper arms as if the sensations rushing through her body are throwing her off balance.

I give her mound the same treatment she gave my neck.

Sucking, kissing, licking, biting.

Her hips work her pussy over my covered cock, dampening the front of my jeans.

When I switch to her other breast and give it the same attention, my free hand drags down her stomach and to the apex of her thighs. She's so wet that my fingers glide through her folds. I graze over her clit, causing her legs to tremble.

I break my mouth off her breast with a pop. "Are you ready, Baby?"

She chants her answer. "Yes, yes, yes."

I pump one digit into her pussy, slipping in and out. Her inner muscles clamp around my finger. She's so tight that my cock hardens almost to the point of pain.

"Look at me, Blake."

When she obeys, I add another finger inside her, and I watch as her pupils blow wide. Her jaw drops in silent satisfaction.

But I don't want her silence.

I want her screams.

My two digits easily find the rough spot inside her and stroke, while my thumb rubs circles around her bundles of nerves.

"Fuck, yes," she shouts.

When I feel her channel start to spasm, I double my efforts. She moves her hips faster, and my hand keeps pace with her.

Blake's hips jerk, her climax sending her over the edge. Her cum floods my hand, and she screams.

"Santi!"

She comes on *my* hand, in *my* house, wearing *my* hat.

If it were acceptable, I'd pound my chest in victory right now.

I slow my motions as she comes down from her high. She slumps forward, lazily moving her lips over mine.

"I need you inside me now," she demands, and her hands go to the button of my jeans. She has my zipper down in seconds. I lift my hips, sliding my pants and boxers to my knees.

My length springs free, hard enough to pound nails.

Blake licks her lips and encircles my cock with her hand, pumping once then twice.

I grip her wrist, stopping her from continuing. "If you do that again, I'm going to come, and I want to be inside you when that happens."

Blake whimpers as she lifts onto her knees, just as desperate for me as I am for her. She positions the tip and her entrance.

I grip her hips. "Condom."

Blake shakes her head immediately. "I'm on the pill, and I'm clean."

She wants to go bareback?

Shit.

This woman is not just going to ruin me. She's going to kill me with sex.

"I'm clean," I respond. "Are you sure?"

"Yes," she nods resolutely. "Please, Santi. Please."

I don't need more than that.

She wants this.

I want this.

I pull her hips down at the same time I thrust up, filling her up. The warmth of her pussy envelopes my shaft, and I swear, I almost black out.

This feels perfect.

She's perfect.

I hold myself still, waiting for her to adjust to my size. When she rocks her hips forward, I smirk.

"Ready for that ride, *mi Cielo?*"

She grins. "Hell yes, cowboy."

Lifting her up, I pull her back down again, grinding into her clit.

"Oh, my God!"

I capture her mouth with mine in a swift, punishing kiss. When I pull back, I growl, "God isn't here. I am. Your *vaquero*. When you scream, you scream *my* name."

I feel her core clutch my length, my words spurring her on.

Noted.

"Yes," she breathes out. "You and only you."

Satisfied with her answer, I set a grueling pace, thrusting in and out of her pussy. With each pump of my hips, we unwind further and further until we're both completely undone.

Being here, inside her, nothing has ever felt so right.

When I feel her muscles flutter around my cock, I use a hand to pinch her clit.

Blake's scream is louder than the first. Her pussy squeezes, pulling me into oblivion with her. My cock pulses, emptying inside her.

Our bodies relax at the same time, and Blake collapses on my chest.

"That was quite the ride."

My chest shakes as I chuckle.

"Gather your strength," I instruct as I stand, wrapping her legs around my waist.

I kick my pants off my legs, then head for the staircase.

She lets out a surprised squeak and holds on to my shoulders as I carry her up the stairs to my room.

"That was just round one."

Blake's eyes widen.

"Let's see if you can hold on through round two."

CHAPTER 9

BLAKE

"Goodnight, honey," Mama wishes, sweeping my hair back.

"Night, Mama," I wish back, smiling up at her from my soft pillow.

Mama pulls the covers up so they rest under my chin. She steps toward the door and stops. "Oh, you forgot your bear."

A tightness sharpens in my chest, but I keep my smile in place as she tucks him in bed with me.

"Sleep tight."

I hear the front door shut as Mama leaves for work at Main Street Diner. I really like the lady there. Mama's boss. She's nice to me and always gives me extra strawberries with my breakfast.

Heavy footsteps move down the hall, and I hold my breath. I send up a silent prayer to God. Maybe he'll hear me this time and answer. The back of my neck tingles as the footsteps get closer.

I close my eyes and throw the blanket over my head.

I'm not brave. I never will be.

I hear the slow clicks in my doorknob as it turns. A cold sweat builds up on my forehead, and I feel like I could throw up.

"Blake," he gently calls me. "I know you're awake. Let's play our little game."

. . .

My buzzing phone rouses me from the ugliness of my unconscious.

Thankfully.

Ignoring the notifications, I sit up to find myself in bed alone. On the nightstand are two small pills, a glass of water, and a note with three phone numbers.

I had to take care of a few things on the ranch. Be a good girl and take the ibuprofen. Make yourself at home. If you need anything else, call me, Levi, or Walker.

I didn't have any expectations from Santiago after multiple mind-blowing orgasms last night. I like it when there aren't any strings.

So why do I have this itch to see Santiago again?

Possibly because I've been in love with him forever, but I'd rather not dwell on that right now. That's a can of worms for another day.

For now, I'll do what he said. I'll make myself at home.

I don't think he'd appreciate me reorganizing his kitchen cabinets, but everything else feels fair game.

Standing from the bed, I drape the silk sheet around myself like a towel. I pad across the cold hardwood floor and peek inside the first door a few feet away from me.

Shelves of cowboy hats, hangers filled with flannel shirts and thick coats, and drawers full of denim.

Dropping the sheet, I slide my arms into thick wool sleeves and button from the top down. The shirt hangs nearly to my knees, smelling faintly of cedar, laundry detergent, and whatever cologne Santiago wears. Warm. Earthy. Comforting.

I wander into the hallway.

Last night, I hadn't noticed much beyond Santiago himself.

Today, I finally take it in.

The entire house feels like him.

Exposed timber beams stretch across the ceiling. Stone surrounds the massive fireplace downstairs, and every piece of furniture looks sturdy enough to survive another hundred Wyoming winters. Leather. Worn wood. Iron fixtures. Family photographs tucked onto bookshelves beside old branding irons and framed rodeo buckles.

I meander back into his bedroom and find the bathroom.

I swear I can hear angels singing.

It's *huge*.

Much like his...Okay, maybe the multiple orgasms didn't satisfy me last night. Or maybe Santiago's dick has turned me into a randy succubus.

I wander across the black slate tile, past the reclaimed-wood double vanity and the free-standing deep tub big enough for two people. The countertop is spotless. Every towel is folded with military precision. His toothbrush sits beside a bottle of beard oil and the world's largest bottle of ibuprofen.

The man is either incredibly organized or has the mentality of a child.

Opening the medicine cabinet, I search for absolutely nothing in particular.

"Well, I'll be damned."

Hidden behind a bottle of sunscreen sits a charcoal face mask. I stare at it, then the empty bathroom, then back at the mask.

Naturally, I slather it all over my face.

If I'm making myself at home, I might as well commit.

I spend the next twenty minutes snooping without actually snooping.

I inspect every beard product he owns.

Judge his cologne choices.

Open exactly one drawer, then immediately shut it, because that crosses a line.

By the time I'm done, the face mask has dried so tight I can barely move my mouth. Looking around the bedroom, I spot the television mounted across from the bed.

Perfect.

I climb back beneath the comforter, prop every pillow behind my back, and grab the remote. One episode of a home renovation show turns into two.

Then somehow three.

Apparently, watching couples argue over backsplash tile is exactly the kind of drama my brain needs this morning.

By the end of the third episode, my face feels like concrete. I peel myself out of bed and head back into the bathroom. The shower practically calls my name.

I twist the handle, and the rainfall showerhead comes to life overhead, steam curling through the room.

Just as I reach for the buttons on Santiago's flannel, my phone starts buzzing from the bedroom.

Dashing back toward the sound, I answer without looking at the screen. "What's up, babe?"

I'm greeted by the voice of my best friend, Savannah Foster, whom I had to leave back in New York. "Just calling to see how it's going."

I respond as I make my way back toward the shower. "Good."

"How is–Where are you? Are you in the shower?" Savannah asks.

"I'm about to be, but I'm at a guy's house." My response is vague, but that doesn't deter her.

Her pause is loud. "Are you being held against your will or something? Cough once if you're in danger, and twice if I need to ride in guns blazing."

I chuckle in amusement. "What? No. I'm fine."

"Then why are you still there?"

A valid question, but one that I'm actively trying to avoid.

"What do you mean?" I return, my tone as innocent as a fox in a henhouse.

Savannah scoffs. "Uh. Girl. Your creed is: hit it and quit it."

"Hey!" I exclaim, affronted.

"I'm not slut-shaming," she reassures me. "Nothing wrong with two adults consenting in a night of...*pleasure*. I know you don't make promises you can't keep. But..." she trails off.

"But?" I question with a raised brow.

I can feel her fidgeting through the phone, like she's uncomfortable with the confrontation. "You're usually gone by now. You don't stick around for morning pleasantries, let alone a shower."

"I woke up in bed alone, and he left a note telling me to make myself at home, so that's what I'm doing," I explain like my behavior is perfectly logical, which it is for any other human being on the planet.

But not me.

"By taking a shower?" Savannah questions further.

"Uh huh."

"Are you by chance delaying your leave so you can see him again?" I can hear the gears turning in her head.

"No..." I answer.

Savannah gasps. "Oh, my God! Blake Jennings! Have you caught feelings?" Her screeches just about burst my eardrum. I pull the phone away from my ear, saving myself a trip to the ER. "Who? Is it one of your dad's friends? The ones you told me about?"

"No." My response is too clipped, too fast. She instantly knows I'm lying and squeals.

"Which one? Tell me, please. I want all the details." She talks so fast that her words become one long sound.

Not ready to confront the questions she's asking, I do the only thing I can think of.

I fake connection issues.

"What—I—you—can't—" I end the call and drop my phone on the counter.

Steam fills the bathroom, fogging the mirrors and glass. Thankfully. I don't want to see my distressed face right now.

Instead, I strip off Santiago's shirt and slip into the massive walk-in shower. The hot water glides over my muscles, and I suddenly realize how sore I am from last night.

Talk about a workout.

I wash my hair with the only shampoo and conditioner in here, quietly reveling in the fact that I'm going to smell like Santiago.

The thought causes my core to ache, and just like that, I'm buzzing with need—deep, intense need.

I glide my hand over my wet, smooth skin, skimming my nipples. I gasp, needing more. With one hand, I cup my heavy breast, and with the other, I slip two fingers in my folds and circle my bud. I lean against the tiled wall behind me for support, ignoring the loud crash from the shampoo bottle falling to the floor. Pinching my stiff peak, I slip a finger into my core. When I find that spot inside me that makes me explode, I sigh at the sensation. I sink to the floor and onto my knees, stroking and twisting, trying to push myself over the edge.

I'm so lost in the race to climax that I don't hear the bathroom door open.

A blast of cold air across my skin interrupts my bliss.

"Blake?"

I scream, surprised to hear a deep voice.

When I open my eyes and look up, I find Levi standing on the tile with the shower door open, and I'm struck by his beauty.

Levi is made up of clean lines and solid muscle. A strong jaw dusted with permanent stubble. Even in a pair of sweats and a t-shirt, he looks like he stepped out of the pages of an outdoor clothing catalog.

His mouth hangs open as his eyes roam my naked body. His gaze lights with heat when he notices where my hands are, then he lingers on the ink etched on my hip.

The shock passes, and I jump into action, attempting to cover myself. "What are you doing?" My question comes out as an accusation.

"I thought I heard…" Levi's sentence cuts off as his gaze finds the fallen bottle. "Oh."

"Unless you plan on joining me, please leave."

I mean for my words to sound more like a taunt or make him uncomfortable so he leaves. But as soon as they're out, I realize what I've just done, and I find that I don't hate it.

My pussy is a greedy whore. Very greedy.

I shouldn't want this. I can't want this.

I already have to accept that Santiago just wanted one night. I can't do the same with Levi.

Maybe I can be happy with the memory.

Memories don't keep you warm at night. Memories sting, memories burn. But this memory might give me some measure of comfort.

It's hard to think straight with this gorgeous as hell man in front of me, and the fact that I'm touching myself in front of him.

His hands go to the collar of his shirt and pull, sweeping the fabric over his head. "If you insist."

CHAPTER 10

WALKER

A stream of light pierces my sleep. I groan as I sit up and rub my eyes. After a quick glance around, it takes me a moment to remind myself where I ended up after last night's binge.

Oversized leather couches, a massive stone fireplace, and huge-ass antlers above the mantle.

I shouldn't be surprised. I usually end up at Santiago's house when I sober up enough to drive myself somewhere. Sometimes Wes will call Santiago or Levi to come get me, but I haven't let it get that far since Amelia left me.

Finding my coat on the floor at my feet, I search my pockets for my keys but come up empty. Seems I didn't drive last night. Both a relief and an annoyance.

In front of me on the weathered wood coffee table is my phone, an unopened water bottle, and my gun. My keys are on the far end of the table.

Santiago usually leaves them here so I can go to work or my own house as soon as I wake up.

I'm reaching for my phone to call Santiago, who no doubt is

somewhere on the ranch at this time in the morning, when a loud crash and a scream come from upstairs.

That wasn't Santiago. That was someone else.

A woman.

Acting on instinct, I grab my gun and take the steps two at a time. I'm barefoot and shirtless, but that's the least of my worries right now.

I poke my head around the corner at the top of the stairs, hunting for the threat. When I come up empty, I continue forward with my eyes peeled. As I near Santiago's room, I hear a woman's voice. She's shouting, but I can't make out what she's saying.

There's another crash, and I rush ahead through Santiago's room and into the bathroom.

What I find is the last thing I expected to see—the last *person* I wanted to see.

Naked.

A blatant lie.

Blake stands in the shower, under the spray of scorching water, as steam billows out from the open glass door. She has one arm across her breasts, covering her nipples. Her other hand is between her legs, hiding her core. Water sleuths off her skin, and her hair is plastered to her head. A bit of black ink on her hip catches my attention as well.

The things I would do to get my mouth on her perfect body are downright immoral.

My cock swells in my jeans, and I'm ready to explode right here like I'm a boy seeing a naked woman for the first time.

We make eye contact, and the pulse in Blake's neck races. She swallows, then bites her lip.

I shouldn't look. Blake is too young for me. That doesn't stop me from looking my fill. I memorize every line—every curve of her body.

Finally, I notice the other person in the bathroom with us. Levi stands in front of the bathtub, slack-jawed and unblinking.

"Levi?"

"Walk? Why is your gun drawn?" Levi eyes the Glock 45 in my hands.

Relaxing my stance, I move my finger away from the trigger. "Why don't you have a shirt on?" I'm sure to make my question sound more like a threat, but he doesn't so much as try to look remorseful. I turn to Blake. "Why are you here?"

She glances to the side. "Um."

"Santiago," Levi answers for her, and it clicks in my mind.

My free hand tightens into a fist as my teeth grind together. "I'm going to kill him."

I'm not sure if my rage comes from Santiago sleeping with Landon's daughter or the fact that Santiago slept with her and I didn't. It has to be the former because the latter can never happen. If the other choices in my life haven't earned me a permanent seat around the fire of hell, then just thinking about Blake and sex in the same thought would seal my fate.

Blake bites her lower lip as she peers at the tent in my pants. The situation tempts me for a tenth of a second.

"This isn't happening," I snap, my statement is just as much for myself as it is for Blake and Levi. Damn this woman and her ability to slip past my self-control.

If I hadn't been here, would they have...

Shoving my feelings down, I bark out orders. "Levi, get out. Blake, get some clothes on."

"I'm trying to shower! You two are the ones who barged in here!" Blake shouts back.

"Well then...finish up." I wave my hand in an angry dismissal.

Levi smirks, winking at Blake as he turns to leave. He gently shoulders past me, then calls over his shoulder, "Oh, I'm sure she will. See you later, Butterfly."

I follow him out, ignoring the hard-on in my jeans, and slam the door shut behind me.

Levi slips his shirt back over his head. Once we're in the hall, he spins on his heel, a smirk on his face and a knowing look in his eye.

"Are you going to deny it?" He questions with raised brows.

I cross my arms over my chest. "Deny what?"

Levi sees right through me. He always has. "That if I wasn't there, you would've gone right there and fucked the daylights out of her."

"I wouldn't."

He scoffs, shaking his head. "Right. Me either." His tone lets me know he doesn't believe me.

He's not alone. I don't believe my claim either.

"She's clearly into Santiago," I say by way of excuse.

Levi looks like he's chastising me. He knows it won't work, but he tries anyway. He's acting like I'm a little child he caught in a lie.

I keep the focus on Santiago.

"If she's a one-night stand, I'll tie him to my hitch and drive," I threaten.

Levi sighs through his nose. "You know he wouldn't do that to her. But he's probably willing to—"

I cut him off, knowing where he's going with this. "Don't say it. Blake isn't a trophy we can pass around."

"Not pass. Share," he corrects.

"No," I assert.

At least…that's what I believe.

I've never questioned Levi or Santiago's ability to love differently than I do. It doesn't bother me. It never has. I just can't imagine myself wanting the same thing.

Then again, I'd never imagined wanting Blake this much either.

Levi challenges my position. "What if that's what she wants?"

"And how would you know? Did you ask?" I challenge him back.

Levi places his hands on his hips, narrowing his gaze. "Are you opposed to sharing, or are you opposed to the idea of being with her at all? How long are you going to fight it?"

I grit my teeth. "I'm not fighting anything. There's nothing *to* fight."

Levi shakes his head like he's disappointed. "You go ahead and keep believing your own press." He deflates a fraction, and his voice gets softer. "You don't have to be miserable, Walk. You could—"

As he speaks, a thought occurs to me.

"Did something happen between you and Blake?" I ask as if I'm accusing him of murder.

"I thought you didn't care," he accuses back.

"I didn't say that."

Levi blows out a frustrated breath. "Do what you want. I'm going to let myself be happy."

"As is your right. I'm going to go catch a killer."

I stalk past him down the hall, down the stairs, snagging my things off the coffee table as I exit the front door and slam it shut.

I don't deserve to touch Blake. I shouldn't even fantasize about her.

My hands have too much blood on them.

Blood that would make her hate me.

I CAN'T BE THINKING about Blake's naked body when I'm working. Distractions mean I'm not focused. When I'm not focused, I can't do my job, and people get hurt.

The forty-five-minute drive north to Jackson gives me time to get my head on right. My route is surrounded by the Snake River and the Wyoming mountain ranges. Both are covered in crisp, white snow.

When I arrive at the coroner's office in Jackson, I find Dr. Alder weighing a liver, a body on the metal slab next to him.

"Tell me you have something for me, Doc," I say by way of greeting.

"Ah, you're here." He removes his bloody gloves, grabs a manila file from his desk, and leads me to the grid of small metal doors on the back wall. He opens it and slides out a rack with the victim lying on it. "Well, he was burned," Marcus says with a bit of dry humor.

"Is it that obvious?" I return, sarcastically. "ID? Cause of death?"

He looks at the file in his hands. Marcus doesn't actually need the file. He remembers all the bodies he autopsies. "It's Derek Holt, alright. Just like Levi thought."

"Who would want him dead?"

I should have some sort of reaction to finding out the victim is someone I know and have worked with on more than one occasion, but I feel nothing.

Death is death. There's no stopping the end when it comes, and there's no point in crying over someone dying. It's part of life.

Marcus slips a pen out of the breast pocket of his scrubs and uses it to point to a specific part of Derek's neck. "It's hard to tell, but this man's throat was cut. He bled out before he was set ablaze."

"So our murderer doesn't use fire as a method of killing," I deduce.

"No, he does not," Marcus agrees.

Angling my head as my brain turns, I add, "More like a tool for attention."

"Very likely," he concurs. "You know, this case reminds me of my time in Nepal. I was there as part of…"

Marcus dives into a story, recalling "the old days." I've never questioned the accuracy of his reminiscences, but if he's to be believed, this man has lived a full life. Once, he worked with a relief effort in war-torn Somalia to help identify dead bodies, giving their friends and families closure. While there, he was kidnapped by a militant extremist group and forced to perform an autopsy on one of their leaders. His death was suspected of foul play, but it turned out to be natural causes. After the autopsy, Marcus escaped under the cover of night.

I wait until he's done with his story, then give my leave. "It was nice talking to you, Doc. Let me know if you find anything else."

Firing up my truck, I steer out onto the highway, heading back to Evergreen Falls. '

It's time to do the worst part of my job—notify the next of kin.

CHAPTER 11

WALKER

My brakes squeal as I come to a stop in front of a one-story taupe home. The small front porch and the large window beckon me, but I sit in my truck.

I hate this part.

When I knock on an unsuspecting person's door, the last thing they think I'm going to do is tell them that their loved one died. I suddenly become a key character in the worst day of their life. Some people faint, some people blame me, and I don't fight it. There's no judging someone for how they react in moments like that.

Two days ago, Derek's wife reported him missing, and now I have to tell her that he's never coming home.

I force myself onto the iced pavement and through the steel gate. A lumpy snowman with a lop-sided smile in the yard stares at me as I pass by.

Raising my fist, my heart sinks, dreading what comes next. I rap three times on the metal of the screen door. When it opens, a short, thin woman with yellow hair stands there, wrapping a sweater around her frame.

"Afternoon, Julie," I say with an even tone.

"Walk," Julie greets back, like my presence brings good news, and she pushes the screen door open. "Do you have news about Derek?" Dark circles hang below her eyes.

"Can I come in?" I ask with an open hand.

She tilts her head, and I can see her mind working to understand what I'm doing here. "What happened? Did you find Derek?"

Releasing a tense exhale, I respond, "I think it'd be best if we talked inside."

Her eyes widen as it clicks. "No."

"Jules…" I reach for her.

She takes a step back, shaking her head in denial. "Tell me he's okay, Walk. Tell me my husband is coming home," she pleads.

My shoulders droop. "I'm sorry."

Her tears fall, unbidden. "No."

I rush forward as her knees give out and she begins to drop to the floor. Catching her around her shoulders, I hold her to me as she wails and screams. Her cries prick at my heart, making the weight on my shoulders feel even heavier, and the guilt feel suffocating.

I didn't do my job.

I didn't save him.

I didn't protect him.

Coaxing Julie to the beige floral couch, I hand her tissues and offer to call someone for her. When she doesn't reply, I tell her that I'm calling Tad Jensen, the Evergreen Falls fire chief, to come be with her. Everyone at the fire station are family to each other, and I know Julie doesn't have any other family nearby.

After the quick call, I go to her kitchen. I search for a pot and quickly make us both a cup of tea. Returning to the living room, I offer her the plain green mug. "Here you go."

"Thanks." She grabs the warm ceramic cup from me and sips. "How did he die?"

I sit on the matching couch across from Julie. "We're still investigating, but it looks to be foul play."

"Someone murdered my husband?" She sets her tea on a coaster on the short coffee table between us.

"I'm afraid so," I confirm, then set my own mug down as well. "I hate to do this, but I need to ask you some questions."

Julie squares her shoulders. "It's fine. I can handle it."

I start the interview like I would any other. "Had Derek been acting strange lately?"

"No, not at all." She shakes her head.

Leaning forward, I rest my elbows on my knees. "No change in behavior? Was he stressed about anything?"

"Quite the opposite. These last few months, he was happier." Julie's gaze moves to the window beside me, seeming to think back over the time frame in question.

"Did he talk about anyone threatening him?"

Her eyes come back to me. As she answers, her voice gets softer. "No. Everyone loved him. There was talk of him receiving the Medal of Valor."

"Were there any ill feelings in the department because of that?"

Her brows lower. "You don't think any of them killed him, do you?"

"Just being thorough," I placate as I hold up my hands. "I need to get the full picture, so I know where to look next."

She shakes her head again. "None of his brothers at the fire station would do this. They're a family."

I nod, validating her reasoning. "I know, Jules. I didn't mean anything by it. It's natural for resentment or jealousy to build. It doesn't mean anyone there hurt Derek."

Julie sips from her tea again as we hear the hinges on the front door squeak.

A voice hollers. "Julie?"

"In here," Julie calls back.

A broad-shouldered man wearing navy blue cargo pants and a matching shirt steps into the room. His focus immediately goes to Julie. He crosses the distance between them in a few steps and sits next to her, grabbing her hand in condolence. "I'm so sorry, Jules. He was a good man. If you need anything, let us know."

Julie smiles sadly. "Thanks, Tad."

Jensen turns and acknowledges, "Walk."

"Jensen," I return.

"I don't know how I'm going to tell the kids." Julie stares down at the coffee table, but it's obvious she isn't focused on the natural pine wood in front of her. "I don't know if they can handle losing another father."

I sit up straight at hearing the new information. "Another?"

Jensen answers for her. "Julie's first husband was KIA in Afghanistan."

Derek, Julie, and their kids moved here about six years ago. I've never taken the time to get to know them better.

"That him?" I point to the pictures on the mantle above the fireplace.

"Yeah, that's Jason," Julie confirms.

I get up and move to get a closer look at the photo. Jason is wearing his army uniform, standing in front of a plain backdrop. Next to the photo is another of Jason and some other men dressed in fatigues. The entire mantle is covered in pictures of Jason and his medals. In the middle of it all sits a framed, folded flag.

It's like a shrine to Julie's dead husband.

Pivoting, I face Julie and Jensen again. My eyes roam the room, and I notice fewer and smaller photos of Derek.

"How long were you two married?" I inquire further.

"Three years. He was on his second tour when his unit was hit by an IED."

"I'm sorry." Trying to figure out how to frame my next question, I start, "Your children..."

Julie knows what I'm asking and answers without being offended. "Annie and Olivia are from my first marriage, but Derek is still their dad."

"Of course," I validate. "When did you meet Derek?"

Julie shrugs a shoulder. "Not long after Jason passed." She lets out a defeated sigh and gets to her feet. Jensen stands with her. "If you'll excuse me, I think I need to lie down for a bit before the girls get home from school."

Jensen and I give our understanding. When we hear a door click shut upstairs, Jensen starts in with his own questions. "That was Derek, wasn't it? The one burning in the field."

"Jensen, I can't—"

Jensen interrupts me. "Don't give me that bullshit, Walk."

Rubbing the back of my neck, I conclude that I can share this with him. "Yeah, it was Derek."

"Fuck," he mutters. "I don't know how I'm going to tell my guys. This isn't just a huge loss for the department. Derek was family."

"I understand," I console, then lead him on with my own interrogation. "Jules mentioned the Medal of Valor."

"Yeah, Derek was like a bloodhound for fires," Jensen corroborates. "He knew where to go, what to do. He could predict what the fire would do before it happened, and because of that, he's saved almost twenty people. That serial arsonist has had us working overtime."

That's interesting...

"Could I see your reports for the last six months?" I keep my face blank, not offering so much as a hint as to where I'm going with this.

Jensen's brows scrunch together. "What are you thinking?"

"I don't know yet," I lie.

Jensen rests his hands on his hips. "Will it help you catch who did this to Derek?"

"Hopefully."

"I'll have them dropped off at the station later today," he says with an edge of determination I'm relying on.

"Thanks." I reach my hand out to him. "Give me a call if you think of anything."

"Of course." Jensen clasps my hand and shakes.

EVERGREEN TREES BLUR together as I head back toward the station, melding into one green smear mixed with white dots from the snow resting on the branches as I drive along County Road 20 alone. The sky is just barely starting to change colors, signaling the coming of dusk. Static crackles over my department radio, making me tense even more.

I turn up the music, hoping that the melodies of blue-collar life, nostalgia, and faith will help clarify the speculations swirling around in my gut.

Blinding headlights flash in my rearview mirror, obscuring my vision for a moment. I roll my eyes and speed up to get away from the overzealous high beams.

I don't like that someone in my own backyard could be out there committing heinous crimes and I not know about it. Part of me wants to be wrong, but another part wants to catch him and make him pay in blood.

Levi, Santiago, and I are usually on top of the shit going down in Evergreen Falls. We take care of our own.

A quick glance shows me the same truck about forty yards still behind me. He's been there for the last several miles.

On a hunch, I slow and take the next turn and the next after that. When my mirrors don't light up, I slow to the speed limit and go back to the case at hand.

Back to the basics. What do I know?

I know that the victim is Derek Holt, age forty-two, multiple years with Evergreen Falls Fire.

Derek has risen in popularity over the last few months and was up for the Medal of Valor.

Derek was killed by a sharp object to the throat, then tied up on a cross, placed in an empty field, and set on fire.

Blake was first on scene.

The clash of metal on metal scrapes my ears as my body is jolted forward, and I almost bang my head on the steering wheel.

"What the fuck?"

Searching for the cause in my mirrors, I find the same beams, but they're much closer as the lifted truck attached to them rides my tail.

Did that guy just hit me?

I can't make out the plates, make and model, or even the vehicle's color. All I can tell is that it's dark.

The engine revs, closing the distance again for another tap. I push the gas pedal another inch closer to the floor to get myself out of range. At the same time, I reach for my radio.

"Jo, I've got a vehicle—"

Another hit.

This one harder than the last.

Back tires fishtailing over the ice-covered road, I struggle to regain control of my truck.

"Walk? Are you there?" Jolene answers me back.

"Yeah, I'm here. I—"

The car behind me moves to the left lane and speeds up. I slam my foot on the gas pedal, and my engine roars, working hard to push forward. I search for any distinguishing marks on the truck but find none.

But I'm not able to get ahead of him.

"Walk?"

"Jo, I'm on Highway 109, heading north. Please send—"

I'm cut off again when the truck swerves into my lane, ramming into the bed near my tire. I start to spin, slowing everything down. Placing both hands on the wheel, I steer into the turn and take my foot off the gas.

But I'm already going too fast.

My windshield looks out over the trees along the road, and I don't seem to be slowing down, and I'm still spinning.

Metal scrapes again, and I'm headed off the road and into the trees.

There's a blow to my midsection, and my head is thrown backward.

One blink, and it all goes dark.

Ringing.

Static.

Hissing.

"Walker? Walker Robert Maddox, you better answer me right now."

Groaning, I force my eyes open, but it's just a peep before they close again. Something warm and wet drips down the side of my face. I try to take a deep breath, but it's cut short by a sharp pain.

Great, a broken rib.

The sound of a car door shutting reaches me. "Help," I try to shout, but it comes out as more of a moan.

Reluctantly, my eyes close again.

I'm so tired. Maybe I can rest for a bit.

Something cold and sharp presses into my skin, pushing adrenaline through my veins. Opening my eyes again, I discover a knife at my throat.

Angling my head, I try to find the person, but he growls out, "Don't move."

With my right hand out of his sight, I slip it onto the seat belt and attempt to unbuckle myself, but it's jammed.

The man presses the edge of his blade in, and I freeze. A keen sting zips across my throat. It's barely a scratch.

"Be careful what you dig up, Sheriff."

The metal leaves my neck, and I turn my head, but the man is gone. I check my mirrors, but there's no sign of him.

The only thing that lets me know he was here is the burning cut.

He could've killed me.

All he had to do was apply a little more pressure.

But he gave me a message instead.

And now I know…I'm on the right track.

CHAPTER 12

BLAKE

Everything is fine. Everything is fine.

I slept with a man I've been pining over since I can remember, then the second found me in the shower with my fingers in my pussy, and then the third finds me in the shower while the second is shirtless.

It's no big deal. Nothing to see here.

I've never been ashamed of my body, but there's something about my childhood crushes seeing me naked that makes me feel exposed.

My hands tremble with nervous energy as I button up the shirt I found in Santiago's closet, making the task take longer than normal.

I'm searching for my jeans when the door to Santiago's bedroom opens. Practically jumping ten feet in the air, I turn and tug on the hem of the flannel, struggling to hide my lack of pants.

Santiago stands in the doorway with a plate of food. "I come bearing sustenance."

His eyes zero in on my legs and trail up my body. He gets a look on his face that has my thighs squeezing together, which, of course, he notices as well.

I shouldn't be embarrassed, but there's a big difference between last night and this morning. Last night was a fantasy. Today I have to face reality.

Clearing my throat, I scurry forward and snatch the plate from him. "You made this?" I cross the room and plop down on the bed. My stomach growls as I find steaming French toast, hashbrowns, bacon, and eggs.

"Walker called in the order to Main Street Diner and had me pick it up," Santiago admits and joins me on the edge of the bed. "But I put it on the plate."

When he sits down, he leaves no room between our bodies. We're touching from hip to shoulder. "Martha looked ready to rip my head off right then and there."

"Why would she do that?" I ask, ignoring the fact that my mouth is full of delectable carbs and sugar.

Santiago deepens his voice, mimicking a villain. "Because I'm the big bad man who has sullied the fair maiden."

Snorting, I almost choke on my food. "I'm nowhere near fair maiden material, and you're hardly my first."

I feel Santiago perk up next to me, and I realize my mistake.

Never talk about past boyfriends or hookups with my current one.

Not that Santiago is my boyfriend.

"Who was your first?" He questions pointedly.

Still staring down at my delicious breakfast, I steer the conversation in a complete one-eighty. "You had a couple of visitors this morning."

"Oh yeah?" Santiago replies, genuinely surprised.

"Yeah. I was in the shower and..." I hold my fork halfway between my mouth and my plate, realizing that this topic probably isn't any better.

"Did someone walk in on you? Who?" His question has a sharp edge to it that makes me think I'm about to condemn someone to death.

I roll my lips in, hiding the truth.

Santiago's finger hooks under my chin and turns my head to

face him. The intensity in his body almost has him vibrating, but his grip on my face is delicate. "*Mi Cielo,* no one else gets to look at you. I'd lock you in this room where I can come home to your perfect body every day."

Apparently, I'm collecting red flags like it's my job because I'm weak in the knees. If we were standing, I'd collapse right here.

I whisper my confession. "Levi and Walk."

"Oh. Okay." The storm around Santiago dissipates in less than half a second.

"That's all you have to say?" I frown, perplexed.

"I don't see the big deal." He shrugs. "It's just Walk and Levi."

Santiago's whiplash has me reeling.

He doesn't want anyone else to look at me, but he doesn't care if it's Walker or Levi. Maybe he only got possessive to get me to give up the names.

Yeah, that makes the most sense.

Which means last night was just one night, as I expected.

Swallowing hard against the knot stuck in my throat, I set my place aside and turn to face Santiago. "I had fun last night, and I'm not naïve. No rose-colored glasses on these eyes here. I know what we did last night doesn't mean..." My speech trails off as Santiago's jaw visibly squares.

"Doesn't mean what? Say it," Santiago utters bitterly.

I'm a big girl, and now I need to act like it.

Straightening my spine, I look Santiago right in the eye as I continue. "It doesn't mean we're in a committed relationship or anything. You don't owe me anything. It was just a bit of fun. I know how this kind of thing works."

Santiago grits his teeth. "What kind of thing?"

I continue as if he hadn't said anything at all. "And don't worry, I was a full participant and fully consenting."

"I know you were. I was there too," he reassures me, exasperated.

Taking a stabilizing breath, I get to the end. "What I'm trying to say is that I'm content with this being just one night."

Silence stretches between us, widening from a crack to a chasm. Santiago's nostrils flare, and his cheeks flame.

"What if I'm not okay with that?" It's a question, but he says it more like a statement.

I can't help but let out a full-belly laugh. "Yeah, right," I finally get out as I playfully shove his shoulder. "I know your track record, Santi. I remember you always having a different woman with you. Never the same woman twice, and in a town this size, I won't lie, that's impressive."

"Blake..." Santiago says my name like it's a word of caution.

I hold my hands up defensively. "I'm not shaming you. Do what makes you happy."

"You make me happy."

Squinting, I try to decipher his statement like it's a cryptic message. He can't mean that. There's no way. I haven't seen him in over a decade, and he just found out that I'm here. "You barely know me."

"That's not true," Santiago refutes as he grabs my hand. The simple contact jumbles my brain, but I can't let him walk in here, flash a smile, and make me fall at his feet.

I try to pull away, but he holds on firmly. "You know *younger* me. You don't know me now. I'm not the same girl."

"I know that. If you were, then what we did last night would be illegal." Santiago widens his eyes in an attempt to move our conversation into a more humorous tone.

Sighing with aggravation, my shoulders drop. "I'm serious."

"Me too." A hint of a smile tugs on Santiago's lips. It takes everything in me to resist mirroring him.

Shaking my head, I steel my resolve. "I don't need a commitment, and I know you don't want the obligation."

"You're assuming, Blake. And you know what they say when you assume," Santiago teases. When I give him a perturbed look, he sobers.

"Let's be honest. We both know I didn't return to Evergreen Falls permanently—"

"Yet," he interjects.

"What makes you think I want a boyfriend?" I snap back and regard him critically. "Now who's the one assuming?"

"Fine. Honesty." Santiago flips my hand over and begins tracing the lines of my palm, sending a tempting shiver up my spine. "Honestly, I don't want just one night. I don't want just a few days or a few weeks." He pulls me toward him and places my hand on his chest over his beating heart. *"Te quiero aquí. En mi cama. En mi vida."*

My chest constricts, comprehending the enormity of his claim.

I want you here. In my bed. In my life.

"Santi..." I breathe out. My hand slides up his chest to the side of his neck, settling on his cheek. He leans into my touch, turning his face to kiss my palm. "You have no idea how badly I've always wanted to hear you say something like that, but those were the wishes of a starry-eyed teenager. Being here—in this town—it brings up things I'd rather let stay buried."

"Then hand me a shovel. I'm good at burying things," he asserts earnestly.

My chuckle lacks humor. "It's not that simple."

"No," Santiago returns. "You're not *letting* it be that simple."

We remain there in our standstill. My hand on his cheek, his hand holding mine in place, and our eyes locked in a silent plea with each other.

For now, we agree to disagree.

But I have a feeling this is a fight I won't win, and I'm not sure I want to.

I briefly allow myself to picture it. Living here with him. Waking up to each other every morning.

But there's a flaw in my impractical daydream.

Levi and Walker aren't there.

Santiago interrupts my internal crisis. "Time for your second prize."

"My second...Oh." My heart pounds as I recall what I asked for. "On second thought, I'm good. No need."

I don't know why I made that part of the bet. I'm going to blame it on the alcohol.

"What's wrong?" His lips purse skeptically.

Shaking my head, I stand from the bed and move to find the rest of my clothes. "Nothing. I'm just tired."

Santiago follows me, gripping my shoulders and forcing me to face him. "Are you…" His gaze analyzes me, perceiving too much. "Are you afraid of horses?"

"No," I answer too sharply.

His mouth falls open on a booming laugh. I force a frown onto my face even though I want to laugh with him. "You. Blake Jennings. Born and raised in Wyoming. You're afraid of horses?"

"They're huge!" I defend.

Santiago gets a mischievous look on his face. "*Igual que—" So is my—*

My hand flies up and covers his mouth. "Oh my god! Not the same thing."

His response is muffled by my hand. "No shit." He kisses my hand again then removes it from his mouth. "We're going," he asserts with a wink.

Lord, bless my panties. They're not going to survive.

"Let's not and say we did," I sass back.

Santiago smacks my ass as he heads for the door, a smile on his face the whole time. "I'll meet you downstairs in five. A lack of clothing won't get you out of this."

I call after him, "I can't even find my clothes."

"Wear mine," he answers from the hallway. "They look better on you anyway."

My cheeks flame.

"Four minutes!" he warns, and I spring into action. I'm dressed and downstairs in three minutes, dressed in Santiago's clothes as he requested. He gives me his approval in the form of a whistle. I don't let myself think about the four-legged behemoths as we stride toward the barn just over a hundred feet behind Santiago's house. Situated next to the barn is a smaller house that I assume is the bunkhouse.

The barn is eerily still, not a soul in sight. They're all probably out taking care of the ranch.

I completely zone out, and before I know it, we're in the barn standing in front of a horse stall. My hand grips Santiago's as my knuckles turn white. Santiago rubs circles on the back of my hand, soothing my nervous energy.

"This is Shadow. You'll be riding her today." Santiago waves his free hand to the horse staring back at me with her ears pinned forward.

Her raven coat shines as she approaches the gate of the stall. She pokes her head out over the wood, and her nostrils flare as she focuses on me. Shadow's eyes have me pinned in place.

"She's beautiful," I whisper.

Santiago nudges me. "Scared?"

"A bit," I admit.

"Don't be. She'll be able to sense it."

I snort. "Right. Because it's that easy."

"Why can't it be?"

"Because," I explain as I turn to him, "fear is paralyzing. It holds you in place until you can't breathe."

His eyes soften in the corners. "You have to fight it, *mi Cielo.* You can't let the fear win."

The way he says it makes me think he believes I can do it. I can be strong and face the ugly memories I've always tried to forget.

"I'll try."

My optimism is rewarded with a kiss on my cheek.

"Good girl," he growls in my ear, sending flutters through my stomach. Santiago pulls back and looks around. "Get yourself acquainted with Shadow. I'll be right back. I need to find my foreman, Javier."

Before I can argue, he's gone. Shadow's focus is undeterred.

"Guess it's just you and me, huh," I mutter. Shadow whinnies her response.

I force one step forward. Then another. And another.

Shadow dips her head, and I take it as a good sign. On a shaky breath, I place my hand on the bridge of her nose. The contact slows my racing pulse, as if she's giving me some of her calm, letting me know I'm okay.

"Can I help you with something, beautiful?"

Off to my left, a man leans on his shoulder against the barrier of the next horse stall over. I don't know how long he's been standing there, and I don't like that fact.

He looks in my direction with his coffee-colored eyes. The sleeves of his red flannel are rolled to his elbows, and his boots appear to be soaked with a mix of melted snow and mud.

Definitely a ranch hand.

"I'm good," I respond dismissively and return to stroking Shadow's coat, moving to her neck.

Shadow lets out a puff of air from her nose.

The man pushes off the wall, strolling toward me. "It's no trouble. A pretty woman like you shouldn't have to get her hands dirty."

"A little dirt never hurt anybody. So, I'll say it again, I'm good." I turn, giving him my back.

"I like a woman who knows how to work."

"Good for you," I respond curtly over my shoulder.

Shadow moves her head, hovering above my shoulder, then lets out a short chuff in the guy's direction. I may not be a skilled equestrian, but I get the feeling that Shadow isn't a fan.

"How about I take you out for a drink tomorrow?" he pushes.

I feel him standing less than a foot away. The hairs on the back of my neck stand on end. Some men are good at taking hints, and unfortunately, this guy seems to be in the other group. He acts like any woman is blessed to get his attention, which means there's no way she doesn't want him.

This guy is in for a rude awakening.

"No thanks. I don't date cowboys," I quip.

"I saw you walk out of Santiago's house."

He went there. Nope.

Whipping around, I cross my arms. "So?" Shadow's attention remains on the man.

Okay, I admit to being wrong about horses. Shadow is clearly a girl's girl.

I don't like that I gave him what he wants—my attention. But the moment he said Santiago's name, he landed on my shit list, and I'm okay with letting him know it.

A small smirk lights the guy's face. "So if you don't date cowboys, then what are you doing with him?"

"Fucking," I bark with a strong tone of reproach.

"Manny!" A man with a body full of lean muscle storms toward us. The snarl on his face looks like there's hell to pay, and the debtor is the persistent man in front of me. *"Te dije que checaras el pastizal del sur. Mueve tu trasero para allá."*

I told you to check the south pasture. Get your ass over there.

Someone's in trouble.

"I was just—" Manny starts, his bravado nowhere in sight.

The lean man stops between Manny and me and shouts, "Get!" After Manny scurries off like a bat out of hell, the man turns to me and apologizes in a much softer voice. "Sorry if he was bothering you."

Dropping my arms, I no longer feel the need to defend myself. While I'm perfectly capable of getting rid of a pushy man on my own, I'm always grateful for the help.

I wave off the apology. "Nothing I can't handle."

"I'm Javier." He holds his hand out to me, and I clasp it with my own as I connect the dots.

"The foreman."

He drops my hand and nods. "That's me."

"I'm Blake."

Javier's face pinches then brightens as he connects his own dots. "Jennings? I knew your father."

I shouldn't be surprised. Daddy was born and raised here. Just because I never came around Falling Sky doesn't mean he didn't.

But just the mention of him still makes me tighten my hands into fists, my nails digging into my palms.

"Happy to hear it." My platitude has no enthusiasm behind it.

I'm saved from the awkward silence when Santiago finds us.

"Javi, there you are." Santiago comes right to my side. Shadow moves, deeming me safe, I assume, and Santiago places his arm across my shoulders. "We're taking Ace and Shadow. I figured while we're out, I'd check and make sure the snow drifts haven't gotten worse."

Javier tips his hat. "Sounds good, boss." He and Santiago get to work saddling the horses.

When it's time to mount, most of my nerves have dissipated. Shadow and I have officially bonded. After that, things get difficult. Javier and Santiago coach me simultaneously, overwhelming my uneasiness.

"Be sure to look where you're going. Your horse follows your eyes," Javier instructs.

"Squeeze with your calves. Not a kick," Santiago directs from atop his own horse, Ace. Ace is much bigger than Shadow and has shiny copper hair. They wait for Shadow and me and the exit of the barn, the doors wide open.

Leaning forward, I whisper to Shadow, "I just need you to follow Ace. Do that, and I'll make sure you get a big treat."

Shadow cranes her neck, looking at me with one eye. It's like she's making sure I'll keep good on my bribe.

I hold my hand up like I'm taking a witness oath in court. "Cross my heart, babe. Do this for me, and I'll get you..." My attention switches to Santiago. "What's her favorite treat?"

Santiago's brows are pinched together as he watches. "Sugar cubes."

I return to Shadow. "I swear you'll get sugar cubes."

Shadow whinnies and trots to stand beside Ace. Santiago gives me a proud look. "Let's go then." He makes a clicking sound with his mouth, and Ace canters away. Shadow follows closely.

Behind us, I hear Javier comment, "That's one way to do it."

CHAPTER 13

SANTIAGO

Leave it to Blake to convince a nine-hundred-pound animal to listen to her. I'm not surprised in the slightest. Blake and Shadow seem to have bonded in the small amount of time I was gone. I doubt that horse will ever obey me again.

Gift for Blake.

Shadow quickens her speed, bringing her and Blake to my side. I'm not sure if it's from Blake's command or if Shadow just felt like it, but Blake remains calm and composed, adjusting to Shadow's shifting pace.

Blake flashes me an elated smile. The cold air has turned her cheeks pink, but the temperature doesn't seem to bother her.

"I didn't like Manny talking to you." The confession is out before I know it. I'm not embarrassed by it. It's the truth.

Blake tries to make her smile go away, but to my content, I don't think anything could wipe that smile off her face right now.

"You heard that?" she questions, her focus remaining forward, utilizing the advice Javier gave her.

"I might have to fire him for that." I make it sound playful, but I'm seriously thinking about it.

Blake finally looks my way, a puckish look in her eyes. "So you *are* the possessive kind." She fakes a serious demeanor. "But Walker and Levi are allowed to see me naked."

My lips contort into a half-grin. "It's different with them."

"How so?" She's dropped the teasing now that curiosity hangs over her like a cloud.

"With them, it's more like sharing, except I'm not losing out on anything."

My answer seems to leave her speechless when we continue down the trail in silence. After ten minutes of silence, I decide she's been with her thoughts long enough.

It's my turn.

I gently pull on the reins, bringing Ace to a halt, and Shadow follows suit. Standing on the stirrups, I swing one leg over and hop down.

"Are we here?" Blake searches the white fields around us. "I don't see any large snow drifts. Do we just turn around now and go back?"

Rounding Ace's head, I come to Shadow's side and motion for Blake to dismount. I hold onto her hips as she mimics my movements.

She peers up at me, a furrow between her brows. "What are we doing?"

I don't give her a verbal answer. Instead, I grab one of her hands and lead her to a spot beside the trail where the snow is thick. Blake analyzes me with her gaze, her skepticism loud and clear. Dropping her hand, I hold my arms out wide at my sides.

"Are we measuring your wingspan?" she jokes. "I already know you're a tall guy. No surprise there."

I smirk, then fall backward into the snow, performing an impromptu trust fall with Mother Nature. Blake lets out a startled shriek as I land on the icy cloud. Then I move my arms up and down and my legs in and out, dismissing the snow melting and dampening my clothes.

"You gave me a heart attack so you could make a snow angel?" she yells accusingly.

My only response is to chuckle.

"Santiago."

More laughter.

"Santi."

Lifting my head up, I pause my movements. "Yes?"

"You're forty-five years old," she points out like her statement is enough evidence for an argument.

I plop my head back down and continue making my angel. "Forty-eight," I correct.

"That's not helping your case," she returns.

"Then I plead the fifth, Your Honor," I joke back. When she doesn't respond, I taunt her. "So you're scared of horses *and* snow angels."

"No," she snaps.

"Prove it," I challenge.

Her footsteps near as she mutters to herself, "This is ridiculous." Despite her reluctance, she gets in the snow with me, creating her own snow angel. It's not long before she's laughing. I stop and sit up, witnessing the pure joy radiating from her.

I'd do anything and everything to keep her laughing like that.

She sighs and stops moving, gazing up at the sky with content written all over her face. I lie back down and look up with her. The sun is starting to go down, and the stars are making themselves known.

"Why do you call me that?"

I prop myself up on my elbow. "What?"

Blake holds her hands up, gesturing to the wonder above. "My sky. I may not be fluent, but I can follow what someone is saying."

"Because that's what you are," I state plainly, like my reasoning is a given.

Her focus remains upward as her face pinches. "I'm the sky? Big, blue, and full of pollution?" She snorts, then makes a face. Sitting up, she mirrors my position. "Are you calling me a smurf?"

An obnoxious laugh bursts free. "No, smart ass." She raises her brows, prompting me to explain. "You really want to know? Once I tell you, you can't unhear it."

"I want to know," she confirms immediately.

"When I look at you, when I'm near you, I feel like I can breathe. It's like I carry this weight on my chest and half the time I don't even realize it. But when you're here, and everything else is dark, and I can't see, you hold up the stars so I can find my way."

Tears form in the corners of her eyes as she shakily responds, "Don't say things like that unless you mean them."

"*¿Por qué no lo diría en serio?*" Shuffling closer, I reach for her hand, and she responds by holding it out for me. *Why wouldn't I mean it?*

One tear slips free. "Because, as I said earlier, you don't know me anymore. I'm not some faultless beacon. I wreck things. I ruin everything I touch."

I bring her hand to my lips and kiss each knuckle. "Then ruin me."

Her tears fall freely, something stitching together in her eyes. She erases the space between us, wrapping her arms around me as her tears fall from her cheeks onto my coat. I embrace her back, holding her tight.

A minute later, my hat is knocked off my head, and hot breath tousles my hair. "The hell?" I open my eyes, looking for the cause, and I'm met with a black snout. Blake shifts back from our hug, chuckling at Shadow's antics.

"What can I say?" Blake says, lifting her arms into a shrug. "She just wanted to make sure I was okay."

Laughter fills the air around us, and I memorize this moment. I never want to forget it.

My phone rings in my front coat pocket. I contemplate ignoring it but decide against it. "Hey, what's up?"

Walker's voice is serious, as usual. "I need you to get over to Highway 109."

I'm on my feet before he finishes his sentence, dragging Blake up with me. "What happened?"

Blake gnaws on her bottom lip. "What's going on?"

"There's been an accident," Walker informs me.

I don't like where this is going. My mind rolls through the various faces of people in my life, wondering which one of them is injured or worse.

"Who?"

Walker's breath crackles through the phone.

"Walk, who was hurt?"

He still hesitates.

"Me."

CHAPTER 14

BLAKE

Santiago must have been a racecar driver in another life because we're at the crash site in minutes despite the icy roads and falling snow. We pull up to find the ambulance, deputies, and fire department are already on the scene.

I'm out of the cab and running through the snow before Santiago can even put his truck in park.

I don't know where I'm going. All I know is that I have to find him.

"Walk!" I shout, scanning the chaos for his signature hat.

The first responder right next to me reaches for my shoulder as he says, "Miss, you need to get back in your car."

Maneuvering away, I avoid his touch. "Where is Walker Maddox?"

"Miss…" he tries again.

"Don't you dare tell me to leave. I'm not leaving until I know he's okay," I state firmly.

He crosses his arms. "You can't be here."

"Listen, buddy," I rest my hands on my hips and stare him down, even though he's a whole head taller than me. "A SWAT team wouldn't be able to move me, so you sure as hell aren't either. I'm going to ask one more time before I release my inner bitch. Where the fuck is Walker Maddox?"

A hand lands on my arm. "She's with me, Johnson."

"Keep her on leash, Harding," Johnson warns.

Levi drags me away, directing me toward the ambulance as we leave the stick in the mud. Behind us, I hear someone say, in a voice that suspiciously sounds like Santiago, "Talk to her like that again…"

We move too far away for me to hear the rest, and I forget all about it when I finally lay my eyes on Walker.

My stomach drops.

There's a huge gash along his hairline and a sizable bruise on the left side of his jaw. There isn't an inch of visible skin that isn't scraped, cut, or bruised.

He made good on his threat. He tried to hurt Walker. He almost killed him.

When Walker spots me, his shoulders lose a bit of their tension. I'm up and in the ambulance with him, disregarding the lack of space. He opens his arms just in time to catch me.

I bury my face in his shoulder, breathing in his presence.

He's here. He's alive.

I repeat those simple truths, waiting for them to sink in.

Walker rubs circles on my back while his other hand holds the back of my head. "I'm okay, Baby Girl."

"You better be," I mutter into his shirt. When I tighten my grip, I feel him flinch as he grunts. I pull back like I was burned. "You're not okay," I accuse.

"He has a broken rib," the EMT I didn't notice before says.

"Don't lie to me," I scold Walker.

"I won't if you won't." Walker's insinuation lands, but I manage not to let it show.

When I keep my lips sealed, Hudson, the EMT, continues to patch up Walker, and I hover. Santiago joins Levi at the open doors, observing the first aid. They both keep a straight face, but there's no mistaking their relief.

Poor guy has to deal with a grumpy over-grown baby. Hudson rambles as he works, which is how I find out that he just passed his EMT exam, and his reward is Walker.

"I told you. I'm fine. I don't need stitches," Walker grates out from his spot on the gurney, pushing Hudson's hands away from the gash on his forearm.

Hudson sighs, a needle and thread in his hands. "Sheriff, I'm just trying to do my job."

"I understand that, but I'm telling you, there's nothing wrong with me," Walker argues.

Sitting on the thin cushion next to Walker, I scoff, then gesture to the plethora of scrapes, cuts, and bruises.

"You know my mom would kill me if I wasn't thorough," Hudson pleads with his bright green eyes.

Walker shakes his head. "Jolene wouldn't even think of it. You're her only child."

"Maybe, but she'd maim me real good, and I'd rather not go through that," Hudson argues back.

"Just let the boy do his job, Walk," Levi demands with his mouth quirked in annoyance. "You can't do your job when half of your body is broken, let alone when you're bleeding all over the place."

Walker glares at Levi, unwilling to admit that he's right. He waves his hand at his injured arm, giving Hudson the go-ahead to continue.

Hudson beams a triumphant smile in my direction. "Thanks, Harding." With the green light, Hudson stitches up the cut.

Walker doesn't flinch or wince once, and he refuses to let Hudson numb the area. I study Walker's face the entire time, waiting to jump in and help, but I hold myself back. Hudson steps out after he has Walker looking like he's close to being mummified.

Walker finally seems to let some of the exhaustion slip in.

"What happened?" I ask.

Walker answers, "Someone tried to run me off the road."

"Tried?" My voice rises an octave, conveying my outrage at Walker's attempt to downplay the situation.

"It looks like they were successful," Levi mutters.

I huff in frustration as I reach for an alcohol wipe and start to clean off some of the dried blood on Walker's cheek. Walker's fists loosen, and he sinks backward, leaning against the wall of the ambulance.

"You don't need to baby me," he disputes in a low voice, his objection only meant for me.

I snag another wipe and gently swab along his jawline, avoiding the bruise there. "You'd do the same thing if our roles were reversed."

Walker's fingers wrap around my wrist, but he doesn't push me away. Memorizing the warmth of his skin on mine, my heart clenches in my chest.

My eyes meet his aqua gaze, and my breath catches. Even sitting, he's still taller than me. Peering down at me, his attention flicks to my lips.

"How're you doing?"

The question at my back causes us to jump apart, neither of us realizing we had drifted closer together.

Deputy McCreedy waits wedged between Levi and Santiago to talk to Walker. Her muscles flick angrily in her jaw as she sneers at me.

"Fine," Walker answers. "Did you finish with the scene?" His tone is mechanical, lacking the warmth of hers.

Tessa's glare softens as her attention switches to Walker. "Ridge is—"

Walker stays in sheriff mode. "You have seniority, Tessa. He shouldn't be alone." He reaches for his shirt, fastening each button. "When you're done gathering the evidence, send it off to the lab in Jackson. You should be able to pull paint samples from my truck, where the other driver hit me. From there, we should be able to narrow down the make and model."

Tessa schools her features, acting as if she's unaffected by the reprimand. "On it, boss." Before she leaves, her eyes narrow on how close Walker and I are sitting. Her nostrils flare as she stomps away.

Santiago and Levi share a look. I have zero clue what it means, but they seem highly amused by whatever thought was passed between them.

When they face Walker and me again, their somber mood returns. Levi steps an inch closer. "Did you get a look at the driver or the car?"

Reaching for his jacket, Walker finishes with his shirt. "Are you interrogating me?"

"Yeah. Get over it," Levi retorts.

"We were deputized, remember?" Santiago pulls his coat aside and points to a badge clipped to his belt.

Walker sighs, rising to his feet. "Yep. Regretting it."

He can't stand to his full height and has to do a bulky shuffle until he's able to hop down from the ambulance. Santiago and Levi step back to make room for him, and I follow behind.

Walker finally sees the badge and rears his head back. "Where did you get that?"

"Jolene gave it to me," Santiago responds proudly.

"Of course she did." Walker rubs his eyes with his hand, then looks to Levi. "Do you have one too?"

Levi just nods, a gleam of mischievous satisfaction in his eyes.

"You two were deputized? When?" I ask, stepping around Walker.

"A while ago." Levi waves like it's an everyday occurrence.

"The car?" Santiago prompts Walker again.

Walker answers like it's second nature. "Black lifted truck. Couldn't make out the license plate. Tinted windows."

"Anyone who might want you dead?"

Santiago's question pulls all the air from my lungs, and my pulse turns hard and quick in my throat.

"I'm the sheriff. Plenty of people are angry with me." Walker's eyebrows arch high, mocking Santiago.

There's one person in particular...but I still don't know their name.

Levi amends the question. "But how many would actually make an attempt on your life?"

"Who knows?" The corners of Walker's mouth pinch. "That's enough with the questions." He moves to leave, pushing between Levi and Santiago.

Levi's hand on Walker's shoulder stops the escape. "If this were anyone else, you wouldn't stop interrogating until you got what you want. Santiago got in two questions."

Walker's expression shutters minutely as he takes a breath. "That's two more than anyone else would've gotten."

I dart around the three of them, moving in front of Walker with my hands raised, signaling him to stop. "How can we help?"

Walker points a finger at me like I'm a disobedient child. "You need to go back to Moose Gap Lodge. I don't want you anywhere near this."

"I'm a big girl. I can make my own choices." My arms fold across my chest, and the heels of my boots dig into the ground.

Walker bends, getting in my face. "If you try to help, I'll arrest you for impeding an investigation."

My teeth grind together. "Is that your only solution? I piss you off, so you arrest me. Sounds like a *childish game,* don't you think?" I use his own words against him.

The muscles in Walker's jaw tighten as he grits his teeth.

"Butterfly, he's right," Levi chimes in, crowding me from the side.

My head flinches as if I was just slapped. "Excuse me?"

"You can wait at my place," Santiago proposes, approaching the other side. The whisper of space between the four of us charges, ready to blow.

"I'm good. I know when I'm not wanted." My response is for Santiago, but I don't take my eyes off Walker.

We seem to end up here every time we're around each other—trying to wear the other down with a glare. And I'm tired of it.

Giving them my back, I march heavily in the opposite direction.

"Wait." Santiago calls after me, but I don't slow down.

The next moment, I'm flanked on either side by Levi and Santiago. They each easily keep pace with me and my long strides.

"What?" I snap at them. My tone is probably too harsh, but I'm too frustrated to care.

They don't know why I need to be involved, and I shouldn't hold that against them. But with progress running a deficit, I want to scream.

"You don't have your car. In fact, I'm pretty sure it's still in the Timberline parking lot," Santiago points out, and my cheeks heat as I remember why my car is at the bar.

Clearing my throat, I respond brusquely, "I'll walk."

I don't actually want to walk, but I'm too angry and too embarrassed.

"Don't be stubborn, *mi Cielo*," Santiago reproves and grips my elbow, bringing my tromping to a grinding halt.

"I'll give you a ride," Levi offers.

Santiago's hold on my elbow doesn't let up.

They're not going to let me leave here on foot.

"Fine," I concede.

I'll do what they want…for now. They can't hover over me incessantly. As soon as Levi's gone, it's back to continuing my own investigation.

Whatever it takes.

CHAPTER 15

LEVI

Pressing the big circle button on top of the countertop appliance, the steam carries a rich, bittersweet aroma through the small kitchen in Northfork Veterinary Clinic. It's only eight in the morning, and I'm already making my fourth cup of coffee. Impatiently, I tap my fingers on the counter as I wait for my large mug to fill up.

I barely slept last night. After Blake forced Walker to go home and leave the crash site, I went to Santiago's and spent the night in his bed. We comforted each other the only way we knew how—with our bodies.

Every time I closed my eyes, all I could see was the blood flowing from Walker's head wound. When I got there, he was still in his truck. The fire department was grabbing the Jaws of Life to get the driver's side door open—a detail I didn't share with Blake. I didn't want to scare her more. She was already worked up when I found her screaming at Johnson. If Santiago hadn't been there to verbally rip him in two, I probably wouldn't have been able to hold myself back from punching him in the face.

I've always known Blake had a little crush on Santiago, Walker, and me when she was younger. I didn't realize how much that had matured until I witnessed her relief when I brought her to Walker in the ambulance.

"Levi? Are you here?"

The echo of my name from the lobby pulls me from my introspection.

"Can I help you?" Abbott responds.

"Oh! You scared me." The customer's voice registers when I realize it's Blake.

Nabbing my full mug, I head for the front. On my way, I unintentionally overhear their conversation.

"I'm sor—" Abbott's voice cuts off. "Blake Jennings?" A hint of genuine delight enters his tone.

"Yes," she answers plainly.

"Abbott Sutton," he informs her, reminding her who he is.

I forgot that they're the same age. They probably went to high school together.

"Oh my God, Abbott," she exclaims contentedly. "It's so good to see you. How are you?"

My grip on my coffee tightens as pain flares in my jaw from clenching my teeth.

"Good. Just working here," Abbott converses casually, "When did you get back?"

"I'm not really *back*."

We'll see about that, Butterfly.

"We should get a drink sometime. Catch up."

My footsteps storm into the lobby. Blake stands there, alluring as ever. Her hair falls in its natural wave. Her oversized, cable-knit sweater and straight jeans do little to hide the curves of her figure. It takes every ounce of energy not to grab her and kiss her until we're both breathless.

Abbott is situated on one side of the counter, and she's on the other, but anything less than ten feet is too close for my comfort.

"Hey, Blake." I give her a simple smile, then turn to my assistant with a plain expression. "Abbott, you can go home. It's a slow day."

"I don't mind help—" he starts.

"I got it covered," I interrupt.

He straightens his spine, ready to dispute further, but after a moment, he relaxes his shoulders and retrieves his things from where he stores them behind the front desk. "I'll see you tomorrow, then."

Once he's out the door, my muscles loosen. "Did you get back to your motel okay last night?"

"Yep," she answers tersely. "You didn't have to snap at him."

"I didn't snap at him," I deny, taking a swig of coffee.

Blake's raises an eyebrow as she folds her arms across her chest. "Would it make things easier if I let you pee on my leg and mark your territory?"

Bringing my mug to my mouth for another sip, my hand pauses halfway, and I perk up. A smug smile curves my lips. "Does that mean you're mine to mark?"

Pink colors her cheeks. "I—Well—If you—" Blake stammers then shakes her head, changing the topic. "How's Bear doing?"

We'll circle back to this later.

Setting my mug down, I ask, "Bear?"

"The dog needs a name," Blake clarifies as her chin dips.

My expression softens. "It suits him."

"I thought so," she returns with a closed-mouth smile.

"Let's go check on him," I invite, offering her my hand.

Her body shows no reservation as she strides toward me, placing her hand in mine and entwining our fingers together. My chest expands, finally allowing me to take a full breath.

I didn't realize how badly I needed her here after last night until now.

Leading her through the clinic and to the kennels.

Once the pitbull comes into view, Blake releases my hand and rushes forward. "Hey, Bear! How's my guy doing?"

Bear jumps up from his bed, licking Blake's hands through the wire door, and his tail wags behind him.

I stay back, giving them room to reunite. "He's happy to see you."

"I'm sure he just smells the treats in my pocket." Blake reaches into her denim pocket and pulls out a bacon-shaped treat, feeding it to Bear.

"Or he remembers that you saved his life," I debate, challenging the way she's downplaying her role in Bear's rescue.

Blake shakes her head, petting Bear's snout. "I didn't do much. You're the one that nursed him back to health."

"But it's you he wants," I point out.

She seems to accept my claim as she showers Bear with more love.

Unexpectedly, Blake gets a far-off look in her eyes. "I always wanted a dog, but Dad never let me."

The mention of Landon Jennings has my lips pressing together. It's a good thing Blake's back is to me because my body is on the verge of shaking, but my emotions aren't her burden to bear. She's already been through enough.

Exhaling a deep breath, I shove my fury deep down and lock it away. "Well, now you have one."

"That's true. I do." Pivoting to face me, she gets up. "Is there anything I have to do before I take him? Do we need to try to find his owner?" Her second question holds a note of apprehension.

"I already tried. No one's claimed him. I even scanned him for a chip, but he doesn't have one," I reassure her.

Even if I did find out that Bear had an owner, I would still give him to Blake. I wouldn't hurt her by separating the two. She'd act like she's fine, but I know this woman. She'd be heartbroken.

"He's had his shots. His teeth are in good shape. No broken bones." I recite the facts like I'm going through a checklist.

Blake reaches for me without my prompt. She returns her hand to mine, resuming the hold we had before. "Thanks for checking him out."

A fire enters my veins, increasing my pulse and making me want to shed my clothes and hers, but I keep my voice soothing.

"Not a problem. I just need you to sign some paperwork, then he's all yours."

Blake nods her head, and I steer us back the way we came and into my office. At my desk, I pull out the proper papers and point to two signature lines. "There and there." Blake snags a loose pen and scribbles her signature. "Congratulations, Blake Jennings. You are now the proud owner of a very happy pitbull."

Her smile is bright, lighting up my whole world. "Thank you, Levi."

Blake has the body of a woman—a very beautiful woman. Nothing like the fake and over-edited pictures of women in magazines that have become the standard today.

Unable to hold myself back any longer, I step into her space, backing her up against the edge of my desk. Her chest rises and falls rapidly, and her pupils are blown wide. My cock grows hard in my pants. I lift my hand, brushing her cheek with my fingers as I tuck her hair behind her ear.

She swallows, and her gaze drops. "Levi…"

I rest my hand on the side of her neck. "Don't push me away." My other hand grips her hip, and I seal our bodies together. "If you don't want me, then say it."

"It's not that." She gives me a pleading look, her eyes gathering tears. "You don't know what you're getting yourself into."

"I know," I state firmly, cupping her face with both hands. "Look at me, Blake." Her eyes flash up to mine. "I *know*."

Blake shakes her head vehemently. "You deserve someone with less baggage—someone easier."

My thumb wipes the tears that fall free. "I don't want easy, Butterfly. I want you."

Her shoulders relax as if my statement has lifted a weight from her.

As Blake lifts onto her toes, I lean down, and our lips meet in a furious passion. Blake immediately opens her mouth for me, and I take the opportunity to swipe my tongue inside. A feral groan rumbles in my throat.

One of my hands glides down her chest, around her hip, and grips her ass while my other hand cups her breast. I swipe my thumb over the peak, causing Blake to whimper into my mouth.

Blake's hands dive into my hair, scraping my scalp with her nails and eliciting another moan from my chest. Her teeth scrape my lower lip, biting me with just enough pain to make me want more.

One moment, Blake and I are losing ourselves in each other, and in the next moment the world goes pitch black. The animals back in the kennels go into a full-blown pandemonium, barking and crying at the top of their lungs, alerting me to whatever is coming.

My reflexes take over, rotating me to face the door to my office and shielding Blake with my body.

Blake tries to peek around me, but I swing my arm back to hold her in place. "What was that?"

I remain silent, listening intently for any sign of life. When one doesn't come, I dart to the cabinet along the wall and retrieve my Sig Sauer P320. "Stay here."

Blake tracks my movements as her hands shake. "Where are you going?"

"To check the fuse box. It's back by the kennels," I answer, checking the slide and turning off the safety. "I'm sure it's nothing."

"Then what's with the piece?" Blake holds her hands out at her sides in frustration.

"Just in case," I lie. "Wait in here and lock the door."

"But—"

I don't give Blake time to argue with my plan. On light feet, I enter the hallway. The dim emergency lights are the only source of luminance out here. I don't like it, but I've been in worse situations.

My blood pumps in my veins with anticipation of what I might find. I check both exam rooms and the storage closet, coming up empty. Sweat drips down my back as I approach the door that leads to the kennels.

God help the motherfucker who threatens me and mine.

My hand brushes the cold metal of the handle when someone grabs my sleeve. Whirling around, I break the person's hold on me.

"Chill out," Blake whisper-shouts at me.

Sighing, I roll my eyes. "Blake, I almost hurt you. You can't sneak up on me like that. I told you to—"

Blake holds up a hand for me to stop talking. "Too bad. I'm coming."

I don't have time to take her back, so it looks like she's my shadow. "Stay close and hold on to the back of my shirt."

When I finally feel Blake's hand grip onto the fabric, I place my hand back on the handle and pull down slowly. The door opens without a sound upstairs, and I peer around the large space. The commotion and barking of the dogs and the kennels are my only indication that something is amiss. I lied to Blake earlier to keep her calm, and I'll probably go to hell for that.

"Do you see anything?" Blake whispers into my ear.

I hold my finger up to my lips, urging her to be quiet. Staying low, I proceed forward with Blake on my heels. With all of my senses on high alert, I scan the room. Everything seems to be in its place.

Leashes on the hooks.

Clipboards hanging by the door.

Kennels locked shut.

The only thing wrong is the lack of lighting and the mop bucket next to me lying on its side, which is more than enough to put me on edge.

My breaths come quick, but I keep them quiet. I told Blake that there was nothing to worry about, but the truth is I have nothing but panic and worry in my veins right now. It's not normal for the lights to just go off like this. The only other time that has happened was during a blizzard, and that was over five years ago.

Guiding us forward past the first row of kennels, I go down the second, leading us by Bear. I know Blake will want to check on him.

Every few steps, I feel Blake's grip getting tighter and tighter.

He barks vigorously, jumping at his cage. He thrashes wildly to get out. Blake's hands tighten the fabric further, and I can hear her light gasp behind me as she witnesses Bear's behavior.

We turn and go down the third and final row, which is empty of occupants. As we clear the end, I'm barely past the last kennel when a shadow shifts in my peripheral vision.

My only warning is the light scrape of boots on the concrete.

In half a second, the shadow is on top of me.

My body is knocked into the hard cement of the floor. A jolt of pain zings from my hip to my shoulder. My gun goes skidding across the floor out of my reach, and the body on top of me is weighing me down.

A fist lands in my gut, knocking the wind out of me, but I was born here. I was raised here—I know how to take a hit.

Twisting onto my side, I keep my elbows tight against my ribs to block the rain of punches at my center. It's too dark in here for me to see his face.

I wrap my left hand around one of his wrists, tightly holding it against my chest. The motion pushes his sleeve up, and I'm barely able to make out the outline of a tattoo on his arm.

Barbed wire?

On the left side, I hook his foot with my own and, with my free foot, plant it flat on the ground. Using my foot as leverage, I push my hips violently upward toward the ceiling and turn my head to the left. Utilizing the momentum, I roll my attacker onto his back, gaining the upper hand.

I return a few punches of my own to his middle and his face. He holds his arms up with his forearms together, creating a shield.

In the split second between punches, he wraps his arms

around my torso and pulls me to his chest, burying his head into my shoulder. He tries to perform the same move I did, but I widened my knees to prevent the switch.

A fast learner.

He switches his tactics and pulls my weight over his shoulder, throwing me off balance and rolling me under him.

He draws his fists back, ready to exchange blows again. But before he can lower his fist to my body, a female enraged cry catches my attention, and a smaller form tackles him from the side just like he did to me moments earlier.

A wave of acid wells up in my stomach as I realize that Blake has come to my defense. "No!"

Rushing to my feet, I don't make it in time to the lake before the man throws her off of him, her body making a loud thump on the hard floor.

Blake doesn't move.

For the first time in my life since I was fourteen years old, I freeze.

I'll never forgive myself for this moment of hesitation—for this moment of fear.

Instead of avenging Blake, I let our attacker run out, and I hurry to her side. "Blake? Blake, are you okay? Butterfly, I need you to talk to me."

A pained groan rumbles in Blake's throat, and she rolls onto her back. "That hurt like a bitch."

My hands hover above her body, afraid to touch her and make her pain worse. "Don't you ever do that again."

Blake pushes herself up onto her elbows. "Don't save your life? Sure. Next time I'll just let you get hurt."

"You're infuriating," I growl.

Needing to remind myself that she's OK, I place my hands on her cheeks and guide her mouth to mine.

It's a kiss of comfort—of solace.

Releasing her lips, I rest my forehead on hers. "Please don't do that to me. I wouldn't be able to live with myself if something happened to you because of me."

She shakes her head. "I can't promise you that. I will always step in when someone I care about is being hurt." Sighing, she sits all the way up, and I give her the space to do so. "Who was that?"

"I don't know. I couldn't see his face." Staring off in the direction he left, I rub my eyes. "But I get the feeling he wasn't here for me."

Blake's head drops to an angle. "What do you mean?"

"In any attack, you take out the biggest threat first," I explain.

Blake brushes off my theory and eyes me as I pull out my phone. "You're going to call Walk, aren't you?" she groans.

I quirk a brow at her. "If you know the answer, why ask the question?"

Rising to her feet, she brushes off her pants, and I stand with her. "I already have one overprotective man with me," Blake gestures to me, "I'm not looking forward to encountering another right now."

"Well then prepare yourself," I chuckle, "because I'm calling two more."

Blake gives me an irritated glare but doesn't say a word.

I'm still trying to keep the moment light for her, even though there was an intruder in the clinic.

Whoever it was that dared to do this, they won't be breathing much longer.

CHAPTER 16

WALKER

Ankle deep in half-melted snow, the chill of the late morning contrasts with the burn in my chest as I remove the cigarette from my lips. My back rests against the brick exterior of the small police station.

This much-needed break couldn't come soon enough. Sleep was scarce last night. Every time I closed my eyes, I was haunted by the bruises on Blake's shoulder and hip. I don't blame Levi. He kept her safe the best he could.

The entire town of Evergreen Falls was turning into one big crime scene.

At six-thirty this morning, my phone rang.

Mayor Bridger Reynolds.

Against my better judgment, I answer.

"What the hell is going on out there, Walker?" Bridger demands before I can get out a greeting. "First a murder, then another body, and now rumors of an attempted break-in? Silver Pines opens in a few weeks. Tourists aren't going to spend money in a town they think is crawling with killers."

I pinch the bridge of my nose.

"My deputies are working every lead we've got."

"Not fast enough."

I bite back a sigh.

Bridger always sounds like an overgrown toddler throwing a tantrum whenever things don't go his way.

"This investigation doesn't move faster because you raise your voice."

"I'm the mayor."

"And I'm the sheriff."

A beat of silence.

"You work for this town," he reminds me, his tone seething.

"I work for the people in it."

His tone sharpens.

"If this keeps affecting tourism, I'll take it to the town council. Maybe Evergreen Falls needs a sheriff who can actually keep this place under control."

There it was.

The weekly threat to fire me.

I've lost count of how many times Bridger has tried to use my badge as leverage over the years.

"If you think you can do better," I return, allowing my tone to convey my annoyance, "come down to the station and take it."

"I'll remember you said that."

"I doubt it."

I ended the call before he could have the satisfaction of getting the last word.

With the cigarette burned to the filter, I drop it into the snow and put it out with my boot.

The crunching of footsteps alerts me to Santiago's approach. "We found the partner."

"Whose partner?" Pulling out a new cigarette from the pack in my pocket, I place the filtered end between my lips and use my lighter to ignite the other end as I take a gentle puff.

"Evan's," Santiago states.

"I thought he didn't have one." I remind him.

"He denied it, but Levi decided to dig through Evan's phone and computer," Santiago explains.

With a sigh, I prematurely put out my cigarette. "You and I can pick him up. Tell Levi to meet us at the cabin."

Santiago glances around. "Did you get another car already?"

"I finished fixing up the 1985 W250," I inform him.

Santiago dangles his keys. "I'll drive. Wouldn't want to get into another wreck."

It's not a far drive to Evergreen Falls High School. The school is located just at the edge of town. The building looms there like a giant steel warehouse. The tan and navy metal siding is weathered by decades of snow, wind, and neglect. Surrounded by a patch of dead grass covered in Wyoming snow, a stone monument in front bears the school's mascot.

Santiago parks his truck along the red curb, and we stroll up the short sidewalk. The heavy front doors give way to a wide commons area filled with trophy cases and announcement posters. Championship banners hang from the rafters overhead, and decades of class photos are displayed on the walls.

Having attended here myself, just like half of the people in this town, I couldn't forget the layout of the school even if I wanted to. We veer right into the front office.

It's hard to believe that after all these years, Miss Coleman still works as the receptionist. I tip my hat to her and point further into the office, indicating our destination. She waves us on by as she speaks into the corded phone.

We pass administrative offices and stop in front of the one we're looking for. The bright bronze plaque next to the door reads *Garth Henderson, Counselor.*

Knocking on the cracked door, I don't wait for a response as I gently swing it all the way open. "Hey, Garth."

"Sheriff," he returns, setting down the paper he was reading over. "What can I do for you?"

Garth Henderson is basically a carbon copy of half the men in Evergreen Falls. Mid-forties, lean build, with dark hair threaded with grey around these temples. Smile lines bracket his mouth, carved there by years of hard work and Wyoming weather. He's the type of man that someone doesn't think about twice when they see him in the grocery store.

Stepping further into his office, I take a seat in one of the chairs in front of him while Santiago remains in the doorway. "I was wondering if you could help me with an investigation."

"I'd love to. What do you need?" Garth clasps his hands together in front of him, resting his forearms on his desk.

My finger taps the edge of his desk. "Not here. Mind coming with me?"

Garth opens his hands in a subtle gesture. "Not a problem."

We're in the car for a good 5 minutes before Garth even acknowledges Santiago—a fact that grates on my skin.

He'll pay for that.

Garth leans forward, poking his head between the driver and passenger seat. "Santiago, what're you doing here?"

Santiago gives his reply without a care in the world. "I'm just playing chauffeur. You hear about Walk's car accident? Totaled his truck."

Garth nodded his head. "Oh yeah. I heard about that." He swivels his head to me and asks, "You doing alright?"

"Right as rain," I confirm, and Garth sits back in his seat.

It's taking everything in me to hold back. I have to keep reminding myself that justice will come soon.

A few minutes later, Garth leans forward again. "I thought we were headed to the station."

"We are," Santiago reassures him. "I just need to get something from Falling Sky first."

When we get to Falling Sky, we don't go through the front entrance. We drive further down and take a fire road to our normal spot.

This is the cabin that we used to play in as boys—me, Levi, Grant, Santiago, and Landon. We would get into all kinds of trouble out here, sometimes with girls and sometimes just from being stupid young boys.

The cabin sits at the edge of Falling Sky Ranch, half swallowed by the forest. The branches of the pines crowded around the structure on all sides hang low enough to scrape the roof.

Santiago's great-grandfather built it from rough-hewn logs that are now darkened by time and weather. Most of the windows are broken. The surviving panes are cloudy with age and coated with dirt. The front porch sags beneath the weight of neglect, the railing missing several slats.

Directing his question to the back seat, Santiago puts the gear into park. "Could you come help me, Garth? It's a little heavy for me, and Walk's back has been bothering him."

"I thought you said you were okay," Garth directs at me.

"Old age," I answer by way of excuse. This is the only time I'll admit that the years have been rough on my body.

Garth accepts my lie. "Oh, okay. Yeah, I'll come."

As Santiago and Garth exit the vehicle, I follow behind them. "I'll hold the door for you two."

Santiago ushers Garth through the front door ahead of him. Garth hesitates as he walks across the dilapidated wood floors, stirring up dust with every footstep. The dim light makes it nearly impossible to see the inside. But I know this cabin better than my own home.

I pause in the doorway.

Something feels off. I can't put my finger on it.

The place should smell like old pine, mildew, and decades of dust. Instead, beneath the musty air, the sharp scent of fresh cleaner lingers.

Faint. Almost hidden.

My gaze sweeps the room, finding that everything looks the same.

Garth juts his head forward as if he's trying to see what's in front of him. "What exactly are we grabbing?"

"There's a table in the corner." Santiago points with his finger.

Garth shakes his head. "I don't see a—"

A shape breaks from the shadow behind Garth, wielding a wooden baseball bat. Garth is completely unaware as the bat comes down on the back of his head. He falls to the warped floor, a pile of dead weight. Levi keeps a hold on the handle and rests the end on his shoulder, standing over Garth's collapsed body.

Santiago moves to stand next to Levi and nudges Garth with his boot. "I think you hit him too hard."

"No, I didn't," Levi argues.

Santiago nudges Garth again. "He's not moving."

"He's not *dead*," Levi corrects.

Santiago flops his arms at his sides in complaint. "But now we have to wait for him to wake up."

Levi waves to Garth with his free hand. "Just throw some water on him."

Santiago swings his arms wide, gesturing to the land around us outside. "Do you see a well around here?"

"Shut up, you two," I interrupt, stepping between them. "We need to get him into position before he wakes up."

Levi makes a face at Santiago.

"What?" Santiago raises his brows. "I'm not the one who hit him."

Levi grumbles, dragging Garth to the center column in the room, while Santiago gets the fire going.

After Garth is tied up and the fire is crackling, Santiago steps outside and returns with a handful of snow. Santiago tosses it into Garth's face, and he sputters awake. "Wakey, wakey."

"Wha—What's going on?" Garth struggles against the ropes. "Did you tie me up?" He glares up at Santiago. When he spots me, he begs,

"Sheriff, you have to help me."

My arms cross my chest. "I don't have to do shit."

"Why are you doing this?" The color drains from his face as he realizes that I'm not his savior here.

I'm his consequence.

Santiago squats, getting in Garth's face. "You're not *that* stupid, are you, Garth?"

"I haven't done anything wrong." Garth struggles to control his quavering.

Levi stands behind Santiago's shoulder. "Evan told us everything."

"N—no. He wouldn't," Garth stammers.

Santiago drops his head to an angle, faking sympathy and pointing to the floor. "Oh, but he did. He sat in this very spot and spilled his guts."

Garth's breathing increases as he thrashes. "Let me go!"

"Shut up." A loud slap echoes in the room as Santiago brings his open hand across Garth's face. "Be a man. Own your shit." Santiago rises to his full height.

Garth is adamant in his denial. "But I didn't—"

Santiago bends, pulling his fist back and punching Garth in the eye. "This can be over quickly if you stop lying."

Garth leans forward as far as he can, groaning from the pain.

Levi tilts his head and informs Garth pointedly, "We have Evan's photos."

"We have Evan's photos."

"I didn't help him with that. I tried to get him to stop." Garth's brows tip up. Santiago makes a show of signing and trudges over to the fire to retrieve his branding iron.

When Levi pulls a hunting knife from his belt and cuts Garth's shirt open, Garth's eyes take on a haunted terror. "No, no, no."

Santiago ignores Garth's plea, pressing the red-hot end into Garth's flesh. Garth screams, on the verge of passing out from the pain.

The stench of burning flesh used to make me sick to my stomach, but now I'm used to the unpleasant smell.

Santiago hands over the branding iron to Levi to return to the fireplace. "Try again. How many?"

Tears track down Garth's cheeks. "I'm sorry. I'm so s—sorry."

"How many, Garth?" Santiago asks again.

Garth continues to weep, barely able to get out the words. "I didn't mean to do it. I didn't mean to."

My blood heats as I listen to him. "That's another lie."

"Why do you have to make me do this?" Santiago shakes his head in mock disappointment as Levi hands over the branding iron.

"Stop! Please, stop!" Garth kicks his legs, trying to keep Santiago away, but his efforts are fruitless.

The Falling Sky brand sizzles against his abdomen, and Garth's cries fill the room once more. He begs for mercy, begs for the agony to end. Even though the branding iron isn't as hot, it still mars Garth's skin. Santiago doesn't stop until Garth's torso is littered with the letters "FS."

Levi crouches down, yelling over the whaling to be heard. "Answer the goddamn question!"

Garth snaps, letting the truth free. "They wanted it!"

Bile rolls in my stomach. "Excuse you?"

Garth's face is blotchy from crying as snot drips from his nose. "They wanted it, I swear. They begged me."

Reaching into my pocket, I pull out one of the photos depicting the heinous acts of Garth and Evan and shove it in Garth's face. "Do you really think this girl wanted you to coerce her into having sex? Does her face look like she's having a good time?"

Garth has the good sense, at least, not to look aroused by the photo. "Sh—she—"

I cut him off, letting a fraction of my fury show. "*She* was a sixteen-year-old girl who just wanted to make it to the eleventh grade."

"She did!" Garth says it as if the girl achieved it on her own.

But we all know the truth.

"After you told her you could help her with her failing grades," Levi adds.

Retrieving another thing from my pocket, I continue, "Last

question," I growl as I hold up a sheet of paper with various teenage girls' school pictures, "are there any more?"

"No. None." Garth lets out a sigh as if he's finally relieved that all of the facts are finally out in the open, and somehow I know it's not an act.

"No. None."

"Don't you dare lie." Santiago threatens.

"I'm not, I swear on my children."

Garth shakes his head vigorously. "I'm not, I swear on my children."

Levi scoffs. "You don't have any children."

Without warning, I pull my Glock 19 from its holster. My index finger squeezes the trigger, sending a bullet through Garth's head.

Santiago mutters a curse as Levi flinches.

"No habíamos terminado," Santiago snaps. *We weren't done.*

[shoot]

"What the hell?"

Switching the safety on, I return my gun to my belt. "He was telling the truth. Besides, we have bigger cases to investigate." Striding back for the door, I stepped out onto the unstable porch.

One case solved.

Another twenty to close.

And I'm not giving up.

CHAPTER 17

LEVI

My back aches, reminding me of my age. It was a long day at the clinic, running between farm calls and appointments. Walker asked me to meet him at Santiago's house after I closed the clinic, and I obliged.

Not that it would take much to get me here.

Even though the sun has just dropped below the horizon, the inside of Santiago's home is lit up as if it's still day.

Santiago's kitchen looks like it was built for feeding an army. A massive island made of dark wood sits in the center of the room beneath wrought-iron pendant lights. The black cabinetry contrasts with the weathered timber beams overhead.

Snow taps against the windows outside. Inside, a cold bottle of beer slides across the kitchen counter toward me, and I catch it, popping off the lid with a bottle opener. Santiago stands on the opposite side of the island from where I sit on a wooden stool.

The creak of the front door and the familiar cadence of boots on the hardwood floors alert us to Walker's arrival.

"In here," Santiago calls.

Walker crosses the kitchen in three long strides and drops a large stack of manila folders on the dark granite between Santiago and me. "This is how you can help."

Santiago takes a sip of his beer, then uses it to point at the mountain of reports. "You're joking."

Walker scoffs, folding his arms. "Did you think you'd be kicking down doors and getting in shootouts?"

"I mean…" Santiago trails off.

"Well, police work includes researching and analyzing data." Walker gives Santiago a look that is full of smug satisfaction.

"We're on it," I claim as I grab the first file from the top and open it in front of me. "What exactly are we looking for?"

"I have a theory," Walker informs us with a nod.

Santiago waves his hand out. "Care to share with the class?"

Walker shakes his head. "I don't want there to be any bias. Just look for patterns." He taps the pile, then turns on his heel and heads back out the door.

As Santiago picks up the next file, I remind him teasingly. "Don't forget to put on your grandpa glasses."

Santiago gives me a miffed look. "Ha. Ha. Very original."

I smile into my beer when I spot Santiago retrieving his glasses from the living room.

Two beers later, I've filled half of a legal pad with notes. Santiago has his own organization system that only makes sense to him. To me, it looks like a tornado came through the kitchen and only hit his files.

Opening the next manila folder, a certain detail sticks out to me.

I've read this before.

Flipping back through my notes, I count the number of times the detail has come up, and a sickening wave of realization wells up in my abdomen. "Oh, my God."

Santiago discards his file into his mess. "What is it?"

I don't give him an answer as I stare down at the papers in front of me. "That bastard."

"Who's a bastard?" Santiago rises from his seat, rounding the island.

"That dirty, rotten bastard!" I shout as I throw my pen down.

Santiago searches for the answer, hovering over my shoulder. "Gotta give me a little more to work with."

I point to the words I just read in the case file. "I think this is what Walk wanted us to find."

Santiago picks up my notes, flipping through the pages. "Are you saying that Derek Holt was the arsonist?"

Retrieving specific files, I show him what I found. "He was first on the scene for every arson fire, and he saved each person who was caught in the fire. And look here. The direction the fires spread seems to be away from the people who were in the buildings."

Santiago strides back to his side, somehow able to find exactly what he's looking for in his clutter. He flips through each file he pulls, reading the same few words aloud over and over. "First on scene: Derek Holt." He drops the folders, adding to the disarray. "Why would he do it?"

Shaking my head, I shrug my shoulders. "I'm sure Walk has an idea."

"I'll call him." Santiago sighs as he grabs his phone.

Walker is back in Santiago's kitchen in less than 10 minutes. He looks at us expectingly, impatiently waiting to hear our analysis.

"Derek Holt is the arsonist," I state plainly. "He was first on scene at all the arson fires. And not just first. He got there more than ten minutes before the truck. At each one, he saved at least one person."

Santiago rocks on his feet. "I'd bet my entire herd that he knew where the people were every time, making it easier to save them."

Not a single muscle twitches on Walker's face.

Santiago narrows his gaze. "You already knew, didn't you?"

Walker lets out that disappointed breath. "I had a hunch."

My lips curved down, forming a small frown. "How?"

"When I talked to Julie Holt, her mantle was basically a tribute to her first husband, who died while in the army," Walker explains, rubbing the back of his neck. "There were only a few pictures with Derek. I didn't search the whole house. I was only in the living room, but I assume it's the same everywhere else."

My eyes stare blankly at nothing, attempting to put together the entire picture. "So...what? You're saying Derek set fires so his wife would think that he's a hero like her late husband?"

Walker shoves his hands into the pockets of his brown wool-lined coat. "Exactly."

I would think that after taking such a huge step in this case, Walker would look relieved, but instead it's as if Santiago and I confirming his theory has added to the stress weighing him down.

Santiago corks abroad. "You get that from your cousin, the hot shot FBI man?"

"I didn't call him," he pauses, "Yet." Walker blinks, and the haunted look in his eye is gone. "Next step is to figure out who would hold a grudge against Derek for this."

"That would mean someone else put two and two together." I presume.

Santiago's eyes dart between Walker and me, waiting for one of us to confirm. "Do you think someone figured it out?"

Walker's tone turns grave. "I think so. According to Derek's wife, everyone loved him. The fire chief said the same thing. So who does that leave?"

"A person who lost something because of the fires he set," I deduce. "No one died, but there was plenty of property damage."

"It could be someone from his past," Santiago suggests

Walker nods. "Always a possibility."

"What do we do next?" Santiago inquires.

"Let me guess," I interject, "more research."

Walker tilts his head. "Exactly."

Santiago and I groan in unison, bringing an amused smile to Walker's face.

CHAPTER 18

BLAKE

"You dirty girl!" Savannah shouts through the phone so loud that I have to pull it away from my ear. "All three?"

I scoff, keeping my eyes on the road as I drive down Main Street away from the diner. Martha made me eat a salad tonight. She scolded me when I ordered my usual like I was a child. She said that I needed a more balanced diet.

Most unpleasant experience since I returned to town.

"You're one to talk," I reply. "And it's not all three. Just...two."

"But you want it to be all of them," Savannah surmises correctly.

My teeth gnaw on my bottom lip. "Maybe."

Savannah gasps, dramatically. "Oh, God."

"What?" I sit up straight.

"You're in love with them," Savannah squeals giddily.

"I am *not*." A bold lie.

Savannah continues to tease me like we're on the playground in middle school. "Yes, you are. Big, fat, triple dip in love."

"Triple dip?" My voice rises an octave.

"Three hunks. Triple. Duh," Savannah explains.

My face pinches. "But 'dip?'"

"If I have to explain that part to you, then we need to have a whole different conversation."

I can't keep a smile off my face at her joke. "Shut up." We laugh together until my abdomen hurts.

Savannah turns the conversation. "Just…be careful, okay?"

Not ready for the shift, I crack another joke. "Of course. I always stretch before and after."

"That's not what I mean, smartass," Savannah admonishes lovingly. "I know what these guys mean to you, and I don't want to see you get hurt."

"Thanks, babe."

"I need to go but call me with updates."

"Promise."

"Love you."

"Love you too."

I'm almost to Moose Gap Lodge when my phone chimes.

Unknown: Did you figure it out yet?

My mouth goes dry. Pulling over on the side of the road, I scramble to type my reply.

Me: Who is this?

Me: I'm going to find you.

Unknown: I know Walker got the ID on the body. Did you figure out why he died?

Did he kill the guy in the field? Or is he talking about someone else?

Me: Who is it?

Unknown: I left you a present at Riverbend Trailer Park.

Unknown: Missing anyone? Have you done a head count lately?

Me: Don't you dare touch my mother.

I get an automated message in return, letting me know that my text can't be delivered.

He blocked me again.

Pressing the gas pedal to the floor, the engine revs as I speed through a quiet Evergreen Falls. Thankfully, most of the town is at home and asleep. Weaving in and out of traffic right now would be a pain.

What am I going to find when I get to the trailer park? Another fire?

I can't let myself drown in all the what-ifs, but it's hard not to wonder.

Get there first, then worry about what to do.

I'm not even a quarter mile away when I see the flames up ahead. My heart just about stops in my chest, and my stomach contracts into a tight ball.

"No," I whisper as my throat threatens to close up.

Just getting to the entrance feels like I'm trying to run through knee-deep mud. It's like I can't get there fast enough.

When I finally pull in, I find that the flames aren't coming from Mama's trailer, but they're in front of it. The fire could easily spread.

I stop and park my car a few trailers back. Jumping out, I run to Mama's trailer and pound on her door.

"Mama! Are you in there?" I try opening the door, but it's locked. "Mama!"

When she still doesn't come out, I turn to the fire, finding that someone is in there hanging on a cross like a scarecrow.

And they're not moving.

After this, I'll never be able to get the smell of burning flesh out of my nose. I hold in a gag as nausea rolls through my stomach.

Pushing past my discomfort, I move to a pile of snow so I can try to put out the fire like last time, but I stop myself and pull my phone out of my pocket.

I don't need Walker even more pissed at me than he already is, so I start to dial 911. But as soon as I press call, red and blue lights almost blind me. I squint, but still try to see who it is.

Before I can make out the shadowed shapes behind the emergency lights, a voice barks my name.

"Blake!"

Shit.

I would recognize that voice anywhere.

"Walk, I was just calling you." I motion my hands in a calming gesture.

"You're under arrest." He grabs me by the shoulder and spins me around. Cold metal locks around my wrists in less than a second.

"Not this again," I complain.

Walker doesn't bother to explain. "You have the right to remain silent. Anything you say can and will be—"

I groan, cutting him off. "Save your breath. I know the spiel."

The door to Mama's trailer flies open. Mama, wrapped in a robe, stomps out, yelling and screaming. "What the hell is going on out here?" Her jaw drops as she waves her arms. "Did you do this?" She directs at me.

My face goes slack, and my chest hollows. "No."

Mama sneers, storming toward Walker and me. "You ungrateful bitch."

Walker steps in front of me, holding his hand up. "Lor! That's enough. The fire isn't spreading. The snow is keeping it in place. Firefighters are on their way. Go back inside your home."

The implacable expression on Mama's face doesn't fade, but she does as Walker directed and goes back inside.

She hates me. She'll always hate me.

Walker's hand on my arm guides me to his truck. He opens the passenger door, ushering me to slide in.

Spinning around, I hope Walker has the sense to hear me out. "Walk. Just let me explain."

"Sure thing. Down at the station." He lifts me by my hips, sitting me on the seat and buckling me in. Walker shuts me in and marches off to coordinate with the fire department.

I hope he listens long enough to hear the full story, and I pray that he won't kill me when I tell him the truth.

CHAPTER 19

BLAKE

I've been waiting so long that I'm wondering if Walker is pulling some kind of elaborate prank on me.

When we got to the station last night, Walker emptied my pockets and locked me in here. I've been in this interrogation room for hours. I wouldn't be surprised if the sun has come up.

Peering into the two-way, I make note of the dark circles under my eyes. I tried sleeping, but a metal chair and table aren't exactly the ideal bed.

The warm beige walls and the gray tile flooring of the interrogation room are nothing special to look at. So much so that I feel like I'll go cross-eyed any second.

Despite my exhaustion, I get to my feet and yell through the door. "Hello? Anybody there?"

I try to turn the doorknob, something I've done periodically, but find it locked. Frustrated, I groan and plop back down in the chair.

As I'm rubbing my eyes, the tumblers in the doorknob click, and Walker strolls in, a paper cup of coffee in each hand. He sits down in the chair on the opposite side of the table, passing one of the cups to me. The smell of freshly brewed coffee makes me perk up in my seat.

As I'm bringing the cup to my mouth, Walker starts, "Miss Jennings—"

I interrupt him with the sound that is halfway between a groan and a growl. "Oh, God. Not this bullshit again."

Walker gives me a look, telling me to behave. "What were you doing at Riverbend Trailer Park?"

Taking a quick sip of the coffee, I keep my answers simple. "I was checking in on my mom." Walker scrutinizes my answer, and I know he sees right through my half-truth. "I need to—"

It's Walker's turn to interrupt me. "This is the second time you were the first person at the scene of a homicide. Both people were killed in the exact same way." As he says the second statement, he lays out two photos of the bodies from each crime scene as well as headshots of two Men.

"Tell me something I don't know." I quip back, then look more closely at the pictures of live people. "Are these the victims?" The two pictures look like DMV photos.

Walker slides the pictures closer to me across the table. "Do you know them?"

"That's Reverend Ricks." I answer, pointing to the first photo, then I indicate the second as I respond, "I don't know who that is."

Walker taps his index finger on Rick's photo. "What's your relationship with the reverend?"

Shrugging a shoulder, I lean back in my chair. "He presided over my dad's funeral services and burial."

"Is that all?" Walker interrogates as if I'm not telling the whole truth.

His suspicion is understandable. He's right. I was at both crime scenes before anyone else, but he doesn't know that it was by design.

"Yes," I answer firmly.

Walker points to the unknown man's picture. "And you don't recognize this man?"

I shake my head, giving the same answer as before. "No. Should I?"

"This is Derek Holt," he informs me. "He's a firefighter."

"The first victim," I deduce, then scoff. "Well, that's ironic."

If dark humor is the only thing that makes me smile right now, I'll take it. I'm at the point where I'm either going to laugh or cry hysterically, and I'm choosing to laugh.

Walker tilts his head to the side inquisitively. "How so?"

Raising my eyebrows, I speak slowly, emphasizing each word condescendingly. "He's a firefighter, and he was set on fire."

"And?" Walker mirrors me, leaning back in his own chair.

I know he's just doing his job, but it is annoying the hell out of me.

"If I need to explain irony to you, then public education failed you," I retort.

Walker gives me another chance to come clean. "Blake, tell me the truth. Why were you there?"

"I already told you," I reply with tight lips.

"Tell me again," he insists.

"I was checking on my mom," I repeat.

Walker rests his forearms on the table, leaning toward me and lowering his voice. "That's not the real reason."

Rolling my eyes, I respond. "If you would just list—"

Walker jumps to his feet, his chair scraping against the tile floor. He slams his hand on the table, causing me to jump. "The body was found right next to your mother's trailer. You got there before me, my deputies, and the fire department. I want to know how."

"Lucky guess," I lie again.

Walker's jaw flexes, irritation rolling off him. "Bullshit."

"I had a hunch." My eyes drop to my lap.

"How?" he pushes again.

My hands ring together as I swallow dryly.

Do I tell him? Will he believe me? Will he be angry?

I guess Walker's anger is better than him believing that I'm a murderer.

My heart races as I chew on my bottom lip. "I've been getting these texts."

"What texts?" Walker grits out.

"The reason I came back..." I trail off, then choose to start at the beginning. "I was at a club with my best friend, Savannah, when I got these text messages from this guy."

Walker sits back down. "Who?"

"I don't know who it is. I actually don't even know if it's a man. That's just what I say in my head."

"What did the texts say?" Walker's tone is deceptively even.

"If you give me my phone, I can show you," I offer.

He's gone and back in less than a minute with my phone in his hand. I type in the passcode and pull up the text thread, sliding my phone back to him. He takes his time reading them, possibly more than once. His body becomes more and more tense the longer we sit in silence.

"When were you going to tell me about these?" He fumes at a low volume.

I shift incessantly in my seat. "I'm showing you now."

Walker holds my phone up, shaking it. "Whoever this is has threatened not just me, but Santiago and Levi as well. You didn't think I should know?"

Guilt eats at me, causing my stomach to twist into knots. I have to live with my choices. I'll never know if things could have turned out differently, so there's no point in wasting time sorting through all the "what ifs."

"Do you need your eyes checked? He told me not to," I huff. "Besides, I know you know I've been following you all and my mom. If something had happened, I would've stopped it."

"You're one person attempting to surveil four. If I need to do that math for you, then public education failed *you*," he throws my sarcasm back in my face, but his statement carries more weight.

Tightening my jaw, I turn my head to the side. "I know what I'm doing."

Walker holds up a finger for each of his rebuttals. "You have no law enforcement training, no weapons training, and no hand-to-hand combat training. Do you even know self-defense?"

My hands tighten into fists as I give Walker a piercing stare. "You don't know that. I could be an MMA fighter for all you know."

He raises his brows. "Are you?"

"No," I answer quietly. My voice grows in pitch and ire as I add, "But again, he told me not to."

"You still should have told me," he asserts again.

My eyes widen. "And risk something happening to you? No."

"I can handle it." He seems so convinced of that statement as if there is no alternative.

My fists slam down on the table, my frustration exploding. "I don't want you to have to handle it."

"Why not?"

I stammer my response. "Because."

"Why?" he asks again.

My pulse pounds in my ears, my heart feeling like it's about to jump out of my chest.

"I hate seeing you hurt!" I shout at Walker as if my outburst is all his fault. The emotional temperature in the room is at an all-time high, and it's not regulating any time soon. Tears clog my throat as I continue. "I can't bear it. Please don't make me. Seeing you in pain, it feels like I've been stabbed in the chest. I can't breathe. I can't think straight." Wiping away the tears on my cheeks, I look him right in the eye. "So don't ask that of me. I won't do it."

I don't know how to decipher the look on Walker's face. It's similar to the face he made when we were in the back of the ambulance. It's as if he might...

No. He wouldn't. He doesn't see me that way.

Walker gets to his feet, rounds the table, and pulls me from my chair by my hand. His hands land on my hips, causing my heart to leap in my chest for a whole different reason than before. His eyes flick to my lips, but I tell myself I must have imagined it.

"How do you think I would've felt if it were *you* who was hurt?" His eyes search mine. "You think I'd survive that?" His grip tightens on my hips. "Because I wouldn't." His jaw flexes. "I don't want to walk into a scene and find you there." His voice turns rough. "Don't ask that of *me*, Baby Girl."

My heart clenches, unsure what to do. I've never seen him so raw.

I'm still trying to figure him out when he breathes out, "Fuck it."

Walker hauls my body to his and seals our lips together. My mind goes blank. It takes me a second to understand what's happening.

Flinging my arms around Walker's neck, I pull him closer and kiss him back. His facial hair deliciously scrapes against my skin. One of Walker's hands slides to my ass while the other glides to the small of my back as if he needs me closer even though our bodies are fused together.

His length hardens in his jeans, and I feel it pressed against my lower belly. My center pulses, throbbing.

Walker's tongue licks at the seam of my lips, and I open for him. Our tongues duel for control, neither of us willing to concede. My teeth scrape his lower lip, and he moans, his grip on my ass tightening.

"Fuck," he whispers. Walker drops his forehead to mine, closing his eyes. The muscles in his jaw stand out as he grits his teeth together. Releasing me, he steps back. "I shouldn't have done that."

Following his retreat, my hands latch onto the front of his shirt. "I don't regret it." Tugging on the fabric, I compel him to make eye contact with me. "I would never regret you."

He closes his eyes again, pinching the bridge of his nose as if he's fighting some internal battle. Walker's hands wrap around my wrists and gently push, forcing me to let go.

Opening the door, he gestures to the hallway. "You're free to go."

"Walk," I start, but he's out the door and gone before I can get the rest of my sentence out.

My fist presses against my chest as the ache becomes overwhelming. I knew he'd do something like this, and I knew it would hurt. I just didn't think it would hurt so bad.

I can't fall apart now, especially not here.

Blinking away the tears, I snag my phone from the table and saunter out. In the hallway, I'm blocked by Tessa. She stands there in her full deputy getup and hands me my purse.

"Thanks." Slinging the strap across my body, I duck my head and step to the side to continue down the hall.

Tessa moves with me, blocking my way. "If it were me, you'd be booked for homicide."

My forehead pinches. "Good thing it's not up to you."

Tessa does a head-to-toe sweep like she's slowly scanning my appearance and finds me lacking. "You're lucky you were cleared by a witness."

My brows shoot upward as an idea comes to mind. "There was a witness?"

"Sheriff Maddox didn't tell you?" Tessa squints at me.

"Um. No. He didn't." I sway back and forth, trying to see past Tessa. "Who's the witness? Can I talk to them?"

"And risk witness tampering?" Tessa ridicules.

I frown mockingly. "How would I manipulate the witness? They already cleared me. Besides, I could help."

"Tessa, we need someone to finish logging in the evidence," Jolene instructs from her desk. "It's in Walk's office."

Tessa spins, still not letting me by. "Where's Ridge?"

"He's finishing the canvas," Jolene informs, then holds up her hand, motioning for Tessa to stand down. "I got Blake. Don't worry."

Tessa gives me one last glare from over her shoulder, then stomps off.

With daylight highlighting the space, I finally get a look around the station. It's not nearly as intimidating as the TV shows make police stations seem.

It's smaller.

Older.

More human.

Jolene's desk operates as both reception and dispatch. It's both chaotic and organized at the same time.

Out here are the same beige walls and gray tile. The most accurate description for them is "government-issued."

When the door to Walker's office snicks closed, I'm pulled from my reverie, and Jolene waves me over. I readily comply.

"Don't mind Tessa. She doesn't trust anybody," she consoles as she shuffles through the papers on her desk.

Discreetly, I wipe under my eyes, hoping that it's not obvious I was about to cry. She may not know it had nothing to do with Tessa, but I still don't want to discuss my relationship with Walker with Jolene.

"I'm fine," I lie. "Can I help with the witness? If they saw someone, I can help with a sketch."

Jolene finally stops what she's doing and looks up at me. "Do you have any experience?"

"Not in forensic art," I specify, "but I am an artist."

Jolene returns to her earlier task, her thumb pointing over her shoulder at an older woman sitting beside two desks facing each other. "Cheyenne Talbot, manager of Riverbend. She already gave her statement to Tessa. She's just signing it."

Did I just get Jolene's approval?

Unsure of the meaning behind the information, I stand there glued to my spot.

Jolene looks up again. "Go on," she says, tilting her head in Cheyenne's direction.

"Oh, right," I startle. Traipsing to Mrs. Talbot, I snag a blank white paper from the printer on one of the desks and a yellow number two pencil from the other.

My sketchbook and charcoal pencils are in my car, which is still at the trailer park, but if there's one thing I've learned over the years, it's that fancy supplies don't make a masterpiece. The artist does.

A half hour later, all I have is a generic sketch of a man. Mrs. Talbot couldn't see much, not even the color of his skin, hair, or eyes.

But the sketch proves one thing.

The person who lured me back to Evergreen Falls is a man.

And he knows what he's doing.

CHAPTER 20

WALKER

Ambling up the sidewalk leading to Santiago's front door, I'm plagued with the memory of how it feels to have Blake's lips on mine—her body against mine.

I lost control for a moment, and I can't take it back. It may have felt good, but it can never happen again.

Pushing open the large front door, the smell of coffee and bacon greets me. I head straight to the kitchen and find Levi and Santiago enjoying a late breakfast together.

Santiago's kitchen looks as if it popped right out of the magazine. The dark cabinetry. Exposed timber beams. The stone fireplace crackles in the adjoining great room.

Unfortunately, the spread of crime scene photos and homicide files disrupts the illusion.

"We need to talk," I declare, getting their attention.

Santiago turns his head toward me. "On a scale of one to super nuclear, how urgent is it?"

"I know why Blake came back," I inform them.

They both jump from their seats, abandoning their food as if a threat looms nearby.

If only it were that simple.

"What did she say?" Levi questions at the same time that Santiago asks, "Is she running from someone?"

"More like running to someone." My shoulders tighten. "Or more than one someone," I add.

Levi's expression goes slack. "You're not making sense."

"Someone threatened us in order to get her to come back." My words stumble over each other to get out of my mouth.

Santiago's voice turns thunderous. "Who?"

Shaking my head, I let out a tired breath. "I don't know, and neither does she."

"We're going to need to get a look at those texts." Levi insists.

"Here." I hand over my own phone, having taken pictures of Blake's exchange with the culprit.

Santiago snags my phone from my hands, and he and Levi read the messages together. Their expressions range from murderous to shocked.

When they're done, Santiago states the obvious. "This guy lured her to Riverbend Trailer Park."

"Yes," I confirm, reaching for my phone as Santiago returns it to me.

Levi tilts his head at me, "You gave her shit for this, didn't you?"

I roll my neck to relieve some of the tension. "Of course, I did. She should've told us from the beginning."

Santiago gives me a sharp look. "If you were in her shoes, would you say something?"

"I don't know." I grind the words out between clenched teeth.

Levi cocks a brow. "Then maybe give the woman a break."

Santiago's expression is smug. "I'm actually flattered. She's been protecting us this whole time like a damn rottweiler."

"More like an innocent doe," I mutter.

Santiago points to me. "I'm telling her you said that."

"Don't you dare."

"While we're on the subject of bad news, you need to see this."

Levi snags the newspaper from the counter behind him and tosses it to me.

Flipping it open, the bolded headline catches my eye.

Vigilante Justice in Evergreen Falls

My gaze flits over the article. "How did Emmett figure it out?"

Emmett Bailey is a writer for the Evergreen Falls Gazette. It's a small newspaper, but everyone in town reads it.

Santiago rubs his chin. "Does he have access to the police reports?"

Returning the paper to Levi, I pace the kitchen, tracing the same path repeatedly. "He shouldn't because it's an ongoing criminal investigation."

Returning to his seat, Levi taps his fingers on the counter as he thinks out loud. "Did someone talk to him?"

Stopping in my tracks, my eyes narrow on him, insulted by his insinuation. "Are you saying one of my deputies talked to the press?"

Levi ignores the hint of a threat in my question and pushes further. "Is it possible?"

"No." My answer is exact and cold.

"Then who?" Santiago questions as he takes his seat next to Levi.

"Maybe he put it together himself." Levi articulates his theory like it's a question.

Placing my hands on the island countertop across from Levi and Santiago, I drop my head forward. "He'd have to have figured out on his own that Derek is the arsonist."

"Which isn't possible," Levi opposes.

"Unless…" Santiago adds.

"He looked through the fire station reports after we did." Levi sighs. "But that's also a criminal investigation."

"Meaning he doesn't have access," Santiago finishes for him.

Levi voices another theory. "Maybe Emmett has listening devices at the station."

My head snaps up, and my hands clench into fists. "He better fucking not."

"There's another possibility." Levi's focus bounces between Santiago and me as his thought hits us.

Santiago's mouth morphs with contempt. "There's no way this killer is that stupid."

My index finger points to the crime scene photos. "But he is *that* narcissistic."

Santiago tilts his head back, gazing up at the ceiling. "How do we even check something like this? Emmett isn't going to give up his source."

Having given up on his food, Levi takes his dishes to the sink. "Before we get a warrant for his phone records and computer, we should just ask him."

"Ask him if he's been in contact with a killer that he deems to be a hero? Yeah. That'll go over well," I answer my own rhetorical question.

Santiago scratches the side of his neck as he studies the pictures of the two crime scenes. "Do we even *want* to catch this guy?"

Levi turns to face us, leans against the sink, and sways his head from side to side, weighing Santiago's question. "He's kind of doing our job for us."

"Yes," I state firmly.

Santiago gestures to Levi and me, his indication clear. "You don't see the hypocrisy here?"

I raise my chin. "We're different."

"How?" Santiago asks, exasperated.

Copying Santiago's gesture, I argue my point. "We don't make a spectacle of ourselves. We work in the shadows. We don't wave a big red flag saying, 'Look at me! Look at me!' This guy does." I hold up a photo from each crime scene for emphasis, then slide them to Santiago across from me. "There are easier and quieter ways of getting rid of a body. This guy chooses to set them on fire. He wants to be seen. He wants our attention."

Levi's brows furrow. "Us specifically?"

Pushing off the counter, I straighten my spine. "I don't know. I doubt it. He wants recognition though. It could be from us or the town in general." My hand massages my eyes as a thought occurs to me. "Narcissists aren't selfless. They're self-serving by definition. This 'vigilante,' as Emmett calls him, is going to step outside the gray area and into the black at some point."

Levi shrugs. "Then how do we catch him?"

"I have an idea."

They won't like my plan, but it may be our only chance.

CHAPTER 21

BLAKE

Plotting through the half-melted snow covering the parking lot of Main Street diner, I make my way inside. The mouth-watering aroma of all-day breakfast mixed with lunch gives me just enough energy to make it to my usual booth.

After I finished the sketch with Mrs. Talbot, Jolene called Ridge and told him I needed a ride back to my car. It's past lunchtime now, and all I want to do is sleep, but I found myself turning to the diner parking lot I drove by.

Martha saunters over. "You look like hell."

Lifting my head from the table, I barely open my eyes to respond. "Thanks, Martha." "It's been a long night."

"It's lunchtime." Martha lifts a single brow.

I mimic finger guns in her direction. "My point exactly."

Did I just use finger guns?

Martha chuckles. "French toast?"

Folding my arms on the table, I rest my head on top. "Please."

I'm half asleep when I feel someone draw close and sit beside me. A familiar voice begins speaking. "I want to try something different."

"At Falling Sky?" Another familiar voice.

Wearily, I crack open an eye and find that my table is now full. Santiago sits beside me, sharing the bench, our hips pressed together. Directly across from me is Levi, and next to him, Walker.

I try not to draw conclusions in my head, but it's hard not to assume that Walker purposely sat as far away from me as possible.

"No, the menu." Santiago holds up a menu so large it would give any other diner a run for its money.

Sitting up, I feel something slide off my shoulders, and I realize that one of them put their jacket on me like a blanket. With a quick glance, I notice that Levi wears his parka, and Santiago dons his thick thermal work coat.

Which leaves...

Walker sits upright on the bench, sporting the usual flannel and rolled sleeves.

But more importantly...

No jacket.

My mind whirls, and I choose to put aside Walker's mixed signals.

My hands rub the sleep from my eyes. "What are—"

Before I have a chance to ask why all three of them are here, a familiar perfume wafts through the air.

Expensive, floral, and overbearing.

"Well," Victoria Reynolds sneers, stopping beside our booth. "This is...cozy."

I peer up at her, my expression bored.

She stands there in an ivory wool coat that probably costs more than my monthly rent back in New York, her copper curls perfectly styled despite the Wyoming wind outside. Her smile is pleasant enough that anyone passing by would think she's stopping by to say hello.

I know better.

Her gaze drifts over the four of us.

"I didn't realize you'd settled in quite so quickly."

Levi leans back against the booth. "We're eating lunch."

Victoria barely acknowledges him. "I'm talking to Blake."

I sigh. "What can I do for you, Victoria?"

She folds her arms. "I just wanted to make sure you're adjusting."

"How thoughtful," Santiago comments.

Victoria doesn't even look in Santiago's direction. "It wouldn't do for you to find yourself in trouble.

If there's one thing I know about Victoria, it's that she likes to talk a big game. At the end of the day, she'd never get her hands dirty.

"I've managed several years without your guidance." I retort. "I think it'd be best if you kept that long nose of yours in your own business."

Her smile never wavers as she glances toward Walker. "I'd just hate to see the sheriff distracted."

Walker barely gives Victoria a glance. "Tell your husband that if he wants my badge, he knows where he can find me."

"I'll be sure to relay the message," Victoria replies sweetly.

The words sound polite, but her tone doesn't.

She looks back at me. "Enjoy your stay, Blake."

She turns on her heel and heads toward the exit, and I watch her leave. "Does she ever get tired?" I mutter.

"No." Santiago snorts. "Back to the menu."

"The menu hasn't changed in years. What could you possibly get that you haven't tried already?" Levi argues back.

"Pumpkin pancakes." Santiago drops the menu on the table, emphasizing his answer.

Levi's expression goes flat. "It's January. Pumpkin is seasonal."

"Excuse me." I try speaking up again.

Levi turns his face toward me. "What's up?"

"You see me sitting here, right?" I gesture to my spot.

Santiago makes a confused face. "Of course. Why do you think we sat down?"

My face scrunches. "Because you're so tired that your legs were about to give out?"

Santiago snorts. "That's a good joke."

"Why are you here?" I ask all of them.

Unexpectedly, it's Walker who responds for all of them. "I'm hungry. I had a long night of interviews, collecting evidence, putting out a fire."

I should be an adult about the situation. I should take the high road.

But the high road wasn't built into my DNA.

"I figured that after this morning, you'd ignore me." My nostrils flare.

Santiago narrows his eyes at me with a hint of a grin on his lips. "Why would Walker ignore you?"

"No reason," Walker answers for me, his tone cold and disapproving. "I'm going to head back to the station."

Holding out Walker's coat to him, I don't realize how much I wanted it until it's about to be taken away. It's as if Walker can see the hesitation in my eyes. He holds his hand up, refusing the jacket.

With only his measly flannel to keep him warm, Walker heads out into the cold.

Levi raises his brows. What's going on?"

Not ready to tell them about what happened, I play dumb. "There was another murder last night, and—"

Santiago cuts me off, clearly not buying my act. "Not what we meant. We know about that already."

I try again. "But I was there and—"

Levi rests his forearms on the table. "Walker arrested you and interrogated you this morning. We know that."

"We want to know what's going on between you and Walker," Santiago states, leaving no room for interpretation.

My gaze drops to my hands. "Oh. Um. Nothing."

Santiago nudges me with his shoulder. "You're a bad liar, *mi Cielo*."

"I'm not lying." I assert.

"That's one, Butterfly." Levi holds up his index finger. "Lie again, and that's two."

I can't stop the smirk that tugs on my lips as I interpret his tone and insinuation with my mind in the gutter. "What happens when I get to three?"

Levi lowers his voice to a sultry tone. "You don't want to find out."

I lean closer toward him. "What if I do?"

He smiles back at me, a playful glint in his eye. "We can talk about that later."

Santiago shifts in his seat next to me and I realize the exchange he just witnessed. "Oh my God." I bury my face in my hands. "What am I doing?"

"You and Walker hooked up." Levi assumes out loud.

I peek through my fingers at both of them.

Santiago tilts his head. "No," he states as if reading my mind. "But you wanted to."

Levi snaps his fingers. "They kissed."

Groaning, I drop my forehead to the table. "I'm just going to hide under the table now."

Shame swarms me. What I wouldn't give for a cenote to open up right under my seat and swallow me whole.

Santiago rubs circles on my back. "Are you afraid that we'd be upset?"

Propping up, I rest my chin on my fist. "Honestly, I'm not sure I want to know what you guys think at all."

Levi covers my free hand with his. The warmth of his touch soothes my anxious thoughts. "Why not?"

I sigh and close my eyes, not wanting their expressions to sway me from telling them the truth. "Because if you care, that's not good. And if you don't care, that's still not good."

Santiago shifts to playing with my hair. "How do you figure?"

"Caring means you're angry with me. I can't handle that." I open my eyes and speak directly to Santiago. "Not caring means our night together didn't mean anything." I turn to Levi. "And our moment at the clinic doesn't mean much either. Again, I can't handle it." I drop my gaze again.

Levi flips my hand over, tracing random lines on my palm. "You know, there's a third option you're overlooking."

"What's that?"

Levi lifts my hand, planting a tender kiss in the center. "We don't care because we just want you to be happy."

Martha interrupts the moment, setting my food in front of me, and Santiago and Levi place their own orders.

My meal remains untouched as I belabor Levi's words.

Is he suggesting that they'd be fine with an unconventional arrangement?

Like the three of us together?

I'm not opposed to the idea. Quite the opposite actually. I just never thought it would be something Levi and Santiago would be interested in.

The thought of the three of us together stirs something in me.

Happiness.

Would I stay here in Evergreen Falls for them? Is that what I want?

Even if my answer is yes, a part of me would always yearn for a fourth to join our trio—a surly small town sheriff who drives me crazy in every way.

CHAPTER 22

BLAKE

I woke up this morning thinking the last two days were a dream. The smell of diner coffee, the feel of cold handcuffs on my wrist, and the taste of cinnamon and maple syrup still linger in my memory.

Yesterday was a distraction. Fun but a distraction nonetheless.

It was a few hours where no one talked about serial killers, dead bodies, or threatening text messages.

I blame Santiago and his stupid charm, Levi and his stupid smile, and Walker and his stupid face.

These three men somehow occupy every available inch of space inside my brain.

But the illusion of easy times shattered the moment my phone rang this morning. Jolene called asking for my help with a witness sketch, and it all came flooding back to me.

A burning body. An interrogation room. An unforgettable kiss.

Walking across the station lot, I watch as the morning sunlight turns the windows into mirrors. For a moment, all I can see is my own reflection.

Tired eyes.

Messy hair.

A woman who thought she could stroll into town, save a few lives, and be on her merry way in no time.

So much for that plan.

"You're here," Jolene exclaims as I walk into the station.

I look toward the desk right inside. Jolene isn't even pretending to sound annoyed.

"I brought my supplies this—"

Bear trots in behind me, nails clicking against the old linoleum. His nose immediately goes to work, sniffing every chair leg and desk corner like he's conducting an official inspection.

Jolene's face lights up.

"Well, would you look at you." She rounds the desk before I can warn her and crouches in front of him. "Aren't you handsome?"

Bear sits automatically, tail thumping once against the floor.

"Oh, you're one of the smart ones." She fishes around in her desk drawer before producing a dog biscuit wrapped in plastic. "Every police station needs emergency treats."

"You just happened to have those?" I laugh.

"I have granddogs." She tears open the wrapper and offers the biscuit to Bear. "And deputies who forget to eat lunch. Somebody around here appreciates snacks."

Bear accepts the treat with surprising gentleness.

"Well," Jolene says, scratching behind one floppy ear, "I think you can come to work whenever you want."

"Thank you." I smile.

Jolene switches back into work mode. "We got a hit and run. Wait for the witness over there." She points to the same spot behind her where Mrs. Talbot sat yesterday.

"Thanks." I dip my head as I make my way to two empty chairs beside the two desks. The desks are vacant just like before. The only sign that anyone uses them is the coffee rings stained on the wood and the mess of paperwork.

A printer hums somewhere deeper inside the station while a radio crackles softly overhead with dispatch chatter. The lingering smell of burnt coffee competes with old paper and pine cleaner. Small-town police station.

A large body stops me in my path. "What're you doing here?"

Jolene answers for me. "She's working. Same as you."

Walker squints at me. "You don't work here."

Clearing my throat, I stand to my full height and pull my shoulders back. "Actually, I do."

"Since when?" Walker's large frame looms over me, but he doesn't intimidate me. I know he would never hurt me.

"Yesterday. Jo hired me." I sass at him.

If he's shocked, he does a good job of keeping the emotion off his face. "Well, I'm firing you."

My eye twitches. The man has spent less than thirty seconds in my presence today, and he's already testing my patience.

And yet, the way his arms fill out his shirt and the fact that I can count the ridges of his abdomen through the fabric have me clenching my thighs together.

My lady bits need to get with the program. We're mad at Walker, not ready to jump his bones.

"No, you're not," Jolene interjects. "We need her." Jolene rises from her chair, places her hands on my shoulders, and steers me around Walker. "Ignore him, Blake. Go do your thing."

Doing as she says, I overhear Walker continue to object. "I don't want her on the damn payroll."

"Good thing she's a volunteer." Jolene quips back. "Now go get the Delaney kid, so Blake can do the sketch."

Dropping my head, I bit my lip to keep an amused smile off my face.

"Sometimes I wonder who's the boss around here," Walker grumbles as he strides toward his office. On his way, Ridge passes Walker, heading in my direction. Walker pulls a plastic bag from his pocket and shoves it onto Ridge's chest.

Ridge stumbles a step backward, catching the bag before it can fall to the floor. "What's this?" Ridge spins toward Walker.

"The paper from Derek's mouth," Walker voices over his

shoulder. He stops in the doorway of his office and faces Ridge. "The partial symbol on the paper is the fire department logo."

I can only guess the look on Ridge's face, but I have a good idea by the way his shoulders sag. "How did I miss that?"

Walker keeps his tone even, but knowing him my whole life, I know it's his way of going easy on someone. "You missed it because you were looking for what you expected to find. When investigating, you have to leave all bias at the door."

"How?" Ridge angles his head to the side.

"You have to learn how to be your own devil's advocate," Walker explains.

Ridge shakes his head. "I..."

"It's easier said than done," Walker cuts in. "You'll get there."

"Thanks." Ridge sighs, then trudges straight to the desk next to me.

The exchange between Walker and Ridge lasts less than thirty seconds, but in those brief moments, it's clear to me how and why Walker has held the position of sheriff for so long.

He may be gruff, but he's also patient and knows how to teach without shaming.

Bear wanders over to Ridge, sniffing curiously at the evidence bag before I quietly snap my fingers.

"Leave it."

Bear sighs dramatically and returns to my side.

Walker brings out a teenage boy actively biting their nails, who is accompanied by a woman sporting what I would call a resting bitch face. If that were my mother, I would probably be biting my nails too. Walker brings out an extra chair for the woman and guides them toward me.

He gives me a nod, and I take that as his mark of approval. The glee that lifts my chest is almost inebriating.

I get to work asking questions and drawing with my charcoal pencils. When I'm just about done, my attention catches on a familiar face strolling in and out of a room next to where Walker interrogated me.

He's carrying boxes of files, piling them next to a foldable table in front of Walker's office that wasn't there yesterday.

Grant, one of Daddy's best friends, sits beside a woman I vaguely recognize. She's somewhere around my age with chest-nut-brown hair twisted into a practical bun and oversized tortoiseshell glasses sliding down her nose every few minutes. She types with impressive speed, barely looking at the keyboard as the scanner hums beside her.

Bear's head lifts, and his ears prick forward. A low rumble vibrates in his chest.

I glance down. "Bear."

His eyes never leave the pair across the room. Another growl.

Nora startles slightly, looking over her shoulder.

"Oh." I gently touch Bear's neck. "It's okay."

Bear calms, but not before one last hard stare.

Poor Nora.

I return to my sketch, adding the finishing touches. When I'm done, the mother and her teen return to Walker's office. I remain in my chair, adding bits of shadow and highlight to bring the portrait to life.

My light is blocked when I hear a voice state, "Jelly Bean, I didn't know you were an artist."

Peering up, I'm met with Grant's disarming smile. "Something like that," I answer with a shrug. A quick glance informs me that everyone has left. Jolene and Ridge's desks are vacant, and even the woman who was sitting with Grant is gone.

Maybe it's lunchtime?

Grant lifts his brows a fraction, nodding his head like he is impressed. "Looks good. Who is it?"

Before I can answer, movement catches my eye. Walker steps out of his office carrying another file. His gaze lands on Grant. Grant notices at the exact same moment. Neither of them says a word.

They simply stare.

It lasts barely two seconds before Walker keeps walking, and Grant returns his attention to me.

Maybe I'm imagining things, but the air suddenly feels tighter.

I turn my sketchbook toward him, allowing him to get a better look. "Someone involved in a hit and run." When he nods again, I return the sketchbook to my lap. "What're you doing here?"

"I've been helping my girlfriend, Nora. She's with the county clerk's office. Her job is to upload all the files in the county to a central system. Evergreen Falls is going digital."

"That sounds like a load of fun." I return sarcastically.

"As fun as watching paint dry." He jokes back.

Since he's already going through all the police records, maybe he won't mind doing me a favor.

"Hey, could you possibly pull some files for me?" I ask with a slight wince, anticipating his reluctance.

Grant shrugs his shoulders. "Sure. What're you looking for?"

"Cases concerning Walker Maddox." My response ends on a high note as if I'm asking a question rather than answering one.

Grant's brows practically shoot up into his hairline. "He's the sheriff, Jelly Bean. It's safe to say most of the cases in these filing cabinets concern him."

A sense of defeat and disappointment pokes at my shoulders.

"You're right." I rub my lips, searching my brain for a better solution. "Um...What about cases where Walker is the intended victim or cases where Walker really pissed someone off? Same thing for Levi and Santiago."

Grant nods in agreement, then inquires, "Care to tell me why?"

Tired of lying to everyone around me, I reply with a simple, "The less you know, the better."

Grant seems to accept my reasoning. "Give me a minute, and I'll see what I can find."

He marches back to the table and gets to work, digging through the files around him. I return to my sketch to pass the time, losing myself in the slope of the man's nose, the sharpness of his mandible, and the arch of his zygomatic bone.

I'm retracing lines I've already created when something lands on the desk next to me with a plop. "Here you go.

Jumping in my seat, my heart calms when I see that it's just Grant. Three light brown folders are stacked next to me.

Like a dog with a bone, I snag the first one and flip it open. I scan the document, hoping to find what I need. "Excessive force complaint against Walk." Closing the file in my hands, I set it on my lap and pick up the next, repeating the process. "Police report. Officers respond to a call at Falling Sky Ranch. A land dispute." Close and repeat. "Another report. Officers break up a fight on Reynolds Family Farms between Sterling Reynolds and Levi Harding."

My mind spins with the possibilities. I feel like a crazy person with a conspiracy board and yarn.

I probably am that person.

I pat files in my lap. "This is a good start. Thank you."

"Not a problem, Jelly Bean. I hope you find what you're looking for." Grant spins on his heel, heading back toward his spot. He only gets a few steps when he turns back and suggests, "There's a room over there if you want to spread out."

"I think I will." Gathering my things, I beeline for the simple pine door. Inside, I find a large table, several mismatched computer chairs, and a large empty bulletin board. No windows and only two unforgiving LED lights.

This will work just fine.

I pick the most comfortable-looking chair and settle in. Pouring over the reports in detail, I flip to a new page in my sketchbook and begin taking notes.

Bear circles twice beneath the table before flopping onto the floor with a dramatic sigh, resting his head across my boots.

Lucky. At least one of us knows how to relax.

I'm just finishing up with the complaint against Walker when the door swings open.

"What're you reading?" Walker strides into the room, swiping the files from me.

"Nothing." I scramble like I was just caught reading his diary. "Give that back!"

Walker opens Santiago's file first. He nods as if the memory of the instance comes back to him in a wave. "I remember this. Santiago's neighbor shot one of Santiago's cattle. He claimed the heifer was drinking water from his property. Santiago and the man got into a standoff."

I furrow my brows. "What happened?"

"Santiago ended up purchasing the neighbor's land. The guy was up to his eyeballs in debt and was looking for a way to weasel money out of someone." Walker shuts the file and unceremoniously drops it on the table.

"Oh."

So that's one file that won't be of any use to me.

Walker flips open the next. "Levi got into a brawl with a farmer when he was on a farm call and realized the guy was abusing his cattle."

Knowing Levi, that other man definitely had it coming.

"And this one," Walker lets out a humorless chuckle as he finally gets to his own file. "It was a drunk and disorderly. I had to restrain the guy when he started to go after innocent bystanders."

Probably another bust with that one, too.

"Great," I say, dropping my head into my hands as I prop my elbows up on the table. My fingers dig into my hair as defeat mixed with frustration makes me want to pull out the roots.

Walker slides the files into my view. "You're looking in the wrong place, Baby Girl." His voice is full of amusement, like my amateur detective skills are gifting him with a good laugh.

He can think this is funny all he wants, but I refuse to see the humor when his life is being threatened.

Releasing my hair, I bring my hands together into two fists and rest my chin there as I glare at him. "Then where should I be looking, Obi-Wan?"

The comedy lifts from his face, shifting his features into an expression as cold as stone. "I don't know. That's the problem."

Walker's confession bequeaths me with a sense of hopelessness as my stomach sinks.

He leaves me alone in the multipurpose room, the stillness of the space becoming too great for my need to act.

What hope do I have of figuring this out if the man whose job it is to investigate doesn't even know where to start?

CHAPTER 23

SANTIAGO

Notes of ammonia layered with sweet fermentation and dust are pungent as hell, but they remind me that I'm home—doing what I love. Most people might look at my job and prefer their nine-to-five.

That's just fine.

I'll take shoveling horse shit, waking up every morning before the sun rises, and riding for days at a time on a cattle drive over sitting behind a desk any day of the week. Rain or shine.

The last few days have been eventful to say the least. We finally got rid of the predators at the high school, we found out what made Blake come home, Walker arrested Blake *again,* Walker finally kissed Blake…

Oh. And there was another dead body.

I'm not about to get in the middle of Blake and Walker to play referee. They're going to have to figure things out themselves.

I'm halfway through brushing Ace's coat when the most perfect ray of sunshine strolls into my barn with her furry best friend at her side. Her curves are swathed in black pants that are tight as hell, laced-up brown boots, an oversized cream sweater, and a puffy parka.

"Need a hand?"

Stepping around Ace, I slide my thumbs into my belt and greet her. "Well, this is a surprise. What're you doing here?"

She shrugs with a smile. "Just wanted to see my—"

"Boyfriend," I finish for her.

Blake tilts her head to the side. "Is that what you are?"

Snagging her around the waist, I pull her to me and dip my head. My mouth hovers above hers. "You bet your ass it is."

Closing the distance, I drown myself in the feeling of her lips on mine. Her hands fly into my hair, knocking my hat off my head, and I don't mind it one bit. The amber and vanilla scent on her skin is another reminder of what I love.

Blake slows the kiss, bringing it to an end. The bright smile she flashes up at me is one that I'd do anything to see every day for the rest of my life.

"Well, if you're going to be here, then..." I nod my head toward the horse stalls.

She nods her head, understanding my implication. "Put me to work. I am yours to command."

I shoot her a suggestive look. "Are you?"

Blake takes a step back and shoves her shoulder. "You know what I mean."

I stumble a step back, letting her think she actually pushed me. "I could use some help feeding the horses and cleaning the stalls."

"I want to see Shadow anyway." Blake walks right past me, heading toward the horse that has become her friend.

I follow behind her. "Thanks. I'm down a man today."

"Oh? Is everyone okay?" Blake doesn't stop until she's feeding Shadow a sugar cube.

"Manny left," I explain.

Blake pauses, her hand halfway to her pocket, probably to fish out another sugar cube. "Did you..."

"Did I what? Kill him?

Blake whirls on me and quirks a brow, her question clear.

"No," I scoff. "After our little talk, it was his choice to leave entirely."

"We'll pretend I believe you," she replies, half in teasing and half in candidness. "Let's get to work, *vaquero*."

I show her how to brush Shadow's coat, comb her mane and tail, and check for ticks and scratches. She doesn't waste any time diving in and getting the work done.

Around midday, I have to drag her away for lunch. I made us simple deli sandwiches and a bowl of dog food for Bear. We enjoy them together under heat lamps on my porch. I may not have the cooking skills of a five-star chef like Walker, but I know the basics.

We are close to finishing when one of the younger wranglers, Todd, comes running up the steps to us.

In spite of the cold, sweat drips down the side of his face. "Boss!"

Todd's frantic energy has me jumping to my feet. "What's going on?"

"Shadow got out, and she's going crazy." He informs me, out of breath.

In lieu of a verbal reply, I take off jogging toward the barn. Footsteps follow behind.

Blake catches up to me quickly. "I'll help."

Rejecting her offer, I reply, "Nope. Too dangerous. Go back inside the house."

Blake doesn't argue with her words. Instead, she displays her defiance by continuing to tag along.

On the backside of the barn, Shadow bucks wildly. Four of the workers, including Javier, attempt to grab hold of Shadow's reins. Skidding to a stop, I glance around to assess the situation.

Javier directs some of the more inexperienced wranglers. "Get your asses away from her hind legs. Are you trying to get yourself killed?"

"Get back," I shout at everyone. The last thing we want is for

Shadow to traumatize herself or us. The men do as I say, backing away slowly, giving Shadow her space.

A figure darts past me, and my stomach knots into a hardball. "Blake!"

Javier reaches out to grab hold of Blake. He's able to grab the hood of her coat, and without missing a beat, she slides out of it, leaving Javier standing there with her jacket in his hands.

Bear tracks behind Blake, staying back a few feet.

Blake slows her steps as she gets closer to Shadow, and my heart lodges in my throat. She holds her hands up in a calming gesture and speaks to Shadow in a voice so low that none of us can hear.

I want to rush forward and drag her away, but sudden movements like that could spook Shadow and injure Blake in the process. So now my only option is to watch the woman I care about most stare danger in the face and pray that she walks away unscathed.

Blake stands in Shadow's line of sight, still speaking in hushed tones. Shadow stops her pitching, swinging her head toward Blake. My focus is locked on the distance between them as Blake takes her time closing the gap. Shadow remains calm, but that can change at any moment. A whinny vibrates from Shadow's mouth, causing Blake to freeze.

I don't know how she learned the different sounds and what they mean. But Lord knows I'm happy she did.

Continuing her shuffle forward, Blake's hand lands on Shadow's muzzle. She smooths her touch up and down the bridge of Shadow's nose.

The wranglers all stare with flat jaws and wide eyes as if the scene before them is some kind of miracle.

They're not wrong.

Shadow lets out a snicker, and my heart finally settles in my chest, relaxing my shoulders. Blake still doesn't attempt to grab the reins, instead remaining by Shadow's head and soothing her with soft words.

Javier sneaks forward and snatches the reins himself. Besides Levi, me, or Walker, Javier is the only person I'd trust in this situation to make sure Blake is okay. Blake presses her forehead to Shadow's, and Shadow dips her head, allowing the touch. Blake says one more thing to Shadow, then Javier leads her away.

Blake remains in her spot and lets out a deep breath. The remaining ranch hands still stare at Blake, all of them frozen in place.

I can't blame them for being dumbstruck, and if I didn't need them to work at Falling Sky, I'd fire them all for the way they're looking at her.

At least they're not dumb enough to speak to her the way Manny did.

Javier gets Shadow put away, then returns outside and barks orders. "Get your asses back to work! Todd, grab a horse and join Samuel in the west pasture. He's checking on the herd there. Jack, double-check the hatches on the horse stalls. I want to know how Shadow got out. Brandon, get the plow out and find a path that needs clearing. Aaron, I need you to break the ice on the water troughs."

Everyone scatters to do as Javier demanded, and Javier tosses me Blake's jacket.

Striding for Blake, I reach her just a few steps, slide her arms into the sleeves of her coat, and wrap her in my arms. "You should add horse whisperer to your resume."

Blake let out a shaky exhale. "Shadow just likes me because I give her sugar cubes."

Bear trots over to us and sits, tucking his hind legs underneath him and giving us his back like he's standing guard.

Good boy.

Holding her a little tighter, I buried my face on the top of her head, inhaling her scent. "I didn't see a single sugar cube in sight this time."

When I feel Blake's body release all its tension, she leans back but keeps her arms around my waist. "Back to work?"

My brows raised. "I think you've more than earned yourself a break for the rest of the day."

"I'd rather keep busy," she insists.

Searching her face, I look for a hint of uncertainty.

I understand her need for a distraction. She may have handled that like a pro, but that doesn't mean that her body didn't flood with adrenaline.

"Whatever you want."

Entwining my fingers with hers, I lead us back into the barn. She heads straight for an empty stall and begins to clean it out.

Unwilling to leave her alone, I snatch a stall fork and join her. We work together in silence, moving from stall to stall. We don't need to communicate. She anticipates my moves just as I do hers, enabling us to work seamlessly.

We're on the last stall when Blake disrupts the quiet. "Did you always want to own Falling Sky?"

Without pausing the work, I respond. "Since I was a boy."

"Really?" Blake questions from the other side of the stall where she continues to separate the straw from waste.

"Yep. My parents adopted me when I was a baby. Ranch life is all I've ever known," I admit. "After my mother died, I had to step up. My father needed the help. Then he had multiple hip replacements and couldn't work anymore."

Blake pauses and faces me. "I had no idea. I'm so sorry."

I don't want to see the pity in her eyes, so I keep my head down and continue to muck. "It's okay. Death is a part of life. It happens."

"How..." she hesitates, then shakes her head and returns to our chore. "Never mind. That's none of my business. I'm being nosy."

I'm a fucking idiot.

If anyone understands, it would be her. Landon was a piece of shit, but losing a parent is never easy.

Turning in her direction, I rest my forearm on top of the staff work. "It was an armed robbery. She pulled over on the highway to help someone who was stranded. Turns out it was a ruse. My mother was a fighter. She pulled her shotgun, and they all pulled their own guns as well."

Blake mimics my stance, her face filled with shock. "That's awful."

Shrugging off her sympathy, I pick up the stall fork and muck again. "They got what was coming to them. God made sure justice was served."

I can feel her eyes analyzing me. Part of me wonders if she's abhorred by my insinuation, but I'm not ashamed of it. I've never been one to avoid doing what needs to be done.

She's silent a moment longer then finally says, "Good."

We finish mucking, then wheel the waste out to the designated dry stack outside the barn. Bear waits for us at the barn doors, declining the opportunity to wade in the snow.

Heading back inside, I find a small pile of mud on the floor next to one of the water troughs. Done with the somber tone of the last hour, I reach into the mud and swipe a finger across Blake's nose.

Blake jumps back with a Yelp. "Did you just…" she touches her nose then examines her finger. "You're going to pay for that!"

"I'd like to see you try." I taunt her.

Blake searches the ground, finding her own spot of mud. She dips her hand in, and I do the same in my pile, then we go at each other. My arms are longer than hers, so I am able to get more mud on her than she can on me.

She brushes mud through the strands of my hair, while I lift her sweater and smear a blob across her stomach. Blake screeches from the cold, then gets me back by ripping open the buttons on my shirt and slathering my chest in mud with both of her hands.

Five minutes later, we're both mottled with patches of mud on our clothes, skin, and hair. We pant in unison—our smiles are mirrors of each other's.

The stress and burdens weighing her down are temporarily lifted.

Mission accomplished.

Talking a lock of dirt caked hair behind her ear, I smirk at her dirty clothes and skin. "I made a mess of you, mi Cielo."

Blake inches closer, placing her hands on my pecs and rising onto her toes. "What're you going to do about it, cowboy?" Her question is low and full of temptation.

Sweeping her into my arms, Blake lets out a startled shout followed by uninhibited laughter. With long, determined strides, I head for the house. "I'll show you what I'm going to do."

She giggles again then swipes my hat from my head, placing it on her own. "Save a horse," she says with a wink.

"Ride a cowboy," I finish for her as something inside me loosens.

I could get used to this.

CHAPTER 24

LEVI

Some memories linger longer than others. No matter how many times I replay the attack from last week, the outcome never changes, despite how badly I want it to.

I can't move. I can't scream. It's like a nightmare where my feet are glued to the ground.

Blake tackles a man twice her size. She hits the concrete. I freeze.

Every damn time.

The sound of her body striking the floor echoes in my head louder than the barking dogs and the clinic, louder than my own heartbeat.

I should have protected her.

Instead, she protected me.

I'm rechecking the schedule for today at the clinic's front desk when the door swings open and a gust of wind chills the entire room.

I glance up, expecting a client. Instead, I find the source of my peace, but she's also the source of several recent headaches.

Blake breezes in, dressed in her usual sweater, leggings, and boots, with Bear trotting at her side.

That dog has somehow become a permanent fixture in my clinic along with his owner.

And I'm not upset about it.

Smirking at her, I ask, "Are you here to babysit me too?"

My question pulls Blake up short. "Babysit?" she repeats like she's offended. "Can't a girl—"

I finish her question for her, lifting a brow. "Check in on her boyfriend?"

She squints, dissecting my words, then concludes, "You've been talking with Santiago."

"He's my best friend," I reply by way of explanation.

Blake nods. "Obviously."

"And a little more," I add.

Blake gawks, her eyes blinking with incredulity and her lips forming a mute O. "I—I didn't—Did I—If I have caused any—" she stammers.

I hold up my hand, cutting her off. "You haven't done anything wrong."

She analyzes my words again, directing herself to the correct conclusion. "It's an open relationship."

"Yes."

The line of Blake's brow jumps. "Oh. Do people…"

"Know about us?" I finish for her again then shrug. "Probably. We don't flaunt it, and it's not like Santiago gives a spiel to his hookups."

"Walk?" She questions.

I dipped my head in confirmation. "Of course."

"Is he…" she trails off, like she's searching for the right words, something she seems to be struggling with today.

"Supportive?" I failed to keep the smile from my face. Her inquiry is predictable yet amusing.

Blake narrows her eyes. "Quit doing that."

"Then use your words, Butterfly," I quip.

Blake crosses the floor, placing herself on the opposite side of the desk. She plants her hands on the surface, leaning towards me as she quirks a brow. "Is he?"

"Yes," I answer with a small smile. "Very. No need to defend my honor or anything."

"Good," she says, like if my answer were different, then Walker would be in for a world of hurt. Blake pushes off the desk, standing straight. "Well, I'm here."

"With your shadow." I tilt my head to Bear.

Blake raises her shoulders as she holds her hands out palms-up in an innocent gesture. "I can't leave Bear at Moose Gap Lodge," she defends.

Unable to suppress a chuckle, I shake my head. "I could use some help walking the animals in the back and feeding them."

Blake's lips curve into a comical frown. "Where's Abbott?"

"On a farm call," I inform her.

"Without you?" Blake asks as her face scrunches up.

"It's a simple checkup." I clarify.

Blake lets out a measured hum, accepting my explanation. "Well then, let's get to it."

Heading for the back, Blake strolls right past me, knowing I'll follow right behind her, which I do.

When we get to the kennels, I give her a brief tour, instructing her on how to complete each task. She jumps right in, zero hesitation, and once again, I follow suit.

Caring for animals has always been easy for me—it comes naturally to me. Animals are honest. They don't pretend to be something they're not. They don't hide when they're hurt. They don't lie about being afraid. Most people could learn a thing or two from them.

I'm lost in the work when a shout comes from the other side of the room. "Levi!"

Sprinting to Blake, I find her staring through a gate with haunted eyes. She doesn't look my direction as I approach, so I keep my movements slow, placing my hand on her shoulder. "What's wrong?"

Lifting a shaky hand, she points inside the kennel. "The dog. She's bleeding."

I allow her hand to guide my gaze, and I find the German Shepherd I found on the side of the road the other day. She was cold and starving, something I come across often this time of year.

After the holidays, I come across more pets left to fend for themselves. Adults buy a pet for themselves or their children, then quickly realize they weren't prepared for the responsibility and ditch the animal.

The concept of abandoned animals is nothing new for me, but it still causes a cold fire to settle in my chest.

"Dammit," I curse, then open the gate, slipping inside, not allowing Blake to follow. The dog scurries into the corner, trying to get as far away from me as possible. I take a seat in the middle of the kennel, giving her space but letting her know that I'm here when she needs me. "She gets nervous and chews on her legs."

"Animals do that?" Blake asks from behind me.

"When they're scared or anxious, they can." I keep my tone calm and composed. Raging over what someone did to this dog won't change anything. It'll just make her more afraid of me.

Blake continues her questioning. "How do you help something like that?"

Peering over my shoulder, I answer, "You make them feel loved."

"You seem to be good at that." Sadness mixed with awe swells in her eyes.

Breaking eye contact, I turn back around. "It's easy when the one time you fail, the consequences were irreparable."

"What do you mean?"

Nausea wells in my stomach as images run through my head like a slideshow of my worst memories.

I haven't talked about this in a long time. Walker and Santiago were present when I went through it. They were a constant presence, offering various comforts and distractions. Landon and Grant were also around, but not in the same way.

"When I was fourteen, my best friend hung himself in his closet. When I found him, it was already too late." Licking my lips, I force myself to hold my head high.

I shouldn't feel the shame. I shouldn't feel the guilt.

But it's always there, waiting to suffocate me.

"Oh my...I'm so sorry. I can't imagine." Blake's voice breaks then firms like she's trying to instill me with strength through her words. "You can't think that it's your fault. Like you said, you were fourteen."

Angling my feet to the side, I spin around halfway toward her, but I keep my focus on the chain link. "I may not have been able to prevent it," I admit out loud, the truth more for me than for her. "I'll never know. But I often wonder if he knew how much I loved him. He was my friend. We were together every day."

A single tear slips from the corner of my eye, and I wipe it away. Not because I'm embarrassed, but because I don't want to think of my friend and only feel sadness. I want to remember him for how he lived.

"He knew."

Blake's platitude draws my attention to her. It's one I've heard many times, but hearing it from her feels different.

Her eyes swim with a million thoughts and emotions—so many that I can't interpret them all.

But one shines above the rest.

Empathy.

A warmth I don't deserve wraps me in a comforting embrace.

A tear slides down Blake's face, but unlike me, she lets the streak stay. As if she's letting me witness her vulnerability—trusting me with it.

A cold, wet nose pushes on my elbow. Peering down at the dog, I lift my arm and let him crawl into my lap.

"That's how I know your friend knew you loved him," Blake comments, and I let the confidence of her words fill a hole in my chest that I've purposely kept empty. I didn't think I was deserving.

But she does.

And if she can give me her trust, I can give her mine.

I'm not sure how long I sit there with the German Shepherd in my lap, but when I glance over at Blake again, she's curled up on the floor with her head resting on Bear. Her eyes are closed, and her breathing is even.

This woman.

This foul-mouthed, sassy, wonderful woman.

Gently, I remove the dog from my lap and place her on the cushion in the corner. I barely have enough room to open the gate and slide out. Bear stirs, but Blake remains still. Bending down, I scoop her up into my arms and carry her into the kitchen. I set her down on the old couch in there, covering her with the blanket from one of the cabinets. Bear hops up on the couch with Blake, taking up the space behind her knees.

"You can cuddle her this time, but next time, it's my turn," I whisper to Bear.

He rolls his eyes at me and grumbles.

Great. I have a sassy woman and a dog with an attitude to match.

I crouch down, sitting on the tiled floor and ignoring the way it makes my back tighten. Settling in, I rest my back against the couch.

This time, when I close my eyes, there are no nightmares, no injured Blake.

Just me and the people I love, enjoying the peace we bring each other.

CHAPTER 25

SANTIAGO

My eyes glaze over as I sort through the monotonous stack of junk mail. Credit card offers, store catalogs, fast food coupons.

Groaning, I collapse onto the floral sofa. "I hate going to the coroner's office. It's cold as hell."

"We live in Wyoming." Levi's voice is monotone as he searches through Reverend Ricks's kitchen cabinets.

Our assignment today was to meet with the coroner in Jackson, then search through the reverend's home.

"Yeah, but it feels significantly colder in there."

Ricks's two-bedroom home sits on a corner lot only a block away from the church. The modest home is well-maintained without being extravagant. The beige siding, white trim, and neatly shoveled walkways feel as if there was no room for chaos.

Nothing about this house stands out.

But that's probably the point.

I rest my head against the back of the couch and close my eyes. "Did Walk say anything else on the phone when you told him that Adler confirmed that the victim was Reverend Ricks?"

"Nope," Levi answers in the same tone, his attention on the task in front of him.

Heaving myself up, I meander to the plain roll-top desk in the corner of the living room. Using the knob, I pull the roll-top upward. Just like the rest of his home, everything is neatly in place.

Sliding open the center drawer, I find ballpoint pens, paper clips, and several church bulletins perfectly organized. The small side drawers contain nothing more than stationery and tax documents.

Hunched into a crouch, I open one of the lower file drawers. "If the killer is 'collecting debts,' then what's the reverend's debt?"

"Who knows?" Levi responds, still scouring the kitchen. "Or maybe Emmett has it wrong, and this killer isn't some kind of vigilante."

I shake my head as my eyes scan over old insurance documents. "I don't think so. It doesn't feel like random acts of violence."

"So…" Levi's voice draws closer. "Are we going to talk about the elephant in the room?"

"What elephant?" I ask back.

Levi enters the still living room, leaning his shoulder against the wall and facing me. "Blake."

"Blake."

Interlocking my fingers together, I place them behind my head and sit up, resting backward in the old chair as it creaks. "I'm telling her you called her an elephant."

"That's not what I meant, and you know it." Levi gives me an annoyed look.

I jokingly roll my eyes. "Okay. What about Blake?"

"We both like her," Levi states, leaving no room for argument.

I nod. "That's an understatement."

Levi folds his arms with a sigh. "What are we going to do? Sharing someone in bed is different than sharing full-time."

"Communicate. Duh." I shrug like the solution is apparent.

"We should talk to her about it," Levi emphasizes.

I flash a wry grin. "Stating the obvious, *mi amor*."

"But what about Walk?" Levi chews on his lip, finally getting to the point.

My brows lift. "Ah. Yeah. That's a different conversation."

"One that needs to happen."

"We'll make it happen," I assure him, then return to my search.

"I told her."

I ask for clarification as I open another drawer. "About what?"

"Us."

Levi's answer pulls me up short. I pause and look up at him, needing to see his expression as much as I need to hear his words. "How'd she take it?"

He nods his head and gives me a half smile. "I think we're good to keep going."

"Then we'll keep going." I agree with him.

Levi nods, satisfied with my response, then returns to the kitchen to finish the search. I follow his lead and do the same.

In the last drawer, a small black leather planner is stashed beneath a stack of envelopes and stamps. I lay it out on the desktop and flip through the pages.

I raise my voice a fraction to get Levi's attention. "The reverend's calendar is color-coded. Green for medical, blue for church duties, yellow for social or recreation."

"At least he's organized," he shouts back.

"Come here," I call to him. When Levi reenters, I scoot the chair to the side, making room for him, and point to my observation. "He has three hours blocked off in his calendar every Saturday."

Levi flips from week to week, discovering the same thing I did. "Does it say anywhere what he's doing?"

"No. It's just marked in red." I shrug.

"Anything else in there marked red?" He questions.

"No," I respond.

Levi slides the book closer to me. "What do you think he was doing?"

"I'm not sure. Whatever it is, it might be what made him a target." I suggest.

"You think his weekly appointment is what connects him and Derek?" Levi asks for clarification.

Shifting my posture, I remark, "I think we're looking at a killer who doesn't care who you are. I think he judges your actions."

Levi pulls out his phone, shooting off a text. "I'll let Walk know we need to pull phone and financial records."

"That'll go over well with a judge." Changing my voice, I imitate a young naïve officer. "Sir, we need a warrant to search bank accounts for a local church that you probably attend."

Levi sticks with his optimism. "Walk probably knows a judge who would sign."

"Not a single judge would sign the last warrant he drafted," I argue, resting my chin in my hand.

Levi gives me a sidelong glance. "That warrant was for Emmett to identify his source. Warrants like that usually don't get signed. Freedom of speech and all that."

Done with the debate, I bury my nose back in the planner, scouring for a key or something that will help me understand what the red means. Levi stocks off, probably going to search another part of the house.

"Do you smell that?" Levi shouts to me from another room.

Sticking my nose in the air like a dog, I sniff. "Is that a gas leak?"

"I don't smell anything burning, so it must be," Levi replies.

"I'll check the kitchen and living room. You check the bedroom and bathroom." I direct as I hop to my feet and head for the kitchen.

I examine every line, hose, and connection, anything that could possibly have a gas leak, but I find everything in working order. Returning to the living room, I hunt for anything that could possibly use gas.

Again, nothing.

The sound of a splash catches my attention. At first, I assume it's Levi in the bathroom, but when I hear it again, I discern that the sound is coming from outside.

Peering through the curtains of the large window in the living room that looks out over the front lawn, I discover the source.

A man dressed head to toe in black holds a red gas can upside down, spilling its contents across the front porch. The man must feel me watching because he stops, his attention snapping to me. A ski mask covers his face, and all I can see are his steel eyes. They narrow, sharpening with a venomous anger.

I keep my eyes on him as I holler, "Levi!"

"Levi!"

"What's going on?" Levi questions as he comes running. I point to the man who has resumed pouring out the gas. Levi's eyes stare at the man, unable to blink. "Shit!" Levi darts for the front door, turning the knob to pull it open, but it stops with a rattle. "It's chained," he communicates to me with a frustrated grit.

Lifting his foot, he braces it on the frame of the door and grabs the doorknob with both hands. Levi uses his foot as leverage as he yanks on the door, trying to break the chain.

"Stop that," I command. "You're going to pull a muscle."

Levi glimpses at the man through the small window at the top of the door. "Is that a match?"

My heart hammers in my chest as I glance out the window and find the masked man holding a lit match. "Fuck!"

"We can't just run at him," Levi reasons. "He'll just throw the match at us, and we don't know all the spots he poured the gas."

"So we're just going to sit here?" I questioned frantically. Taking another peek, I don't want to lose sight of the man. Our situation is precarious enough.

The man's focus ping-pongs back and forth between Levi at the door and me at the window.

I can't see more than his eyes, but the way they pinch at the corners tells me that he's enjoying this. He tips his head toward the sky and belts out a maniacal laugh—one that chills me to my bones. He takes one more look at us, then turns and walks down the lawn toward the street.

My eyes squint quizzically. "Where the hell is he going?"

Levi remains silent as we both observe the man, waiting for any sudden movements that will force us to spring into action. He's about to step off the curb when he tosses the match over his shoulder, and it lands in the grass, instantly igniting it.

"Get a fire extinguisher!" I yell at Levi as I run to the desk, pick up the chair, and hurl it through the window.

The glass shatters, breaking into a million pieces with a high-pitched crack. Having found a fire extinguisher like I told him to, Levi jumps through the broken window and sprays the chemicals on the fire.

I rush out after him using my boots to stomp out the smaller fires.

I assume someone called 911 because by the time we have the fire extinguished I can hear sirens speed in our direction.

"Where did that sucker go?" I ask as I pant from exertion, resting my hands on my hips and tilting my head back.

"I don't know," Levi answers. "But look."

I glance in the direction he points to with his finger. Tilting my head to the side, I tried to make out the burned letters in the grass. "What does that say?"

"What does that say?"

"Hypocrite." Levi breathes out in a whisper.

Our eyes connect, and the paralyzing shock emanating from his person matches my own.

"We need to call Walk."

CHAPTER 26

BLAKE

If this is what it's like to be a detective, I'm sure glad I chose art. I want to run my head through the wall.

My room at Moose Gap Lodge isn't much bigger than a shoebox. The knotty pine paneling covering the walls gives the space a rustic charm that would be cozy if I weren't slowly losing my mind. A double-sized bed occupies most of the room, leaving just enough space for a small desk, a dresser, and a pair of nightstands.

Snow clings to the outside of the window, shading the world beyond the glass a mixture of white and gray. The heater beneath the window rattles every few minutes, struggling to keep up with the freezing Wyoming winter.

When I first checked into Moose Gap Lodge, the room looked like another ordinary motel room.

My clothes were neatly placed in the closet and dresser. My toiletries were organized in the bathroom.

Not so much anymore.

Sketchbooks and charcoal pencils litter the desk. Evidence photos blanket the bed. Sticky notes occupy every available surface. Empty coffee cups crowd the nightstands, plus the empty mug that was filled with nasty motel coffee. I downed it like a shot of bourbon.

I'm pretty sure I've consumed enough caffeine this week to kill a horse.

The wall opposite the bed has disappeared beneath a collage of photographs, timelines, sketches, newspaper clippings, and handwritten notes. I even have colored string connecting victims to locations, suspects to evidence, and theories to dead ends.

The only untouched part of the room belongs to Bear, who has claimed the patch of carpet directly in front of the rattling heater. He lies there wrapped in a blanket like a puppy burrito.

Most people would walk in and probably assume a conspiracy theorist had taken up residence. They'd see trash, chaos, and obsession. All that's missing is the string to connect the thumbtacks.

I see a pattern trying to emerge.

Emphasis on *trying*.

It feels like a painting that isn't quite done. A shadow too dark or a highlight too bright. The wall gives me the same feeling.

The answer is here. I know it is.

The problem is that I've been staring at this wall for so long that everything is starting to blur together.

There's Derek Holt. He was setting fires around town—a fact that I'm not supposed to know. I may have taken a peek at the open file on Ridge's desk this week while I was helping with another sketch.

Then there's Reverend Ricks. I still don't know what he was doing that got him on The Debt Collector's radar.

I'm still wondering how the Evergreen Gazette figured out the motive.

Another item on the investigation list.

And the big question: How the hell does this connect to my stalker?

He lured me to the trailer park. Maybe he's trying to tell me something, or maybe he's trying to set me up.

Hopefully, he doesn't figure out that I told Levi, Santiago, and Walker that he's the reason I'm here.

As if the three of them weren't already overprotective.

I think I'm going to have a heart attack just trying to figure this out.

A sharp knock at the door pulls me from my fun game of How-Long-Will-It-Take-Blake-To-Scream-And-Run- Away.

The notes slip from my fingers and scatter across the floor.

Bear sits up on his bed by the heater but doesn't make a sound.

Assuming it's safe, I shout through the door, "Who is it?"

"It's me, *Cielito*."

Glancing around the room, I determine that there isn't enough time to hide the evidence.

Or the evidence board.

Or the evidence connected to the evidence board.

Making a face, I ask in a whisper, "What do you think, Bear? Should I answer the door?" Bear sighs and angles his head. "You're probably right."

Opening the door a few inches, I block the space with my body. "Hey, Santi. What's up? Can I help you with something?"

Santiago stands taller, peering over my head. "Are you hiding something?"

Closing the door a couple of inches, I leave enough room just for my face. "No. Why would you ask that?"

His gaze drops to the exposed skin of my legs, and my belly turns into a fluttering mess. Then I remember that all I'm wearing are a pair of loose sleep shorts and an oversized off-the-shoulder tee.

That's my Friday night.

"Then why are you standing like that?" Santiago leans left.

I lean left and sport a fake frown. "Like what?"

He leans right. "Like you're guarding Fort Knox."

I lean right.

He gives me a look that is probably supposed to make me feel disciplined. "Blake."

"Santiago," I retort.

He pinches the bridge of his nose. "You're making this weird."

"I'm not making anything weird," I argue. My mouth pinches as a thought occurs to me. "How did you find out which room I was in?"

"Blake," he says with a squint, skipping over my question, "Do you have someone in there?"

Santiago doesn't wait for me to answer and pushes his way inside.

Stepping out of the way, I sweep my arm out to my side and shut the door after him. "Come on in. I don't need privacy."

"What's mine is yours, and what's yours is—" Santiago pauses, taking in the room. He points to the wall. "That's a murder wall."

"No." My arms fold across my chest as I shrug. "It's how I organize my thoughts."

"Pictures of dead bodies." He points again. "Murder wall."

His amusement fades as his eyes evaluate all the notes, photographs, and sketches tacked up on the wall to the empty coffee cups. "You've been doing this by yourself?"

I simply nod.

Santiago takes his time looking over my mess as if he's able to follow my thought trains. "Do you think it's all connected? The texts and the Debt Collector."

Sighing, I rub my eyes. "It's one theory among thousands."

Santiago examines the wall for another moment before looking back at me, and his expression changes.

"When's the last time you slept or ate?" He studies me attentively.

My brows push together. "I don't know."

Santiago's expression softens as he takes a step closer. "Blake."

My hands shoot up defensively, warding him off. "I'm fine."

He disregards my silent request and doesn't stop until his arms are wrapped around my waist. The heat from his body pours into mine, sending ripples of anticipation through my veins.

Santiago traces a single finger under my right eye. "These dark circles beg to differ."

My mouth pinches as I reply flatly. "You know just what to say to make me swoon."

"You're no help to anyone like this." Santiago sweeps my hair over my shoulder.

"It's not like Walk would actually let me help anyway," I grumble.

"Walk knows you're going to do what you want to do, but if he saw you like this," Santiago gestures to the whole room, "he'd flip his shit. And who knows what Levi would do."

"I can't just ignore it," I whisper into his shirt. "This is the whole reason I came back."

"What I'm hearing is that you're here for me."

My stomach drops, and Santiago's grin widens.

I rear my head back and widen my eyes. "That's not exact—"

Santiago interrupts me with a swift, hard kiss, backing me against the door. "You're here for me."

He swipes his tongue into my mouth, forcing a moan from my throat.

"And Levi."

His hands grip my ass as he kisses me again. My knee slides up, my leg hooking around his hip.

"And Walker."

Pulling back, I narrow my eyes at him.

"You can't deny it," he disputes as he suppresses a smile. "How did you get the case files anyway?"

"You're not so old that you don't know what a copy machine is, right?" I tease.

"Brat," he teases back. "Does Walk know you copied the files?"

Did I tell him? No.

Is it possible that Jolene did after she let me use the copier? Yes.

Santiago shakes his head. "Come on. We're going out." His hand reaches for the doorknob.

My fingers wrap around his wrist, stopping him. "Where to?"

"Timberline."

My brows shoot up. "Right now?"

"Why not?" He returns with a shrug.

"Because of this," I return, dropping my hold on him and gesturing at my mess on the wall and my outfit.

Santiago waves his hand at the wall. "That'll all be here tomorrow." He takes a couple of steps backward. "As for this," he motions to my clothes, "I can help with that right now."

He spins on his heel and heads for the closet. He digs around, looking through my wardrobe.

"Santi, I'm tired," I complain as I trudge over and toss myself onto the bed.

Santiago pauses his search and puts his hand on my mug. "Your cup is empty, and it's still warm. I'm pretty sure you're wired." Then he pulls out a simple pair of wide-leg pants, a cropped tank, and a chunky cardigan and tosses the clothing at me.

Of course, he picks out an outfit that's the perfect mix of cute and comfortable.

What is he? A fashion guru?

Setting the outfit aside, I shake my head. "I'll pass this time." He approaches me with a determined look. "What're you—" He dips, wrapping his arms around my waist and digging his shoulder into my gut. When he stands, my world gets flipped upside down. "Santiago Ramirez! Put me down!"

"You'll thank me later," he says proudly as he gives my ass a calming pat. Santiago jostles me around as he squats, gathering my clothes.

"When pigs fly!" I shout. "Bear, get him!" I snap my fingers, hoping he comes to my rescue.

Bear stands, looks to Santiago and me, then turns in a circle, lying down with his back to me.

"Traitor."

Santiago chuckles as he strides for the door. "Even Bear thinks you need a break."

"I saved your life," I plead with Bear.

"Technically, that was Levi," Santiago corrects as he hauls me outside and marches to his truck. My body instantly freezes, and I momentarily regret not changing first.

However, being kidnapped by a six-foot-something rancher technically moves the accountability to him.

Reverently, Santiago sets me in the cab and buckles me in.

"I can do that," I snap.

He just smirks. "But I do it so much better."

When he rounds the hood, heading for his own door, I contemplate running back to my room and locking the door, but then I remember that I don't have shoes on.

Great.

As Santiago slides in with me, he turns the key in the ignition and tosses me the clothes again. "You can change in here."

"In front of you?" I question outraged.

"Nothing I haven't seen before, *mi Cielo*." He returns smugly.

"I don't have any—"

"Shoes?" He reaches his hand down to the floor and flings a pair of boots at me.

My boots.

When did he grab these?

My eyes narrow, and Santiago smiles back.

Looks like I'm going to Timberline tonight.

CHAPTER 27

LEVI

Timberline is a smidge bit louder tonight than I prefer. Obnoxious laughter and drunken shouting spill from a table near the dartboards. Resin pool balls crack together behind me as blue-collar workers place bets on their games. The scent of fried food and beer hangs thick in the air.

The waitress weaves through the crowd with practiced ease, balancing more plates and cups with one arm than any person should be able to. Wes catches her eye from behind the bar and silently points toward a new group of patrons that just walked in. She nods once before emptying her tray and changing course.

They've been doing this song and dance for years.

Most of the residents of Evergreen Falls come here to unwind after a long week of hard work, and soon, Timberline will be overrun with tourists.

I'm here because Santiago sent me a text.

Santiago: Timberline. Twenty minutes.

Now there's a man who works hard but also plays hard.

Recently, my "playtime" has consisted of daydreaming about Blake Jennings. The problem is that I'm always thinking of her. When I'm working, when I'm sleeping. She more than haunts my thoughts.

She consumes them.

And I'd be lying if I said I wanted it to stop.

The label on my beer is half destroyed when I glance at the entrance for the sixth time. On the seventh, the door swings open, and relief slumps my shoulders, but then confusion has my spine straightening.

Santiago walks inside, and his eyes find me quickly. When he strides for me, I notice that Blake trails behind, followed by Walker.

When I get a good look at her, my mouth practically waters. A fitted cropped top has her breasts ready to spill free. Part of me wishes it would happen, but then I'd have to kill every person in here for getting a glimpse at her tits.

I force my gaze back to her face.

I last all of three seconds before I fail spectacularly and settle my eyes back on her chest.

Suddenly, I'm grateful she's wearing a cardigan.

They each take a seat at the square table I saved for us. Santiago pulls out a chair for Blake, placing her on my right, Walker takes up the seat on my left, and Santiago sits down opposite me.

Walker removes his coat, placing it on the back of his chair, and the other two do the same, except Blake just has a cardigan.

Where's her jacket?

It's below twenty degrees outside.

Did Santiago forget her coat or did Blake?

The waitress stops by, knowing our usual, and places a beer in front of Santiago and Walker. "The same for you?" she questions Blake.

"Sure," Blake answers compliantly.

"Wait," I say to the waitress, then turn to Blake. "Have you eaten?"

Blake raises her eyebrows as if I just dumped a load of audacity in her lap. "I'm capable of feeding myself, thank you. I've been doing it for decades."

I give her a look and reply, "I know, but humor me."

Blake's stomach chooses that moment to let out a grumble comparable to that of a mama bear whose cubs are being threatened.

After shooting Blake a smug smirk, I place a large food order. I'm not sure what Blake prefers besides French toast, so I play it safe and order most of the menu.

The waitress nods and heads to relay the massive order to the kitchen.

"Nice of you to finally join me," I direct to Santiago and Walker. "Are your phones broken?"

Walker's face remains blank. "No."

Santiago pulls his from his pocket and taps on the screen. "Mine seems to be fine."

I shrug, gesturing to Santiago and Walker. "And neither of you thought to let me know you'd be late?"

"I got held up at the station," Walker defends himself.

Santiago points a thumb to his left and flashes an infuriating grin. "I was picking up Blake."

Blake crosses her arms and leans forward. "*Kidnapping* Blake," she remedies for him.

Santiago tilts his head from side to side and takes a sip from the dark bottle. "Semantics."

Blake's nostrils flare, then she turns to Walker. "I'd like to report a crime, Sheriff. Your deputy has forced me here against my will."

Walker looks her dead in the eye, takes a chug of his drink, and answers smartly, "You'll live."

A laugh bursts from Santiago and me at the way her face

grows scarlet, and a small smile tugs on Walker's mouth as he takes another drink.

Blake's eyes turn cold as she points a stern finger at each of us. "You three are on my shit list."

Holding up my hands innocently, I proffer, "I have French fries coming. Is that enough to get me off the list?"

Blake glares. "It's going to take more than French fries, Levi Harding."

"Cheeseburger?" I add.

Her glare softens. "Closer."

"I'll take it," I say with a smile.

The waitress returns carrying the food, setting down a basket of fries, onion rings, mozzarella sticks, soft pretzel bites, nachos, cheeseburgers, and beers. The smell of grilled onions and fresh-cut potatoes replaces the lingering scent of earthy fermentation for a moment.

Blake snatches a fry and an onion ring before anyone else has a chance to touch them. She munches away, then gives the three of us a flustered glance.

"Why am I the only one eating?" she questions as her eyebrows form a deep, puzzled crease. "Here," Blake offers as she hands me a soft pretzel.

"I'll wait," I answer with polite refusal.

"Is it because I touched it?" Blake frowns at the food she tried to feed me. "Do you think I have cooties or something?"

Santiago snorts, and Walker just shakes his head.

"No, Blake. I'm making sure you eat first."

Even under the neon beer signs and dim fluorescent lights, I track how her cheeks color with an abashed hue.

Beautiful.

Santiago's hand hovers above the untouched mozzarella sticks, and I give him a look that promises pain if he picks one up.

He lets out an annoyed huff. "Seriously?"

Walker shrugs apathetically. "Apparently."

Santiago nudges the fries closer to Blake, and Walker quietly reaches across the table and places the ketchup next to the fries. Sheepishly, she takes the bottle and squirts out a blob, eating the small mound without another word, and a stream of pride has me ready to puff up my chest.

I don't like that she isn't used to having someone take care of her. Granted, I know that when Santiago, Walker, and I are together, we can come off as intimidating. But we've always taken care of her. The dynamics of our relationship have shifted, but she should still expect us to care.

For the last several years, seeing Blake was something I imagined would happen at some point. I just never imagined she'd be sitting beside me, snacking on bar food, bantering with Santiago, and arguing with Walker like she was always meant to.

The conversation settles into something easy for a few minutes. The kind of conversation that makes you forget about dead bodies, stalkers, and everything else waiting for us outside Timberline's walls.

A microphone squeals through the speakers, cutting across the chatter throughout the bar.

"Easy there," Wes calls out to the person messing with a wad of cables and cords from his spot toward the front of the space, adjusting the stand to a taller height. Once he has the setup ready, he saunters to my side. "Hey, Harding—"

"Not tonight, Wes," I interject swiftly.

He sighs, exaggerating his disgruntlement by moving like he's a rag doll. "Don't make me beg."

Blake watches our interaction with an intense, keen awareness.

"I'm good tonight," I state firmly.

"Come on, man..." Wes mopes.

Blake clears her throat, inserting herself into the exchange. "Excuse me, what's going on? Why aren't you willing to help Wes? He's the keeper of the drinks."

Santiago groans.

"This should be good," Walker mutters into his beer.

Santiago implores me. "Don't do it. Please."

"Do what?" Blake's lips twist as her head leans at an angle.

Wes tries to entice me with the promise of convenience. "I have an axe over there you can use."

Blake tilts her body toward Santiago across the table. "Why does Levi need an axe?"

"I'll do anything," Wes begs. "Free beers for the table? All you have to do is—"

"I'll be up there in a few." The words are out of my mouth before I realize it.

Wes pats me on the shoulder in appreciation and strolls away.

I wanted to enjoy myself tonight with a beer, some food, and friends. But it looks like I'm due for something else.

Actually...

Blake came here carrying the weight of the world on her shoulders, and for the first time all week, she's taking a break.

Forced to take a break, but I'm not going to pass up this opportunity.

And if I can give her a reason to smile tonight, I'll do it without a second thought.

Blake motions her hands, expressing her vexation. "This monkey in the middle thing we have going on here isn't helping any of you get off my list."

"Just give it a minute," Walker says by way of explanation.

Blake groans in exasperation, rolling her eyes. "Give what a minute?"

Jumping to my feet, I tuck in my chair and plant an unexpected kiss on Blake's cheek. "I'm sorry, Butterfly, but I'll make it up to you."

I leave Blake with her mouth hanging open as I head straight for the microphone and remove the guitar Wes pointed out from its case. Slinging the strap over my shoulder, I give each string a good pluck and tune the ones that sound off.

A quick glance shows me that Blake still gapes in my direction, and her forehead is wrinkled in surprise.

When I'm ready, I step up to the mic and tap on the grill. "This thing on?" My voice echoes through the bar and draws the attention of every single person, and the one woman I want to notice me isn't looking anywhere else but me.

My introduction is announced to everyone, but I keep my eyes locked with a set of mocha-colored irises. "This is for a special someone."

I easily fall into a rhythm, strumming my fingers across the strings and moving my other fingers over the fretboard. The tones that flow from my instrument perfectly complement the words and pitch I free from my soul.

The song is one of devotion—it's a promise.

With every verse and chorus, I ask her to stay. It's a big ask, I know, but I'll always regret it if I don't.

Somewhere during the second verse, Timberline disappears, and there's only Blake.

Blake's hands cover her nose and mouth as tears well up in her eyes, and instantly, I know they're tears of affection.

When the last notes fade into the crowd, a tear drops from the corner of Blake's eye and disappears into her hands.

Applause, whistles, and cheers erupt from the audience. I lean the guitar against the back wall and stride for Blake, overlooking the various calls for my attention.

There's only one person I want right now.

When I'm a few steps away, Blake leaps from her seat, and I catch her in my arms. She moves her lips over mine, pouring passion into each swipe of her tongue.

More whoops and hollers ring out around us.

When she pulls back, I question with a smug grin, "Does that mean I'm off the list?"

In lieu of a verbal answer, she kisses me again.

"I'll take that as a yes."

Blake nestles closer as our kiss becomes more heated.

I pull back, trying my best not to laugh at the way she frowns.

"If we keep going right here, Walker is going to have to arrest me for public indecency and lewd conduct."

"Then take me somewhere." Blake flashes me a smirk. "Now."

My brows lift. "Now?"

"Right now," she confirms.

The crowd around us has dispersed, and I glance around the bar, searching for a place to go.

My eyes accidentally meet Santiago's as he mouths the word "bathroom."

Snagging Blake's hand, I head in that direction. "Follow me."

"Whatever you say," Blake replies enticingly.

I stride past the bar and down the narrow hall. At the end are two clearly marked doors, each leading to individual bathrooms.

The first is locked, but the second swings open.

Urging Blake ahead of me, I usher her in, then shut the door behind us, making sure to turn the deadbolt.

Even if someone walked in, I don't think I could stop.

Blake whirls, jumping into my arms. I catch her easily, my hands gripping her ass. Her legs encircle my waist, and our mouths crash into each other.

"I need you to fuck me right now, Levi Harding."

"Don't have to ask me twice."

Carrying her over to the sink, I set her on the edge and pull her flowy pants down along with her panties, taking her shoes off as well. Blake lifts her hips, making the process quicker. In a matter of seconds, her shirt is over her head, and her bra is sliding down her arms, freeing her beautiful tits.

I step back, allowing myself this moment to take in every inch of her smooth skin. "Goddamn, Blake."

She smirks, lifting one leg and placing her foot on the sink. My eyes widen at my unobstructed view of her core. Pink and glistening.

"If you don't get over here right now, I'm going to have to finish the job myself."

Her hand glides over her stomach, and just as she's about to reach her core, I lunge. Landing on my knees, I grip her wrist and pull it away.

"Mine," I growl and bury my face in her pussy.

I sling her other leg over my shoulder as my tongue slides through her folds. Her delicious taste fills my mouth, and I'm instantly addicted. I know I'll never get enough of this–of her.

Blake moans, collapsing back against the mirror.

Another swipe of my tongue has her back arching, pushing her tits into the air.

Needing more, I dive back in like a starving man. I circle her entrance, sliding my tongue back and forth from her entrance to her clit.

Blake's hips begin to move, like she needs more.

I circle her clit, giving it a small flick, then drag my tongue down, over her entrance, and to her puckered hole.

Her body tenses as she sighs, "Levi."

My cock stirs in my pants at hearing my name on her lips like that.

If I could record it, I'd play it over and over on a loop.

Her hips thrust forward again, and I return to the apex of her thighs, starting with her ass. My tongue licks and sucks, and she throws her head back, panting and moaning.

I move my tongue, returning to her clit as my finger slips between her ass. I move my tongue and finger in tandem, circling where she wants me but not giving it to her just yet.

Her breath comes faster, moaning louder.

"Please," she lets out on a desperate breath.

As I coax my finger past her ring of muscle, I swipe my tongue back and forth over her bundle of nerves. I don't stop until my finger is all the way in her ass.

Then I flick my tongue faster and faster as I move my finger in and out.

Her body locks up as her cum floods my facial hair, bathing it in her fluid. Her ass tightens around my finger, and my tongue slows, guiding her through her climax.

When her body releases the tension, she's gasping for air.

Rising to my feet, I go to unzip my pants, but Blake bolts upright and knocks my hands out of the way. Blake has my jeans undone and my cock free swiftly.

"Shirt," she clips as she shoves my pants and boxers down my thighs.

I do as she says and remove my shirt, lifting it over my head, not bothering to take the time with the buttons.

All the air leaves my lungs when Blake wraps her hand around my length and moves her fist up and down.

"Shit, Blake," I choke out.

I let her pump my shaft as I embrace the pleasure she gives me. When a bead of precum appears at the end, Blake pauses, bending down and swiping it with her tongue.

I step back, pulling myself out of her grasp.

"The first time we're together, Butterfly, I'm not coming all over your face. We'll save that for another time."

Blake's eyes light up at the idea.

Oh, yeah.

Definitely doing that later.

Blake fixes her seat on the sink, scooting to the edge. She places her hands on the rim of the sink and leans back, spreading her knees wide. Her folds are drenched and swollen

I have half a mind to fall to my knees and lick her until she screams again.

But the need to be inside her is stronger.

Returning to her, she guides my cock to her core. "I'm on birth control."

My eyes almost pop out of my head.

"Are you sure about this?"

She nods eagerly.

I'm frozen, still shocked that she's going to let me do this.

Impatiently, her hands grip my hips and pull me forward, sliding my length inside her.

Blake clasps my shoulder with one hand, like she's searching for something to ground her. I know the feeling. I need the same.

My hand slaps the wall next to the mirror, propping me up.

When I finally move my hips, sliding out of her heat, we groan together in unison. Then, without warning, I snap my hips forward and pump back inside.

Blake's nails dig into my shoulder.

I repeat the movement, and her nails bite harder, allowing me to revel in the thought that she'll mark me.

Together, we find a rhythm, wringing pleasure from each other.

I want this.

I want this with her every day for the rest of my life.

Blake's pussy grips my cock like a vice as her orgasm starts to build, causing my hips to falter. When her inner muscles convulse, Blake leans forward, muffling her scream by biting my chest, propelling me forward into a state of intense ecstasy.

My heart still races from my climax, causing my breath to come out short and quick.

Blake rests her head in the center of my chest and lets out a small chuckle.

I smooth my hands over her back, rubbing in circles. "Can't say I've ever had that reaction before."

"That was amazing." Blake tilts her head up, her face beaming. "I'm surprised we didn't break the sink."

I shake my head at her, my smile matching hers. "We can always try again later."

She laughs harder, wrapping her arms around my neck and pulling me in for a kiss.

When her stomach grumbles, I step back. "Round two is going to have to wait. Let's get you fed."

Grabbing paper towels from the dispenser, I clean Blake, then myself. We gather our clothes and dress. I pause before we walk out and grab her hand, lacing our fingers together, and a blush colors her cheeks.

We meander back to our table, stopping at the bar to order more food

When we sit, Santiago wiggles his eyebrows at me, and I lean over, punching him in the arm.

Walker refuses to make eye contact, so I ignore him.

He can act uninterested all he wants, but I know the truth.

More importantly, he does too.

CHAPTER 28

BLAKE

Levi has a voice that would make any woman throw her panties at him. I would know. I practically did that in the Timberline bathroom.

What else is a girl to do after a super sexy man sings *My Wish* while making eyes at her the whole time?

But the recovery time I'm going to need after mine and Levi's bathroom shenanigans is going to set a world record.

Swallowing another bite of my cold burger, I exhale a breath of stupefaction and ask, "Since when?"

Santiago, knowing exactly what I mean, gives me a look. "Since forever."

Swinging my head toward Walker, I question accusingly, "And you knew?

"Yep." Walker uses the tissue-paper-thin napkin to wipe his hands as he finishes the onion rings.

Levi just sits there smug as a bug, and I can't fault him for that.

My phone buzzes in my cardigan pocket. I had to fight with Santiago in the car earlier to get it from him. He claimed that I would spend time on it instead of spending time with him.

The phone number is one that I recognize, prompting me to answer. "Hello?"

"Blake, I need you to come back to Moose Gap Lodge as soon as possible," Mason, the owner, requests. His tone causes my chest to grow so tight that I have a difficult time breathing.

"What's wrong?"

My question has Levi, Santiago, and Walker perking up in their seats.

A horn blares through the earpiece. "Just get back here."

"Mason, is Bear okay?"

Silence.

"Hurry."

All of the color drains from my face as I hold my phone in front of my face and find that Mason hung up.

Levi's hand lands on my knee, but I can't feel it. "What happened, Butterfly?"

Walker whips out his own phone, and we all attempt to listen in despite the person wailing into the microphone. "Jo, what's going on?" Nodding his head, Walker's face grows serious. "I'm on my way." He stashes his phone back in his pocket and stands as he pulls me up from my seat and slips my arms into his coat. "Come on," Walker directs to Levi and Santiago, who are already on their feet and ready to go.

Walker places his hand on my back to guide me forward, but I dig my heels in, panic overtaking my body.

Levi wraps an arm across my shoulders. "We need to check on Bear."

My heart hammers as my stomach drops.

Bear. I need to find Bear.

I allow Walker to lead me to his truck, and Levi joins us as Santiago jogs to his own. Walker hops in the driver's seat, and holding my hand, Levi slides into the passenger seat and pulls me in after him. He places me on his lap, shuts the door, and somehow gets the seatbelt over the two of us. We're a jumble of limbs, but it still soothes me.

Walker peels out of the parking lot, and Santiago zooms behind us.

Levi traces circles on my back, releasing the tension there.

When we pull up to the motel, I have no trouble recognizing a scene I've become too familiar with—wild embers.

My car is on fire.

The flames climb several feet into the starry night sky. The windows have already blown out, and a tire pops like distant gunshots.

The billowing smoke rolls from my car windows. The smell of burning rubber fills the car before we're even in the parking lot.

"Oh, my God," I breathe out.

Red and blue lights flash in the evening darkness, reflecting off the white snow.

Yellow turnout gear darts through the smoke, and reflective stripes catch the rotating emergency lights. A firefighter braces the hose while another enters the cloud of steam and smoke. The firetruck sits at an angle across the motel entrance, its emergency lights washing Moose Gap Lodge in red and white.

The few guests staying at the motel are outside, wrapped in blankets and robes, looking as if they had haphazardly dressed to watch the show. One guest is filming the entire scene on their phone while another tries to wrangle a grumpy child in their arms. Mason is running around placating the guests and tending to their needs.

I'm out of the cab and running forward before Walker can bring the truck to a stop.

Levi's voice trails behind me. "Blake!"

Arms encompass my middle, yanking me backward. "Slow down, *mi Cielo*."

Walker strides past us, approaching one of the firefighters.

When I stop flailing about, Santiago sets me back on my feet, and he and Levi escort me to Walker.

"We're almost done putting it out," the firefighter informs Walker.

"Thanks, Tad." Walker pats him on the shoulder. "Was there a dog in the car?"

"Not that I could see," Tad answers honestly.

"I'm going to check your room for Bear," Santiago mentions, then jogs toward my room on the second floor.

Another fraction of tension releases in my shoulders.

Levi grabs my hand, interlocking our fingers together. "It's a rental, right?"

I nod.

"Did you have insurance on it?" Levi follows up.

I nod again.

"Everything will be okay. We can replace anything that was in there," Levi assures me.

"Okay," I return in a whisper.

"Do we know how this happened?" Walker questions Tad.

"I'll know more once I can get a closer look." Tad points his thumb toward my car.

Walker's gaze lingers on the side of Tad's face as he watches the fire, perceiving something the rest of us don't see. "But you have an idea."

Tad nods. "The driver's side window looks broken."

"Which means..." Walker prompts Tad to explain further.

Tad expels a rigid breath. "It might have been intentional."

"Shit." Levi curses next to me.

Tad advances into the fray, and Walker spins toward me.

"He could be wrong." I proclaim in hope.

Walker shakes his head. "Tad has good instincts for investigating fires."

"Maybe the broken window was an accident." I try again.

Santiago returns to my side, taking hold of my other hand. "Bear is fine," he comforts me. "Walk—"

Walker angles his head, directing his question toward Santiago. "Was the window broken when you left?"

"It wasn't." Santiago's response dispels my optimism. "But—"

"It could have been a rock." I try one more time.

"Hey, Walk—"

Walker gives me a flat look. "A rock picked itself up and jumped through your car window?"

Narrowing my eyes, I quip, "Stranger things have happened."

"Walker Maddox!" Santiago yells, causing me to flinch.

"What?" Walker's tone sounds put out.

Santiago shifts his weight from side to side, and my focus bounces between them. Walker's eyes scrunch while Santiago's dart to the side.

Their wordless conversation has my jaw clenching, but Levi has no problem following their cues.

"Oh, shit," Levi curses again, then the attention of the three of them shifts to me.

My brain rattles, scouring for the meaning, but then the fog lifts. Levi, Santiago, and Walker all know when I figure it out.

I drop Levi and Santiago's hands and pretend to fix my hair, pretending to be completely unbothered.

But I'm not fooling them.

Walker's voice is almost threatening. "Don't you dare, Baby Girl."

Eyeing each of their positions, I duck low as Santiago's arms attempt to snag me. Walker and Levi bump heads when they both try to bend down and grab hold of me.

Sliding backward, I move myself out of their reach and sprint for the stairs. My legs are long enough that I can take them two at a time.

"Blake, no!"

"Butterfly!"

Skidding to a stop in front of the door, I notice that it doesn't sit quite right in the frame. The brass cylinder looks as if someone punched it inward, leaving a jagged ring of exposed wood around where the knob is holding on for dear life. Long cracks spiderweb over the painted doorframe where the deadbolt tore free. Even though the door hangs open an inch, I still have to ram my shoulder above the knob to wrench it open.

Bear whines, circling my legs. Once he's satisfied that it's really me, he jumps, placing his front paws on my stomach, and sniffs, searching for anything amiss. When he goes back down onto all fours, my stomach drops, and my breath grows thin and uneven at the sight in front of me.

"My stuff..."

The lamp lies shattered on the floor. The mattress has been shoved halfway off the bedframe. Every dresser drawer hangs open along with the closet doors. My clothes litter the room as if someone tossed them over their shoulder, one armful at a time.

Whoever did this wasn't just searching for something.

They were ripping my life apart.

"Blake, you can't be in here," Walker says as more of a command than a suggestion.

"Walk, *ya déjenla." Leave her alone.*

"Fine, but don't touch anything," Walker commands

"Her fingerprints are already all over the room," Levi asserts.

"I mean you two," Walker points to Levi and Santiago. "Gloves. Now." Walker steps out of the room, and I overhear his side of a phone call. "Jo, call in Tess and Ridge. I need them down at Moose Gap Lodge ASAP."

Leaving Walker to his conversation, I move around the room, inspecting for anything else out of place.

On Bear's bed, I find one of my sketches torn apart. I drop down onto my knees and sort through the pieces, putting them together like a puzzle.

I only have a few pieces in place when I realize that it's a sketch I drew weeks ago. Levi, Santiago, and Walker were hanging out together in front of the police station. Flurries floated through the air as bits of sunlight reflected off them, showcasing how they danced in the breeze. The guys were having a moment. I don't know what was said, but whatever it was, it had them all smiling and laughing together. For a brief moment, they were carefree and unburdened.

Why would someone destroy this moment?

The sketch was in my nightstand drawer.

Shaking off the dread, I ask myself out loud, “Who would do this?”

Santiago’s head pops out of the closet, and in his gloved hands, he holds a few of my clothes. “Piss anyone off lately?”

Where did he get the gloves?

I don’t think I want to know.

“Besides Walk?” I retort.

“This is serious.” Walker chimes in. I didn’t hear him come back in.

“I’m not laughing,” I return.

Walker looms over my shoulder, gazing down at my pieced-together sketch, and a knot of anxiety twists in my stomach.

I don’t like him seeing this. It’s like he’s peering into my soul. I know it’s just a simple charcoal sketch, but I feel as if this paper reveals too much about myself.

I don’t know when Levi and Santiago come over here, but Levi is the first to speak up.

“Butterfly...” His voice is softer than usual. “You drew this?”

Heat creeps up my neck. “It’s just a sketch.”

Walker doesn’t take his eyes off the page. “It’s us.”

Santiago crouches beside me, carefully picking up one of the torn pieces. His thumb brushes the edge without disturbing the charcoal. “You even caught the way Walk scowls when he's pretending not to laugh.”

Walker shoots him a look.

Santiago only smiles.

Levi studies the page for another second before looking at me. “You’re incredible.”

I duck my head, suddenly fascinated by the floor. “They’re just drawings.’

“No,” Walker says quietly. “They’re moments.”

Scooping the shreds into a pile, I hide the image and begin to pace the length of the front wall. Levi and Santiago go back to searching the room, but Walker observes me, which only serves to tighten my stomach into a ball of nerves.

Maybe if I keep ignoring him, he'll lose interest.

Fat chance.

That man's concentration is like a laser beam—narrowed and piercing.

Thankfully, Levi steps out of the bathroom, uncomfortably tenting his gloved hands together in front of his chest. "I think it's safe to say you may owe Mason some damage fees."

My forehead wrinkles. "What're you talking about?"

Santiago diffidently raises his hand as he declares, "I found Bear locked in the bathroom and barking his head off when I came in and..."

"He chewed up parts of the bathroom door and the frame, trying to get out." Levi finished for Santiago.

"What?" My eyes widen, then swing to Bear, who is standing guard in the open doorway.

"Whoever did this," Levi waves to the mess in the room, "locked him in there."

"Asshole," I curse.

Levi crouches down, sliding his finger over a spot on the tile in front of the bathroom door. He rubs his fingers together, analyzing them like they hold important information. Then he crosses the room to Bear and takes a knee.

"Open," he commands, and Bear instantly obeys.

My arms cross loosely over my chest. "What're you doing?"

"Checking Bear's mouth." Levi's focus doesn't waver. "Bingo!"

The rest of us gather around Levi and Bear.

"Nice catch," Santiago commends.

Walker passes Levi a few forensic swabs while Bear holds perfectly still as if he's a professional statue.

Another conversation that I'm unable to follow. This is getting old. "What are we looking at?"

Levi wipes the cotton between Bear's teeth and holds it up for me to inspect. "DNA. Bear bit your intruder."

Dropping to their level, I wrap my arms around Bear. "That's a good boy. Someone is getting extra treats. Yes, he is."

Walker places each swab in a plastic bag. "There's no guarantee we'll get clear results from this, but it's worth a shot."

Santiago shrugs. "Worst case scenario, results are inconclusive, but it won't be hard to find the person in town with a dog bite."

After the swabs are taken, the guys disperse to resume combing through my room, but I stay with Bear and shower him with love.

Santiago meanders over to my murder wall, as he calls it—the only untouched thing in the room. He carefully scans over the photographs, sticky notes, and papers tacked up there.

"Is this different? I don't remember this being here earlier." Santiago points to a piece of yellow paper with bold print all over it. I recognize the paper as an advertisement for the grand opening of Silver Pines, the ski resort. They're all over town.

Stepping forward, I examine alongside Santiago. "Some of this has been moved."

Someone. Touched. My. Wall.

I've spent days putting all of this together. It's not some mix-and-match game.

Walker moves to my other side, joining Santiago and me. "I'll get my deputies to take some pictures. You can look at them with fresh eyes later."

Levi appears on the other side of Santiago. "Why do you have a murder wall in your bedroom, Butterfly?"

A groan reverberates through my chest. "It's not a murder wall."

"It's a murder wall," Walker contradicts me.

Santiago lowers his head toward me and whispers, "I told you."

Walker peers closer at a paper. "I don't want to know how you got these copies."

My eyes dart around the room, looking everywhere but the guys.

I'm not sure if what Jolene did was legal, but I'm not about to rat out my inside woman.

Slapping my hands on my thighs, I change the subject. "So, I assume I can't take any of my stuff."

"It's evidence," Walkers says by way of confirmation.

"That's what I thought." Releasing a fake sigh, I pretend to be put out when I'm just happy that they accepted my segue. Sauntering toward the open door, I'm stopped by a hand on my upper arm. When I spin around, I come face-to-face with my three overbearing protectors. They stand shoulder to shoulder with Walker in the middle.

To anyone else, they'd be intimidating.

But not to me.

Levi raises a single brow. "Where are you going?"

My lips purse together, confused as to why I'm being asked to state the obvious. "The front desk. I need to book another room."

Walker scoffs derisively. "No, you don't."

My fists clench at my sides. "Did I miss the moment you became the boss?"

Santiago frowns as he rubs the back of his neck. "Technically…"

"I'm a *volunteer*," I clarify. "That doesn't make him my boss."

"Blake…" Levi starts to beseech me.

"No." My teeth grind together.

"None of us should be alone right now." Walker's voice of reason is getting on my last nerve. I don't want to admit that he's making sense.

Instead of rationality, I go with obstinacy, but something in his wording has my spine straightening. "Why not?"

"Do I have to explain it?" Walker's question is meant to be rhetorical, but I caught what he said, and I'm not letting it go.

"You said 'none of us.' Meaning all four of us," I point to each person, including myself. "I want to know why."

"Shit." A momentary shadow of unease flashes in Levi's eyes.

"I told you we should've told her," Santiago admonishes Walker.

"Told me what?" My mouth thins with displeasure.

Santiago spills the beans about the day before. Searching the reverend's home, the man with the match, the fire on the lawn, and the word "hypocrite."

My fists fly, pounding on whatever I can reach. "And you didn't think to tell me?" Levi secures one of my wrists while Santiago secures the other, preventing me from taking out my frustrations on them.

But it's not just that.

It's the thought that they could've died, and there was nothing I could do to prevent it.

"That's the pot calling the kettle black, don't you think?" Santiago gives me a look that says he knows that I know he's right.

And I don't like that he's pointing out my duplicity.

"That doesn't matter now." Walker's interjection is dismissive, but at the same time, I understand that he's encompassed in distress.

Levi and Santiago release my arms.

My mouth hangs open, stunned that he isn't taking the opportunity to call me out like Santiago did.

Instead, Walker gives orders. "You can go shopping in the morning. Accompanied. For now, we're staying together. Two at minimum."

Throwing my hands up in annoyance, I complain, "You're enforcing a buddy system? This isn't summer camp."

"The snow on the ground makes that apparent," Levi murmurs shrewdly.

"If I'm not allowed to stay here at Moose Gap Lodge—" I start.

Walker rubs his fingers over his mouth uneasily as he articulates a very good point. "I don't think Mason is willing to rent you another room after this."

"And I'm not allowed to take any of my belongings," I continue, "then what do you expect me to do?" My mouth is tight and grim as I eye the three men in front of me.

Santiago's face lights up as if he just had a world-changing epiphany. "You can stay at my house."

My head flinches backward. "What?"

"We all can." Santiago opens his arms, gesturing to the four of us. "I have the space," he points to Walker and Levi, "and you two are there often enough anyway."

All these men have to do is look at me, and my willpower turns into dust. They tempt me at every turn.

The more memories I make with them, the harder it will be to walk away.

Squaring my shoulders, I level them with a cold glower. "I'm not going."

None of them are happy with my response.

Go figure.

Walker shoots me a challenging look, Santiago's expression promises he'll tie me down if he has to, and Levi's gaze sharpens to a lethal point.

To my surprise, Levi bends, encompasses my thighs with his gigantic hands, shoves his shoulder into my stomach, and stands.

Twice in one night.

What the hell?

The yelp that comes out of my mouth is anything but ladylike. "Levi!"

"There's no messing around when it comes to your safety." Levi's declaration leaves no room for argument as he marches outside.

I catch Santiago holding in a laugh as he ambles behind us. I give him the middle finger, causing his laugh to burst free, and Walker smirks.

"Two peas in a fucking pod," I mutter irately. Bear trots at Santiago's side, and I give him a chastising scowl. "We need to work on your guard dog training."

CHAPTER 29

BLAKE

By the time we left Moose Gap Lodge, midnight had come and gone. My muscles felt heavy in a way that had nothing to do with exhaustion.

I wasn't just tired. I was wrung out.

Before we headed to Santiago's home, Walker's deputies collected evidence around my car as best they could, then made their way to my room. Levi and Santiago spoke with Mason for a time, then they shook hands and Mason ushered the remaining guests to their rooms. Walker moved about, directing Tessa and Ridge, speaking with the firefighters, and working the investigation.

When we pulled up, Falling Sky greeted us with a quiet stillness.

Snow blanketed the corrals, softening the ranch beneath the porch lights. The horses had long since settled into their stalls, and the wranglers were passed out in the bunkhouse. The only sound was the wind whispering through the pines.

I practically crawled up the stairs and right into Santiago's shower. I don't even remember taking off my clothes.

Bear followed me with a little more pep in his step, but

stopped at the bathroom entrance. He sat down on his hind legs with his back to me like he was appointing himself to stand guard.

After washing away the smoke, ash, and dust, the hot water runs clear.

Stepping out of the shower, I wrap myself in one of Santiago's oversized white towels. Steam fogs the mirror, causing my reflection to disappear.

When I reach for my clothes, my hand pauses.

I don't have any of my things with me.

My suitcase, my sketchbooks, even my favorite sweater. Everything I brought to Evergreen Falls sits behind yellow crime scene tape.

Wonderful.

With damp hair and dressed in nothing but a towel, I exit the bathroom in search of the three brutes.

I don't have to go far because they're all on the staircase.

They're carrying a mattress at an odd angle, making it look like it's about to topple over the railing at any moment. Santiago is in the front, walking backward as he pulls on the mattress with an awkward grip and barking directions. Levi is in the middle, doing what can only be described as a sideways crab walk up the stairs while in a half crouch, holding the bottom of the mattress. Walker brings up the rear, jaw tight as he muscles the entire thing upward like sheer willpower is fueling him.

I blink once.

Twice.

Am I hallucinating?

"What's going on here?" I question loud enough for the struggling trio to hear as I lean against the railing of the overlook on the second floor.

"What does it look like?" Levi's retort comes out as a grunt.

"It looks like you're lugging a giant-ass bed up the stairs," I return, holding in a laugh.

Walker's voice is strained with exertion. "There's your answer."

"But why?"

Santiago wipes a bead of sweat from his forehead on his sleeve. "What do you think? What beds are used for."

They finally reach the top step and stop to readjust their positions.

"Fucking?" Santiago snorts at my sass, but when Walker's and Levi's cheeks turn scarlet, I smile to myself and decide to push it further. "I don't know about you guys, but I'm kind of beat. I only have one pair of clothes now. I don't even have a goddamn toothbrush. I'm not exactly in the mood to scratch anyone's itch tonight."

Three pairs of flabbergasted eyes stare at me.

Worth it.

If I'm being forced to sleep on a communal bed, I'm raising hell.

"Good God, woman." Walker lets his end of the bed thump against the hardwood with enough force to rattle the picture frames on the wall.

Santiago groans from the added weight. "Really?"

Walker deadpans, "I needed my hands free."

Levi follows Walker's example. "It's for sleeping."

My mouth gapes. "For who? An entire NFL team?"

Santiago releases his grip and whirls around to give me a look. "It's for us. Obviously."

My fists rest on my hips. "Us? Who is 'us'? You got a mouse in your pocket or something? I don't remember agreeing to this. I was planning on taking the couch, you know, seeing as how I was forced to be here against my will."

"Baby Girl, cut the shit." Walker strides past the mattress. He doesn't stop until we're toe to toe. He's close enough that I have to tip my chin up to see his face. Close enough that I catch the clean scent of soap, sending a zing of need through my bones.

Damn him.

"You know damn well that Mason wouldn't have let you rent another room after Bear tore up the doorframe in the bathroom. We both know that Silver Pines is too expensive for even God himself. So unless your plan was to sleep on a park bench, you don't exactly have any other option. Now quit your whining and sleep on the damn bed." Walker gestures to the mattress.

My nostrils flare.

I hate it when he's right.

Mostly because it happens more often than I'd like to admit.

Instead of responding to Walker, I lean to the side and inform, "Santi, I'm stealing your clothes."

Santiago waves his hand as if my statement is no big deal. "Take all the clothes you want."

Spinning on my heel, I stomp back into Santiago's bedroom. I lock myself in the closet and wait for the heat to leave my face.

I'm not embarrassed.

But my dignity deserves a little privacy.

The closet smells faintly of Santiago—oakmoss and leather. Most women would probably be thrilled to rifle through his clothes, but I'm annoyed.

One of his shirts probably costs more than my entire wardrobe.

I've done well for myself in New York, but not *this* well.

I throw on a pair of boxers and a shirt so large that it almost reaches my knees.

Exiting the closet, I'm met with the sight that tests my control. The need to laugh rides me hard.

Levi stands at the top left corner of the bed, while Santiago is positioned at the bottom left. Together, they tuck the corners of a fitted sheet between the mattress and the floor, but after they do, the other corners come undone.

It's almost alarming how quickly they got the old bedframe and mattress out of here.

"Bite your tongue," Levi chastises. I'm not sure if he's serious or playing around, but either way, I snap.

I laugh so hard that every inch of my abs cramps up. When I calm myself, I wipe the tears away and am pulled up short.

Levi and Santiago have discarded their task and openly stare in my direction. The tension in their bodies is almost too much for me to handle. I feel myself dampen between my thighs.

Clearing my throat, I stride to Bear's makeshift bed, a couple of pillows covered with a blanket, and kneel next to him. "I need to go shopping,"

Santiago shrugs and goes back to securing the sheet. "No need."

My eyes narrow as I pet the top of Bear's head. "What do you mean? I already told you that I only have one pair of clothes. I'm not wearing yours every day until Walk decides to release mine from evidence."

Levi finally gets both corners on the right side to stay in place. "Just let us take care of it."

I quirk a brow at him. "You don't know my size."

"Yes, we do," Santiago disputes, his side also tied down.

Excuse me?

I'm not sure if I'm flattered or concerned.

Glancing around the room, my mind wanders to the missing third in their trio. "Where's Walk sleeping? Ya know, buddy system and all. Is he even here?"

Levi strips off his shirt. "He's showering in one of the guest bedrooms."

Santiago does the same, then unbuttons his pants.

My eyes fall to my lap. "Oh."

I fiddle with the hem of Santiago's shirt, unsure if I'm suddenly bashful from the idea of Walker in the shower or from all the skin on display.

Either way, my imagination betrays me.

Absolutely not. We're not doing this today.

Santiago snickers. "Is that a blush?"

Levi teams up with Santiago. "That's definitely a blush."

My head snaps up toward them. "Shut up."

Levi sports a smirk. "I'm sure he won't mind if you take a little peek," he teases with a wink.

These two together are all sorts of trouble.

I throw my arms up. "Who are you kidding? I wasn't born yesterday. That man would kill me."

"Walk wouldn't touch a hair on your beautiful head, *mi Cielo*, and you know it."

They finish making the bed and getting ready to sleep in silence, but the knowing looks they shoot my way feel louder than a gunshot.

When Walker joins us, his hair is wet, curls twist the ends. He enters the room, wearing only a pair of small boxer shorts. He shuts and locks the door behind him, then crosses the room to the windows and checks those locks as well.

If paranoia burned calories, Walker would've disappeared into thin air by now.

Levi climbs into bed, followed by Santiago, who spoons him from behind. The sight has my heart warming in my chest.

But then I'm reminded that I'm now locked in a room with three sexy men who are wearing less than I am.

Keeping my eyes on the floor, I tuck Bear in and saunter to the side of the bed opposite Levi and Santiago. I nestle down under the thick comforter and silk flat sheet, leaving about a foot of space between Levi and me.

Heavy, long breaths come from Levi and Santiago already.

Walker snags a simple navy wingback chair situated by the windows and drags it right in front of the door. He takes a seat, attempts to make himself comfortable, and flips off the lights.

The only light in the room streams in from the minuscule amount of space under the door, but it's enough for me to see.

The sight of Walker in the small chair is comical.

His shoulders are wider than the armrests, and his head is much higher than the top of the chair.

Scooting closer to Levi, I flip back the corner of the covers in invitation. "There's enough room on the bed for you."

"Someone needs to keep watch."

I sit up in bed. "If you're going to watch me sleep, I'm going to start calling you Edward."

"Why would you do that?"

"I'll let you borrow the book," I return.

Walker's silent for a beat before he explains, "I'm not watching you. I'm watching the door."

His back is to the door, but he's supposed to be *watching* the door?

Sounds like an excuse.

The weight of the entire day slowly seeps into my bones, causing my next argument to come out wearily. "Bear is on guard duty. Get your ass in bed."

"Blake." He says my name like it's enough to get me to let this go.

It's not.

"You can be the little spoon," I jest.

"Blake," he says again.

Sighing, I lie back down, my hands above my head for dramatic effect. "Walk, you won't be able to do your job if you're barely able to keep your eyes open tomorrow. We all need sleep. It's been a long night." I peek my head up. "Please."

I watch his shoulders droop as he gives in.

A bed is always better than a chair.

He heaves himself up and pads on light feet to my side. He lifts the blanket, and I slide over an inch as he lies down beside me.

I turn onto my side and face Levi, with less than an inch of space on either side of me. Then I feel Walker's arm slide under my head and his other arm drape over my hip. His warm, naked chest rests against my back.

"Keep your hands to yourself, Baby Girl," he mumbles sleepily.

Closing my eyes, I nuzzle backward into him. "I don't make promises I can't keep."

Santiago's groggy voice stretches across the bed. "If you two need to fuck it out, feel free."

I feel Walker jostle about a bit, then a thwack echoes in the room.

"Ouch!" Santiago whisper-shouts.

"Shut up and go to sleep," Walker demands as he returns his arm to my hip.

The room rests in silence.

The jokes cease.

Snores begin to pick up—both human and canine.

And the snow falls outside.

It's strange. Not too long ago, I felt alone.

Now three stubborn, infuriating men won't let me out of their sight.

And it feels good.

Like home.

CHAPTER 30

WALKER

Last night was the best sleep I've ever had, and that is not a good thing. Even with Santiago's snoring, which is so loud it's like he's actively trying to wake the dead, I had a good, deep sleep.

At some point in the night, Blake turned over, facing me, and tucked her head beneath my chin. The position felt so natural, it was as if we'd been sleeping like this for years.

She trusted me to keep her safe.

That's the problem.

I can't.

Last night at the motel proved that.

I'm too attached. I'm too close to all of this.

Not just the investigation.

Too close to *her*.

But I can't seem to backpedal. There's no going back to the way things were.

Somewhere over the last few weeks, the line between my role as sheriff and something else disappeared, and I don't remember crossing it.

Maybe...

The line never existed.

Blake doesn't know I'm standing in the doorway of the multipurpose room, watching her work.

Good.

She's been in here poring over photos of her motel room for hours. She's almost completely recreated her murder wall.

I think.

I've been in law enforcement for almost thirty years, and even I can't make heads or tails of her complex web. So I doubt the person in her room last night was able to either.

She has printouts of the photos Ridge took spread out across the conference table, as she sits cross-legged in a computer chair with an open sketchbook in her lap. Pens, pencils, highlighters, and other writing utensils are scattered all around her on the floor, the table, and her lap. A pile of processed snack foods rests on the chair next to her. Neon sticky notes in a plethora of colors are covered in her handwriting and placed indiscriminately all over the place.

Whatever system she has set up only makes sense to her.

Blake scribbles on another sticky note, rips it from the pad, and slaps it down on one of the photos. A determined wrinkle seems to be permanently etched between her brows.

The pink eraser at the end of a number two pencil is on the receiving end of her frustration as she chews it to bits. I'd bet my next pack of cigarettes that she doesn't even realize she has the habit.

The multipurpose room isn't much to look at, and in all honesty, it doesn't get much use. Blake could move in here, and none of us would notice.

The beige walls are a few shades darker than the rest of the station due to the lack of natural light in here. Blake appears to be content to work among the scratched-up whiteboards, fluorescent lights, and cramped filing cabinets.

Blake's head snaps up, pointing right at me. "I survived many years without a babysitter."

Leaning a shoulder against the door frame, my eyebrows lift. "Funny. I think Levi, Santiago, and I can say the same."

"And you all are still alive because of it," she returns in a cheeky tone.

"And you can say the same thing," I retort.

She gives me her signature you're-annoying-me look. "You're impossible."

My palms make a slight upturn in response. She can be irritated with me all she wants, but at the end of the day, if she's safe, I'll happily take her ire.

Blake returns to her sketching and note-taking for a few moments. Even the crease between her brows makes a comeback, but it's not long before she's circled to irritation again. "I can't focus with you hovering like that."

Arching a brow, my head falls forward an inch in consternation. "I'm all the way over here. You have every office supply we have in the station besides a stapler, plus food," I emphasize my pointing by nodding toward the pretzels, chips, and other snacks. "What more do you need?"

Blake drops her arms onto the table. "Space."

The amount of time I've been standing here without her notice could be considered creepy, and I understand her need for room. No one likes it when people hover.

Pushing off the frame, I point my index finger at her. "Fine, but I'm not leaving the building."

Leaving the door wide open, I head back for my office located right next to the meeting room.

Blake wants space, so I'm giving it to her. She deserves that at the very least.

Hell, she deserves a whole hell of a lot more than I've been giving her lately.

I let my door remain wide open as well, and I tell myself it's not because I want to be able to see if Blake leaves the other room.

Collapsing into my desk chair, I kick my feet up and rest them on top of the desk. My office is exactly the way I left it this morning.

Incident reports are stacked neatly in a tray on the corner of my desk. My department radio charges next to my computer monitor. My coffee next to the keyboard is in the same place, but it's long since gone cold. A heap of case files waiting for signatures sit neatly in the center of my desk.

The stark contrast between my office and the absolute chaos that Blake has turned the conference room into is drastic.

Flipping open one of the case files, I attempt to focus, but after rereading the same section several times, I still don't know what it says. I swipe a pen from the top right drawer and jot down my signature. A brief review lets me know that I signed the wrong line.

So much for productivity.

I toss the file back on top of the pile and rise to my feet. Fiddling with the blinds over the one window in my office, I make note of the dust. Retrieving a napkin from another drawer, I give the horizontal slats a quick wipe and chuck the napkin into the trash.

Pacing the length of my office, my mind finally does what I've been trying to avoid.

Think.

There was someone in Blake's room, someone who means her harm.

I hate that there's nothing I can do about that now. All I can do is work the case.

The lock was broken, which means that the person doesn't know how to pick locks. From the canvas Tessa and Ridge performed last night, no one heard the person breaking into the room, nor did anyone hear Bear barking like a rabid dog.

Hard to believe, but it is what it is.

Then Bear was trapped in the bathroom and attacked the person. The full DNA report will likely take months, but I greased a few palms this morning to get a Forensic DNA Phenotyping report. That one won't take as long and will at least help us narrow down the search.

Blake could've returned to Moose Gap Lodge while the person was still inside.

I don't let myself finish the thought. I don't have to.

My imagination does it for me anyway, causing my mouth to twist wryly as every muscle in my body contracts.

I should have put one of my deputies outside her room. I should've made her move into Santiago's house sooner.

Blake would've laughed in my face, but I have no qualms about kidnapping to ensure Blake's safety.

My radio crackles from where it's plugged in, ripping me from my apprehensive pondering.

Jo laughs at something in the lobby. She's probably on the phone.

The ancient printer in the bullpen rattles as it spits out a file. That thing could be heard from a mile away.

Closing my eyes, I do my best to focus, but I find myself listening for Blake.

Is she thirsty?

Does she have a headache from being in that room for so long?

Should I get her to take a break?

My fingers massage my brow ridge as I ridicule myself for acting like this—obsessed. Checking the clock on the wall, I discover that only five minutes have passed.

Just.

Five.

I wait for the five minutes to turn into six before I lose the argument with myself and find a reason to go back to Blake.

Whipping up a coffee in the little breakroom, I search for anything I can add to it. I fill half of the mug with milk and the other half with drip coffee. I send a thank-you to the deity upstairs when I find a can of extra-creamy whipped cream and cinnamon in the cabinet.

At the station, we pretend Tessa is the reason we have all the things for a latte, but it's me. Although I'm not the one who supplies the mugs. That's Jolene. A fact that is made apparent when I get a look at the words on the mug in my hand as I take it to Blake.

Chaos Coordinator.

Nothing says, "I'm not thinking about you," quite like this mug.

Entering the room, I find Blake in the exact same position she was in when I left.

"I figured this might help," I say by way of announcing my presence as I carefully find a spot to set down the mug.

"You're an angel." Blake snatches the coffee from my hands and takes a gulp, a smile brightening her face. "Oh, sweet bean juice." She takes another look at the ceramic cup. "Did you make this?"

Unwilling to answer, I ask a question of my own and pull out the empty chair opposite her. "How's it going?"

Blake lets out an aggravated groan so loud there's no mistaking that she's ready to throw a chair through a window.

"That bad?" I keep my hands in my lap so as not to disturb

She smacks her fists on the table as she scowls at all the papers. "I know every paper, picture, and Post-it that was moved. I marked them with these little yellow stickers." She holds up a full sheet of bright yellow circular stickers, shaking it around as if it personally offended her.

Leaning back in my seat, I get comfortable and cross my arms. "That's a start."

She waves her hand over her hard work. "But I did all of that hours ago. Nothing else makes sense. None of it."

"Want to talk it out?" I suggest.

Blake falls back in her own chair, sighing up at the ceiling. "I guess it couldn't hurt, unless my brain explodes."

"Drama queen."

She sits up, giving me the same scowl that she gave the table. "Overbearing oaf."

Cuing the discussion, I start. "Santiago mentioned you thought the Debt Collector and your stalker could be connected."

Blake nods in confirmation. "The more I look at it, the more I think they may be working together." She holds up one of the photographs containing a yellow sticker. "My intruder—"

"You mean attacker," I correct.

"*Intruder,*" Blake persists, widening her eyes, "moved the Silver Pines flier next to my stuff on the Debt Collector."

A detail we all noticed last night.

Sitting up, I point to the photo in her hand. "What do you think that has to do with the texts?"

"He wrote the word 'present' on the flier." She indicates the bolded letters on the flier. "The texter—"

"Stalker," I correct again.

Blake continues as if I didn't speak at all. "—also called the body at the trailer park a present."

That is a bit alarming.

"That does feel significant," I agree.

Returning the picture to its place, she gestures to the Debt Collector's victims. "But I can't figure out what Silver Pines has to do with Derek Holt and Reverend Ricks."

The riddle of the century.

"I'm not sure either, but I put Neil Redford under police protection. Ridge has been on him since last night," I inform her.

Her face scrunches. "Who?"

"Neil Redford," I reiterate.

Frowning, Blake squints.

"Silver Pines."

The dots still don't connect for her.

"He's the owner and developer of Silver Pines," I clarify. "And the manager at Evergreen Community Bank."

Her brows lift with understanding. "That makes sense." She takes another hearty gulp of the coffee. "Why are you doing this?"

Casually, I drag my hand over my mouth. "What? My job?"

Blake closes her eyes, pauses, then opens them slowly, communicating her lack of amusement. "Doing an award-winning impersonation of a helicopter mom."

"No, I'm not," I deny, shifting in my chair.

"Coffee, hovering in the doorway," she lists, "you even waited for me outside the bathroom earlier."

Weaving my fingers together, I recline and rest my hands on my chest.

Blake angles her head, and her tone softens. "Nothing is going to happen to me here. We're in a police station, for God's sake."

For a moment, it's as if Blake takes some of the weight I carry around on my back and places it on her own.

She reaches her hand across the table toward me.

Sighing, I sit forward and clasp her hand. Sincerity tinged with trepidation leaks through my voice. "I can't risk it."

Blake's mouth curves into a light frown. "What're you talking about?"

Something inside of me snaps. It's like a bomb goes off, tearing down the walls I built around my heart, and there are too many pieces to put them back together. I don't want to lose it here in front of her.

But it's too late.

Dropping her hand, I list the close calls. "The clinic, your room, your car. How many more times do you think you'll get lucky?"

Blake sits up straight, her gaze too perceptive. "You're scared."

"No, I'm not." Strenuously, I shake my head in denial. "I'm realistic."

Blake bites her lip as sympathy colors her eyes.

"Fine." Abruptly rising to my feet, I cause my chair to roll backward and crash into the wall. "I'm scared." I throw my hands up, feelings spilling all over the place. "From the moment I found out you were back, everything has gone to hell in a handbasket. I know you didn't do any of it, but it seems to happen around you, which means you're going to get hurt. I can't let that happen."

Blake gets up, scurrying to the door and closing it. She approaches me, her palms making a calming gesture.

"Take a moment and breathe with me," she entreats in a soothing tone.

Shaking my head, I reply, "Three times, Blake. Three times you could've been hurt or worse, and I wasn't there to step in for any of it."

Her hands land on my chest, her right one resting over my heart. Maintaining eye contact, her eyes rim with tears. "I'm not worth saving, Walk."

Is that what she really believes—what she actually thinks about herself?

As a sheriff, I've encountered the scum of the earth. Blake Jennings is nothing like them.

Cupping her face with my hands, I stare right back. "Then why do I keep trying?"

"I believe someone once said that's the definition of insanity." Blake flashes a sad smile.

"Maybe." My eyes trace the slope of her neck, the beauty in every inch of her being. "But I'd do it again." A few tears slip free, and I use my thumbs to wipe them away. Infusing each of my words with vigor, I bring my face closer to hers. "I'd choose you every time, Baby Girl."

The words leave my mouth before I can stop them, and there's no going back.

"Why me?" Blake's voice cracks.

This woman.

"Because I don't know how not to."

My heart pounds as Blake's eyes search my face.

Something between us snaps.

"Fuck it," I curse.

We move at the same time. My arms wind around her waist as hers lock around my neck, and our lips meet in an explosion of heat. We battle each other for dominance of the kiss, our tongues dueling and teeth nipping, making the connection all the more intense.

Her hands shove into my hair, knocking my hat to the ground.

I want her. I *need* her.

My cock throbs in my pants, desperate for her touch.

Guiding Blake backward, I pick her up by her hips and set her down on the edge of the table. Blake swipes her hand backward, sending the photos and notes flying in every direction.

Blake spreads her knees, making space for me between her thighs, and I eagerly accept her invitation.

Her hands find their way to the buttons of my shirt and get to work. I help her efforts by removing my utility belt and setting it aside. When she finishes with the buttons, she pushes my shirt off my shoulders, and I let it fall to the ground.

I find the hem of her sweater, remove the knitted fabric, and toss it over my shoulder. I make quick work of her pants, panties, and bra.

I step back and drink her in. Her curves, her breasts, her smooth skin.

My mouth practically waters.

My eyes are drawn to a tiny bit of ink on the inside of her hip. "A butterfly?"

"I got it after I sold my first painting."

Dropping to my knees, I work my lips up her thigh, kissing and nipping at her skin. When I reach her hip, I place a light, tender kiss on the butterfly, causing a contented sigh to slip from her lips.

Rising to my feet, I snag a chair, rolling it toward Blake. I plop down in the seat between her legs peer down at the juncture of her thighs. Her slit glistens with her arousal, and a moan works its way up my throat.

Blake's hips lift as she leans back on her elbows. "Please, Walk."

"From the moment I saw you at my crime scene, I've wanted this, Blake."

I drape her right leg over my shoulder, kissing the inside of her knee.

Blake whimpers.

"I'm not going to rush it."

Her hips lift again, and I place my hand on her stomach, holding her in place.

"I'm going to take my time, Baby Girl."

My lips land a little higher on her inner thigh. She fights my hold, pushing against my hand.

"Stay still," I command.

Blake lets out a frustrated grunt, and I smirk.

Drawing out the process, I return to her inner thigh, making my way north with my lips. When I get to her center, I blow out a breath, causing Blake to gasp.

"You may want to keep your cute little noises to yourself, Baby Girl. You never know who might hear them, and I'd hate to have to cut someone's ears off because they heard you moan from my mouth on your pussy."

Blake bites her lip.

Hard.

Squirming at my promise.

Instead of licking her arousal from her folds, I switch to the other leg and start all over again.

Blake flops onto her back, throwing her arm over her eyes and lets a frustrated snarl.

"Something wrong?" I tease.

Blake sits back up. "I swear to God, Walker Maddox. If you don't get your mouth on my pussy soon, I'm going to use my hand."

"Don't threaten me with a show," I smirk.

Blake bites her lip again, and without warning, I go right for her core. She has to bite her hand to keep herself from shouting.

My tongue dips between her folds, licking up her juices, and I savor the taste.

I'm going to need this every day until I die.

My tongue circles around her entrance, and her hole contracts, needing to be filled. Giving her what she wants, I spear my tongue inside her channel, and her whole body shivers.

I dip my tongue in and out, gliding up to her clit and back

down. She soaks my face and the table, a wet spot forming beneath her.

The next time I slip my tongue inside, she explodes.

I reach my hand up and cover Blake's mouth, her teeth biting into my palm.

Her legs tremble as she writes, riding out the wave of her release, and it's the most beautiful thing I've ever seen.

When she relaxes back into the table, I remove my tongue from her core, licking her clit. Blake spasms, shoving my face away.

"Too much," she whines.

Standing up, the chair slides back, and I undo my pants and push them down my legs along with my boxers.

Blake lifts her head, her gaze going right to my hard length, and her mouth drops open.

"Holy shit."

My fist wraps around my shaft, pumping as I gaze at her body. Blake watches me intently, licking her lips.

"Fuck, Baby. We don't have time for that right now, but next time, I'll let you choke on my cock."

Her eyes widen as she clenches her thighs, thrilled at the idea I put in her head.

Craving her lips on mine, I wrap my hand around her throat and guide her to lie back on the table. I follow her down, crawling on top and thrusting my tongue into her mouth.

Blake sucks my tongue into her mouth, and I feel my length ready to spill.

Blake lifts her legs, wrapping them around my waist. She uses her position to push her hips, trying to get my cock in her channel.

"Patience," I growl.

Her voice turns pleading. "I need you, Walk. I need to feel your cock move in and out. I need you to fill me with your cum."

"Fuck, Baby Girl," I swear, my control snapping.

Adjusting her hips, I angle my own and notch my tip at her

entrance. At an agonizingly slow pace, I move my hips in small, shallow thrusts to work my way in.

A crease forms between Blake's brows as she chants, begging for more.

Once I'm completely seated inside her channel, I clench my jaw, holding my release back. I haven't been on the verge of a climax this quickly since I was a teenager.

Moving my hips back, I almost pull all the way out, leaving just the tip inside. Then abruptly, I snap my hip forward, filling her.

"Good God, Walker," Blake pants.

"Hold on to something," I warn her.

Blake scrambles to grip the edge of the table, then I pull back again and pump again.

I pump in and out.

In and out.

The conference table rocks, creaking with the pace I set. I repeat my motions, holding back my release.

My Baby Girl comes first.

A drop of sweat trickles down from my temple, exertion and pleasure stealing my breath.

I use one hand to cup her breast, twisting and plucking her turgid peak, forcing her to ride that line between pain and pleasure.

"You need to tell me now, Blake. Am I pulling out or coming inside you?"

"Inside me." Her answer is immediate. "I take the pill."

"Fuck yes," I breathe out.

Her pussy clamps down on my shaft unexpectedly, her orgasm hitting her without warning. She opens her mouth to scream, and I cover her sounds with my hand.

The next squeeze of her channel, thrusts me into the blissful high of my own climax, her pussy milking my cock dry. My orgasm feels as if it goes on forever.

Coming down from the high, I rest my forehead against hers. Neither of us utters a word, basking in the glow.

Placing my lips to hers one more time, I stand up straight and pull up my pants. I don't care that my dick is covered in our mess.

Blake snaps her bra in the back and searches for her sweater.

Snagging her panties off the floor, I slide her legs in and bring them up to her hips.

Blake squirms. "I need to clean up."

"Leave it," I command. My hand covers her pussy possessively. "I want you to remember."

She slaps my arm half-heartedly. "You dirty man."

We turn away from each other, searching the room for the remainder of our clothing. Blake flings my shirt in my direction, and I throw her leggings to her.

Reaching for my belt, my hand freezes, hovering in the air.

The light reflects off the polished brass.

My chain and my freedom.

My responsibility to this town.

My badge.

I'm the sheriff of Evergreen Falls.

What the hell have I done?

CHAPTER 31

WALKER

Blake is vulnerable. Someone is terrorizing her. She trusted me enough to lower her guard. I should've had more self-control than that. She deserves more than a quick fuck in the conference room at the police station.

Blake doesn't even know the truth. Levi, Santiago, and I never told her. If she knew, she'd never look at me the same again.

The line that I thought didn't exist earlier becomes crystal clear, and I crossed it.

It's as if Blake can feel the shift in my mood. Her hand falls on my shoulder, grabbing my attention, concern filling her features.

"Walk, are you okay?"

My eyes drop, and I spin away, sliding my belt through the loops on my jeans. Her hand drops away, and I lose her touch.

I try to convince myself that this is how it has to be.

I can't look her in the eye. Not now. I don't want to see the look on her face. "Get your things. We need to leave."

If I look at her now, I'll stay.

"Where are we going?" Her voice relays the hurt I've caused.

We finish dressing in silence. I'm done before she is and wait for her to tie her boots. She slips on her coat, or rather, Levi's coat. Blake did some online shopping this morning, and until her purchases arrive, she's borrowing whatever clothing of ours she can make work.

When she's ready, I open the door and gesture for her to go ahead of me. Thankfully, Tessa and Ridge are still gone, but Jolene shoots me a knowing look as she sits dutifully at her desk. To my relief, she doesn't comment. She gives us a polite goodbye and leaves it at that.

I shut the passenger door to my truck after Blake enters, then I climb in on the driver's side.

Blake doesn't waste a second trying to remedy the situation. "Are we going to talk about what we did?"

Unable to articulate the appropriate words, my lips remain shut as I pull out of the parking lot and head toward Falling Sky.

How do I tell her without hurting her? Is that even possible?

The cliché phrase sits in my throat. I try swallowing it down, but it won't go away.

My only option is to rip off the band aid.

In my next life, I'm coming back as a rusty dumpster.

Staring straight ahead, I tighten my grip on the steering wheel. "This can't happen again."

The silence between us expands, pulling taut like a rubber band. When Blake opens her mouth again, the rubber band snaps. I'm left with a welt on my soul, and I deserve it.

"Did you not like it?" Her tone is timid, the complete opposite of Blake.

Regardless, her question throws me off. "I came, didn't I?"

"That doesn't always mean it was enjoyable," she disputes.

"I liked it. I liked it a lot," I answer honestly. "But Blake, you don't know everything."

I can feel her mood flip as her eyes attempt to bore a hole into the side of my face. "Are you saying I'm not smart enough for you?"

I grimace. "What? No."

"Then what is it?" The sound of her hands slapping her lap resonates in the cab of my truck.

"I mean about me," I amend.

"You think you're some big mystery to me? Sorry to burst your bubble, but you're not that complicated, Walker Maddox," she claims belligerently, but she doesn't stop there. "I know it's been a while for you, but that's the point of a relationship—to get to know the other person."

She has a point, but that doesn't change the facts.

She doesn't know the truth.

And I'm not sure I can be the one to tell her.

Blake sighs, some of the fight leaving her bones. "What are you afraid of, Walk?"

What am I afraid of?

The answer is simple yet complex.

Losing her.

I assume I'm silent long enough that Blake's patience wears out as soon as I maneuver my truck into Santiago's driveway.

"Right. Roger that, Sheriff. Loud and clear," she snaps as she hops out of the cab.

On instinct, I reach for her, but she dodges my hand. "Blake—" Her name leaves my mouth too late.

With her hand on the door, she uses her other to scold me. "Let me know when you get your head out of your ass."

Shutting the door, she stomps off into the house.

Blake slams the front door hard enough to rattle the windows.

Resting my head along the back of the bench, I tell myself repeatedly that I did the right thing.

Every instinct in my body tells me to go after her. Instead, I sit in my truck like a coward.

Of all the fuck ups in the world…

I can feel sorry for myself at any time. Someone is threatening Blake.

Scrolling through the contacts in my phone, my thumb hovers

over a particular name. We grew up more like brothers than cousins, even though we only saw each other in the summer, and if there's anyone I trust with this case besides Levi and Santiago, it's him.

After I tap his name, the phone only rings once before he picks up. "Special Agent Roman Cassidy."

Despite everything going on, the corner of my mouth still twitches upward. "Still making people call you that?"

"Only when I know it's you," he quips back, then his tone shifts. "What's going on?"

Silence grips me for a heartbeat.

"Walk, who died?"

"It's a case."

"That doesn't answer my question."

Sharp as a tack as always.

I exhale through my nose. "No one else. Not yet."

Roman lets out his own quiet breath on the other end. "Okay. Start at the beginning, and don't leave anything out."

I spend the next several minutes taking him through the details of Derek Holt, Reverend Ricks, the crime scenes, the notes—everything we've uncovered up to this point.

Roman doesn't utter a word until I'm done. He just listens.

"Have you figured out why the reverend was targeted?" he asks.

I shake my head even though he can't see me. "Not yet. One of my deputies is tracking down a judge for warrants on his phone and bank records."

"Good," he commends.

The rapid clicking of keys echoes through the phone.

He's taking notes, possibly doing his own research as well.

Of course he is.

"Your killer is organized," Roman deduces after a moment. "Patient and purpose-driven."

I lean farther into my headrest. "I gathered that."

"Forget the fires," he instructs, ignoring my sarcasm.

"What do you mean?"

"You were right. The fires are the cleanup. He's using them to destroy evidence and control the narrative," he explains.

My fingers tighten around my phone. I didn't realize until now how much I needed that confirmation.

"If I had to bet," Roman continues, "white male in his forties. Maybe fifties."

I frown. "Why?"

"Confidence," Roman answers without hesitation. "He's comfortable enough to stage scenes, communicate with law enforcement, and he keeps escalating. That kind of thing usually comes with age."

"What do you think about the psychopathy?" I question.

Roman hums in thought. "He doesn't profile as a psychopath."

His answer surprises me.

"He isn't killing because he enjoys it," Roman analyzes. "He's killing because he believes he's right."

My stomach sinks.

Somehow that feels worse.

Much worse.

"There was a clue in the first victim's mouth, but not the second, right?" Roman questions.

"Correct," I confirm.

"Maybe the location of the body is the clue for the second victim," he suggests.

I'll get Tessa on that.

"One more thing," Roman adds. "People lie."

I wait.

"Evidence and behavior don't. Find where your victims actually died. I don't think the original crime scenes are where you found them."

Digging through the glove compartment, I fish out an uncapped pen and an old receipt from Main Street Diner. I jot the note from Roman on the back of the thermal paper.

"We'll start looking." Dropping the paper and pen onto the bench seat, I pinch the bridge of my nose. "What I still don't have is motive."

Roman is quiet for a moment.

"You do."

My brows furrow. "No—"

"You just don't recognize it yet."

"Thanks, Obi-Wan," I retort.

"I'm more like Qui-Gon Jinn."

I huff a single laugh. Roman's attempt to lighten the mood works for a half second, but then that moment ends.

"Do you want me out there?" Roman proposes. "I can have this transferred if you want another set of eyes."

His offer doesn't surprise me.

What does is the part of me that almost says yes.

"No," I respond. "You just got settled in San Francisco."

Roman sighs. "Walk..."

"I'm serious," I affirm.

"Me too," he counters. "If this goes sideways, I don't care what city I'm assigned to, I'll be there."

I stare through the windshield toward Santiago's house.

"I'll keep that in mind."

Another beat of silence.

"Something else is bothering you, Walk."

I scoff. "No."

"You've been lying to people your whole career, Sheriff Maddox, and I hope you're better at it with others than you were just now."

I don't respond. I don't have to. He knows me too well.

"What it is..." his voice softens, "don't carry it by yourself."

"Thanks, Rome."

"Call me when you find the connection," Roman requests.

"*If,*" I correct.

"Not if. When."

The call ends before I can respond.

All I can do is hope he's right.

Because if I don't find the motive, this guy is going to get away with murder.

CHAPTER 32

BLAKE

Men are damn exhausting.

Multiply that by three?

Impossible.

This can't happen again.

I don't know what made Walker suddenly change his mind, but he can take his regret and shove it where the sun don't shine. He's maddening. I might rip my hair out from Walker stress alone.

You don't know everything.

The words replay on a loop that I can't seem to shut off.

I kick a corral fence post with my boot in frustration, and pain shoots through my toes, causing my to ball my hands into fists. Bear nudges me with his nose, and I reach down to scratch behind his ears, which he loves.

I'm so mad at Walker.

So why does this hurt so much?

An hour after Walker and I got back from the station, Santiago left on horseback to check on some pasture or whatever, while Levi and Walker headed back into town. I'm not sure what they were doing, but I'm not sure I want to know. It'll probably enrage me even more.

Fine. If Walker wants space, I'll give him space.

They left me with Javier like I'm some sort of incapable child.

My fingers yearn for the feel of a brush, but all of that is sitting in storage in New York City.

Even my clothes aren't really mine anymore.

Everything I'd brought to Moose Gap Lodge is sealed up as evidence after someone tore the room apart. Levi and Santiago insisted on replacing my entire wardrobe before I had the chance to argue. My side of Santiago's closet is somehow fuller than his now, stuffed with cozy sweaters, jeans, boots, and enough flannel to survive ten Wyoming winters.

I should probably be annoyed that they made the decision for me. Instead, I kind of love that they wanted me to be comfortable.

"Everything okay?" Javier's question pulls me from my pouting.

Pivoting toward him, I lean back against the fence and rest my elbows along the top.

Javier has been repairing tack beneath the overhang of the barn with leather stretched across his lap. His fingers move with practiced ease, weaving new stitching through old cracks. The rhythmic scrape of his awl is curiously soothing.

I force a smile. "Just tired."

"Mmm," he returns as if he doesn't fully believe me. "Sometimes the hardest thing to do is to let the bull run in circles until he's worn out. A tired bull is more amenable."

"I'll go crazy if the only time we get along is when he's tired." A sigh causes me to tilt my head to the sky. "I don't think Walker would be a bull. Maybe a mule."

Javier chuckles.

"It'll pass," he encourages. "Can you grab the halters from the equipment room?"

"Can do," I answer with a thumbs up, then march off toward the barn in search of halters.

I'm not entirely sure what a halter is, but I'm sure I'll figure it out.

Treading into the barn, I'm struck by the tranquility inside. Usually, one of the horses nickers as soon as they hear footsteps.

But there's nothing.

They all must be too tired.

Turning the corner toward the equipment room, I find that I'm not alone.

"Hey Abbott," I greet with a smile. "What're you doing here?"

Abbott shifts a case from one hand to the other. "Just picking up some equipment."

After Walker implemented the buddy system, Levi moved some of his veterinary equipment to Falling Sky. Santiago cleared a room in the barn for Levi to work in, but Abbott has taken over most of the day-to-day back at the clinic.

Abbott looks at me expectantly, but I'm not sure what I'm supposed to do. So instead, I give him an awkward wave.

"Okay. Well...See you later."

"Actually," Abbott rubs the back of his neck, and his eyes dart to the floor. "I was wondering if you'd maybe like to get a cup of coffee sometime." Abbott's ears turn pink, and his grip on the handle tightens.

My brows shoot up. "Oh. Um..."

"Just to catch up," he adds.

"I'll let you know," I compromise.

"Thanks." Abbott scurries past me with long strides.

Maybe it's not the best idea to get coffee with someone I once dated in high school. Especially after I learned that my guys have a jealous streak.

Finally entering the equipment room, I search for something that could be considered a halter.

I should've asked Javier what a halter is...

The click of boots from outside the room has me turning around to face the open door. A shadow creeps up the wall as the last person I expected to see comes into view.

"Manny?"

"Hey, Blake." He stops in the doorway, resting his shoulder against the frame, and smiles at me politely.

What is he doing here?

I stumble over my words. "I thought you were..."

"Fired?" His smile fades into an empty expression. "Guess he decided to give me a second chance."

"That's good." I nod my head. "Wouldn't want to be out of a job."

"I'm sure you wouldn't."

Something in his tone nags at my senses like a splinter beneath my skin.

"What?" I question with a frown.

"Nothing." He pushes off the frame, straightening himself. "I should get going."

"See you later," I say with a wave.

"Yeah."

I watch him disappear the way he came, a blaring question pushing to the front of my mind.

Reaching into my back pocket, I pull out my phone and type out a text to Levi, Santiago, and Walker as Bear prances out of the equipment room. He's probably going to find Shadow.

Me: I thought Manny was fired.

Santiago: Don't defile my phone with that cabrón.

Levi: He was.

Walker: Why do you ask?

Me: He was just here.

Santiago: I'm on my way.

Levi: Us too.

Me: It's not a big deal. He left.

Those overbearing, aggravating…

Shaking my head, I stow my phone back in my pocket and laugh. It's either laugh or rage, and I'm choosing to laugh.

I take another look around the equipment room and decide to swallow my pride and ask Javier what the hell a halter is.

Stepping out of the equipment room, I let out a whistle. "Bear?" I call out, but he doesn't come.

I whistle again. "Bear?"

A muffled bark rings out sharply.

I guess I'm coming to you.

"You know, it's usually the opposite," I shout to Bear as I follow the sounds of his woofs and yaps. "I whistle, you come running, then everybody wins."

Rounding the corner, I find Bear next to Shadow's stall. "There you are," I say in relief.

Shadow stands at the gate, her head poking out over the top. I stroke my hand down her face, between her eyes, and let myself vent. "They're being a bunch of overprotective idiots."

Shadow blows out a breath through her nose, and I take it as a sign that she agrees with me.

"Did you miss me, girl?" Shadow grunts in response. "Yeah, I missed you too."

Bear lets out a growl. My hand pauses on Shadow's snout.

"Bear?"

He lets out a booming bark, his head facing the barn door, which I notice is now closed.

Did I close it? I don't remember doing that.

Then again, it's been one hell of a day.

A sweet aroma enters my nose, and Bear barks again. Goose bumps break out over my skin, sending a chilling shiver up my spine.

The smell, pungent and sharp, gets stronger.

I'm not sure where it's coming from, but I recognize it easily.

Gasoline.

My stomach drops.

In a full sprint, I run to the doors and tug on the handles, but they don't open. Instead, there's a metallic rattle on the other side.

I'm locked in.

My pulse stutters.

Bear works to claw at the wood. When that doesn't work, he begins using his teeth. The horses in their stalls whinny and snort, stomping their hooves in alarm.

No.

No, no, no.

"Javier!" I shout in a panic. "Javier!"

Only the frantic cries of the horses answer me.

Where is he? He should just be around the corner. He should be able to hear me.

Breathe, Blake. Fucking breathe.

Panicking isn't working. The guys are on their way, but who knows how long they'll take.

Turning in a circle, I search for something I can use.

Riding blanket? No.

Grooming supplies? No.

Sledgehammer? Hell yes.

I don't know who left that against the first stall, but God bless this forgotten tool.

Heaving the heavy hand tool, I lift it over my shoulder and lug it toward the door. I give it a swing, but all that results is a bang. Not even a loud bang because the ruckus around me drowns out the sound.

Examining where I hit the door, I find that I didn't even make a dent. I dig deep and lift the sledgehammer again.

After a few more hits, I have loosened one of the planks. Sweat drips down the side of my face. Dropping the sledgehammer, I find I can push the single plank a couple of inches, giving me a limited view of the outside.

A wet drop lands on my finger, causing me to draw back. I rub the liquid between my fingers and sniff.

Definitely gasoline.

Pushing the plank again, I peer through the crack and freeze. Another wave of chills numbs my body.

He stands there in the cold, watching me. A bright red gas can hangs in his hand at his side. In his other hand, he fiddles with a lighter. Flicking it on and off.

On.

Off.

On.

Off.

"Manny…" My voice barely works. "Don't."

His eyes lift. I'm not sure if he can actually see me through the small gap, but the way he glares, it's as if he can see right through the wood. "You ruined everything."

Blinking, I shake my head, hunting for his meaning amongst the synapses in my brain. "What are you talking about?"

He doesn't speak again.

Doesn't even acknowledge my question.

He flicks the light again and lets it fall from his grasp.

A scream scrapes against my vocal cords as it reverberates in the air.

Manny turns his back on the barn and marches away.

"Manny, wait!"

Either my shout is overpowered by the roar of the flames, or he ignores me.

Maybe both.

The embers spread, wild and unpredictable. A fleck of ash lands on my finger, burning the flesh on my knuckle. Flinching backward, I clutch my hand to my chest.

"Fuck, fuck, fuck," I curse.

Thick gray smoke curls beneath the rafters. The horses slam against their stalls. Bear becomes more aggressive with the door. The blaze licks up the wall, heating my skin.

My heart pounds in my chest, on the verge of paralyzing my limbs.

I can't give up.

Not now.

CHAPTER 33

SANTIAGO

Winter has a way of making the world feel bigger.

Ace's hooves prance over the snow as we ride along the fence in the northern pasture, checking for broken posts. The Snake River Mountains stand tall against a cloudless sky, and for the first time in days, I almost relax.

The only thing that would make this better is having Blake here with me.

Brandon and Sam trot along with me. Jack and Todd rode out to the west pasture to take hay to the cattle there since the snow covers the grass, effectively cutting off the natural grazing.

My phone vibrates in my inside jacket pocket, and I contemplate ignoring it. I pull it out anyway and bring Ace to a stop as Brandon and Sam ride ahead.

A smile overtakes my face when I see Blake's name on the screen, but that quickly fades.

Blake: I thought Manny was fired.

Brandon turns, directing his horse back toward me. "Everything okay, boss?"

"Yeah." My answer isn't fooling anyone.

I type out a light response, attempting not to alarm Blake.

Me: Don't defile my phone with that cabrón's name.

Levi: He was.

Walker: Why do you ask?

Blake: He was just here.

A chill unrelated to the cold disables me.

Brandon must sense my shift. "Boss?"

With my eyes still on the screen, I instruct, "Back to the barn." My head snaps up. "Now!"

I type out my response and return my phone to my pocket.

Me: I'm on my way

Ace must feel my panic. He takes off at a breakneck speed before I direct him.

Wind whips against my skin, threatening to blow my hat off my head. But I don't care. I'd give up anything if it meant protecting Blake.

The images of all the possibilities flash through my mind. None of them brings me a semblance of peace.

Ahead in the distance, a column of smoke rises into the air like a skyscraper.

My heart stops.

"Faster!" I shout in demand, and Ace obeys.

The sound of wood splintering meets my ears before the barn comes into view, confirming what I already know.

I didn't think my dread could get any worse, but it does.

When the barn comes into view, the fire engulfing the walls pulls all the oxygen from my lungs. The velvet dance of light could be considered enchanting if it weren't also destroying my love and my livelihood. Before Ace can come to a stop, I'm off his back and sprinting right for the flames.

My legs move faster than I ever thought was possible. "Blake!"

"Santi!" Blake's reply is muffled by the roaring fire and thumping sound coming from the other side of the barn door.

I'm only a few feet away when I see the chain around the door handles. Without a second thought, I run for the bed of my truck on the other side. The large metal toolbox that permanently sits under the back window of the cab holds a variety of tools that I haven't checked for some time.

Throwing open the top, I dig around. Wrenches, hammers, jumper cables...

Come on.

Come on.

There!

The fire breathes its embers toward me as I approach the doors. Ignoring the heat is nothing compared to hearing Blake scream for me.

"Santi! Help!"

The blades of the bolt cutters encircle a link on the chain. I take a deep breath to gather my strength, but my lungs fill with smoke. Pushing through the coughing, I thrust my hands together and break the chain. The ends dangle, and I grab hold of one end and tug.

The stench of burning flesh meets my nose, and it takes a moment for the pain to register in my hands.

But I can't let go. I can't leave Blake in there.

The metal drops to the ground, and I use my boot to push the handle and slide the left door open. The large wood only moves an inch, the fire having already warped the metal on the track.

"Shit!" I exclaim as I refuse to give up, kicking the handle repeatedly.

The horses' cries and the shouts from Blake almost cripple me. Instead, I use them to fuel my strength.

Kick.

Nothing.

Kick.

Nothing again.

For the next kick, I throw all of my weight into it.

The metal screams, and the wheel on the track finally jerks loose. The door shudders, opening just an inch.

"Come on," I grit out through clenched teeth.

I won't give up.

When there's enough space, Blake and Bear dart through the opening. Blake lands in my arms, and a bucket of relief pours onto my heart.

My arms wrap her in an embrace, and I move us back a few feet to get out of range of the fire. *"Estás a salo, mi Cielo. Estás a salvo. Estoy aquí." You're safe, mi Cielo. You're safe. I'm here.*

When she pulls back, I'm struck by the ash smudges covering her face. Another reminder of how close things got.

Brandon and Sam rush by us on foot, affirming how fast Ace got us here, and dart into the burning barn.

"The horses," she breathes out as her eyes widen, and tears streak through the soot on her cheeks.

"Don't you dare go back in there," I warn her.

"But—" She attempts to move out of my arms.

I tighten my hold. "Stay out here. I mean it."

I don't release her until she nods in agreement.

"Take Bear and stand about a hundred yards away," I instruct.

She nods again, and I dash back into the flames.

The horses squeal as they kick the gates of their stalls. Smoke builds, obscuring my vision, but I can still make out shapes. The acrid scent of burning pine, scorched hay, and gasoline rolls into me. Heat slams into my face hard enough that I instinctively shield myself with an arm.

Brandon is approaching our only viable exit, a howling chainsaw in hand. Sam is with him, wielding an axe.

"We need to widen it!" Brandon informs me, and I spring into action.

Scanning the immediate area, I find a sledgehammer on the concrete near my feet. "Let's get it done."

They nod their heads in understanding, and we get to work.

As we exert ourselves, the heat builds in layers. Smoke builds in direct result from the fire spreading. The loose bits of hay are our greatest adversary.

One spark is all it'd take.

My eyes water from the smoke, and my chest aches from all the coughing.

Brandon has his side done before Sam and I clear ours, and it's enough space for a horse. As three of us disperse in unison to unlock the latches on the stalls, I hear the blare of a fire engine horn.

Gracias a Dios.

A beam overhead lets out a long groan. I look up just in time to spot glowing embers raining down from the rafters.

"Look out!" I shout and shove Sam to the side as a burning board crashes where he'd been standing moments earlier.

The first horse I come to is Willow, a chestnut mare with white spots all over her hindquarters. "Easy, *niña,*" I say in hopes of calming her, but it doesn't work. Instead, I lift and slide the latch. Willow kicks the gate open and sprints to the way out. Duke follows Willow. Bandit nearly knocks me over trying to get outside.

When we're done, I follow the same path the horses took. My ribs ache from coughing. Every breath burns from the thickening smoke.

Being the last to exit, I stumble out and fall on my knees in the snow.

A breath of fresh air has a whole new meaning for me now, as I finally breathe in untainted oxygen.

I'm almost tackled to the ground as a pair of feminine arms enwrap me in a desperate embrace, and the scent of amber, sprinkled with vanilla, fills my nose.

Blake.

When she pulls back, I search every inch for an injury. "Are you okay? Let me look at you."

Her brows almost lift off her face. "Me? You're burned."

Blake's statement brings the pain to the front of my mind. A few spots on my arms feel as if they have the world's worst sunburn, but they're nothing compared to my right palm. My hand throbs in a way I've never felt before.

"It's fine. I'm fine."

Blake reaches for my wounded hand and carefully flips it over. Her motions reveal the blisters covering my palm.

"This looks like a second-degree burn."

"That's all?" I question sarcastically.

Blake doesn't laugh at my humor. "Come on. The ambulance just pulled up."

Sure enough, the red and white truck comes to a stop behind the fire engine.

Blake helps me to my feet, and I suppress a groan. Every muscle in my body is sore. Blake places my arm across her shoulders and attempts to carry my weight.

I take a rough swallow and ask, "Did everyone get out?"

"You got everyone. Man and horse," Blake assures me.

As we hobble in the direction of the ambulance, Hudson jumps out of the cab and rushes toward us. Hudson takes my other arm with my injured hand and helps us the rest of the way.

Glancing around, I find the entire fire department present, rushing about to put out the fire.

My eyes snag on the burning building, and it hits me.

My barn is gone.

My father built half of this place with his own hands. I grew up here. My mother walked those aisles every day.

Now it's gone.

And someone tried to kill the woman I love.

CHAPTER 34

WALKER

"Can you drive any faster?" Levi complains from the passenger seat.

"I'm going as fast as I can without causing an accident," I grumble. Even still, I push the gas pedal further toward the floor.

We saw the smoke about a mile back. The dread only grows the closer we get.

"Neither of them are answering," Levi complains, pulling his phone away from his ear.

All I can think is that I need to get there. I need to see Blake.

We had sex this morning, and then I fucked it up.

I pushed her away.

If she's hurt...

No.

I shove the thought aside.

We pull in through the front gate and circle the main house to the back, where all the commotion is going on.

I scan the crowd for Blake and Santiago, but come up empty. Instead, I find the fire department is in the midst of putting out the fire while the wranglers gather the horses in a nearby corral.

Where are Blake and Santiago?

Parking my truck, Levi and I hop out at the same time and dart forward.

Relief cools my alarm when I spot Blake standing outside the open doors at the back of the ambulance.

"There," I shout to Levi, pointing to Blake.

Darting toward the EMT, I call for her. "Blake!"

She whirls, almost too quickly, like she's on edge. But when her eyes land on Levi and me, her body visibly relaxes. Her movements turn sluggish as she runs toward us.

Reaching her first, I wrap her up in a comforting hug.

She doesn't argue. She doesn't tease. She doesn't tell me to put her down.

And that's what scares me.

She's afraid.

Blake nestles her nose into my neck like she needs to reassure herself just as much as I need it.

Levi taps me on the shoulder and raises a brow when I look at him, his implication clear.

I pass Blake to him, and he holds her close. I search her back for anything amiss.

"I'm okay," Blake claims.

Levi pulls back and refutes, "I think we'll be the ones who decide that."

We each give her a thorough scan as we ask a million questions, looking for signs of burns, smoke inhalation, blood, a concussion...

Blake holds up her hands and backs up a step. "You two need to chill."

Levi turns to me. "We should have Hudson check her out again."

I nod my agreement, Blake scoffs.

"I'm fine," Blake asserts as she crosses her arms.

"Please," I beg.

"Give us some peace of mind," Levi adds.

Blake concedes, lets out a reluctant breath, and nods. Then

points her thumb over her shoulder toward the ambulance as if she already knows the next person Levi needs to see.

Santiago.

I love the man like a brother, but Levi and Santiago are different. They make each other happy, and that's all I want for them.

Levi is up and in the ambulance before I can blink.

Blake takes a shaky step forward, and I scoop her up in a bridal carry. When she doesn't resist or complain, something inside my chest just clicks.

She's in my arms.

She's safe.

When we close the distance, we find Santiago sitting in the same spot I was in just two weeks ago. Levi sits at his side, holding Santiago's hand in his lap. Hudson sits across from Santiago, wrapping his hand in a white bandage as Santiago holds a clear mask over his nose and mouth. His face is gray beneath the soot.

"Whoa," Hudson holds up his hand. "One at a time."

I nod in acknowledgment. "What's the diagnosis?"

"I'm fine," Santiago grumbles, removing the mask from his face.

Levi forces Santiago to put the mask back in place. "Hush."

"Mild smoke inhalation and first and second-degree burns. He'll need to change these bandages every twenty-four hours. I recommend continuing the oxygen through the night, and tomorrow he needs to go in and see a real doctor."

Levi sits up straighter.

Hudson quirks a brow. "A doctor for humans. Not animals."

Santiago pulls on the mask again. "Why are you telling them all of this instead of me?"

Levi pushes the mask back. "Because he knows you won't listen to him, so we are going to be the ones who make sure you're following his instructions."

Santiago sighs, shaking his head.

"But he's going to be okay?" Blake questions Hudson in a small voice, her fear coming through.

"Definitely," Hudson answers.

Blake sags in my arms, resting her head on my shoulder.

"Now that that's taken care of," I start, "what the hell happened here?"

Blake's voice only shakes once as she fills us in.

When she gets to the chain.

Throughout her story, I feel my face growing hotter and hotter. I do my best not to grip her tighter, but I need the reminder again.

She's in my arms.

She's safe.

When Blake finishes, Levi whips his head to Santiago, his body tight and his voice taking on the harshness of shattering glass. "What the hell were you thinking? You ran into a burning building?"

Hudson finishes dressing Santiago's burn and sits back, awkwardly twiddling his thumbs and moving his eyes to look anywhere but what's happening right in front of him.

Santiago rolls his eyes. "I didn't do it alone."

"One idiot following two more doesn't make this better."

Santiago's expression turns serious as he drops the mask once more. "You didn't hear them screaming. I needed to get the horses out."

Levi deflates, his borderline-belligerent demeanor fading. If anyone understands the need to rescue an animal, it's Levi.

"Didn't you leave Javier with Blake?" I question Santiago.

He nods.

"Could he have—" I start

Santiago sits up straight. "Absolutely not. No way. Javier would never do something like this."

"Then where is he?" I interrogate.

Santiago's face tightens with strain. "I don't know."

I nod in understanding. "Jolene radioed Tess and Ridge when Levi and I left the station. They should be here any minute. I'll have them start a search ASAP. We'll be losing daylight soon."

"I can help with that," Hudson volunteers. "Unless someone else gets injured."

"Thank you," Blake expresses.

"Now," my tone turns menacing, "where's Manny?" I spin in a slow circle, scanning the entire area for any sign of him.

Levi's eyes narrow. "Yeah, where is that asshole? I need to have a talk with him."

"Get in line," Santiago snarls.

"I don't know," Blake answers. "He dropped the lighter and walked away."

My jaw locks as I growl at Santiago. "If that wrangler of yours—"

"That's enough," Blake scolds the three of us, "Santiago, this is not your fault. Levi, I know you're worried, but tone it down a bit, please. Walk, no one could've seen something like this coming. We need to focus on finding Javier and Manny."

Releasing a pacifying breath, I nod. "I agree."

"Santiago needs to stay on oxygen, so the rest of us can start the search," Blake directs. "You can put me down now, or do you plan on carrying me everywhere while you do your sheriff thing?"

Nice try.

"Not a chance, Baby Girl. Stay with Santiago. Hudson, don't let him leave until he's all patched up. Blake doesn't leave either." I maneuver Blake, setting her feet inside the ambulance and urging her inside. "Levi, let's go."

Levi places his hands on Blake's hips and guides her into his spot as he stands.

"Hey!" Blake shouts in indignation.

"I should help," Santiago argues.

Levi points a punitive finger toward Santiago. "Stay put."

Blake and Santiago sulk as Levi and I get to work. Tessa and Ridge pull up just as we're about to start. I fill them in, then it's all hands on deck, aside from Blake and Santiago. I give Levi my spare radio and make sure we're all tuned in to the same channel before we spread out.

Ridge starts out on the main trail. Tessa circles the wreckage of the barn, weaving in and out of the firefighters as they clean up their equipment. Levi takes the shed and secondary trail. That leaves me with the main house.

It's not long before we find something.

Tessa's voice crackles through the speaker of my radio. "I have an 11-24."

Abandoned vehicle

"It looks to be a Chevy C/K 1500," Tessa adds.

"Give me the license plate," Jolene responds like she's been waiting by her radio this whole time, which she probably has. There's a reason she's had this job for so long.

Tessa reads off the seven-digit license plate, and within seconds, Jolene has a result. "The truck is registered to Manuel López."

"Thanks, Jo," I chime in. "Ridge, join Tessa and you two search the area for any sign of him."

"On it," Ridge confirms.

I'm just finishing with the side of the house when Levi radios in. "10-54. Send Hudson to the shed."

Person down.

"10-4," I reply and take off in a jog back to the ambulance.

"I have a pulse, but there's a lot of blood," Levi remarks.

I rip open the ambulance door. "You're needed in the shed. Bring your kit," I order Hudson, and he jumps into motion immediately.

Jogging ahead of him, I glance over my shoulder and find that Blake and Santiago have joined us.

And they say I'm stubborn...

The door to the shed hangs open, and when I'm over the threshold, I'm struck by the scene. Levi kneels beside an unconscious Javier, who is lying in a small pool of what appears to be his own blood.

Hudsons pushes past me, but I hold Blake and Santiago back.

Santiago has been close with Javier his whole life. He's more of an uncle to Santiago than anything else.

Blake gasps, covering her mouth, and Santiago tries to move around me.

"No." Santigo takes a sharp inhale as his face drains of color.

Hudson leans over Javier, assessing him, as Levi states, "His pulse is about sixty BPM and dropping, and he's breathing on his own."

"Head injury. Possible blunt force trauma," Hudson observes. "The bleeding has slowed, which is a good sign, but I need to get him to the hospital in Jackson for an MRI."

"Whatever he needs," Santiago demands.

Hudson is efficient as he orders us around to help. Somewhere in the ruckus, Hudson radios dispatch to request a volunteer EMT. The volunteer arrives just in time to hop in the back of the ambulance as Hudson takes off.

"That explains why Javier didn't come running when I yelled for him," Blake mutters.

Santiago stands in the wake of the ambulance, biting the side of his lower lip as his brows pull together.

"He'll be okay," Blake comforts as she wraps an arm around him.

"We still need to find Manny," I declare. "You two can stay here, and Levi and I can get back to the search." I rest my hand on Santiago's shoulder, offering my own version of solace. "We'll take care of everything."

Santiago shakes his head. "No, I want to help."

"Me too," Blake chimes in.

Giving up on arguing with them, I yield. "Alright. Blake, you're with me. Santiago, you're with Levi, but if you start to wheeze, I want you to put the oxygen mask, that Hudson left for you, back on."

"Deal." Santiago pats my arm as he and Levi head back to the shed.

Dipping my head, I signal to Blake that we're going to the back porch, then stride in that direction. She follows closely behind.

The sun has almost dropped completely below the horizon, so I pull out my flashlight to illuminate my path.

The snow here has been shoveled, leaving the porch clear, which means no footprints. Just as I'm about to declare the porch cleared, my light catches on something small and reflective along the railing.

"What is it?" Blake whispers.

"Shh." I hush her.

Drawing closer, I find that it's a drop of blood. I find another one further down.

Then another.

And another.

My body goes into a state of extreme calm, bracing for a storm, and my pulse slows.

I know what I expect to find.

But that doesn't make it easier.

The trail leads us to the edge, and when I shine my light over the side, I spot a dark lump a few feet below.

Shit.

"Don't look," I instruct Blake over my shoulder.

She ignores my instruction and moves around me. "Look at wha—" Blake cuts herself off when she finds the body with a loud, shocked inhale.

On instinct, my arm reaches out, sweeping her backward.

Blake's breaths come fast and turn shallow.

Removing my radio from my belt, I inform everyone else. "I found him. Back porch."

Ridge's reply is immediate. "On our way, boss."

"Us too," Santiago notifies.

"Levi. Santi. Hurry up. I don't want Blake near the body."

Returning my attention to Blake, I place my hands on her shoulder, back her up, and bend so we're eye to eye.

"Breathe, Baby Girl."

"H—He's."

Pant.

"D—Dead."

She's right. Manny is dead, and I can't change that. If he were alive, he'd be dead now.

I can't offer her empty platitudes.

"I need you to breathe with me, Blake."

She nods.

"In." I take a dramatic inhale, and I feel her shoulders lift as she copies me. "Out." We exhale together.

I repeat the method with her three more times before Blake calms.

Sometime during our breathing, everyone arrived. Tessa and Ridge have taped off the crime scene and begun collecting evidence.

I move Blake inside the house and into the living room, sit us down on the couch, and place her on my lap. Blake relaxes into me, and my heart warms.

Levi and Santiago follow Blake and me, offering her comfort. Levi runs his hands through her hair as Santiago rubs her back.

In minutes, Blake starts taking long, deep breaths, and her body unwinds the last fraction.

Levi keeps his voice hushed. "She's asleep."

"Good," Santiago says in the same tone.

"She's had a long day," I add.

"If you want to take her up to bed, I'll stay down here until Tessa and Ridge are done," Santiago volunteers.

I shake my head, refusing his offer. "I need to figure something out." Shifting, I indicate that I want Santiago to sit down next to me. After he does, I move Blake to him and stand.

Manny didn't survive long enough to watch the barn burn.

Which means someone else was here.

"If Manny started the fire, then who killed Manny?"

CHAPTER 35

LEVI

After always being with someone over the last few days, the quiet in the clinic feels off. Northfork Veterinary Clinic has been the place where I spend most of my time for years.

Now the stainless-steel tables, antiseptic smell, and fluorescent lights almost feel unfamiliar.

Blake is in the clinic, but she's passed out on the couch in the kitchen down the hall. Bear naps with her, curled up on Blake's legs.

Yesterday would be too much for anyone to handle. She fell asleep in Walker's arms last night, but she tossed and turned most of the night.

This morning, Walker announced that he needed to go to the station. Neither Santiago nor I wanted to leave Blake, so we did a quick round of Rock, Paper, Scissors to determine who would go with Walker.

Santiago lost.

Which means I got to lie in bed with Blake in my arms for another hour.

It was difficult to make the decision to wake her up. I could've stayed in bed with her all day, but work won't get done itself.

In a stupor, Blake ate breakfast and got dressed. I practically had to carry her to the car, then into the clinic.

Dr. Marcus Adler asked me to preserve any evidence and store the body here because he doesn't know when he'll be able to perform the autopsy.

As always, I obliged.

Abbott continues seeing patients in the other room. He got to the clinic shortly after Blake and me. I sat in on his first appointment, and the poor guy was so nervous that he wrapped gauze around his own finger rather than the calico's paw. When I pointed it out, his face turned a bright shade of scarlet that I'd never seen before on a person. Other than that, he did great.

Deciding to give the guy a break, I left him to finish up the appointment on his own. I assume it's all gone smoothly since then because he hasn't come to me with any questions.

Santiago and Walker should be here any minute, so I wash my hands at the surgical sink as I wait for them to arrive.

I finish gloving up when Santiago and Walker stroll into the exam room. Santiago places a chaste peck on my lips, ending the kiss too quickly.

I think we both could use a distraction and blow off some steam with each other.

Another time.

"Ready?" Walker questions as he hops up onto the counter, taking a seat.

"Ready," I emphasize my answer by giving my blue nitrile gloves a good snap.

Santiago finds a plain, uncomfortable chair in another room and drags it in, plopping down in the seat.

I retrieve Manny's body from cold storage and get him situated on the surgical table. After I get my prep tray together, I fall into a mindless routine. I've done this so many times before that I don't have to think about it too hard.

Once I've removed his clothes and sealed them in evidence bags, my eyes stop on Manny's forearm.

"Is that..." I trail off as I bend to get a closer look. A memory struggles to rise to the surface.

"Don't contaminate the body," Walker warns as he jumps to his feet.

"It's my clinic."

I get Walker's apprehension. We're all feeling it, but it's different for him. Santiago and I have stakes in this, but even if Blake wasn't a factor and Walker failed to produce results, the town would lose trust in him.

"It's my investigation," Walker argues back, marching forward.

"I just need to see his damn arm."

"You two need to calm down," Santiago says from his seat by the door.

Ignoring Walker's hovering, I finally examine the skin on Manny's forearm, and the detail strikes me in the face.

Blinking slowly, I right myself.

"Happy?" Walker sasses as he crosses his arms.

"It's him," I declare breathlessly.

Santiago joins us around the table, responding to me as if I've lost my mind. "Yes, this is Manny. We hate him."

"No, it's *him*." I repeat.

Walker's mouth pinches. "Are you okay?"

"Manny is the one who was at the clinic," I try to explain.

Santiago arches a single brow. His response comes out slowly, like he thinks I'm stupid or losing my mind. "I'm sure you've had a lot of people in and out of the clinic."

"Smartass," I snap. Finding the right words, I attempt to clarify again. "He's the one who broke into the clinic when Blake was picking up Bear."

The muscles in Walker's jaw tense. "Are you sure?"

I nod, convinced, and point to the inked barbed wire on Manny's arm. "Yes. This is the same tattoo I saw on the attacker."

Santiago lets out a low whistle. "So we *really* hate him."

"Understatement of the year," Walker grumbles.

Walker drags a hand down his face. "He attacks you and Blake at the clinic."

Santiago clenches his fists. "He shows up at Falling Sky and locks Blake in the barn."

"And he sets fire to the barn," I add.

"But what doesn't make sense is," Walker starts pacing back and forth, "he was reckless. He talked with Blake. She saw his face. Calculated criminals don't usually make that mistake."

Santiago works his jaw back and forth. "Manny wasn't patient. One time, a gate jammed, and he kicked it until it opened. Another time, Willow wouldn't obey him, so he tried forcing her."

I let out a single sardonic laugh. "He tried forcing an animal more than five times his weight to do what he wanted? What an idiot."

Walker's pacing pauses. "He was impulsive." Walker looks between Santiago and me.

My head slants to a curious angle. "Do you think he was the Debt Collector?"

Walker shakes his head. "There's no way. The Debt Collector is the complete opposite of Manny—calculating, manipulative, intelligent. He leaves messages, he stages the bodies, he cleans his mess. Manny poured gasoline on a barn in broad daylight."

I nod my head.

"The Debt Collector is sophisticated. Manny is too young, too impulsive," Santiago concurs.

"Exactly." Walker snaps his fingers. "Then why was he trying to kill Blake?"

I review the facts in my head.

Manny hits on Blake. Blake rejects him, but Manny won't take no for an answer. Manny runs his mouth and gets fired, which means no job.

No job, no income.

"I don't think it was about Blake," I speak up. "I think this is good old revenge."

Walker purses his lips, contemplating. "Let's assume it's about Blake. Convince me I'm wrong."

I take them through my thought process, laying it out perfectly.

"I think killing Blake was to get back at Santiago, the man who fired him. Blake was just the means by which he could exact his revenge."

But there's one problem...

"Then who killed Manny?" I follow up.

"Who murdered the attempted murderer?" Santiago rephrases sarcastically. "Now that's the real brain teaser."

"If we figure out why, that should point us toward the who." Walker rubs his chin.

Santiago and I start spouting off theories.

"Someone could have followed Blake from New York."

"Someone protecting Blake."

"Blake's stalker."

"Someone who had a personal grudge against Manny."

Walker straightens his spine. "That's it."

Santiago scratches the side of his head. "A personal grudge?"

"No." Walker chews on his lip. "The stalker."

"Why?" My face scrunches up.

"The stalker needs Blake around. He wants her to see something. He's tormenting her. He wouldn't lock her in the barn and set it on fire without telling her who he is and why he's doing it."

"What did Manny say to Blake again? She told you, right?"

"He told her that she ruined everything." Santiago looks as if he just ate a lemon.

I know he probably blames himself for this. He fired Manny, and then Manny went after the people he cares about.

Wrapping an arm around his shoulders, I pull him closer, offering comfort.

He knows what I'm going to say.

And I know what he's going to say.

So nothing needs to be said at all.

"That rules out Manny even more. The stalker wanted Blake to come back to Evergreen Falls," I point out.

Santiago's eyes narrow as he tries to decipher the same puzzle we're all struggling with. "Are we sure that the stalker and The Debt Collector aren't the same person?"

"I haven't wanted to jump to conclusions, but I've been trying to investigate through two lenses. They're two different people, or they're one and the same." Walker rubs his eyes.

I don't think he slept at all last night.

My forehead wrinkles. "Walk, that's a lot for one person."

Santiago's mouth pinches. "And you're leaving out another lens."

"What's that?"

"The Debt Collector and Blake's stalker are two different people who are working together." Santiago brings his hands together in demonstration.

"How about we each take a theory?" I suggest. "Walk, you take different people. Santi, you take different people working together. I'll take the same person."

"Alright. Let's do it." Walker heaves a sigh, pinching the bridge of his nose.

"I need to take five." Walker pushes away from the table and heads for the back exit, pulling out his pack of cigarettes as he goes.

Santiago and I exchange a look.

The same look we've exchanged several times over the last week.

Now?

Now.

I guess this is happening.

And without jackets.

How fun.

We follow Walker and join him outside while he smokes, standing side by side. We find him leaning against the building, a cigarette in his mouth, his lighter held to the tobacco end.

I clear my throat. "Walk."

"Yeah?" he answers, taking an inhale from the filtered tip.

"We need to run something by you," I return.

"That sounds ominous."

"We know you have feelings for Blake," Santiago states.

He doesn't answer.

He doesn't have to.

A minor twitch in his jaw is the only indication he heard us, but it's enough.

"No use in denying it." Santiago widens his stance.

Walker lets out a dark chuckle. "What's your point?"

"We do too," I explain, gesturing to Santiago and myself.

"I know."

"So," My hand moves to the back of my neck and squeezes. "What if we came to a certain type of agreement?"

"Are you suggesting we become..." Walker's brows pinch. "What? Brother husbands?"

Santiago shrugs a shoulder. "We could call it that."

Walker studies the two of us for a moment. "You're serious."

Neither Santiago nor I answer.

We don't need to.

"I know you two have done the sharing thing," he vaguely motions between the three of us, "but *I* haven't."

Santiago holds up a hand as if to pause Walker's spiral. "We're not asking you to decide today."

Walker drops the cigarette butt into the snow, grinding it into the earth. "Then what are you asking?"

Santiago answers honestly. "If Blake wanted all three of us, would you consider it?"

Crossing his arms, Walker blows out a humorless laugh. "That's not how it'll go."

My eyes narrow. "What makes you so sure?"

Walker scratches at his forehead, moistening his lips.

I've never seen Walker so unsure of himself. He's not cocky, but he has an air of authority about him that exudes certainty.

Walker looks away. "She doesn't know."

Oh.

He means...

The secret—the one thing we've kept from her.

"Then we'll tell her," I reply, taking a confident step forward.

Walker looks back at us.

Really looks.

"If we tell her everything, and she still chooses us..." Santiago steps up to my side. "Would you be willing to try?"

"I don't know."

I know Walker well enough to recognize when he's lying.

But this time he wasn't lying to us.

He was lying to himself.

CHAPTER 36

BLAKE

Apparently, it's Bring Your Roommates to Work Day at the Evergreen Falls police station, and Walker is gung-ho for it.

I planned on sleeping in for the next week or year after my near-death experience—an event I do my best not to think about. I cuddled up to Walker in the ginormous bed that Santiago insists we all sleep on.

The first night in bed, Walker got in begrudgingly, but every night since then, it's been assumed. Like we all have a "spot" on the bed. Except for Levi and Santiago. They switch sometimes. It depends on who wins their nightly thumb war.

Today, I was relaxing in a nice bubble bath when Walker barged in and informed me we were all going with him to the station and that I needed to get ready. I made an obscene hand gesture and forced him out of the bathroom.

Being the hellion that I am, I decided to take my time.

And then some.

So when I'm the last person to the truck, it's no surprise.

"Are you sure you're ready? I think you may still have a hair out of place," Walker sasses from the driver's seat as I stride toward him.

"You're just jealous that you can't look this good," I tease, pretending to primp my hair. When my arms fall to my sides, I find something amiss.

Santiago and Levi are already in Walker's truck.

And there's only one bench.

Which means three seats.

My mouth turns down into a frown. "Are we recreating what it's like to drive in a clown car?"

"It's easier this way. Just get in." Walker motions to the cab.

I arch my brows. "Where is Bear supposed to sit?"

"He's staying here with Javier," Walker decides.

As if they rehearsed this, Javier strolls our way, stopping at my side, and I gape at him.

My arms open wide and automatically wrap around him, and I bombard him with questions. "When did you get out of the hospital? Should you even be out of the hospital? How is it that you look perfectly fine? Does your head still hurt at all? Did you get Jello in the hospital? What if—"

"Slow down, *princesa*." Javier's hands clasp my upper arms, gently pulling me away from him.

"Let the man breathe, *mi Cielo*," Santiago shouts through Walker's open window.

"I'm fine. Everything's fine. I'll keep Bear with me today. I promise he's in good hands," Javier reassures me.

I nod to him, then drop to my knees to hug Bear goodbye. "Be a good boy, okay?"

Bear grumbles like a grumpy teen who's embarrassed to be seen with his mom.

Rising to my feet, I disregard social norms and hug Javier again. "I'm happy you're okay."

Javier returns my embrace. "You too, *princesa*."

With one more goodbye, I cram myself into Walker's truck,

and Walker peels away, probably irritated with me taking my time.

The entire ride, Levi, Santiago, and I are a jumble of limbs. There's an elbow or knee in my stomach, and what I think is a hand on my ass. Getting out of the car is a relief.

Jo greets us as we all go inside. Tessa bats her lashes at Walker, then squints at me. Ridge waves enthusiastically.

Aside from waking up, it's a good morning. That is, until I see who is waiting for Walker in his office.

A woman, looking worse for wear, sits in one of the chairs in front of Walker's desk. Her hair's wild waves are stringy, and her skin, which used to match mine, is an unhealthy shade. Dark circles pull on the bags under her eyes.

I freeze in place, my heart stumbling over its rhythm. "What's going on?"

Levi wraps his arm around my waist as Santiago and Walker continue to his office.

"Walker had Ridge pick your mom up this morning for questioning," Levi whispers in my ear as his hand rubs comforting circles on my back.

A worthless, good-for-nothing burden.

"Why?"

"The financial records for Reverend Ricks finally came in. He withdrew three hundred dollars in cash from the church account every Saturday for the last six years," Levi explains.

You do nothing but take.

My chest constricts. "What does that have to do with Mama?"

Levi brushes my hair back. "That's what Walker intends to find out."

"Then why am I here?"

Before Levi can answer, Santiago exits Walker's office, and his eyes land on us. "What's going on?"

"I knew we should've told her before we got here," Levi argues with Santiago in a hushed tone.

I eye Tessa, discreetly watching our exchange, though I doubt she can hear anything that's being said.

Even if she could hear, I'm not sure I would care.

There's a reason I haven't spoken to Mama since the day I found the first body. The things she said were nothing new, but that doesn't mean I want to hear them again.

Walker quietly closes his office door behind everyone. The room suddenly feels much smaller.

I stay near the door while Loretta sits in the chair, arms folded.

Walker remains standing and doesn't waste time.

"Loretta, we received Reverend Ricks' financial records this morning."

My mother's expression doesn't change.

Walker opens a folder and slides several printed bank statements across his desk. "For six years, Reverend Ricks withdrew three hundred dollars in cash every Saturday."

Mama's eyes dart to the side.

"Can you explain that?"

Mama barely glances at the papers. "No."

Finally, he asks, "Do you know where that money went?"

Mama rolls her eyes. "I don't know anything about the church's finances."

Walker slides another document toward her. "We do."

Mama doesn't respond.

"The withdrawals stopped the week Reverend Ricks died," Walker continues.

Mama still doesn't utter a word.

"And according to the bank," Walker looks directly at her, "those cash withdrawals match deposits into your account."

My brows knit together.

Mama's jaw tightens minutely, but I notice it.

Walker sees it too. "Loretta?"

She lets out an irritated sigh. "He was helping me."

My stomach knots.

Walker folds his hands together. "Helping you with what?"

Mama rubs her forehead. "Bills."

"Helping how?" Walker questions further.

"Money was tight." Mama folds her arms.

Walker doesn't let her off the hook. "So Reverend Ricks gave you three hundred dollars every week." Walker doesn't blink. "For six years?"

She sighs dramatically. "I'm a single mother."

Levi quietly speaks for the first time. "Blake hasn't lived with you for twelve years."

She shoots him a glare. "My husband is still dead."

"What did you have to do for the reverend in exchange for the money?" Walker presses.

Mama refuses to look at him, shooting a glare my way instead.

"He was paying me for sex," she finally spits out.

My mouth hangs open, unsure how to respond.

Mama pivots in her chair to face me. "Don't look at me like that."

"Mama, if you would've told me, I could have—"

"You're one to talk," she snaps.

My brows wrinkle together. "What?"

Mama sits up straight in her seat. "Whoring around now?"

I flinch as if she just slapped me.

"Watch your mouth, Lor," Santiago warns.

"Blake is my daughter, and I'll speak to her however I please," she sneers at him. "Answer the damn question."

I shake my head. "No, I'm not."

"Rumor has it you went home with Santiago last week, then fucked Levi in the bathroom at the Timberline the other night."

I cross my arms. "Who I sleep with is none of your business."

"It's my business when your choices reflect poorly on our family," she snaps.

My eyes widen as I point at my chest. "My choices? What about yours?"

"Don't you take that tone with me." Mama narrows her gaze.

I throw my hands up, done with this hypocritical nonsense.

"You're a goddamn alcoholic, and you're worried about *my* choices."

Mama looks down her nose at me. "I'm allowed to have a drink or two with dinner."

I scoff. "More like a drink or two every ten minutes."

Mama gets to her feet to face me. "I'm not the one sleeping with your daddy's friends. Have a little integrity, Blake."

"Lor," Levi barks.

Mama turns to Levi. "She's been whoring since she was a little girl. Did you know that?"

A pit opens up in my stomach, and I struggle to breathe.

"Mama...D—did you know?"

"Of course, I knew. I know how you seduced him. How you told him you'd lie to the police about it if he didn't do what you wanted." Mama looks me up and down with contempt.

My voice hollows. "I was a little girl."

"A little manipulative bitch," Mama snaps. "Landon was so disgusted with himself, with what he had done," she turns back to Walker, gesturing to me, "what she *forced* him to do, that he ended his life early."

"I—I didn't..." I shake my head, struggling to swallow it all. "When did you know?"

Mama's glower punctures a hole in my chest. "I found his journal after he died. He wrote about the whole thing."

Santiago steps between Mama and me. "You don't know what you're talking about, Loretta. That's enough."

Mama makes for the door to leave, shooting me one last repulsed. "You disgust me."

Walker follows Mama out. "Ridge, take Loretta home. Now."

Nobody notices me move, or maybe they do. I don't know. I can't hear anything anymore.

Not Walker. Not Levi. Not Santiago.

The office door opens beneath my hand, and the hallway blurs. Someone says my name. Then again louder.

I keep walking.

Jo looks up from the front desk.

I don't stop.

The front door swings open, and winter air slams into me hard enough to steal my breath.

Good.

“Blake!” Walker’s voice.

I don't turn around. If I look back, if I let one of them touch me, I'll fall apart.

So I run.

The snow crunches beneath my boots as I sprint across Main Street, not caring where I'm going.

Only that it's somewhere.

Anywhere that isn't here.

CHAPTER 37

BLAKE

Every inch of my body is numb, and it's not from the freezing temperature tonight. I can't feel or hear a thing. My consciousness is too full, flashing between the past and the present.

Problem. Burden. Whore.

After Mama said her piece, I ran. I don't even remember consciously making the choice. All I remember is thinking, "I need to leave. I can't be here." I didn't realize where I was until the cold metal of the bridge railing was biting into my palms.

I know my overprotective men aren't going to be happy about it, but there isn't much I can do about that now.

The heels of my boots are the only thing keeping me from falling into the raging Snake River below.

The moonlight shines across the rippling water, crafting a shattered reflection of its source. The water, painted the deepest blue, surges downstream, devouring everything in its path.

A little manipulative bitch.

My shoulders droop, resignation and denigration etching their way across my body and filling every limb.

I didn't plan this, but now that I'm here, I'm wondering if this is always where I was going to end up.

Maybe the reason I never wanted to come back to Evergreen Falls wasn't that I didn't want to be reminded of what Daddy did or remember Walker's rejection.

Maybe the reason was that I knew I'd end up right where I am now, thinking over if I should jump—just like Daddy did.

Landon was so disgusted with himself.

"Blake!"

The call of my name is so faint that I believe it's coming from inside my head.

"Butterfly."

"Mi Cielo."

"Baby Girl."

Blinking, my head pivots to the left.

They're here. All of them.

Levi's knuckles are white from the grip he has on Santiago's arm—to hold him back or for Levi's comfort, I'm not sure. Walker stands slightly in front of them, his hands up and palms facing me as if he's begging for mercy. A quick glance in each of their eyes shows me their pain, their fear.

"Baby Girl, what are you doing?" Walker's voice shakes.

My attention returns to the water as I ask, "Do y'all ever think things would be easier if you just stopped existing?"

"I won't lie to you, Blake." Walker takes a deep breath. "It's crossed my mind a few times in my life."

"Once when I was fourteen," Levi answers.

Santiago clears his throat, but his response still comes out shaky. "After my mother died."

"Thank you for being honest," I return.

"Blake, how about we all take a step back together and talk about what's on your mind?" Walker suggests.

I don't answer. I can't answer.

Instead, I voice some of my thoughts and sniffle. "You know Daddy wanted a boy, right? That's why he named me Blake."

"Yeah, we know, *mi Cielo*." Santiago sounds pained.

Tears line my lashes as I turn to him and ask in earnest, "Do you think that's why he wanted a boy? Because he knew what he would do?"

"Blake—" Santiago starts.

The river slams into the rocks not twenty feet down from where I stand on the ledge. "Is this how he did it, you think? Is this where he went?"

"No, Baby Girl. It's not." Walker's answer holds a well of sadness and remorse.

Does he miss his friend?

"I know you all figured it out. Mama was clear about what Daddy did."

For the first time in my life, my truth is out there, lingering in the frost-bitten air. The release causes my heart to race as I wait to see where it lands and how they react. It's only a split second, but it feels like an eternity. I've feared this moment since the first time Daddy came into my room at night.

She forced him.

"We know," Levi confirms.

My heart stills.

"We've always known," he clarifies further.

Shaking my head, I struggle to digest *their* truth. As I turn my head toward them, I'm met with grief and sorrow. "How?"

"Do you remember that night—the night Landon died?" Walker asks, sympathy colors his face.

Furrowing my brows, I nod. "You all were yelling with Daddy outside, then it got quiet, and you came into my room."

Walker tilts his head. "Do you remember us coming in your room before the yelling?"

Focusing on a spec of dirt on top of the snow at Walker's feet, I search for the recollection. "There are some holes in memory. I've always chalked that up to trauma."

"That's perfectly normal," Levi assures me.

My eyes remain on the dirt as they take turns reminding me of what my brain is blocking out.

"The three of us came over to watch the big NBA game, LA Lightning versus San Francisco Knights."

I remember Daddy loved watching the Lightning. His schedule revolved around the Lightning's games.

"The front door was always unlocked, so we went right in."

Yes. That changed when Mama and I moved to Riverbend Trailer Park.

"We knew Loretta had already left for her shift."

That adds up.

"We went down the hall looking for Landon when we didn't find him in the living room with the pregame show on."

Make sense.

"He wasn't in his bedroom."

Because he was in mine.

"We heard a noise and opened your door."

My body goes rigid, and my pulse quickens in my throat. I can see the glow-in-the-dark stars on my bedroom ceiling. They're so clear, so bright.

"SHIT!" Daddy curses as I feel him jump to his feet, rattling my bed.

He's not supposed to do that. Mama always tells him he can't swear in front of me.

I'm lying on my bed, flat on my back exactly how he tells me to. When he comes in here, I look up at the stars Mama put on my ceiling and find shapes like I'm making my own constellations. I even started giving them names.

Elanor the elephant.

Millie the monkey.

Hailey the hippo.

"Shit, shit, shit," Daddy curses again as his belt buckle clinks.

I recognize the sound.

"Lan?" I hear someone ask as my doorknob turns.

Who is that?

I turn my head toward the door and find Daddy's friends there. Levi, Santiago, and Walker.

Mama says I've known them since I was a baby. They're really nice. But why are they in my room?

One of them flips the light switch, and I squint from the brightness.

Santiago runs in, grabbing Daddy by his shirt, and throws him up against my dresser. I sit up in my bed and yelp.

Why did Santi do that?

Levi moves into my room and stands next to Santiago. "What the fuck, Landon?" His mouth barely moves because he's gritting his teeth so hard.

"This isn't what it looks like, guys." Daddy's voice shakes. I've never heard him sound like that before.

Santiago grabs the collar of Daddy's shirt and holds him up. "Oh yeah? Because it looks like you're standing in your daughter's room with your pants unzipped and the lights off."

"That's enough," Walker shouts. He's still standing by the door. "Take him outside."

"Oh, my God." My breath saws in and out of my lungs, the cold creating an uncomfortable burn, but I can't slow my heartbeat.

Did they...?

"Blake?" Footsteps pad closer.

Three pairs of hands grip my torso and each of my arms, and I'm hauled backward over the railing.

"Let me go!" I shout, thrashing.

I'm set on my feet, but I can't run because I'm being held against a solid chest.

Peppermint.

Walker.

He spins me in his arms as two more bodies crowd me, trapping me between the three of them. My fists fly, pounding against his chest even though he's not the one I'm angry with. Walker just stands there, taking the brunt of my self-loathing.

"Let me go," I shout again.

"No," Walker firmly rejects.

"Yes!"

His hands wrap around my wrists, ceasing my onslaught. "Never, Baby Girl."

My chest heaves from my exertion. "What did you do to him?"

Walker's face is grave.

"Did you kill him?" I spin, looking them each in the face.

"Yes." Walker's tone is gruff behind me.

My shoulders shake as I bow my head. The crushing weight on my chest is too much. I can't carry it anymore. The tears that have been swimming in my eyes finally fall down my cheeks. It takes me second before I realize the wailing I hear is coming from me.

I did this. Me.

I made them kill someone. I made them kill Daddy.

"We couldn't ignore what we saw. We couldn't just leave you there with him."

Whirling on him, I lash out, pointing my finger in his face as I raise my volume. "I didn't need you to save me! I didn't need it then, and I don't need it now!"

Walker crosses his arms, keeping his tone lethal but even. "You were seven years old."

I throw my arms up. "I would have figured it out!"

Levi scoffs, prompting me to turn on him next as he patronizes, "Seven years old versus a full-grown man."

"Not even a gambling addict would take those odds," Santiago adds condescendingly.

I level a glare toward him. "You guys didn't have to step in."

The abuse would've continued, but I would have survived, and their hands wouldn't be stained with Daddy's blood because of me.

"Stop it," Walker barks.

I spin in another circle, feeling their presence even closer. It's as if the walls are closing in on me, but the walls are three grown men to whom I owe everything.

"You killed him," I state.

Walker drops his arms, leaning toward me. "And we'd do it again. Landon was a monster, a sick, depraved monster. He was molesting you, his *daughter*. No man deserves to take another breath after hurting a child like that."

I don't deserve this.

Their devotion. Their care.

My head tilts to the side. "Is this what you were talking about last week? The reason for 'you don't know everything about me'?"

Walker clenches his jaw, like he's not going to give me an answer, just like the other day. I don't grasp how much I need his response until he lets out an unshakable, "Yes."

He thought I'd reject him for this? He's the one who has to live with killing his best friend. He risked everything. *They* risked everything. I'm the one who was rescued.

Nausea turns in my stomach, and a sob escapes my throat.

"*Mi Cielo*," Santiago vocalizes, guiding me to face him. "You need to know that we don't have any regrets."

"But it's because of me." My voice cracks with emotion. "I made you do it."

Levi places his hand on my cheek, urging my attention to him. "We all made a choice that night, Butterfly. We knew what we were doing."

"*Todos tomamos decisiones y tenemos que vivir con ellas*," Santiago adds. "Landon made his choice. We made ours. Now it's your turn." *We all make choices and have to live with them.*

Their words land on my heart and reverberate in my head, creating a stillness. The voice telling me that I'm the one who has to carry around the guilt and shame quiets.

The truth settles inside me.

I'm not responsible for the actions and feelings of another person.

What does that mean for me? Can I accept that? How do I move on from here?

"So what's it going to be?" Walker questions.

One small step at a time, I face him. "What?"

He nods his head, indicating the bridge. "Are we going to move aside so you can jump, or are you coming home with us?"

My chest contracts.

I know my answer. It floats to me like a gentle breeze, easy and simple.

"I'm coming with you."

Levi blows out a breath, wrapping his arms around my shoulders from the side, and buries his face in my hair.

"*Gracias a Dios*," Santiago shouts to the sky, then emulates Levi's position. *Thank God.*

Walker cups my face, his touch tender on my skin. "Good. I wouldn't have let you go no matter what."

He dips his head and catches my lips with his own, immersing me in a fervent kiss. My hands grip his clothes and pull him closer.

This. This right here is what I'm choosing.

Levi Harding, Santiago Ramirez, and Walker Maddox.

My choice is them.

CHAPTER 38

SANTIAGO

Blake has made herself at home in the dining room. I have no problem with that. In fact, I welcome it. I just wish it were because she's doing something she loves, rather than something that makes her so stressed she doesn't eat.

Which has been the case.

She didn't even touch the food we got her from Main Street Diner.

Two days ago, she was ready to end it all—an event I don't like thinking about. I'd prefer to focus on the result.

She made her choice, and it was us.

But as soon as we got back to the house, she hopped right into the investigation. Now my dining room looks exactly like the wall did in her room at Moose Gap Lodge, except it's bigger.

The first floor of my home is open-concept, yet Blake has managed to create an invisible barrier around the dining room that not even Bear dares to cross.

When I got up this morning, Blake was already awake, dressed, and sipping a coffee. Her ass was planted in the dining room as I stalked off to the temporary horse stalls for morning chores. It's past noon now, and she still hasn't moved.

Levi already held a few appointments in the space I'm lending to him in the barn. Now he's resting on the couch, with his feet up on the coffee table, a book in his hand.

And no shirt.

Just his scrub pants and a pair of thick-rimmed glasses. His lickable abs on full display.

Yeah, I'll lick those later.

I have a more pressing matter in front of me.

It's a nice day outside. Temperatures are above freezing, the sky is clear, and the sun is shining.

Time to touch some grass.

Or snow.

Strolling into the dining room, I deliberately step on a pile and knock it over. "What're you working on?"

Blake doesn't look up from the notes in her hands as she responds. "Same thing I've been working on for the last few weeks."

This won't do.

I stomp straight for her and mess with her *system*, as she calls it, along the way, trying to draw her attention. Her focus doesn't even waver until I'm right beside her. Snatching the papers from her, I toss them over my shoulder.

Blake reaches for them as she shoots me a disappointed look. "Hey!"

"You're coming with me," I inform her, offering no alternative.

She quirks a brow, leaning away from me in her chair. "Excuse you?"

I shoot her a smirk. "Wasn't a request, *mi Cielo*." Gripping her waist, I bend and lift her onto my shoulder.

She lets out a yelp. "Levi!"

From his spot on the couch in the next room, his nose remains in his book as he replies, "I'm not getting in the middle of this."

"Traitor!" Blake shouts back, sounding so indignant that momentarily, I fear she'll smother Levi in his sleep tonight.

But she made her choice.

Blake kicks her feet as I grab her coat off the hook by the back door. "You can't do this every time I refuse to follow you around like a dog."

"Watch me," I taunt her.

"Bear, this is your time to shine," she prompts the pitbull.

I fail to stifle my amusement. "He won't."

"Yes, he will," she argues back.

With my hand on the knob, I wait, letting Bear prove my point. "No, he won't. Dogs don't bite the hand that feeds them."

Bear lifts his head from where he lies on his cushy bed that Blake insisted on buying for him. That dog is going to be spoiled, but he does his job when needed. Bear assesses the situation, humphs, rests his head, and resumes his nap.

"*I* feed him," Blake contends.

"So do I."

She pushes on my back, attempting to straighten her spine. "Have you been sneaking him treats?"

I let my silence speak for me.

"Santi, you can't do that!" She pounds a fist on my back.

Returning her blow with a slap on her ass, I carry her out onto the back porch. "Too late."

The heat from the sun warms my skin, and I relish it. I may have lived here my whole life, but a change of pace is always nice.

Marching across the worn path in the snow from the porch to the barn, made by my treks back and forth, I tote Blake to the spot where Jack waits with Ace and Shadow. I asked him to get them saddled when I went up to the house earlier.

I deposit Blake on her feet and slip her arms into the sleeves of her coat. Securing the zipper, I whip out the gloves I stashed in my pocket and slide them on.

Blake frowns at me like a petulant child. "Are you done dressing me, *Dad*?"

Her insult has the opposite effect, and I feel my cock stiffen.

"You can call me Daddy any time," I reply with a wink, and her cheeks fill with a perfect pink color. Motioning to the horses, I retrieve the reins from Javier. "Let's ride. Shadow is already tacked up for you."

"Have fun," Javier salutes, making his way deeper into the barn to get back to work.

Blake's obstinacy dies as she caves, seizing Shadow's straps. "This feels irresponsible."

I wave off her concern, mounting Ace. "You'll be fine. The case will still be there when we get back."

"Santi..." Blake expresses her hesitation as she places one foot in the stirrup and swings her other leg over Shadow's back.

"Shadow missed you. She told me herself."

"If the horses are speaking to you when you talk to them, then it's probably time to put you in a home, old man," she teases.

Widening my eyes, I repeat her last two words. "Old man?"

Blake's smile is wide from our banter, lighting up her face. "You're the one going senile."

"I take offense to that," I return, faking my affront.

Her answering smile is all I need.

Urging Ace forward, I begin our distraction, and Blake follows behind with Shadow. Just like the first time she rode, Blake coaxes Shadow so we're trotting side by side.

From the moment she saddled up, I could see the difference in her eyes. In the dining room, her gaze was troubled. Out here with nothing but a horse, the earth, and the sky, her eyes are bright, and the tension in her shoulders is gone.

"Tell me about your life in New York," I prompt her.

She shrugs, her eyes fixed forward. "Not much to tell."

"I doubt that."

Blake sighs, her gaze going far off. "I rent—used to rent—a studio. I canceled the lease when I came here. My best friend is Savannah. I miss her like crazy." Her head tilts to the side as her smile becomes more subtle.

I understand Blake's longing. She has spent a large portion of her life in New York City. Of course she's going to miss it.

But I'm selfish enough to keep her here with me—with us.

"Why art?" I question.

Blake shakes her head, returning to our horseback ride. "What?"

"Why did you choose to pursue a career in art?" I ask again.

Blake flashes a contemplative frown, shrugging a shoulder. "I guess because it's how I express myself."

Wanting clarification, I inquire, "What do you mean?"

Blake nods her head as if the motion helps her find the words. "It's cathartic. I started drawing after my dad died, then it just sort of stuck. I won a couple of awards in high school, and when I got to New York, I got my paintings in a few galleries, and it took off from there."

"Do you miss it?"

She switches her attention to me, scrunching her brows. "What? New York?" Swaying her head from side to side, she seems to fully contemplate my question. "Sometimes. I miss painting more."

It's not hard to sympathize with Blake. If I had to walk away from my life at Falling Sky, homesickness would paralyze me.

Needing to see her smile again, I firmly squeeze my calves together, make a sound with my mouth, and tap Ace's croup. Ace obeys my cues and widens his stride, quickening his pace.

"Santi!" Blake shouts after me.

Glancing over my shoulder, I shout back, "Come on, *mi Cielo*." Lifting my face to the sky, I let out a loud, triumphant bellow and instruct Ace to run faster.

With the chilled wind numbing my face, I let a warm feeling spread through my chest. It's moments like this that make the early mornings, little sleep, and grueling labor worth it.

In my peripheral vision, Blake and Shadow gain on Ace and me. I never taught Blake how to instruct a horse to run, but I'm not surprised she figured it out.

Blake's hair whips behind her, and the expression on her face matches my own.

I direct Ace to pull back a hair, so I can watch Blake in this moment. She drops the lines to Shadow's bridle and hesitantly spreads her arms wide. Her head tilts up, and the cheer she bellows is unleashed in the Wyoming air, dancing to a rhythm that is solely Blake Jennings.

This is what *I* choose.

Her.

This life.

This moment.

We race in tandem for another hundred yards, then slow. Blake releases a thrilled laugh, ending on a contented sigh.

I shake my head, unable to suppress a chuckle. I could watch this woman all day.

"There she is," I say as if I'm uttering a reverent prayer.

Blake brings Shadow to a complete stop, angling her head toward me. "What do you mean?"

Halting Ace, I dismount, rounding to Blake's side. I peer up at her and answer, "You're free. Nothing weighing you down. Just you."

Blake swallows and descends from the saddle, her eyes glassy. Engulfing her in my embrace, I add, "You've spent so much time surviving that you forgot how to live."

"Don't you dare make me cry," she whispers, shaking her head. Her watery smile causes my chest to clench. "You going to teach me how to live?"

"Damn straight," I promise her.

Blake lets out a humorless laugh. "Good God." Her arms circle around my neck as she pulls me in for a soft kiss. "I love you, cowboy," she says against my lips.

My breath catches, and a sweet warmth unfurls low in my stomach. Everything narrows to her—just her. I can't stop smiling because she is my missing piece. With her, Levi, and Walker, the ranch truly feels like a home.

Pressing my head to hers, I whisper back, "*Te amo, Mi Cielo.*"

I love you, my Sky.

CHAPTER 39

BLAKE

Lazy Sundays are my new favorite.

I convinced the guys to relax with me. Yes, the world around us may be a complete nightmare, but it's Sunday. The day of not giving a fuck.

I exerted the most energy when I went down the stairs to lie on the couch.

We've watched TV, cuddled, napped, read books—all the things necessary for a carefree day.

Even my outfit matches the occasion.

I stole Santiago's wool socks, and they keep my feet at the perfect temperature. Levi's tee almost reaches my knees, and Walker's sweatpants barely stay on my hips. It feels like I'm wrapped in a large blanket.

Santiago wakes me from a nap on Levi's chest on the couch. "It's time to wake up," he coos gently.

"Why?" I question with a yawn.

Levi stretches, waking up with me.

Santiago grasps my hands and guides me to my feet. "We're going to dinner."

I give Santiago a teasing smirk. "Are you asking me on a date, cowboy?"

"If you want to see it that way," he attempts to hide a knowing smile. "But do dates include parents?"

The P-word chases away the last of the fog from my mind as I stand up straight.

"Parents?" My question comes out higher pitched than intended.

Santiago doesn't clarify. He either doesn't notice my apprehension, or he ignores it as he heads up to his bedroom to, I assume, get ready.

My gaze swivels to Levi.

"No, not mine," he answers my unsaid question as his hands flick outward. "They travel around the country in an RV."

I turn my head toward Walker, who sits on the other end of the sectional couch.

"Nope. My parents passed away years ago."

My brows pull together. "But Santiago..." I trail off.

"His mother was killed when Santiago was thirty-five." Walker stands, grabbing my hand and leading me to the stairs. Levi tracks behind us.

I nod, already aware of the tragedy. "He told me."

Walker guides me up the stairs. "His father lives in a cabin on the west end."

Blinking, my mouth opens in shock. "Santi never mentioned him, so I figured his dad wasn't around."

"Well, we're going to dinner at his house." Walker shrugs as we enter Santiago's bedroom.

Steam rolls through the cracked bathroom door as Santiago showers for the occasion. Levi and Walker disappear to find more appropriate clothes to wear.

Wear.

Shit.

"Wait!" I shout in alarm after them. "What do I wear?"

Their only answer is to laugh at my distress, causing me to curse them in my head.

Spinning on my heel, I stare blankly at the closet. Santiago moved his clothes aside, making room for the brand-new ones he, Levi, and Walker had purchased for me.

Blindly, I grab the first two items my hands touch. Thankfully, they work. I end up with a pair of rust-colored wide-leg pants and a soft ivory sweater that slips off one shoulder, no matter how many times I tug it back into place.

Casual enough not to feel overdressed.

Cute enough that I don't look like a bridge troll.

Outfit: check.

I keep my makeup minimal and throw my hair into a messy updo.

As I'm about to head back downstairs, I'm hit with a barrage of anxious thoughts.

Am I supposed to bring dessert? Do I call him Mr. Ramirez? What if I say something stupid? What if I have to pee a ton because I'm anxious, then he thinks I have health issues?

Levi appears in the doorway to the bathroom. "Butterfly."

Peering at him through the mirror, I'm practically speechless. It's not fair that he looks that amazing in a simple pair of jeans and a white scoop neck tee under a red flannel.

Not fair at all.

"Yes?" My voice quavers.

"You're pacing." Glancing down, I discover that he's right.

Levi approaches with a calming presence. He soothes his hand over my upper arms in comfort. "Don't be nervous. You look beautiful."

"Thank you," I whisper.

As if he knows I can't make my feet budge, he entwines our fingers together and leads me out of the bathroom and back to the first floor.

At the bottom of the staircase, we meet Santiago and Walker. I'm momentarily struck by the sight of their styled hair and lack of cowboy hats. Each man wears the same thing as Levi–something I doubt they did on purpose. Secretly, I'm hoping they don't notice it either.

"Damn," Walker mutters under his breath as his eyes land on me, but still loud enough for me to hear him.

Walker's curse causes Santiago to turn toward me, and his jaw drops. *"Esto es el paraíso." This is paradise.*

Their praise and appreciation give me the boost of confidence I need. Straightening my posture, I descend the last few steps, feeling like a million bucks.

"Put your tongues back in your mouths," I tease as I strut toward the exit.

Walker's hand finds the handle to the door and opens it for me.

"Thank you, handsome," I say with a wink as I cross the threshold.

Santiago and Levi do their little bit of debating over whose truck to take. The one thing we all agree on is that we're not piling in Walker's truck.

After an infamous game of Rock, Paper, Scissors, we end up in Levi's F250 with Levi driving, Bear nestled between Santiago and Walker in the backseat, and me in the passenger seat.

Tired of the silence, I ask, "What was Santi like as a kid?"

Levi and Walker answer at the same time.

"Loud."

"Sticky."

Santiago makes an indignant sound. "Rude."

"More like accurate," Walker retorts.

"Sticky?" I roll my lips to hold in a laugh.

Levi answers, keeping his eyes on the dirt road. "He was one of those kids who somehow always had sticky hands. It was like he put his hand in a jar of honey and let it dry."

Failing miserably, a laugh bursts from me. Santiago pouts in the back seat while Levi and Walker join me.

Levi slows the truck as we pull up to a single-story ranch

home sitting back from the road beneath a cluster of towering whitebark pine trees. It isn't large or flashy. It's a modest home wrapped in faded cedar siding with a deep front porch stretching across the entire length. Rocking chairs flank the front door, and a wooden porch swing on the far right gently creaks in the breeze.

As Levi brings the car to a stop, I turn toward the back. "Anything I need to know before we go inside?"

"Be yourself," Santiago answers immediately.

"I'm serious." I lift my brows for emphasis.

"So am I." His warm smile gives me a sense of comfort.

We exit the vehicle, marching through the snow-covered path and up the porch to the front door. I expect one of them to knock, but they step right on it. Even Bear shows no hesitation.

Striking honey-colored oak floors that stretch through the main living area are softened by woven rugs. A fire lights a river-rock fireplace anchored to one wall, its mantel crowded with framed family photos instead of decorations. The deep cognac leather couches appear crisp and clean, the cushions sinking just enough to hint at their years of use.

One wall holds a plethora of family photos–Santiago as a kid covered in mud, a family of three riding horses across a pasture, a teenage Santiago and a middle-aged woman who I assume is his mother. A pair of muddy work boots rest on a rubber mat just inside the front door, and Navajo-style blankets are draped across the back of each couch.

Levi, Santiago, and Walker each slip off their boots, placing them next to the first pair on the mat like this is their ritual. Awkwardly, I do the same as if I were going to take my shoes off all along.

"*Mis hijos.*" A man strolls from around the corner, holding out his arms. *My sons.*

Shifting my weight back and forth, I hide behind my men with Bear at my side.

"*Hola, Papi.*" Santiago greets and walks straight into the man's arms.

Santiago's father looks older than I imagined. Thick salt-and-pepper hair curls slightly around his ears, and laugh lines fan from the corners of his warm brown eyes. His skin looks like it's been bronzed by decades of hard work under the Wyoming sun, and a neatly trimmed beard streaked with silver frames his easy smile. He's not particularly tall, but carries himself with a quiet confidence only a man who has done a lifetime of honest work could possess. His dark sweater stretches across a pair of sturdy shoulders that age hasn't quite managed to steal, and a frilly pastel pink apron is tied around his waist.

Levi steps up next. "Ángel," he greets. Their hug is no less affectionate.

Walker doesn't move from his spot and tips his head. "Sir."

Ángel closes the distance and wraps his arms around Walker despite his obvious discomfort. "How many times do I have to ask you not to call me that?"

Walker's hands ineptly pat Ángel on the back. "You'll always be sir to me."

Ángel pulls back, giving Walker a penalizing look. "I work for a living, son."

"You're retired," Santiago deadpans.

Ángel waves off Santiago's comment and moves Walker aside, coming to me.

"You must be Blake," he says gleefully and opens his arms.

My face flushes as I step forward, outstretching my hand for a shake. "It's nice to meet you, Mr—"

A huge grin stretches his lips as his warmth envelopes me in an embrace. "Call me Ángel, *hija*."

My entire body freezes.

My daughter.

He called me his daughter.

I return the hug as a spark lights up the dark recesses inside me.

"Ángel." I repeat.

Ángel releases me and looks me over. Not in a way that causes discomfort, but rather in a way that feels like he's measuring.

Bear takes the pause as an invitation to give his own greeting. He jumps up, placing his front paws on Ángel's chest and licks his face.

Ángel half flinches, closing one eye as he pets Bear, but Ángel doesn't seem put out by the affection. "I wouldn't forget you, Bear."

Bear, satisfied that he was acknowledged, hops down and prances into the living room, finding a comfortable spot to relax in.

Ángel wipes his face and turns back to me. "So you're the woman who has captured the hearts of these three."

"Oh, dear God." My mouth becomes dry, making it impossible to swallow.

Walker's eyes widen. "Jesus, Mary, and Joseph."

Levi and Santiago snicker, covering their mouths with their hands.

I didn't think about how the town would react to our unconventional relationship. I didn't care. It's no one's business but our own.

But now I care.

I care *a lot*.

Ángel rests his hands on my shoulders. "Breathe, *mija*. I wouldn't dare cross you with four pitbulls around."

His comment causes the corner of my mouth to tug upward, releasing a fraction of my worry. "They all love you. I doubt they'd turn on you for me."

He gives me a look, making me feel like I should know better. "Don't underestimate the heart."

Santiago claps, rubbing his hands together. "What's for dinner?"

Ángel drops his hands from my shoulders and strides for the kitchen. "Slow-cooked pork chile verde."

Levi rubs his stomach. "Say less."

The guys saunter after Ángel, so I do the same.

The kitchen is large enough to fit all five of us comfortably without making me feel claustrophobic. The knotty pine cabinets and worn butcher-block countertops look polished and smooth. Copper pots hang over a large island while a cast-iron skillet rests permanently on the stovetop. Every available surface holds evidence that someone actually lives here.

A heavy oak table dominates the dining room just beyond the kitchen. Each chair is slightly different from the next, as if they have been collected over the years rather than purchased as a set.

Nothing in this home matches perfectly to something else.

Nothing looks so expensive that I feel like I'll dirty it by touching it.

Somehow, that makes Ángel's home feel even more beautiful.

Each room is used.

Lived in.

Loved.

Ángel stirs something in a pot at the stove, the smell making my mouth water.

"What can I help with?" I question, holding out my hands to show I'm ready to be put to work.

"Nothing," he waves me off . "You go on and have a seat." Ángel points the wooden spoon in his hand at Levi, Santiago, and Walker. "You three are a different story."

Santiago's face falls as he jokes, "I get the feeling that I'm no longer the favorite."

"You never were," Ángel roasts, then directs each of the guys, leading them to their working stations. "Levi, you're on the rice. Walk, set the table. And Santi," Ángel marches back to the stove, slapping Santiago's hand, "stop eating the pork and start warming the tortillas."

Santiago playfully pouts as he drags his feet. "This feels unfair."

Ángel gives Santiago what can only be described as a fatherly look. "Blake gets to put her feet up because she has to deal with you three every day."

They all hop to it before Ángel can scold them again.

Timidly, I tiptoe into the dining room as if I'm not supposed to be here even though Ángel specifically told me to relax.

Ángel's hospitality was unexpected. I'm not sure what I was expecting, but I know it wasn't a welcome with open arms.

I choose the chair that looks the most comfortable and sit down, folding my hands in my lap.

The guys do as they're told. Set the table, warm the tortillas, and prepare the rice. When they're all done, they bring out the food and sit with me. Ángel sits at the head of the table with Santiago on his right and Walker next to him. Levi takes the seat between Ángel and me.

Ángel instructs us to "dig in" and Santiago takes that quite literally. The man always eats with gusto, but this is something else. He clearly loves a home-cooked meal.

Levi fills my plate before dishing his own food. Walker waits to get his food last.

Taking care of everyone else first as always.

The meal passes in relative silence aside from Ángel demanding life updates from Levi and Walker.

When my plate is almost empty, I ask Ángel, "Do you have any good stories about these guys?"

"He doesn't," Santiago answers too quickly.

"Tú solo mastica. Hablar te va a dar indigestión." Keep eating. Talking will give you indigestion. Ángel pats Santiago's shoulder, then sets his elbow on the table and rests his chin on his fist.

"One time, when Santiago was about two or three, he got into his mother's spice cabinet," Ángel starts.

Santiago groans while Levi and Walker chuckle.

Ángel ignores Santiago's obvious objection. "He found the nutmeg and got it everywhere. I mean *everywhere.* Then he stripped off his clothes, and the nutmeg got on his...willis and doodleberry. Poor boy screamed and screamed."

"Oh, no." My eyes widen as I chuckle. Levi drops his fork on his plate, throwing his head back in laughter. Walker holds his stomach, curling over from laughing so much.

"Willis and doodleberry?" Santiago criticizes.

Ángel lowers his brows at Santiago and gestures to me. "I'm talking to a lady." Dismissing Santiago,

Ángel turns his attention back to me. "He'd freak out any time he smelled nutmeg after that."

Santiago shivers. "Still don't touch the stuff."

I try to compose myself as I question Ángel again. "What about these two? Any embarrassing stories?"

Levi and Walker sober.

"None," Levi snaps, then says to Ángel, "I'll give you a hundred dollars to not say a word."

Walker keeps his lips sealed.

I squint at him. "No objection from you?"

Walker shrugs.

Ángel points to Levi. "This one used to bring me injured animals all the time. I'd let him use the barn and whatever he could find to nurse them back to health. One time he even brought a raccoon."

"A raccoon?" My mouth falls open.

"It followed me home," Levi defends himself.

"Because you fed him marshmallows the whole way," Santiago ripostes, shoveling another bite of rice into his mouth.

Ángel moves to point toward Walker. "And this one was arrested for destruction of property when he was about sixteen. I got a call in the middle of the night to pick him up at the station. I had to post his bail."

Rearing back, I place my hand on my chest dramatically. "Sheriff Maddox, I am shocked."

Walker rolls his eyes at my teasing. "I was trying to free the man's horse."

My head tilts to the side. "A horse?"

"Neighbor wasn't feeding it, and Walk cut the fence," Ángel explains further.

"I was *liberating* it," Walker responds.

"He actually used the word liberating when he was questioned by the sheriff at the time," Levi interjects.

Ángel continues with the tales. "Well, there was one time when they dared each other to—"

"And on that note," Santiago slaps his hands on his lap, interrupting the story and stands. "I think it's time to clean up and get going. No more stories from a senile old man."

Santiago takes the initiative and starts the cleaning process.

Ángel narrows his eyes playfully. "Who are you calling senile?"

Walker rises to his feet, gathering plates. "We should be heading out anyway. I have to be at the station early in the morning."

Levi piles dishes on his and carries them to the kitchen.

I get up to do the same when Ángel stops me, holding up his hand. "Sit."

"But I can help," I reason.

"I know." Ángel gets to his feet and grabs the remaining dishes, then heads for the kitchen. "That's why I'm telling you not to."

His demand confounds me.

No expectations.

No conditions.

Just kindness.

Once the dishes are done and leftovers are put away, we move to the front door and put on our shoes. Bear rises from where he lies on a rug in front of the fireplace, stretches, and trots to my side.

The guys each hug Ángel, thank him for dinner, and head to Levi's truck. I do the same, but Ángel stops me before I exit.

"If any of them ever give you a problem, you call me. *¿Sí?*"

I nod. "Yes, s—Ángel."

His expression turns serious. "I heard about the barn. If you need anything, anything at all, call me. You're always welcome here."

I let out a contented sigh. "Thank you, Ángel."

"You know," Ángel gestures to the truck, "those boys haven't smiled that much in years."

My lips purse. "Really?"

He nods. "You're good for them."

Ángel's sincerity has me grinning from ear to ear.

"I think they're the ones that are good for me."

Ángel smiles back. "That's usually how it works."

Confusion takes over my expression. "What works?"

He pats my shoulder. "Love."

In a daze, I turn and amble to the truck.

I don't remember buckling my seatbelt.

I don't remember the drive back.

I don't even remember getting ready for bed.

There's only one thought going through my mind.

I'm actually happy here–thoroughly and unequivocally happy.

And it's all because of them.

Levi, Santiago, and Walker.

CHAPTER 40

LEVI

My stomach grumbles as I look over my appointment schedule at the front desk of the clinic for the hundredth time today, hoping that time for lunch magically appears on the computer screen.

It doesn't.

I had to move my appointments back to the clinic after the barn burned down. I lost a good portion of my equipment, but that stuff is replaceable. I've actually already replaced most of it.

The barn is coming along great. Santiago paid extra for the construction crew to work overtime. The only downside is the banging of hammers, the piercing screech of circular saws, and the rumbles of heavy machinery waking me up every morning.

And I've made little headway in my "two people working together" theory. I'm finally understanding why Blake looks as if she wants to rip her hair out when she's sitting at Santiago's dining room table going through case files.

The bell above the clinic door jingles. A tired sigh escapes me before I even look up. When I do, my shoulders loosen.

"Knock, knock." Blake walks right up to me and plops a large brown takeout bag on the desk.

Santiago enters right behind her.

My smile is automatic. I couldn't stop even if I tried. "Aren't you two a sight for sore eyes?" I tilt my head to the side. "Where's Bear?"

"With the other ranch hands. I figured he needed time to run around." Blake shrugs. "Santiago and I thought you might like some lunch."

Reclining in the computer chair, I interlock my fingers behind my head. "Butterfly, if you two keep bringing me lunch, I'm going to become completely useless."

Santiago drops his head to an angle. "Food is fuel. You need it to keep up with your busy schedule."

I let out a deep exhale. "Unfortunately, my busy schedule doesn't allow for midday meals."

"Bullshit," Blake barks, marching past the desk toward the back. She searches every room until she finds Abbott and asks him to take my next appointment.

I know he's capable, but I typically take a hands-on approach to veterinary medicine.

Abbott eagerly agrees. Though I'm not sure if it's to impress Blake or because he wants to do more appointments on his own.

Satisfied she's done her job, Blake herds Santiago and me into the kitchen for a nice Main Street Diner meal. We sit at the small round table, and Blake hands out the to-go boxes. I practically swallow my food whole, having skipped breakfast.

Reaching over, I tuck a lock of hair behind Blake's ear. "Thank you, Butterfly."

She gives me an easy smile in return. "You're welcome."

"What about me?" Santiago waves to himself. "I drove."

Blake shoots Santiago a mild scolding look. "Only because you three refuse to let me go anywhere alone."

"Buddy system," Santiago reminds Blake.

Blake throws her hands up, dropping them into her lap. "I'm the only one who has to have a buddy. You all loosened the reins for each other, but not me."

"And there's a good reason for that," I defend.

"You all decided you don't mind being hypocrites?" Blake surmises cheekily.

"No," I answer patiently. "You're too important."

"But you all are no less important to me," she returns.

"Escúchame, mi Cielo." Listen to me, my sky. Santiago holds her hand in both of his. "Walker whole-stubborn-heartedly agrees with us, so it's three against one. You're not going to win this battle."

Blake narrows her gaze. "We'll see."

Santiago's right. She's not going to win this one. Blake can probably get us to do a lot of things, but this isn't one of them. Even after everything settles, we're still going to worry about her.

Glancing at my watch, I make note of the time.

"I have an appointment that's going to be here any minute," I announce.

Blake whirls to face me, brows raised in outrage. "Are you kicking us out?"

I'm not sure whether I should laugh or kiss her.

Patting her knee, I shake my head. "I would never. I'm just letting you know that I won't be in here for a bit."

Rising to my feet, I start to gather the trash, but Blake snatches it out of my hands. "I got this. You go do your sexy vet thing."

She says it so casually, like she doesn't realize that she just destroyed every coherent thought in my head.

Lifting a brow, I smirk. "You think it's sexy?"

Instead of answering, Blake shoos me away. "Get out of here."

"Alright, alright," I return, holding my hands up as I leave the kitchen.

I meander to the second exam room to prep for Fluffy, Harold Whitcombe's sheep.

The appointment itself is routine. The elderly ewe with an abscessed hood and Harold, who apologized every ten seconds as though the infection were somehow his fault.

Normally, work demands every iota of my attention.

Today, however, every few minutes, my mind wanders to the woman down the hall.

Blake has a habit of making herself at home. If I know her at all, she's already cozied up in my desk chair in my office, raiding my snack drawer.

The thought makes me smile.

The appointment lasts longer than expected. Sheep don't appreciate having their infected hooves cleaned, and Fluffy proved particularly tenacious in expressing that opinion.

By the time I finish bandaging the leg and sending Harold home with antibiotics and instructions, nearly an hour had passed.

Abbott volunteers to handle the paperwork for which I thank him repeatedly, then I head toward my office.

An odd silence greets me. "Blake? Santi?" I call out.

"Here." Blake's voice is a little shaky.

"Sorry that took so long," I apologize as I enter the room. "That poor sheep had—"

Blake stands perfectly still behind my desk.

A hidden closet door hangs open.

Shipping tubes and packages are scattered on the floor.

An unstretched canvas rests in her hands.

The sensation of a trapdoor opening in my stomach brings on a wave of nausea as my skin turns clammy.

"Levi, what is this?" Blake holds up the tube and gestures to the others inside the closet.

Oh shit.

CHAPTER 41

BLAKE

My thoughts go a million different directions as I stand there holding a painting—*my painting*.

I painted this piece about a year ago after a particularly terrifying encounter with a man named Anthony Cole. I'll never forget him. He attended one of my showings and spent an uncomfortable amount of time asking me questions unrelated to my art. His southern accent sent chills up my spine. I couldn't wait to get away from him. Then I thought I saw him following me home after the show.

The next day, I started this painting of a woman sitting in silence in the middle of a crowd.

"Levi?" I prompt him again.

He rushes forward, outstretching his hand for the canvas. "I can explain."

I pull it out of his reach and take a step backward. "Please do, because I can't make sense of it."

Levi spears his fingers into his hair, pulling at the roots as he paces. He takes a steadying breath, but his hands still quiver.

"I tried finding you as soon as you left Evergreen Falls. I needed to know that you were okay. That's all."

Tipping my head forward a fraction, I raise my eyebrows as I point to the rest of the shipping tubes and other stretched canvases still in the closet. Morbid curiosity pushes to the front of my mind as I set the painting in my hands on his desk and reach for another in the closet.

"It took three years, but I finally found you. When I did, you were on your fourth showing."

I flinch as if he slapped me across the face. "You—you were there?"

Levi does a quick swipe with both hands, slicing the space between us in a clear sign of denial. "No. I never flew out to New York. I purchased these online."

Flipping the canvas in my hands, I show him the painting of a man on a horse in the middle of a field of wheat. "But this one was a commission."

Levi takes an unsteady inhale. "Yes."

"You're my patron in the west?"

"What?"

"My agent had told me that there was an anonymous person out west who was buying up a lot of my work," I explain, then wave a hand at all the art pieces. "I think she undersold how many you bought."

Levi chews on the corner of his bottom lip. "Some of it was after the fact." He points to the canvas in my hands. "I found out who originally bought that one. It was some guy on the Upper East Side, and I convinced him to sell it to me."

A flutter rolls through my stomach.

"You bought all of these?" My gaze moves over the shipping tubes and canvases, trying to count them all.

He has so many of my paintings.

Like he was collecting them.

I don't understand it.

Levi gives me a single nod.

"Why?" My question comes out on a light breath,

Levi takes a jittery gulp. "At first, it was a way to check in on you—a way to make sure the girl I knew hadn't disappeared. I saw how talented you are, and I wanted to see that every day." He takes a step forward, gently removing the painting from my hands. He holds it like it's the most precious thing he owns as admiration fills his face. "Then it stopped being about the art." His eyes move to my face as he smiles. "It became about you."

Tears prick at my eyes, rolling freely down my cheeks.

My voice comes out as a squeak. "Damn, you Levi Harding."

Levi's brows lower over his eyes. "For what?"

"For making me fall in love with you."

"I love you too, Butterfly."

I yank the painting out of Levi's hands and place it on his desk. My arms wrap around his neck and pull, bringing my lips to his.

Levi's hands land on my waist, tugging me closer.

I pour every bit of my heart into the kiss, communicating everything my words can't.

His teeth scrape my bottom lip, then his tongue invades my mouth. My core pulses as need overtakes my senses.

His length grows hard in his pants, and my thighs squeeze together as my panties dampen.

One of my hands slides down Levi's chest, undoing the drawstring and reaching into the waistband of his scrubs.

"Levi, one of the shepherd mixes keeps trying too—Am I interrupting something?"

I spring back from Levi, and my face turns a deep shade of scarlet. Santiago steps inside, shutting the door behind him. Levi pulls me back toward him, and my hands land on his chest.

Santiago strides closer. "I'd tell you two to get a room, but..." He gestures around Levi's office. "You already have one."

My eyes dart between them, an idea forming as I back up and place myself behind the desk. "Then what do you say we make the most of the opportunity?"

Their eyes bulge, and they seem to be frozen in place.

Lift my sweater over my head, I let it fall to the ground.

Still frozen.

Their attention does something to me.

I feel beautiful.

Confident.

I smirk, reaching my hand behind my back. With a simple twist, the clasp is undone, and the straps loosen. Using my other hand, I hold my bra in place.

"You want to get Levi ready for me?" I ask Santiago.

A slow smile lights up Santiago's face. "You're a vixen, *mi Cielo*."

I shoot them both a wink, and Santiago moves to Levi. He cups the sides of Levi's neck, bringing their mouths together. Levi's hands grip Santiago's shirt, and their tongues dance together, thrusting in and out of each other's mouths.

My panties flood with arousal just from watching them together.

They say I'm the vixen? Then what does that make them?

When their lips part, Santiago moves behind Levi and faces him toward me. Then Santiago slips Levi's shirt over his head, giving me a view of Levi's muscled chest.

Santiago places his hands on Levi's hips, gliding his hands forward and dipping them below the waistband of Levi's pants. Santiago finds Levi's cock, and a small cry escapes my lips.

"You want to see, Butterfly?"

I nod my head eagerly.

Levi shoots me a wink as he shoves his pants and boxers down his legs, letting them drop to the floor.

My jaw drops.

I watch as Santiago's hand pumps up and down Levi's shaft in practiced and measured movements.

Levi and Santiago's gaze remain trained on me.

Slowly, I let my bra fall from my chest, revealing my breasts and hardened nipples. Levi licks his lips, and Santiago groans.

"Shit, Butterfly."

I smooth my hands up my stomach and cup my breasts, swiping my thumbs over my peaked buds. My legs shake.

Releasing one breast, the weight of it doing a small bounce, I slip my hand into the waistband of my pants and cup my center.

"Ah, ah, ah, *mi Cielo*," Santiago reprimands. "Turnabout is fair play. You want to see us, we get to see you."

With a nod, I shuck my pants and take a seat in Levi's chair. I prop one foot up on the edge of the desk, allowing them a look right at my pussy. My arousal slides down to the chair, dampening the cushion beneath me.

Levi and Santiago groan in unison.

"You're turn," I challenge Santiago.

He rises to the test, undressing himself completely within a few seconds.

It's like we're playing a game of chicken, but I'm unsure what determines the winner.

Santiago and Levi stand side by side, their lengths hard as steel, their sculpted bodies enough to make me climax just from looking at them.

I whimper, slipping two fingers into my channel and stroking that spot inside that drives me crazy. My other hand returns to my breast, working my nipple to work my need higher.

"Keep working that pussy, Butterfly," Levi directs as Santiago drops to his knees in front of Levi.

Oh.

My.

God.

Santiago's tongue flicks at the head of Levi's cock, causing Levi to curse and grip the edge of his desk to hold himself up.

When Santiago's mouth envelops Levi's length, my jaw drops. My instinct is to close my eyes and make myself come, but I don't want to miss a single second of this.

Santiago's cheeks hollow as he takes Levi's entire length into his throat.

"Oh, my hell," I swear, and swirl my thumb around my clit, sending a jolt of pleasure through my center.

Levi's eyes heat. "That's it, Blake. Come on your fingers. Show me how you get yourself off."

Levi taps Santiago's shoulder, and he pops off Levi's shaft.

Together, they round the desk to where I sit and fall to their knees on either side of me.

Santiago slips a finger into my center with mine, guiding my hand as our digits work my pussy together.

Levi's mouth closes over the peak of my other boob. He licks and nips at the peak, causing a cry to claw up from my chest. Levi's hand covers mine, and like Santiago, he leads me in playing with my breast.

"Come for us, Blake. I need to see it," Levi growls in my ear.

Santiago's face dips to the juncture of my thighs, licking my bundle of nerves like I'm his favorite flavor.

My orgasm hits me like a freight train. Levi kisses me to prevent my screams from echoing down the hall. The hurricane of pleasure threatens to drown me as my channel convulses around mine and Santiago's fingers.

The three of us draw out my climax together. My legs twitch when I come back down.

"Oh my God," I pant out.

"You're absolutely beautiful," Santiago whispers, kissing his way up my stomach, between my breasts, and to my mouth. He slides his tongue against mine, and I taste myself.

My arousal builds again, and I reach for Levi. He leans in, and I pull away from Santiago, nipping at Levi's bottom lip. He groans and thrusts his tongue into my mouth.

Taking a breath, I sit back and look to them. "I need you. Both of you."

"Good," Levi growls as he and Santiago get to their feet.

Levi pulls me up with them, leading me to lean over the desk. My nipples scrape against the cold surface, tightening them further. Santiago moves to my head, and my mouth waters, desperate to get my lips around him.

Levi, kicks my legs apart, stepping between them. "You ready for us?"

"Please," I beg.

At the same time, they move closer, positioning their cocks at my holes. Levi's tip rests at my entrance, and Santiago's tip sits on my lip.

I tilt my hips, giving Levi better access, and open my mouth, allowing Santiago entry.

They thrust into me together, filling my mouth and my pussy. Santiago's musk explodes over my tongue, and I moan, closing my lips around his length. Levi's hand gathers some of my release on his fingers, and he glides his hand between my cheeks to my third hole.

I moan again, circling my hips.

"Shit," Santiago curses, gathering my hair in his fist. He uses his grip to guide my mouth up and down his shaft, pumping his hips in tandem. "Your mouth feels like heaven. So warm and wet."

Levi's finger pushes into my ass at the same time his cock enters my channel. My knees threaten to give out.

The pleasure is too much, but I can't get enough.

Levi and Santiago work my holes together, setting a rhythm that pushes my bliss higher.

I feel Santiago's dick twitch in my mouth, prompting me to suck harder. Saliva dribbles down my chin, making a mess of my face and the desk.

As I do, my pussy begins to tighten around Levi.

"I'm not going to last much longer," Santiago grunts.

"She's close," Levi replies.

On Levi's next thrust, I come, and I come hard.

I scream around Santiago's cock, and his seed empties into my mouth. I continue to climax as I swallow him down.

Levi thrusts one more time, grunting, sounding like he is half in pain and half in oblivion.

When my muscles relax, I let the desk take all of my weight.

Levi's hand lands next to my head, propping himself up so as not to crush me.

Santiago lowers himself to his knees and captures my mouth with his, tasting himself on my tongue. Our kiss is lazy and messy, but no less perfect.

Santiago pulls back, wiping the mess from my face with the first piece of clothing he swipes from the floor. "You're ours, Blake Jennings."

"Yours," I agree contentedly.

Working together, Santiago and Levi clean me with tissues and dress me in my clothes. I'm half asleep through the entire process.

Then Santiago sweeps me up in his arms and carries me out to his truck and I rest my head on his chest

He drives us back to Falling Sky, and my eyes barely stay open for half of the trip. When we pull up, Levi arrives, parking behind us. He takes his turn carrying me, taking me inside the house and up the stairs and into Santiago's bathroom, where they remove the clothes they just dressed me in and guide me into the shower.

I lean back into Levi's hard body as he and Santiago wash my hair and my body, massaging my scalp and my muscles.

When the water shuts off, I frown, causing Levi and Santiago to chuckle.

They wrap me in a soft, warm towel and dry me off then themselves.

Scooping me into his arms once more, Santiago carries me to the gigantic bed. He sets me in the middle as he and Levi climb in and surround me from either side.

"Sleep, Butterfly," Levi whispers into my damp hair.

As I drift off, I hold onto the feeling in my chest that tells me this is where I'm supposed to be–this is where I'm supposed to stay.

CHAPTER 42

BLAKE

The bell above the diner door jingles as I step inside, and warmth immediately chases away the late winter chill clinging to my coat.

The crackle of bacon floats under the hum of customers chatting among themselves. Fresh coffee perfumes the air. Somewhere in the back, dishes clatter together while country music plays softly somewhere through the speakers.

No matter what time of day it is, Main Street Diner always smells like breakfast.

Walker opted to stay outside in his truck to make a few phone calls, promising he'd only be a minute. Considering his minute usually means fifteen, I meander toward the counter and take a seat on a stool rather than heading for the usual booth.

"Well," a familiar voice drawls behind me. "Evergreen Falls really can't seem to get rid of you."

I suppress a sigh before turning around.

Bridger Reynolds sits a few stools away, expensive wool coat draped over one arm, looking more like he belongs in a boardroom than a diner. His polished boots are spotless despite the slushy parking lot outside.

"Mayor Reynolds," I acknowledge.

He smiles. "Just Bridger."

"I'll stick with Mayor."

His smile thins. "I heard you've been spending quite a bit of time with the sheriff."

Small towns really are allergic to minding their own business.

"I've been helping with a few things."

"Helping." He rolls the word around like he doesn't believe it. "Be careful."

I raise a brow. "About?"

His eyes flick toward the window where Walker's truck sits outside. "Not everyone in this town deserves your trust."

"Funny," I reply. "I was just thinking the same thing."

For the briefest moment, something flashes across his face—annoyance, but then the polished politician returns.

"I hope you're wrong."

He gives me a courteous nod before disappearing toward a booth near the back of the diner.

He's like a damn cockroach that won't die.

Martha meanders over from the back, shining a glass in her hand. "I swear, girl..." She points her rag at me like a weapon. "If you're here to order more of that sweet stuff that rots your mouth, I'm going to shove a salad down your throat."

"You did that last week and look." I flash my teeth. "Still have all of them."

Martha returns the glass to the stack on the counter behind her. "I'll make you something healthy first, and then you can have your syrup-y addiction."

I make a gagging noise. "It's going to be something green, isn't it?"

Martha shoves her hands on her hips and raises her brows at me in answer.

Ugh. It's going to be green.

Spinning on my stool, I lean to the side, resting my elbow on the countertop as my eyes wander to the man outside. He parked right in front of the entrance, claiming it's because as the sheriff he can park anywhere, but I know it's really to keep an eye on me.

Walker holds his cell phone to his ear with his shoulder as he jots down notes in his small notepad. His expression is serious, making me think he isn't having a pleasant conversation.

Martha follows my gaze through the front window and hums knowingly. "You've been spending a lot of time with those boys."

Heat creeps into my cheeks. "Yeah."

No point in denying it. I'm sure half the town has already started taking bets.

Besides, I can't lie to Martha.

Martha sets down a mug and fills it to the brim with coffee. Steam rises from the drink, indicating it's fresh, but I pick it up anyway.

"And I've seen the way Grant has been eyeing you."

The mug stops halfway to my lips, and my mouth falls open at Martha's insinuation. "Grant? No. It's not like that with him."

"I know, honey." Martha's smile disappears as she dries her hands on her apron. "Be careful around Grant."

My mouth twists into a confused frown.

"The history between those four is complicated," Martha explains.

My mind immediately starts rearranging memories.

I search for one where all four of them were together. I remember Grant stopping by on Thanksgiving, but only Grant. Levi, Santiago, and Walker attended my high school graduation, but not Grant.

Even in public—county fairs, farmers markets, the grocery store—Grant was never at the same place at the same time as the other three.

Is that why Grant seemed upset before he left Timberline a few weeks ago?

Is that why I've barely seen him since then?

My brows furrow tightly. "Complicated how?"

Martha shakes her head. "That's all I'm saying. It's not my story to tell."

My hands cradle my head as they pull at my hair. "How did I never realize..."

Martha grabs one of my hands. "You were young, Blake. You weren't supposed to see it."

"But—"

Martha cuts me off, not willing to hear my misplaced guilt. "The problems between those men are their own. They will figure it out. I just didn't want you to go in blind."

My body grows tense as I pull my hand away from hers, and my gaze drops to the laminate counter. "So this isn't because you think it's weird?"

"What?" Martha's expression scrunches up.

"You know." My hands wring in my lap. "Because they're my dad's best friends."

Martha's tone goes flat, suggesting she already knows the answer to her question. "Did they make a move on you before you were eighteen?"

An awkward laugh bubbles up in my throat. "God, no. Never."

Martha plants both of her hands on the counter. "You're a grown woman." She dips her head a fraction. "They're grown men." She straightens her posture. "The only people who get a vote are the ones in the relationship."

Martha strolls away, attending to another customer.

The knot that I didn't realize had been living in my chest since Levi, Santiago, and Walker crossed every imaginable line loosened. I didn't realize how badly I needed someone else to say it.

I'm not broken for wanting them.

And...

She said "relationship."

Singular.

The word settles somewhere deep inside me, and my heart jumps at the sound of it.

I glance over my shoulder toward Walker and find him pacing

alongside his truck, still on the phone. When he catches me looking at him, he ends the call and strides to the entrance of the diner.

The bell jingles again as Walker steps inside. His expression is carefully neutral.

Too neutral.

Walker sits down on the stool next to mine. His hand grips the bottom of my cushion and slides me closer to his side.

"Everything okay?" I ask.

"Yeah."

Liar.

CHAPTER 43

BLAKE

I didn't realize how much I was carrying around on my shoulders until my talk with Martha yesterday. Somewhere between her advice, Levi's confession the day before, and Santiago's inability to stop making me laugh all last night at dinner, the tension in my shoulders had loosened.

It's still there for the most part, but it's relaxed.

Easier to bear.

For the first time since coming back to Evergreen Falls, I wasn't waiting for the next bad thing to happen.

Although waking up this morning to the sound of hammers pounding nails into the studs of the barn could be considered a bad thing.

I'll be honest.

It *is* a bad thing.

Santiago wants the barn completed as soon as superhumanly possible, which I understand. The barn is central to his livelihood, and he has other people depending on him.

But allowing the construction crew to start when the bunkhouse wakes up is inconvenient for the rest of us.

With a warm coffee in hand, the crisp morning air fills my

lungs as I step out onto the back porch with Bear weaving between my legs as if he believes he's a small cat.

Falling Sky is already bustling as the sounds of construction ring through the valley. Someone laughs boisterously near the corrals. Diesel engines rumble somewhere beyond the equipment shed.

The skeleton of the new barn stretches toward the velvet and amber-streaked sky. Every day, another wall goes up, another reminder disappears.

Maybe healing works the same way.

Strolling down toward the corrals, I pass by Todd, who is carrying a fence post over his shoulder.

He tips the brim of his hat in my direction. "Morning, Blake."

"Morning."

Brandon waves from the tractor.

Sam is halfway up a ladder, aiding in the construction. He balances a nail gun in one hand and somehow drinks coffee with the other.

That's ranch life.

I cup my hand next to my mouth and shout, "Pretty sure OSHA would have a problem with that."

Sam's shoulders shake with laughter. "Good thing OSHA doesn't live in Wyoming."

Bear trots between wranglers and construction workers like a foreman making inspections. Every now and then, someone bends down to scratch behind his ears before getting back to work.

Javier stands on the edge of a corral, his forearms resting on the top of the pipe fence. He watches as Jack works with a young, speckled gelding.

Curious, I wander over beside him.

"Buenos días." Good morning.

"Morning," I return. "How's your head?"

"Better."

Jack doesn't hold a lead rope, and there isn't a saddle on the horse's back or a bridle around his head.

It's just the two of them inside the circular pen.

The gelding trots along the perimeter with his ears pinned halfway back, tossing his head every few strides. Jack will change direction arbitrarily with nothing more than a shift of his shoulders and a wave of one arm.

No yelling. No whip. No force.

Watching Jack and the horse, I tip my head to the side and ask Javier, "What's Jack doing?"

Javier smiles. "Listening."

I frown. "Looks more like the horse is avoiding him."

Javier chortles. "For now."

The gelding circles again, blowing hard through his nostrils. Then something changes. One ear swivels toward Jack.

Then the other.

The horse lowers his head and licks his lips before slowing from a trot to a walk.

Javier points at what just occurred. "See that?"

I nod slowly.

"He's asking the horse a question."

My nose wrinkles. "What's the question?"

"Do you trust me enough to stop running?"

Jack turns his body slightly away from the gelding and drops the pressure completely. Instead of continuing around the pen, the gelding hesitates.

One uncertain step. Then another.

The horse walks toward Jack on his own. When he reaches Jack's shoulder, Jack scratches the base of the horse's neck like they've been friends for years.

"That's it?" I question.

Javier nods. "You can't force trust," he says with a shrug. "You can only give someone a reason to choose you."

Give someone a reason to choose you.

Those words echo in my head on a loop.

Javier angles toward me. "Speaking of horses that need a little extra attention..." He nods in Shadow's direction. "Mind taking her for a walk?"

My head jerks back. "You want me to walk a horse?"

"She likes you."

"She likes a lot of people," I return without confidence because I don't know that for sure.

"Not the way she likes you."

My lips press into a thin line as I admit, "It's because I feed her sugar cubes."

Javier gives me a half smile. "Sugar cubes or not, she still likes you."

I sigh through my nose. "Okay, I'll do it, but if she runs away, it's not my fault."

"Noted," Javier replies, like he doesn't believe that'll happen.

Javier gives me a rundown of what to do with Shadow, then fits her with a halter, attaches the lead rope, and hands me the end.

There's no way I'm qualified for this, but here we are.

The south trail has a quality that makes it feel like I'm a princess walking through the woods, waiting for a charming prince to pop out of the trees and serenade me.

Maybe it's the way the morning light trickles through the snow-covered evergreen branches, or maybe it's the fresh pine scent complementing the sounds of running water from the nearby creek.

I even begin talking to Shadow and Bear like a fantasy princess would.

"Ángel is a really good cook. I hope that means Santiago knows how to cook. My skills with a stove are limited to grilled cheese, scrambled eggs, and boxed mac n cheese."

Shadow angles her head toward me and rolls her eyes.

"I'm a pro with the microwave, though," I defend.

Shadow's reply is to blow out a puff of air through her nose.

"Walker has pulled his head out of his ass."

Shadow sneezes.

"Exactly."

As we continue down the path, construction, horse neighs, and chatter fades, the trees effectively shutting everything out–or closing us in.

"I was thinking about–"

Shadow stops, becoming impossibly still. Bear halts with her, scanning the trees.

"What is it, girl?" I ask as I stroke my hand down her mane.

Shadow's ears twist back and forth. I attempt to open my ears, seeing if I can hear what she hears.

Nothing.

The wind still sways the trees, and ravens still caw in the distance.

I shrug a shoulder and guide Shadow forward. Bear resumes the walk with us, practically prancing through the snow like a deer.

"I've come to the realization that I can't go back to New York now. I'm in too deep with these men."

Shadow snorts like she knew before I did.

"I'll have to find an apartment to rent. It needs to have studio space, though. I've missed painting. It's like someone has chopped off my arm and now I have to learn to live without it."

Shadow lets out a small nicker

"I hope the guys are excited about it too," I return with a shy smile. "Worst case scenario–"

Bear pauses mid-step, and his hackles slowly rise.

Shadow and I stop with him, the hairs on the back of my neck standing on end.

Bear's ears point toward the trees.

"What're you looking at, Bear?"

Silence continues to be the only answer.

I wait a minute to satisfy Bear, then guide the three of us to resume.

This time, I don't say a word, listening intently for any sound at all. The trees get closer and closer to the footpath, narrowing the space.

A twig snaps behind us, causing me to jump and turn around.

But the shaded path is empty.

I shake my head side to side, attempting to dispel all unnecessary anxious thoughts, and push on forward again.

I've only taken a couple of steps when a bush beside the path rattles.

My grip on the lead tightens, forcing the polyester fibers to bite into my palm.

It's a squirrel.

Or a bird.

Except it's winter. Squirrels hibernate, and birds fly south.

Quickening my pace, I pull Shadow rather than lead her like I'm supposed to. My breath turns into shallow gasps as my chest rises and falls in rapid succession.

A blur of warm gray darts in my path and emits a low growl.

Bear's protective stance in front of Shadow and me turns into a predatory bow.

A drop of sweat rolls down my spine as my knees tremble, threatening to give out.

My voice is tight, cracking slightly as I shout into the trees. "H–hello?"

Nothing.

My words don't even echo through the wooded area.

Forcing my pitch up an octave, I call out again. "If someone is out there..."

Nothing.

The trees don't sway.

The snow doesn't fall.

The stab of terror in my gut is almost unbearable.

Keeping my attention on our surroundings, I turn Shadow back around. "Okay, that's enough walking for today. Let's go back."

Bear takes the lead this time, setting a jogging pace for the three of us.

My breaths come harder.

Quicker.

Heavier.

I'm no longer a princess in an enchanted fairytale. I'm more like the damsel running away from the mysterious evil spirit that haunts her.

A deafening crash reverberates through the wood.

My heart stops, and I'm unable to move.

Fear takes over every muscle in my body.

Shadow lets out a squeal and stomps her hooves, while Bear takes up his hostile stance, showing his teeth as he growls at the threat.

A crack of a fallen branch.

The snap of a twig.

Oh God.

My breath quickens, and my muscles become so tense to the point of shaking.

A patch of sagebrush shivers in the cold.

Every nerve in my body stands on end, waiting for the doom to reach us.

The snow clinging to the brush explodes outward as a white-tailed deer jumps from behind the foliage.

My heart almost leaps out of my chest as I startle.

The antlered buck stops in the middle of the trail, sniffs the air, and capers off.

The laugh that bursts out of my mouth is involuntary and accompanied by tears. I'm not sure if I'm crying in relief or joy.

"You just took ten years off my life, Bambi!" I bellow.

Blowing out a large breath, I look at Bear and Shadow. "Let's go home."

My hands won't stop shaking. It's so bad that I can't even keep hold of the rope anymore. It slips out of my grasp three times before I just give up and send up a plea to the universe that Shadow doesn't choose this moment to run away.

Sounds of life reach my ears, letting me know we're almost back, when Bear bends his head down and sniffs.

"What now?" I ask exasperated, not in the mood for another critter visitor.

With his nose to the ground, Bear walks back and forth, side to side, and in circles. I'm about ready to pick him up and go straight to Levi to demand a checkup when Bear stops, turns his head to me, and lets out a single bark.

Not one of alarm or warning.

More like trying to tell me something.

Hesitantly, I take measured steps toward him. Shadow keeps pace with me. "What did you find, boy?"

He yips one more time and uses his nose to point to four small twigs.

No.

Not twigs.

Cigarette butts, still smoldering.

Was...Was Walker out here? Was he following me? What the hell? Is this his idea of a joke?

Crouching down, I search the snow. Footprints much larger than mine litter the area. My hands ball into fists.

That fucker better pray he can get into WITSEC because I am coming for him.

Rational thought and I are not compatible right now.

Swiping the evidence from the snow, I march the rest of the way. My fury doesn't diminish even a fraction.

Hammering and whirring of tools causes a throb to stir in my head.

Stepping off the trail, Falling Sky comes back into view. Javier, Santiago, Levi, and Walker all hang on the fencing of the corral where I first spoke to Javier earlier. Their arms hang over the top as they watch Jack work his magic with another horse.

They must feel the raging storm that is my energy because all five heads swing to me.

But the ferocity in my eyes is only meant for one.

Walker Maddox.

He furrows his brows and advances to meet me.

Dead man walking.

Shadow and Bear scamper off together. I'm not sure where, and at this moment, I can't say I care.

When Walker gets within arms length, I thrust my hands forward and shove with all my might.

But he doesn't budge, which angers me more.

I try again.

And again.

No result.

The snarl that rumbles from my chest is purely feral.

Walker, done with being my punching bag, captures my wrists and pulls me close. "What's wrong?"

"You." I attempt to slam my fist into his gut, but Walker is stronger than me. Always has been and probably always will be.

I hate that a part of me loves that right now.

Walker shakes his head. "You're not making sense."

"Were you following me?" I shout.

Walker's brows squish together. "Why would I follow you?"

"You tell me." I rip my hands out of his grasp. I know the only reason I'm successful is because he let me.

Instead of yelling again, I throw the cigarette butts at him. They hit his chest and fall to the ground. He bends and picks one up.

He holds it between us. "What is this? Are you trying to tell me that you're smoking?"

"Those are yours, you prick. I know you were trying to spook me. Probably trying to teach me a lesson for going on a walk without a buddy." My hands tighten into fists at my sides.

"I don't smoke clove cigarettes." Walker raises a brow.

The dread from earlier returns with a vengeance. "If...if those aren't..."

Walker turns his head and lets out a piercing whistle, gaining the attention of everyone in the immediate area. "Hey! Does anyone here smoke clove cigarettes?"

Santiago and Levi make a face expressing their disgust. Javier and Jack shake their heads in denial.

The rush of my increasing pulse makes it feel like I'm underwater, muffling voices and noises.

"Santi, check with the crew," Walker directs, descending into sheriff mode.

My vision is on the verge of going black when large, calloused hands frame my face. "Baby Girl, look at me and breathe."

Blinking, I try to force Walker's face to come into focus. "What?"

He bends, bringing our noses closer. "Baby Girl, I need you to talk to me."

The contact grounds me back to this moment with Walker.

Swallowing, I nod, gathering my thoughts and words.

Santiago and Levi join us, flanking me on either side. Their presence brings an added sense of safety.

"Start from the beginning."

I do.

I tell them about Javier asking me to walk Shadow. About the trail. About Shadow stopping and Bear growling. How the snapping of twigs and branches turned out to be a deer. The cigarette butts. The footprints. The feeling that someone had been there the entire time, watching me.

Throughout my story, no one interrupts me.

The only sounds are hammers striking lumber at the new barn and the distant whinny of a horse.

Walker rubs a hand over his mouth. Levi's jaw is so tight I'm surprised he doesn't crack a tooth. Santiago stares toward the tree line where I'd just come from, his expression unreadable.

Walker crouches down and picks up the rest of the butts,

pulling an evidence bag from his coat and placing the evidence inside.

He must always carry those around.

"Nobody touches the trail," Walker commands. "And nobody leaves until they've been questioned, including the ranch hands and the construction crew."

"Walk—" Santiago starts.

"I'm not asking," Walker snaps.

My phone buzzes in my pants pocket. Tapping on the text, a prickling sensation shoots up my spine. My pulse roars in my throat.

Wordlessly, I hand my phone over to Walker. His eyes narrow, not understanding why I'm giving him my cell. When he reads the message on the screen, a livid spasm crosses his face.

"Fuck."

Unknown: Nice day for a walk.

CHAPTER 44

BLAKE

The week after my walk with Shadow settles into an unexpected routine.

Every morning, hammers echo across Falling Sky while the new barn slowly replaces the one Manny burned to the ground. Every evening, the four of us collapse around Santiago's kitchen table for dinner before arguing over whose turn it is to wash dishes.

The investigation also never really stops.

Walker comes home with another stack of files almost every night. Levi disappears to compare timelines or review autopsy reports. Santiago rides fence lines with the wranglers during the day and somehow still finds time to help Walker chase leads after dark.

The guys haven't officially taken me off the case, but every time I try to help, they steer my attention in a different direction.

Then there are the cameras.

After someone followed me down the south trail, Walker refused to leave anything to chance. Trail cameras now watch every road into Falling Sky, the creek crossing, the tree line, and nearly every game trail leading onto the property.

According to Walker, no one is setting foot on the ranch again without us knowing.

I tell myself they make me feel safer, but really, they remind me that someone is still out there.

The smell of fresh-cut pine greets me before I even step inside the barn's skeleton. Sawdust floats through shafts of Sunday afternoon light filtering between the rafters. The big sliding doors are wide open, allowing a cool winter breeze to roll through.

A week ago, this place still smelled like smoke. Today it smells like lumber.

Apparently, healing has a scent.

I stop in the doorway and watch my three men work for a minute. The construction crew doesn't work on Sundays. Walker cleared them all himself last week after the unfortunate incident on the trail.

I refuse to label it as anything other than an unfortunate incident right now.

Walker's face is so close to a level he balances on the wall, I'm surprised he doesn't go cross-eyed. Levi and Santiago work together to hold up a giant framed wall.

Walker squints at the bubble in the level. "A little more."

Santiago and Levi grunt as they adjust the wall.

"A little more."

More grunts.

"More."

"You're going to have to be more specific," Santiago murmurs in a strained voice.

Levi groans. "You two stop your yammering before one of us drops this thing."

"You're doing it wrong," Santiago criticizes Walker.

Walker snorts. "I've been building barns longer than you've been alive."

"Lies!" Santiago accuses. "You're only a year older than me."

"It *feels* true," Walker grumbles.

I don't interrupt. Watching the three of them bicker has

become one of my favorite pastimes. They fight like family. Five minutes after they threaten each other with bodily harm, they're laughing as if nothing happened.

Santiago notices me first and smiles immediately. Walker gives me a quick glance. Levi blushes.

I wave in greeting. "Hey, guys! How can I help?"

Their heads swivel to each other. They have an entire conversation with just eye squints, frowns, and arched brows. They don't utter a single word. They nod to each other, coming to some sort of an agreement.

Walker snags a few bulky Folger's coffee cans. "We need these separated." He plunks them onto the concrete at my feet.

Peering down, I find each can filled to the brim with a variety of nails and screws. I do a slow blink. "That's the job you're giving me? Organizing nails?"

Levi guffaws unrestrained. "I'm not giving you a hammer."

I frown at him. "Why not?"

"We don't need anyone getting hit in the head," Levi remarks.

I cross my arms. "Human heads don't look like nails. I think we're good there."

Walker quirks a brow. "Between the three of us, we're bound to say something stupid. Something that will probably warrant a hammer to the head."

"Speak for yourself," Santiago smirks.

Lowering myself to the concrete foundation, I cross my legs and start sorting.

The bang of hammers turns into a cadenced tune that fills the comfortable silence. Every now and then, one of them asks for another board or a handful of screws for the wall blocking, and I retrieve it for them.

Without realizing it, I fall into their rhythm, finding where I'm comfortable.

Martha's words of caution from last week drift to the front of my mind.

The history between those four is complicated.

My indecision to bring it up causes me to drop a two-by-four on Levi's hand. He gives me a deadpan look as he tries to shake off the pain.

Levi mutters under his breath, "And you wanted me to give you a hammer."

My eyes dart all over the unfinished space, and my toes curl in my shoes.

"I need to ask you something," I blurt out.

The three of them freeze.

Santiago holds a hammer in the air, ready to swing it at the nail in his other hand. Levi slowly sets his drill down. Walker straightens from his stooped position, leaving his tools on the ground. They face me together, standing side by side.

Santiago's eyes narrow skeptically. "I'm not sure I like where this is going."

"You can tell me it's none of my business if you don't want to answer," I reply, holding up my hands in defense.

"Why don't you talk to Grant anymore?"

No one answers.

Santiago doesn't even try to hide his surprise. Levi's expression is grim. Walker empties his of emotion.

The emptiness of the barn has never felt so full.

Three pairs of eyes meet, silently passing the conversation between them before anyone speaks.

My stomach tightens.

Whatever happened with Grant is bigger than I thought.

Walker cocks an eyebrow. "Why?"

I throw my arms up in frustration. "It's like everyone warns me about him but won't tell me why.

"Grant..." Walker's gaze focuses on the ground as if he's searching for the right words. "He wasn't always the man he is now."

My brows raise slowly as I await clarification. "What happened?"

Levi's chest expands as his shoulders pull back. "Something we should've handled differently." His tone is menacing.

"We all made mistakes." Santiago's fists tremble with rage. "People got hurt."

Blinking, I attempt to see past their vague answers, but their ambiguity is working in their favor.

"Did Grant hurt someone?" My lips press tightly together.

Walker nods. "Yes."

My hand rubs my eyes. "Did he hurt you?"

Levi lets out a sharp breath. "Not directly."

I'm done with this brain teaser.

My shoulders fall. "Then why can't you tell me?"

"Necesito que confíes en nostros, mi Cielo." *We need you to trust us, my sky.*

Levi's expression softens. "We'll tell you everything, just not today, Butterfly."

My fists rest on my hips. "And who decides when I get to know?"

"We do," Walker replies.

"You're choosing for me?" I accuse, frustration charging my tone.

"Yeah," Walker admits. "I am." His eyes analyze my every mannerism and expression, then his shoulders rise and fall with a steadying breath. "And if you hate me for it later, I'll live with that."

Santiago bravely steps forward, rubbing his hands over my upper arms. "I know asking you to trust us isn't fair, especially after everything. But we're asking anyway."

If it's possible to be in a state of unfettered rage and pure, undiluted captivation…

I'm there.

They each carry a real fear that comes from my knowing, and it has them petrified.

They're even willing to carry my hate.

I give them a slight nod. "Okay."

Walker visibly relaxes. Levi lets out a long breath.

Santiago stands there smiling down at me. He places a kiss on the top of my head, and the three of them turn back to finish the wall.

"So..." fidgeting with my fingers, I move a little closer. "Since I'm trusting you with this, do you think you could trust me with a hammer?"

"Absolutely not." Levi's response is immediate. "I've seen your temper."

I shoot him a glare and point. "You're back on the shit list, Levi Harding."

Levi spins back around, a roguish look on his face as he shoves his tools at Walker. "I could always repeat what we did last time to get me off the list."

Santiago feigns ignorance, setting his tools on the ground. "What did you guys do last time?"

Walker drops the power tools, not caring that he very likely just broke them all. "I think we all know what they did."

"Our girl's a screamer," Levi smirks.

Levi, Santiago, and Walker stalk toward me, and suddenly, I feel like prey.

It's exhilarating.

My footsteps move me backward out of the barn as I come up with a way to make this interesting. "Whoever catches me first gets to pick the position."

Santiago's brows shoot up, Walker's eyes smolder, and Levi's lips curve into a sinful smile.

"If we're good with that..." I start, then turn on my heel and bolt out the open barn doors. My heart races as I pump my arms, lengthening my stride.

I don't know where I'm going. I don't have a destination in mind, but I find myself racing up the steps of the back porch.

My hand grips the knob of the door when a pair of arms

encircle my middle and haul me off my feet. I yelp as footsteps thunder closer.

In my ear, a deep voice growls. "Guess I'm the winner, Butterfly."

My core clenches, emphasizing the fact that I'm empty and desperate to be filled.

The four of us pant, catching our breath as Levi rips open the door and marches inside with me in his arms.

Levi leads the way to the living room, where he sets me down on the animal rug in front of the burning fireplace.

I quickly dress down to my bra and thong, sitting comfortably on the rug. "So what's it going to be, Harding?"

"It depends. Walk, are you willing to try something?"

Walker squints, mulling it over for a moment. "What kind of something?"

"You'll like it, I promise." Levi winks.

He actually *winks* at Walker.

Walker shocks us all when he says, "Let's do it."

Walker isn't a prude. He doesn't judge anyone for who they love. But if he wants to try it out, I'm so excited.

Levi rips his shirt off over his head and lies down on the rug. "Butterfly, come sit on my face."

My panties flood.

I crawl over to Levi. When I'm close enough, Levi impatiently grips my hips and hauls me into his lap. "Let's give them a good show."

Something in my stomach flutters in anticipation, more than ready for whatever he has in mind.

Levi unclasps my bra, flinging it toward Santiago and Walker, then he lowers his head and lifts my breast to his mouth at the same time. His mouth closes over the tip and sucks.

I cry out, bowing my back and pushing my breast further into his mouth.

He moans around my nipple, sending a jolt of bliss straight to my core.

Turning my gaze to Santiago and Walker, I find Walker undressing, and Santiago is already down to his boxers with his hand beneath the waistband. The movements he makes behind the fabric with his hand make it clear what he's doing.

And it's just from watching me get my tit sucked.

A sense of pride and empowerment encourages me to continue.

My needy pussy grinds down into Levi's lap, desperate for friction. Levi pushes his hips upward, pushing his hard length right where I need it, but a small sense of frustration nags at me.

"Too many clothes," I whine.

Levi releases my boob with a pop. "In due time, Blake. Patience."

I tilt his head to get him to look me right in the eye. "I've never been a patient woman, Levi."

"I won fair and square, and now you have to deliver."

I growl. A full-on growl. "Then hurry up."

Levi smirks, grips my hips, and flips me over onto my hands and knees with my ass in his face. His hands gently glide over my cheeks, then one palm comes down on the skin with a resounding smack.

I jolt forward in surprise, but the sting quickly turns into a pleasurable tingle.

I feel the thin scrap of my thong soak through.

Levi's palm connects with the other cheek, but this time I'm ready. The sting fades quicker this time, and I shove my ass back toward his face.

"Feeling greedy, Butterfly?"

I nod, unable to form words.

I glance over toward Santiago and Walker again. This time, they're completely naked, each pumps their own shafts, and their eyes concentrate on my ass.

"Are you wet, Blake?"

I nod again.

"I think I need to check for myself."

I moan, burying my face into the rug, thrusting my ass higher in the air.

I feel as Levi kneels behind me and slips my thong over my hips and down my thighs. I lift my legs one and a time to help him get them all the way off.

I peel over my shoulder and find him bringing the fabric to his nose and inhaling deeply. "Fuck," he groans, then tosses my panties toward Walker, who catches them with ease, keeping the slow pace he set with his other hand. He takes his turn breathing in my scent, then passes them to Santiago, who shoves the fabric in his mouth, gagging himself as he tastes me.

An uncontrolled whimper falls from my lips, my center throbbing, yearning for any type of attention.

"You see that, Blake? You see what you do to them?"

I nod again.

"You make us crazy."

"Please," I beg Levi.

"Since you asked nicely," Levi teases.

I feel his heat disappear from my back, then his legs land on either side of me as he grasps my hips and hauls me backward.

I yelp in surprise, then yelp again when I feel something wet and smooth slip through my folds and glide from ass to clit.

I sit up, realizing Levi's face is right under my core, eating me like a starving man.

Throwing my head back, I shout as the sensations rip through my body, overtaking my senses.

Levi stops for a moment, throwing out directions, but I don't hear him. The ringing in my ears is too loud.

Suddenly, Santiago appears in front of me, kissing me and thrusting his tongue in my mouth the same way Levi's was just in my pussy.

A hand guides me to lean forward, as a thick, hard cock enters me from behind. A quick look behind me, and I find Walker kneeling and pushing into my channel. Once he's fully seated, Levi adds his tongue, and I swear I choke on thin air.

"Oh. My."

Santiago cuts me off with another kiss. "Don't you dare scream for God right now. He's not here."

"Santi, please."

"That's right, *mi Cielo*. Beg for *us*."

Walker and Levi work together, licking and pumping into me. Walker's groans grow louder and louder.

Santiago dips his head, taking Levi's dick into his mouth and giving me a front row seat.

Shit, that's hot.

Santiago's mouth glides up and down, Levi's length disappearing into his mouth.

Pure need urging me forward, I dip my head and help. Santiago and I find a rhythm, taking turns sucking and licking.

Walker's thrusts become erratic, and Levi's tongue zeroes in on my clit, giving it extra attention.

I moan around Levi's cock, and in turn, he moans into my pussy, vibrating it.

A chain reaction sets off.

Levi erupts, his cum filling my mouth.

Walker goes next, spending his seed in my pussy, and Levi licks the drops that escape.

My mouth full of cum, I motion for Santiago to come closer. When he does, I use Levi's seed to wet Santiago's dick. His eyes go wide at the sight.

Levi continues eating my pussy as I suck down Santiago.

It isn't long before Santiago is shouting his release, and I'm shouting mine as I'm drowned in bliss, my pussy convulsing

We collapse into a heap. I'm not sure where one person ends, and the other begins, and I like it that way.

Covered in each other's cum and sweat, Walker cuddles me from behind, plastering my back to his chest, while Levi and Santiago hold each other.

We'll get up soon, but right now, we just bask in this moment of complete satisfaction.

As I watch the flames dance in the fireplace, I remember my question from earlier…

They may have fucked me speechless, but I'm no fool.

I'll find out what happened between them and Grant one way or another.

CHAPTER 45

LEVI

The sun rises as Blake and I make breakfast together. It's the perfect scene. Even when she burns the toast. I will happily eat charred bread if it means I get to be with her.

Blake considers the buddy system to be...patronizing.

She complains about it every morning.

And I ignore her every morning.

"When can we eighty-six the buddy system?" Blakes asks around a mouthful of scrambled eggs.

"You know why we're doing this."

I smile and take a bite of my scorched toast. My gag reflex is immediate, but I don't want Blake to feel bad, so I use my coffee to help me swallow it down.

And now I have to eat the whole slice, so she doesn't feel bad.

Maybe I'll make the toast tomorrow.

Blake sighs theatrically, unaware of my toast conundrum. "I know. I'm just getting cabin fever."

Walker treads down the staircase, dressed for another day as Evergreen Falls's finest.

Blake mumbles into her coffee, "*He* doesn't have to have a buddy."

Walker's radio crackles, and Jolene's voice comes through. "Walk." Walker sighs, lifting his face toward the ceiling.

"Walk, pick up the damn radio," Jolene demands.

Reluctantly, he reaches for the radio and responds. "Yeah, I'm here, Jo."

"There's a garage fire at Jill Becker's house. Fire Department is already on scene and requesting law enforcement."

Walker's hand massages his temples. "I'm on my way."

The warmth that had settled over the room vanishes.

My appetite disappears.

Walker is already reaching for his jacket. Blake has her phone out and dials Santiago to tell him what's going on.

Walker opted to drive his own truck, seeing as how he'll probably have to stay longer than us. Blake, Santiago, and I jumped into Santiago's GMC. Knowing we'd argue over who gets to sit next to Blake, Santiago lifted the center console and converted it into a jumper seat for Blake.

Twenty minutes later, we're winding through the back roads north of town.

Smoke looks different to me now. When I see it, my chest tightens before my brain can catch up.

My stomach knots before we even reach the driveway, but I shove it aside.

It's not Blake. It's not Santiago. They're not in the fire.

When we arrive, the worst of the flames have already been knocked down.

Thick gray smoke curls from the open garage, drifting lazily across the driveway. Firefighters move with practiced efficiency, dragging blackened hoses through puddles that reflect flashing red lights. Steam rises where freezing air collides with scorched concrete, wrapping the property in a ghostly haze.

The sharp scent of the smoke hangs heavy in the air. It settles in the back of my throat.

Some smells never really leave you.

We meet Walker by the curb, waiting for his direction.

A flash of déjà vu hits me square in the chest. My eyes blink rapidly as I glance around the scene, searching for the familiar sight.

Scratching the back of my head, I question, "Does this scene feel familiar to anyone else?"

Walker scans our surroundings. "What?"

"Evan Lockhart," I answer.

Understanding dawns on Walker and Santiago's faces.

Blake's face scrunches. "Who is Evan Lockhart?"

Walker shifts on his feet, uneasy. "He..."

"He had a garage fire like this as well," Santiago explains to Blake.

Fire Chief Tad Jenson strolls over to where we stand. "Thanks for coming, Sheriff."

Walker shakes Tad's hand. "Anytime." He turns to Santiago and directs, "You and Blake walk the perimeter and set up the crime scene tape. There's a roll in my truck."

"On it," Santiago replies.

Blake lifts her hands, palms up, while shrugging her shoulders. "I'm in no way qualified for any of this, but sure. I'll help."

"You're a volunteer," Walker reminds her.

"For forensic art. Not forensic science," Blake sasses, and strides after Santiago.

Walker tips his head to Tad, lowering his voice and motioning me to step forward and join the conversation.

"Is there anything about this fire that sticks out to you?'

"Yeah. Lockhart."

"Is it just because the fire is in the garage?" Walker interrogates.

Tad shakes his head. "No. Same burn pattern, same accelerant, and same point of origin."

Walker straightens his spine. "Thanks, Tad. I'll start working things from my end."

Tad gives Walker an appreciative nod and returns to his team.

Walker and I pace away, taking ourselves out of earshot.

"But Derek Holt..." He starts, staring at the concrete as if it holds all the answers.

"Was never setting garages on fire," I finish for him.

"That means Evergreen Falls has," Walker corrects himself, "*had* two arsonists."

"What are the odds of that?" I question out loud with a frown.

"Less than one percent," Walker responds. "And they're usually juveniles, so we're either looking for a teenager or an anomaly."

"If this is a repeat of Evan Lockhart's house, then we should sweep the house," I suggest.

Walker and I are mulling over new theories when we hear, "Blake!"

The way Santiago shouts her name causes the blood to drain from my face.

Walker and I break into a sprint for Blake. There's no hesitation, no pause. I don't know what's happening, but I don't need to.

I will always show up for the woman I love.

Santiago kneels next to Blake in the grass on the side of the house, examining her hand. Dark red liquid drips onto the freshly fallen white powder.

We dropped to our knees beside them, ignoring the freezing snow soaking the knees of my pants.

"What happened?" Walker questions frantically.

"I'm fine, I promise," Blake claims.

"Santiago, go get the first aid kit from my truck. Levi, give me your jacket." Walker directs.

Without question, Santiago and I spring into action. He runs off toward Walker's truck, and I rip off my coat. Walker uses it to apply pressure to her wounds.

Blake lets out a hiss of pain.

Santiago returns, crashing down to his knees and opening the container. He hands Walker the supplies he needs.

Lifting a little bit of fabric from her skin, Walker examines the state of her hands. "Shit," he curses.

I peek at her hand, and my stomach contracts into a tight ball.

A large gash crosses her left palm, and a few smaller ones along her fingers.

"That's it." Walker shakes his head, frustrated. "You're done. No more crime scenes for you."

"Done?" Blake's brows rise. "It's just a cut."

"He's right," Santiago agrees.

"What?" Blake gapes at him.

"Butterfly," I rest my hand on her shoulder. "This isn't a punishment."

"But—" she starts.

I keep my voice low and calm. "We're going to worry, and then we won't be able to do our jobs."

"I work for the police department just like you guys." Her eyes dart to the side. She knows her argument is weak.

Santiago's expression turns inscrutable. "You're a volunteer."

Blake's brows furrow. "Volunteers are people too."

"Then you're fired," Walker clips as he wraps her cut with gauze.

"You can't fire me," Blake argues. "Jo said only she can do that."

"Jo's delusional," Walker quips.

Blake's face softens. "You guys can't keep me in bubble wrap forever."

"Mírame," Watch me.

Blake's eyes meet mine. I silently plead with her to understand.

I would do anything, sacrifice anything, if it meant she never had to know pain again. Just the thought of her being hurt, even by accident, racks me with torment.

She lets out a sigh, and her gaze drops to her hand. "I don't like it, but after what happened in the woods..." Her lips turn downward. "I'm willing to try."

The three of us let out audible breaths. It's like someone just took a portion of the stress off our plates and threw it out the window.

"I'll take you back to Falling Sky," Santiago offers.

We escort Blake back to the truck, but on the way, a small

brown object in the snow stands out. I let them continue, and I crouch down to get a closer look.

It's a cigarette butt.

A *clove* cigarette butt.

My heartbeat kicks hard against my ribs as I stare at the evidence that we could have easily missed.

It wasn't just the woods.

Whoever followed Blake before is still following her.

CHAPTER 46

WALKER

Sweat drips down my neck as I check the level of the floating shelf for the third time.

It's level.

It was level the first two times as well.

Doesn't stop me from checking again.

After the weekend I had, trying to light a fire under the asses of the people at the crime lab in Cheyenne, I was ready to hit something—or someone.

If I had the skills, I'd perform the DNA tests on the DNA from Bear's mouth and the clove cigarettes myself. I thought I'd have the DNA profile back by now, but I'm still waiting.

Waiting isn't my strength.

So I took all that energy and channeled it into finishing this project.

The rest of the barn still looks like a construction site.

Open studs, exposed wiring, half-finished stalls, dust.

But this room just needs the finishing touches.

Moonlight pours in through the three large windows and French door along the north wall, washing the room in soft, natural light. That's the first thing I researched.

Artists want light. Natural light.

The walls are painted a warm ivory instead of unfinished barn wood. The vaulted ceiling leaves the exposed timber trusses visible above, giving the room enough height for oversized canvases without making it feel cavernous. Every light fixture hangs on its own switch, so she can brighten one corner without washing out the entire room. Ventilation ductwork disappears into the ceiling, quietly pulling away paint fumes.

Cabinets and a counter line the south wall from floor to ceiling, and floating shelves fill half of the east wall. Among the cabinets on the south wall is a deep utility sink, and the counter contains jars of brushes. Narrow drying racks slide out from one side of the room like giant filing cabinets. Beside the drying racks, I installed vertical slots that hold blank canvases sorted by size.

If she has to spend most of her time at Falling Sky, I want her to have something here that's entirely her own.

Blake doesn't realize it, but she's always rubbing her fingertips together or opening and closing her hand as if she's missing something.

A paintbrush.

Every time I saw it, I wanted to fix it. I wanted to be able to pull a brush out of thin air and hand it to her.

In the last week, the analytical look in her eye has faded. She used to look at the Snake River Mountains as if she wanted to capture them on her canvas, planning how she'd mix her paints to get the colors right.

Deeming the shelves sufficient, I return to assembling the easels by the windows. I cut enough wood for three.

One large enough for oversized canvases.

One tabletop model.

One lighter so she can drag it outside if she wants.

After these, I just need to finish the patio I started on the outside of the north wall, but I figured she wouldn't use it until the summer.

With my back to the open door, I listen as footsteps tread into the room. Santiago and Levi have come around this time, the last few nights, to help.

"Can you hand me the screwdriver with the red handle? It should be on the counter by the sink."

"Walker?"

My body goes rigid as I slowly turn around. Blake stands in the doorway with wide eyes.

She's dressed like she was about to go to bed. She's wearing one of my hoodies that hangs down to her mid-thigh and slippers. Her legs are bare as if she's not wearing anything underneath.

The thought of being able to slip my hand under the hem and find her bare has my cock growing stiff.

Blake takes a step into the room and wanders to the cabinets to her left. She opens them one at a time and explores their contents. I filled them with supplies this morning. Everything from paint thinner and paper towels to every color of oil paint that I could find.

My stomach turns in knots, waiting for her to say something.

She moves to the drawers, pulling them open one at a time and examining the blank canvases I stocked for her.

Next, her steps lead her to me. She stares up at me, and I can't quite make out the look on her face.

"What is all this?"

I swallow hard. "It's your studio."

Tears fill her eyes, and mine almost follow. "You built me a studio?"

"I built you a studio," I confirm.

"You built me a studio," she repeats, turning back around to take it all in.

I lean to the side, trying to get a glimpse at her face. "Did I get the right stuff?"

"Yes," she answers softly. She moves to the stool beside me, takes a seat, and waves her hand at the wood. "What're these?"

I take a step back to show her. "Easels. This one is heavy and sturdy to hold larger canvases, and I'm finishing a tabletop one and a portable one you can take outside on the patio."

She blinks. "Patio?"

"Yes," I reply, motioning outside the window. "It's not finished yet."

Blake stands and runs her fingers over the finished easel. "I don't think I've ever owned one this nice." She releases a single laugh. "I never owned a new easel. In New York, I bought a lot of things secondhand to scrimp and save."

Words get stuck in my throat.

Blake takes measured steps to close the distance between us. She reaches for my hand, lifting it as she runs her fingers over my knuckles. "Why do you keep doing things like this?"

She peers up at me through wet lashes.

"Because I love you."

For a second, my heartbeat stammers, causing a tidal wave of nausea to build in my stomach.

I've stood in burning buildings. I've had guns pointed at my chest.

But none of that has ever left me feeling this unsteady, waiting for her reply.

Blake smiles at me in a way I've never seen before.

"Good."

My brows shoot up.

"Good?"

She drops my hand, encircling my waist with her arms. "Because I love you too."

My heart stops, and I forget how to breathe.

Her words hit harder than any punch I've ever taken. Not because they hurt.

Because I don't know what to do with something this good.

The only thing I can think is: *She chose me.*

CHAPTER 47

BLAKE

He built me a studio. A fully stocked dream studio.

Love isn't always loud. Sometimes it's in the little things, like a cup of coffee made just the way I like it or giving me his jacket when I'm cold.

But sometimes love looks like an entire art studio because he knows how much you love painting.

I don't know exactly when I fell in love with them—Santiago, Levi, and Walker.

But it happened.

These men have captured my heart, and I don't want them to give it back.

My head rests against Walker's chest with his arms around me as we stand in the studio he built for me.

Santiago appears in the doorway, brushing sawdust from his jeans, and his gaze lands on me. His expression goes through a million emotions. Confusion, concern, shock, love.

A smirk curves one side of his mouth. "I take it she likes it."

A watery laugh slips from my mouth, and I nod. "I love it."

Santiago steps further inside, "I helped pick out the windows."

My watery laugh turns joyful. "Oh, yeah?"

A sly thought makes my smile shift into something downright sinful.

I take a step back and drop my arms, prompting Walker to do the same.

"I guess I need to find a way to thank you two."

Santiago's brows almost shoot right off his face, and Walker does a slow blink.

Reaching the stool, I sit on the edge and spread my legs, revealing my lack of panties. Santiago looks as if he's about to fall on his knees. The heat in Walker's eyes makes me think I might be in trouble.

I tug on the hem, pulling it up further.

"Ay Dios mío." Oh my God.

Santiago practically sprints across the room, but Walker gets to me first, charging at me like a bull. He grips my wrist, yanking me to my feet.

My heart stutters in excitement.

Walker bends, bringing his face close to mine. "Are you telling me that you came all the way out here, risking the possibility of passing wranglers, without any panties on while wearing *my* clothes?"

My thighs clench, needy and empty. "Not *clothes*. I'm only wearing one thing of yours."

"It seems to me you're just wearing one thing. Period," he barks.

"I guess you'll have to find out for yourself," I sass.

"Walker Maddox," Santiago says sternly, "If you're not going to join, then you need to leave because I'm fucking our girl one way or another."

Walker's eyes remain on my face. "Oh, we're fucking her alright. She just may need to learn a lesson in the process.

I can't control the whimper that escapes me.

"On your knees," Walker commands.

The anticipation of what's about to happen is almost too much. I'm ready to explode.

I kick off my shoes and immediately fall to my knees.

Walker quickly works to undo his pants, releasing his stiff length. "You're going to suck us off until we come all over you, Baby Girl. Got it?"

I nod, conveying my excitement.

Walker spears his hand into my hair. "Sweatshirt off." The top is off and cast aside in the blink of an eye.

I sit up on my knees, reaching for Walker's cock, but he steps back. "You take what I give you, Blake."

Shooting him a frown, he lets out a chuckle.

"This is too hot for words," Santiago breathes out, staring at us both.

Walker steers my head in Santiago's direction. "Crawl to him, Baby Girl."

Oh, my hell. I'm going to die. This is how I die.

Death by arousal.

"Santiago, pants down. Unless you want to watch instead."

"I'd like to be an active participant," Santiago stammers, pulling his dick out of his jeans.

Placing my hands on the floor, I let my ass and tits sway with each movement forward. Before I reach Santiago, I take a glimpse over my shoulder.

Walker has his hand around his cock, pumping his fist up and down his shaft, his eyes glued on my ass.

Before I push off my hands, I tilt my hips, flashing my pussy at him. The growl that thunders in his chest, has my arousal dripping down my thighs.

I reach Santiago and immediately go for his hardness. Resting my hands on his thighs, I lick the tip. Santiago sounds like he's about to choke.

Taking him into my mouth, I suck as I slip my lips closer to the base. When he hits the back of my throat, I gag.

Santiago's hand reaches down, brushing my hair away from my face. I peer up at him through my lashes. He bites the fist of his other hand, holding in his shouts.

That won't do.

I want him undone.

I use one hand to cup his balls, massaging them, as I suck him down again. This time, when his tip reaches my throat, I breathe through my nose and swallow him down.

My other hand slips between my thighs, finding my core dripping.

A hand grasps my wrist, pulling my fingers away from the apex of my thighs. Walker grumbles into my ear, "Brats don't get to come yet."

I whimper around Santiago's length, and I swear his knees shake.

Walker stands beside Santiago, and I decide to turn the tables.

Pulling back, Santiago's cock releases from my mouth with a pop. I smirk up at Walker and position myself between him and Santiago.

Walker gives me a suspicious look, and my smile widens.

I balance myself by placing my hands on their thighs.

My mouth closes around Walker, the taste of him gliding over my tongue. I hum in excitement, causing Walker to moan. I take him as far into my mouth as possible, then pull away.

Switching to Santiago, I do the same, then back off.

When I go back to Walker, I pump Santiago's length with my hand. As I suck Walker down, I run my tongue on the underside of his cock. Drool falls down my chin, making a mess of myself, but I don't care.

"Ah, fuck," Walker grunts as I hollow my cheeks, swallowing him down my throat.

I feel the slickness between my thighs, my pussy needing to feel full.

"Keep going, Baby Girl. You're being such a good girl. Your punishment is almost over."

I double my efforts, sucking them harder, flicking my tongue over the parts that make them crazy.

When I start to feel their cocks grow even harder, I sit back, using my hands to finish them off.

Santiago's release comes first. He shouts, his words echoing off the walls.

I aim this tip toward my chest, allowing his warm ropes of cum to paint my chest and my neck.

Walker follows shortly, Santiago is still working through his climax. Walker's seed mixes with Santiago's landing on my tits and covering my hands.

Once I've wrung out every drop of pleasure from them, I release their cocks, and they stare down at me, their eyes wide with amazement.

I keep my eyes locked with theirs as I drag my finger through the mess on my chest and bring it to my mouth. I suck my finger the same way I sucked their shafts.

They groan in unison.

"Damn, that's sexy."

"So damn hot."

"Punishment over," Walker declares, lifting me up by my arms. "Santi, on your back."

Santiago rushes to do as Walker demands, lying on the floor. As he does, Walker leans down, capturing my lips with his, tasting a mix of himself and Santiago, groaning into my mouth.

When the kiss ends, he clenches his teeth, as if he's holding back.

Straddling Santi's thighs, I press my chest to his, my sensitive nipples dragging across his chest hair.

Walker kneels in between Santiago's legs behind me. He bends forward, placing his mouth by my ear. "We're both going to take your cunt, Baby Girl. At the same time. Think you can handle that?"

I nod vigorously, my channel clenching around nothing but air.

"Santiago, you first," Walker instructs.

"Don't have to tell me twice," Santiago comments.

We move our hips together, and I'm so wet that his shaft easily slips inside. We moan together, reveling in the sensation of our connection.

Walker presses a hand to my back, tipping me all the way forward, so my chest rests completely on Santiago's.

"Relax, Blake."

I nod, feeling his tip at my entrance.

I don't know how the hell he's going to fit, but I can't say I'm not excited.

At an agonizingly slow pace, Walker enters in shallow thrusts, less than an inch at a time.

My vision blurs, all I can focus on is how full I feel.

So incredibly full.

"Damn, Blake. You're so wet that I'm sliding right in," Walker grunts in my ear.

Santiago wraps his hand around the back of my head, pulls me down, and our lips meet. He nips at my lip, causing me to tense.

"Fuck, Santi. I need her *relaxed*."

Santiago lets out a remorseless laugh. "My bad."

Walker huffs, continuing to work his way inside. Each movement sends a rush of sensation throughout my body.

"Feel how good your greedy cunt takes us both, *mi Cielo*."

A small cry falls from my lips as my pussy floods with more arousal, allowing Walker to seat himself all the way inside.

Santiago's face almost looks pained. I smooth my finger between his brows. "Are you okay?"

Instead of answering me, he croaks out, "Walk, I fucking swear, I'm ready to blow."

"Me too," Walker pants, then sweeps my hair over one shoulder. "Are you ready?"

"Please, fucking hell, please," I whine.

I cry out as Walker and Santiago retreat from my heat. I'm readjusting when they plow back into me.

If anyone were listening, they'd think I was being tortured.

In the best way, I am.

The pleasure coursing through my veins is too much to handle. No single person can survive this much sensation at once.

Each hammer of their hips, each thrust into my core, steals my breath.

I sit right on the edge of my climax when Santiago captures my lips, and Walker sucks on my neck, launching me into a whirlwind of ecstasy.

Santiago and Walker find their own releases, slowing their thrusts until we're all spent, lying in a pile of bodies, sweat, and cum.

I've never felt so messy yet so content at the same time.

Walker places small kisses up my spine and to my neck, ending at my ear. "You did so well, Baby Girl."

I can't form words. They've literally fucked all of the words out of my brain.

"Mmm." I sigh with a smile.

I exist in space, somewhere between sleep and consciousness. I'm not sure what happens next. All I have are bits and flashes.

"She's not going to move," Santiago chuckles.

"Alright, come on, Ramirez. Let's get her showered and put to bed."

Next thing I know, I'm under a spray of warm water, and I realize their cum is being washed away.

A small cry falls from my mouth.

"Shh, *mi Cielo*. It's okay."

I'm not sure if I respond, but three deep snickers meet my ears.

I fade again, and when I come back, I'm dry, dressed in comfortable clothes, and lying in our bed. My head rests on a bare, firm chest that rises and falls with deep, sleep-filled breaths.

Our bed.

This is *our* bed.

Levi, Santiago, Walker, and me.

We share this space where we exist together, blocking out the world beyond these four walls.

Walker's arm is draped across my waist. Somewhere behind

me, Levi lets out a quiet sigh in his sleep. Santiago's fingers are still loosely tangled with mine, as though even unconscious he isn't quite ready to let go.

I never understood why people called a bed a safe haven.

A bed has always been a place I feared.

A place where nightmares began.

Somehow, they've turned it into the exact opposite.

Maybe this is what home was supposed to feel like all along.

CHAPTER 48

BLAKE

For the last week, when the guys have to leave for work, I haven't complained once, and I feel like that earns me a gold medal.

Then again, they gifted me a whole damn studio—the perfect place to spend my time.

Tonight, however, they're all acting a little weird. Instead of leaving me to paint, they're all in here watching me.

I've asked over and over whether everything is okay or if anything has come up in the case, but they all insist that nothing is wrong.

The three of them together are either planning something incredibly thoughtful or incredibly stupid.

Both options are equally likely.

I'm washing my hands after cleaning up when they all nod, stand together, and surround me.

I dry my hands, then turn around. "Is this an intervention or something?"

"Date night," Santiago answers with a smirk.

I grin, excitedly. "Riding again?"

Levi tilts his head from side to side. "Not quite."

I lift a single brow. "Where are we going?"

Instead of answering my question, Walker suggests, "You're going to want to wear all black."

My lips pull down into a frown. "Why?"

Walker hands me a bundle of black fabric that I didn't notice he was holding. "Black clothes help you blend in when it's dark."

I narrow my eyes. "Are we doing something illegal?"

They exchange a look and bust up laughing.

My eyes bounce between them as I smile uneasily. "But seriously. Are we?"

They still don't answer. Instead, they chose to guide me to the bathroom and tell me to get dressed. I do as they ask, dressing in a black long-sleeve thermal, black leggings, thick black wool socks, and black combat boots.

What is this? Military training?

When I exit the bathroom, they've changed into all black outfits as well.

Santiago looks around at all of us and beams. "I feel like we need to get some eye black to paint a line under our eyes to complete the look."

"I'm willing," Levi says, raising his hand.

"I'm not," Walker returns with a glare.

"I'll do it if you tell me where we're going," I negotiate.

Walker looks relieved. "Two versus two. No eye black."

"You'll both do it anyway," Santiago says confidently.

Santiago ends up being right. In the car on the way to the undisclosed location, he wears Walker and me down into putting on the eye black, which Santiago had in his pocket the whole time.

When we turn down a road I've avoided for twenty-three years, my chest tightens.

They wouldn't take me there. It's not exactly a date night location.

But then we take a right turn into the parking lot. My palms grow clammy, and my pulse races.

Levi parks his truck and shuts off the engine. Santiago and

Levi turn in their seats to look at me. Walker's hand moves across the back seat and grasps my own.

My eyes stare out the windshield toward the field, sparse with trees. "I don't want to be here," I whisper. "I don't want to see him."

Walker squeezes my hand. "You don't have to."

I can't do this. I don't want to.

But why did they bring me here? What's the point?

He does not control me. I am stronger now.

I repeat the mantra until my muscles allow me to move. Slowly, I climb out of the cab and move to the front of the car. The guys meet me there.

Levi and Santiago each grab one of my hands, while Walker stands behind me. They don't move a muscle until I lift my foot to step forward, and we make our way across Evergreen Falls Cemetery.

Old snow crunches beneath our boots. Bare cottonwoods stand watch over the dead, their skeletal branches creaking whenever the wind stirs. Dozens of footprints from loved ones who have been here recently are scattered among the granite headstones. The lettering on many of the headstones is softened beneath caps of snow, their families and friends not having visited in some time. The cold settles deep in my lungs with each breath.

The farther we walk, the quieter the world becomes. Even the wind seems to die. Every footstep in the snow feels too loud.

Too final.

Like the dead are listening.

I don't need anyone to tell me which grave we're headed to. My body remembers the way, even though I haven't been here since I was seven years old.

The headstone we stop at is a polished black granite. Dirt and snow cover part of his name. I reach forward and brush it away.

Landon Kurt Jennings.

Loving husband and father

A bitter laugh catches in my throat.

Loving.

That's one way to write history—with lies.

Shaking my head, I fold my arms, and my voice turns bitter with venom. "Is this some kind of fucked up way of making me move on? Am I supposed to sit here and tell him I forgive him?"

"Is that what you want to do?" Levi asks.

I can't stop staring at the words.

Loving husband and father.

What bullshit.

"Hell fucking no," I bark.

"What do you want to say?" Santiago questions.

I clench my jaw. "Nothing."

"Then don't." Walker grasps my wrist, forcing a wooden handle into my hand.

Turning to my guys, I grip the handle with both hands and hold it between us. "What am I supposed to do with this?"

"Whatever the hell you want." Walker tips his head in indication.

Hesitantly, I face the headstone again. My grip tightens around the sledgehammer.

Whatever the hell I want.

I know what I want. I want him gone for good.

Loving husband and father.

Wielding the tool like a baseball bat, I lift it over my shoulder and swing it in an arc to the side. When the end makes contact with the granite, a tremor vibrates up my arms, and a small chip falls to the ground.

That's it.

One tiny piece.

He took everything from me, and all I get is a little sliver?

Loving husband and father.

With a roar I didn't know I possessed inside me, I lift the sledgehammer again and use all my muscles to bring it above my head and slam it down.

Loving husband and father.

I can't stop until those words are gone, erased from existence.

I swing again.

And again.

And again.

"You touched me!"

CRACK!

"You took my childhood from me!"

CRACK!

"You hurt me!"

CRACK!

"I hate you!"

CRASH!

Unable to lift the sledgehammer anymore, the handle falls from my grasp with a thud. My breaths are fast and shallow, fatigued from labor.

The headstone lies before me in pieces.

I drop to my knees, my last words to my father thick in my throat.

"You don't get to exist in my world anymore, Landon Jennings. I won't let you or your memory haunt me anymore."

I don't realize tears are streaming down my face until the wind chills the streaks.

My shoulders shake. Not from the cold, but from the sobs wracking my soul.

I cry for the little girl who didn't know any better.

For the girl who thought she was tainted.

Walker kneels behind me and kisses the top of my head, encircling me in his arms. "You did good, Baby Girl. You did good."

Levi kneels on my right, wiping my tears. "He's gone, Butterfly. He doesn't get to take up space in your life anymore."

Santiago takes the spot on my left and brushes my hair out of my face. "*Estoy tan orgulloso de ti, mi* Cielo." *I'm so proud of you, my Sky.*

I close my eyes and let myself lean into them.

For years, I believed healing meant forgetting—that one day

I'd wake up and the thought of Landon simply wouldn't hurt anymore.

I was wrong.

Healing isn't pretending the past never happened. It's refusing to let it decide who I become.

The little girl buried beneath years of fear isn't forgotten tonight.

But she finally doesn't feel alone.

Snow settles over the shattered pieces of granite, slowly covering the lie carved into the stone.

Somehow, it feels less like an ending and more like the first page of the rest of my life.

CHAPTER 49

BLAKE

For the last week, I've barely seen daylight. Apparently, grief and oil paint make excellent roommates.

Every morning, I disappear into my studio, and every evening, one of the guys has to practically drag me away from my paints.

Somewhere between canvas number eight and canvas number twelve, my heart finally unclenched.

So tonight I think I'm done hiding.

The construction crew has already gone home. I'm no expert, but it looks as if they're almost done. A few more days, and things can go back to normal around here.

Inside Santiago's house, everyone has settled into their nightly rhythm. Bear is with Shadow as usual. Walker occupies the couch, paperwork spread out across his lap and the coffee table. Levi leans back in a recliner, reading a veterinary journal that he swears is interesting. Santiago stands in the kitchen making hot chocolate because, apparently, coffee isn't an acceptable beverage after eight o'clock.

I stroll inside and sit down on the arm of the couch. "Any plans tonight?" I ask.

"Paperwork," Walker answers, lifting one of the stacks.

Levi keeps his eyes on the article. "Reading."

Santiago enters the living room, a steaming mug in hand. "Got something in mind?"

"What do we say to a friendly game of poker?" I glance around, gauging reactions.

Walker drops the paper he was reading and gives me a look. "Baby Girl, you don't have a poker face."

I sit up straight. "Says who?"

"We'd all be able to read you like an open book with big, bold text," Levi answers, his nose still in the journal.

I doubt that.

"Can we at least give it a try?"

Santiago gives a look like he thinks I'm up to something. He sits down in the other chair and sips his hot cocoa. "What're we betting with?"

"Money?" I suggest.

Santiago shakes his head. "Been there, done that."

I shrug a shoulder. "Kisses?"

Levi quirks a brow. "Walk doesn't go this way."

I raise my brows. "Sexual favors."

"Again." Levi gestures to himself, reiterating his previous statement.

"We could make it interesting," I smirk.

Santiago narrows his eyes. "Interesting how?"

"Bull poker." I cross my arms like it's the best idea in the world.

Walker's response is immediate. "Hell no."

"No hay forma que te acerques a un toro." There's no way I'm ever letting you near a bull.

Levi finally drops what he's reading. "When pigs fly, Butterfly."

Walker frowns. "How do you even know what bull poker is?"

Sitting forward, I enunciate each word. "I grew up here." I roll my eyes. "Do I need to tattoo it on my face?"

Levi sits up, kicking the footrest down. "Don't tell me you've played before."

"Maybe." My eyes dart to the floor, and I twist my hands in my lap.

"What!" Walker jumps to his feet like he's going to find who I played bull poker with and punch them in the face.

Santiago's jaw drops.

"Blake Jennings," Levi says my name in a disciplinary voice.

"Oh, come on," I beg. "Please." I press my palms together in a silent plea.

"Hell no." Walker imitates how I enunciated earlier. "Do *I* need to tattoo it on *my* face?"

I've been a recluse for a week. I'm not keen on having a quiet night. I don't need to party like a college kid, but I need out. And since they're not going to allow me to go somewhere by myself...

I cross my arms. "I'll do it whether you play me or not."

"Over our dead fucking bodies," Santiago claims for all of them.

I squint. "I don't like that visual."

Levi tilts his head toward me. "Then don't play bull poker."

My brows knit together as I think of a way to bribe them. "How about this: winner gets to take me to bed."

"Always down for that. Don't need to play bull poker to get me into bed, *mi Cielo*."

"Alone," I add.

That gets Santiago and Levi's attention.

Santiago rests his chin on his fist. "Tell me more."

Walker's tone turns threatening. "Don't egg her on."

"I'll do anything the winner wants." I smile coyly.

Levi's brows shoot up. "Anything?"

"Anything," I confirm. "Let your fantasy go wild."

Santiago sports a lopsided grin. "It can get pretty wild."

"Then take me for a wild ride," I challenge.

Santiago rises to his feet and rubs his hands together. "Okay, I'm in."

"Me too." Levi stands as well.

Walker glares at them. "You two are no better than a desperate teenager."

Santiago scoffs. "You say that like it'll make me change my mind."

"Fuck." Walker drags his hand down his face. "I'm coming." He points an accusatory finger at each of us. "Only to make sure none of you get hurt."

"We won't. I'm a pro," I beam.

Walker squints at me. "That doesn't make me feel any better."

Levi gets a folding table and four chairs from Santiago's garage. Santiago gets Javier to help him get the bull into the chute.

A few of the wranglers hear the words "bull poker" and want to join. Walker snaps at all of them in a rage. Not because of the danger, but because of the prize.

Todd and Sam watch, resting their arms against the top of the corral fence. Javier waits for our cue to open the latch of the squeeze chute.

I sit with my back to the bull. On my left, Levi bounces his knee, chewing on his lip. On the other side of the table, Santiago shakes his head with wide eyes. On my right, Walker sits with crossed arms and a tight, grim mouth.

The night has settled over Falling Sky like a heavy quilt. The sea of stars stretches endlessly overhead. Silver light from the moon spills across the round pen.

My breath drifts in white clouds every time I laugh. The cold nips at my skin, but I've readjusted to the Wyoming winter. It's familiar now rather than miserable.

"I haven't done this since my twenties," Levi admits.

"Me too," Santiago adds with a humorless laugh.

"I can't believe you talked them into this." Walker huffs.

"You're sitting here too," I point out, then hold up the bottle of gin I swiped from Santiago's liquor cabinet. "Liquid courage, anyone?"

Levi lets out a nervous breath. "What the hell. Yeah, pass it over."

"We seem to be accumulating an audience." Walker nods to the fence.

We all turn and find that Jack and Brandon have joined the other two.

Levi passes the bottle to Santiago. "The guys want to see their fearless leader in action."

"I'm not feeling very fearless right now." Santiago takes a large gulp, handing the bottle to Walker.

"Need me to hold your hand?" I tease.

Walker glares, passing the bottle to me without taking a sip. "You're enjoying this way too much."

"I told you." I hold the bottle up like I'm giving a toast. "I'm a pro." The gin goes down my throat with a burn.

"Fuck, this is crazy, *mi Cielo*."

"We're here for a fun time, not a long time, boys," I shout, adrenaline rushing through my veins.

The wranglers hoop and holler at my cheer.

"I'd prefer my fun time to last longer than forty-five years," Levi mutters.

Walker cracks a small smile. "You're a wild one, Blake Jennings."

"Damn straight." I nod.

Santiago leans across the table. "Don't judge me if I run."

"Never," I assure him with a wink.

"If we run, you have to run too," Walker demands.

"No promises." I shoot him a mischievous smirk.

Walker narrows his eyes. "This is for your safety."

I taunt him with a quick raise of my brows.

"Cowboys ready?" Javier shouts.

"Excuse me!" I wave my hand in the air.

"And cowgirl," Javier amends.

"Let him rip," I shout.

The clink of metal meets my ears as the bull bellows angrily. That's my cue to remain as still as possible.

"Shit," Levi curses before the bull makes it into the round pen. "Blake, run with me."

"I'm comfortable right where I am."

"Dammit!" Levi shouts and takes off for the fence.

The bull enters the pen and lets out a ferocious roar.

"Oh, fuck no." Santiago is the next to leave.

The bull charges the perimeter of the fence, forcing the ranch hands to back away.

I wink in Walker's direction. "It's you and me."

Walker looks like he's holding his breath.

The bull's stomps get closer.

Walker's eyes move between me and the bull and back.

My pulse roars louder than the bull.

Walker gives me one last look, pleading.

"No," I mouth.

Walker jumps to his feet and runs faster than I thought possible. The bull charges for Walker, and my heart pounds in my chest.

The bull runs right through the table, sending it flying over my head.

I hold myself perfectly still.

Walker gets himself over the fence just as the bull comes up behind him, barely missing Walker and hitting the fence instead.

The wranglers cheer boisterously as the bull runs the fence again. I hear a creak of metal, hooves pounding against the compact dirt, then a click.

Daring to turn, I find that the bull exited through the gate, and Javier closed it behind him.

I can't believe I just did that.

The elation of victory has me rising to my feet, throwing my fists in the air, and joining the others in cheering.

"The queen reigns supreme!" Javier shouts.

I stand on my chair, face my guys, and take a bow. I'm not sure if they want to strangle me or kiss me.

The line between love and hate is thin, right?

Hopping down, I join them on the other side of the fence. Javier ropes the wranglers into helping him get the bull put away.

"Since I'm the clear winner," I start, "I choose me and my trusty B-O-B." I don't wait for their reply and march toward the house.

Levi hollers after me. "B-O-B?"

I stop for a moment and wink at them over my shoulder. "Battery-operated boyfriend."

Walker's chest puffs up in annoyance. Levi's jaw drops. Santiago looks all the more intrigued.

I widen my stride and quicken my pace.

"Blake." Walker's voice holds a note of warning.

I wave my hand in the air. "Enjoy the couch!"

"Blake!"

I break into a run as their footsteps thunder behind me.

I'm in the house and up the stairs before everyone else. As I reach Santiago's door, I spin on my heel and catch a glimpse of the guys reaching the top of the stairs.

"Don't you dare, Blake!" Walker bellows.

I smirk, slam the door, and turn the lock.

Three thuds bang on the other side of the door, and I laugh.

Retreating into the closet, I pull out the box Savannah sent me last week. She told me it would come in handy. I thought she was talking crazy, but now, it seems she was right.

I pull the teal toy and lube from the box, prancing over to the bed. I strip off my clothes and settle into the middle of the mattress.

Shouts reverberate through the door from my men, begging and threatening me to open the door.

I spread the lube on all three pieces of the vibrator–the dick, the anal beads, and the clit stimulator. Pressing the power button, the toy comes to life, and my eyes widen

That's one intense toy.

"I can hear that thing through the door, Butterfly! Put it down!"

With a smirk, I slowly insert the toy one inch at a time, the vibration instantly curling my toes. I work the toy in and out of my channel as the stimulator overwhelms my clit.

"Oh God!" I shout.

The door crashes inward, wood splintering and shattering everywhere.

I gasp, my eyes widening as Levi, Santiago, and Walker prowl inside, but I don't stop the pleasure between my legs.

They surround the bed, their eyes glued to my pussy.

I'm not sure if they're angry, horny, or both.

But I can't make myself care when I'm on the brink of orgasm.

"You're in trouble, Baby Girl."

My moans and sighs almost drown out Walker's threat.

"I don't care," I reply breathlessly.

My pleasure coils tightly in my core, ready to spring at any moment.

"Blake," Santiago warns.

"I'm not stopping," I return and give them a show. I lift my hips higher, moan louder, and thrust harder.

"Shit," Levi groans, stripping off his clothes and climbing into the bed on my right. "Keeping going, Blake. You look so perfect."

I whimper, trying to stave off my climax.

Santiago is the next to cave. "Fuck this," he curses, discarding his clothes and crawling between my legs. He takes the front row seat, licking his lips. He drags his nose up my inner leg, not quite reaching the apex of my thighs. "You smell amazing."

"Dammit," Walker snaps, pacing the left side of the bed like a wild animal.

The vibrations of the dildo are too much and not enough at the same time.

Walker's nostrils flare like an angry bull. "You're going to pay for this," he growls, shedding his clothes as he gets into the bed last.

"You better come in the next ten seconds, because whether or not you're done, I'm fucking you hard and raw."

His threat doesn't scare me.

Especially not when he's threatening me with a good time.

But his fire, his need for me, sends me plummeting into an abyss of pleasure as I scream through my climax.

Before I'm done, the vibrator is swiped from my hand.

"Hey!" I protest.

Levi holds the toy in his hand, clicks it off, and throws it off the bed.

"That's expensive," I complain.

"I'll reimburse you," Levi answers, uncaring, his focus somewhere else.

The guys are ready to pounce, but I hold up my hand, stopping them.

"I won the game tonight, right?" I question rhetorically.

They nod.

"Then this is what I want," I start and point to Santiago. "I want you in pussy and Levi in your mouth."

Santiago's eyes bulge with eagerness.

I point to Levi. "I want you to play with my tits."

Levi licks his lips.

I point to Walker. "And I want you in my ass."

For a moment, Walker actually looks stunned. I didn't think he was even familiar with that emotion.

When I drop my hand, they all spring into motion.

Talk about eager.

"Maybe we need to play bull poker more often," I mumble.

The guys freeze and reply all at once.

"Absolutely not."

"Fuck that."

"Never again."

My smirk is full of sass. "We'll see."

"No we won't," Walker quips, hauling to the side of the bed.

Santiago lies on his back, Levi stands next to Santiago's head, and Walker kneels between Santiago's legs.

Yeah, Eager.

Walker lifts me up, setting me down on top of Santiago, who immediately brings me in for a kiss.

His tongue distracts me from the movements around me. I don't even care what they're doing, as long as Santiago's tongue keeps moving with mine.

Hands maneuver my hips, spearing me on Santiago's cock. The movement sends a jolt through my core, causing waves of aftershocks from my self-induced orgasm.

Santiago feels my inner muscles spasming, and he groans into my mouth.

Levi's hand reaches over, easily finding the stiff peak of my breast. "I want to suck on your tits every day, Butterfly." His voice rumbles as he speaks.

"Fuck me," Walker grits out, like it's taking every ounce of self-control not to rut into me.

Pulling my mouth from Santiago's, I peer behind my back toward Walker, whose eyes are trained on the spot where Satniago's dick slips inside my channel.

I tilt my hips, giving him a better view. The sound that vibrates through his chest is absolutely feral, and I wonder how I can make him do it again.

Walker's hand goes to his shaft, pumping himself. After a moment, I realize he's pumping in time with my and Santiago's thrusts.

I whimper, drawing his attention.

Slurping wet sounds have me turning back around and the sight in front of my face has my pussy clamping down on Santiago's length.

Levi's shaft glides in and out of Santiago's mouth. His hips move in a seductive rhythm that I want him to replicate on me later.

Santiago sucks like he can't get enough of Levi's cock.

I know the feeling. I can't get enough of these three.

A cold liquid drips onto my asshole, causing me to jolt. Walker's finger spreads the lube around my puckered hole, then I feel the tip of his digit dip in.

I cry out the sensation on the verge of shooting me over the edge.

He plunges his finger in and out in time with Santiago's cock hammering in and out of my heat.

I don't know how much time passes before I feel the blunt tip of Walker's cock pushing into my ass.

My responding scream scratches at my vocal chords.

"Too much. It's too much," I chant repeatedly.

"Relax for me, Baby Girl."

I nod, trying to do as he instructs, but I'm so overwhelmed.

After several thrusts, Walker's cock is fully seated in my ass.

I get one breath, that's all they give me, before they unleash themselves on my body. Thrusting, humping. Moving in and out of every hole. Levi's hand plucks and pinches my nipples.

It's not long before I feel my pussy clamp down on Santiago and my ass squeeze around Walker, and everyone's movements falter.

Our moans, cries, and shouts blend as I fall into an earth-shattering orgasm. Santiago and Walker continue pumping in and out of my holes, prolonging my high.

My entire body goes rigid before I finally come back down.

The room gradually quiets until the only sounds left are our uneven breaths. Strong arms gather me close, careful now, where moments ago, they'd been anything but gentle. Someone else brushes damp hair away from my face. Another presses a lingering kiss to my forehead.

I curl closer without thinking. No one lets me go.

Maybe that's what surprises me most.

Not that they wanted me. That they keep choosing me.

I smile to myself as sleep begins to pull me under.

I'm exactly where I belong.

CHAPTER 50

BLAKE

Silver Pines rises from the mountainside. A monument made of timber and stone, looking more like something plucked from Colorado than the little Wyoming town I remember. Snow clings to every roofline, smoke curls from massive stone chimneys, and strings of warm white light trace the covered walkways leading toward the entrance.

Hundreds of people mill around the plaza. Children zip through the crowd carrying helmets bigger than their heads while skiers click awkwardly across the packed snow in rental boots. Somewhere nearby, a group roasts chestnuts over an outdoor firepit, the sweet smell mingling with pine and woodsmoke.

The crowd gradually drifts toward the temporary stage erected in front of the resort's main entrance. Evergreen garlands wrap around the wooden railing, and an oversized red ribbon stretched across the stone walkway leading into the lodge. Newscasters murmur into microphones as their camera people jockey for a position.

Walker scans the people from our spot to the side of the stage. He's working security for the event, being the head of the police department. Levi and Santiago are here as well, along with Tessa and Ridge.

I got to tag along because I argued that this isn't a crime scene. It's a town event.

"Stay close," Walker demands.

"I *am* close."

He lifts a single brow. "You wandered off for a cinnamon roll ten minutes ago."

I roll my eyes. "I wandered less than five feet."

"You still wandered."

The unamused expression on my face doesn't sway him. Regardless, I slip my hand into the crook of his arm, which seems to satisfy him.

A burst of applause ripples through the crowd as a distinguished man in his early sixties steps onto the stage. His silver hair is neatly combed beneath a black Stetson, and his tailored charcoal coat looks far too expensive for Wyoming winters. He smiles with practiced ease, the kind that says he's spent years shaking hands and posing for photographs.

Neil Redford.

"Ladies and gentlemen," Neil begins, his voice booming through the speakers. "Thank you for joining us today."

The applause from the crowd dies down.

"For generations, Evergreen Falls has been a place people drove through on their way to a different destination. My hope is that Silver Pines gives folks a reason to stop, to stay, and to experience everything our little town has to offer."

The crowd erupts into applause again.

Neil continues his speech, talking about new jobs, local businesses, and other opportunities the resort will bring.

I glance toward Martha, who is standing with Gus near the front with a few other business owners, and she's positively glowing.

"So without further ado," Neil says, reaching the end of his speech. He accepts a pair of ceremonial scissors from one of the organizers. "Welcome to Silver Pines Mountain Resort."

The crowd cheers even louder than before as the scissors slice cleanly through the bright red ribbon.

Camera flashes burst like small fireworks. People surge forward toward the entrance, eager to be among the first inside.

Walker doesn't move, which means I don't move either. He watches the crowd instead.

The sea of winter coats bombards the plaza as people funnel through the open doors. Volunteers hand out trail maps while hotel employees welcome guests with steaming cups of hot chocolate.

Walker shifts beside me, his gaze sweeping methodically from face to face, disregarding the celebration.

His radio crackles on his shoulder.

"Walk."

Without taking his eyes off the crowd, he presses the button on the side. "Go ahead, Jo."

"We just got a tip of a suspicious man dressed in black."

Walker lets out a slow breath through his nose. "Clothing isn't suspicious, Jo."

"The caller said he smells like gasoline," Jolene continues. "He's carrying a large duffel bag around with him and was last seen heading inside."

Walker's posture changes subtly. Every muscle in his body goes rigid. His hand drops to the radio again. "Tessa. Ridge."

"Go ahead," Tessa answers immediately.

"Circle the south side of the lobby. Approach from opposite directions," Walker commands.

"Copy."

"Levi. Santi."

Levi's voice comes through the speaker. "We're here."

"Take the west corridor. Check the conference rooms and ski lockers."

"On it."

Walker finally looks at me. "You—"

"If you tell me to stay here, I'm going to scream," I warn.

His jaw flexes. "This isn't the time, Baby Girl."

I shoot him a glare. "If you didn't think it was safe, why'd you bring me?"

Walker raises his brows. "Because I couldn't leave you at home either."

I hate that he makes sense.

Walker studies me for a second, and I keep my face stern. When he comes to a decision, he lets out a harsh breath.

"Fine. Come on."

Victory.

"You stay right on my six."

"I can do that." I nod.

"Hand on my belt the entire time."

"Aye aye, captain," I say, giving him a salute.

His voice deepens. "I'm serious."

"So am I."

His expression says he doesn't believe me, but I'm not leaving him with much of a choice.

Walker turns toward the resort entrance, reaching back for my hand and placing it on his belt.

"Let's move."

Walker pushes through the revolving doors first, his hand hovering near the grip of his holstered gun. I do as he instructed, keeping my hand on his belt.

Warmth rushes over me as we step inside, carrying with it the scent of cedar, fresh coffee, and cinnamon. The soaring lobby, which looked so peaceful from the outside, is now packed shoulder to shoulder with tourists checking into the hotel and hauling skis toward the rental counter.

Chatter bounces off the vaulted ceiling, blending into a constant roar that makes it impossible to focus on any one voice.

If someone wanted to disappear, this would be the place to do it.

Walker moves us through the space as he checks everything.

The balcony, the staircase, people, hands, bags.

The radio comes alive again with Levi's voice. "West corridor clear."

Santiago next. "Conference rooms clear."

Ridge chimes in as well. "South entrance clear."

Walker answers without looking away from the crowd. "Keep moving."

The tension in Walker's body, the clipped instructions, and the procedural sweep has the seriousness of the situation settling into my bones.

My heart starts to pound.

Walker's breathing slows.

I don't know if his calm makes this all better or worse.

"Walk," Tessa radios in. "I have a possible visual."

"Location," Walker replies.

"Main lobby. North side. Standing beneath the chandelier."

Walker's hand reaches back for me, landing on my wrist as if he's making sure my grip is secure as he moves faster through the crowd.

"Converge on Tessa's location," Walker demands.

Everyone around us suddenly feels six feet tall. Puffy coats, wool hats, ski helmets all seem to be closing in on us.

I stretch onto my toes, trying to see above everyone's heads, but Walker's broad shoulders block my view.

Tessa gives the person's description. "Male approximately five-ten. Black jacket, gray beanie, carrying a large black duffel."

Walker's hand settles on his pistol, not yet drawing the weapon. He stops and takes a deep breath, speaking quietly into his radio. "Hold positions."

My stomach twists into knots.

The people around us continue on, laughing, sipping warm drinks, and excitedly waiting in line, completely oblivious to the potential danger.

I lean to the side, trying to get my own visual.

My eyes snag on Abbott.

I didn't know that he skis.

A tear rolls down his cheek as he blinks.

My lips purse as I attempt to understand what's wrong. He doesn't seem to be with anyone.

I follow Abbott's line of sight, turning my head.

Neil Redford stands a few feet away, shaking hands with guests and laughing.

Did Neil say something to him?

My head cocks to the side. "What the—"

A scream reverberates above the chatter.

"He has a gun!"

A deafening crack tears through the lobby.

Chaos ensues. People run in every direction. Glass shatters. Parents grab their children and run for cover. Furniture gets knocked around.

Walker whips around, shoving me behind a nearby stone pillar with one arm. "Stay down!"

Walker runs out of view.

"Tessa!"

"Drop the gun!"

"On your knees!"

I peek around the pillar to make sure Levi, Santiago, and Walker are okay.

Santiago shoves people so they're covered.

Another crack.

Walker sprints forward.

Levi tackles someone to the ground.

"Walk!"

My head turns toward the shout.

Tessa sits against a wall. One hand pressed to her abdomen.

My feet are moving before my brain catches up. "Tessa!"

I skid to a stop in front of her and drop to the ground. "Tessa, look at me."

Tessa's chest moves rapidly as she struggles for air. I move her hand so I can look at the damage.

A bullet is lodged in her bulletproof vest.

"It caught the plate," I inform her.

"I'm okay." Tessa winces. "Mostly."

Walker lands on his knees next to me. His hands are shaking. "Talk to me."

I'm not sure if he means Tessa or me, but I answer him anyway. "No blood. Her vest caught the bullet."

Walker lets out a breath, his shoulder relaxing.

Tessa coughs. "Damn, that hurt like a bitch."

A laugh bubbles up in my throat, and I'm unable to hold it in. Walker joins me, but when Tessa lets out a laugh, she flinches from the pain.

EMTs rush in, arriving quickly, having been on standby for the grand opening.

I move to make room, but Tessa catches my wrist. "Hey."

Turning back to her, I place my hand on hers.

"Take care of him."

My face scrunches in confusion, and Tessa nods to Walker, who is helping Santiago and Levi with the suspect.

"He acts tough." Tessa flashes me a painful grin. "He's not."

Tessa releases me, and I finally step back as the EMTs work on her.

Unsure of where to go, I awkwardly shift on my feet. I know my guys don't want me near the shooter, and the EMTs need space. It's not like there's a good place to sit, either.

I shuffle to the side and choose to hold up the wall.

The guys get the suspect cuffed and haul him to his feet.

My breath catches.

Abbott?

CHAPTER 51

LEVI

Violence is rarely as loud as people imagine. Movies make it seem like it's always rapid gunfire or swords clashing together.

Today, it was two gunshots.

But it's the screams that linger with me.

And when I saw Blake run to Tessa, I thought I was having a stroke.

The image returns to the front of my mind, and my chest tightens all over again.

Every few seconds, my eyes drift from the road in front of me to the passenger seat.

Blake stares out the window as her hands rest in her lap, fingers laced together so tightly her knuckles have turned white.

I don't think she realizes how tightly she's gripping.

The truck hums steadily beneath us as snowflakes drift through the headlights.

Usually, Blake fills every quiet moment with questions or observations, but she hasn't said a word since we left Silver Pines.

She's going to make herself bleed if she keeps chewing on her lip.

"Butterfly?"

"Hmm?" she returns, eyes still focused out the window.

"You with me?"

She answers with a small nod.

I'm not sure if she's lying to herself or me.

I reach across the center console, prying one of her hands from the other and lacing our fingers together. She squeezes my hand almost immediately.

Relief settles deep in my chest.

She's here.

Falling Sky comes into view. Porch lights cast warm pools of light across the snow, turning the house into a welcoming beacon against the shadowed mountains.

At the end of the driveway, Javier waits outside, Santiago having called ahead, while Bear rolls around in the snow.

I put my truck in park, hop out of the cab, and round the hood to the passenger side. Opening Blake's door, I offer her my hand to help her out.

She refuses my hand and jumps down by herself.

Javier strides toward us, his eyes studying Blake. Bear stops his frolicking and runs ahead of Javier. He sniffs her legs, checking to make sure she's okay.

Blake turns to Javier. "I'm okay."

"I wasn't asking," he replies and opens his arms.

She leans into him, melting into the embrace. Her shoulders finally relax for the first time since we left Silver Pines.

She needed this.

They release each other at the same time, and Javier looks at me.

"There was a shooting at the grand opening."

Javier's brows knit together.

"Tessa took one to the vest, but other than that, no one else was hurt."

He lets out a sharp exhale.

"We have the shooter in custody at the station."

Javier nods once, understanding why Santiago called.

"I'll keep an eye on her."

"I know," I confirm.

Blake crosses her arms, narrowing her eyes at me. "You're seriously going to leave me behind?"

"Blake."

She holds up her hand for me to stop. "Don't."

I sigh. "Walker and Santiago need my help."

Blake drops her hand. "I know." Her eyes fall to her boots. "I just don't want to sit here when I could be of help."

Stepping closer, I brush a strand of hair behind her ear. "This isn't because we don't trust you."

She snorts. "Could've fooled me."

A sad smile barely curves my mouth. "It's because we need to be sure that you're safe."

"You can be *my* babysitter," Javier interjects.

Blake and I slowly look toward him.

Javier shrugs. "I've been told I'm very easy to babysit."

Blake cracks a laugh, her smile taking over her face. When she stops, her attention returns to me. "Tell Santiago and Walker that you three owe me big time for this."

"I will happily pay on my knees," I say with a wink.

Blake playfully shoves my shoulder. "You're a shameless flirt, Levi Harding."

I kiss her forehead, then watch as Javier leads Blake inside with Bear following right behind them.

Every instinct tells me to stay and spend the rest of the night making tea, wrapping her in blankets, and convincing myself she's alright.

But Walker and Santiago need me.

And right now, I'm only going because Blake is breathing.

I arrive at the police station swiftly. The parking lot is overflowing with news station vans. Each news reporter and their cameramen mill about, waiting for the opportunity to pounce.

I park my truck in the back, avoiding the mob out front.

Inside, Ridge nods, acknowledging my arrival. Jolene sits at her desk, her eyes rimmed red from crying. She's probably worrying over Tessa, who is still at the hospital getting checked.

Walker and Santiago wait for me at the end of the hall that leads to the interrogation room.

Walker notices my presence first. "Blake okay?"

"Javier's with her," I answer.

Walker and Santiago nod.

I move to go down the hall to the observation room, but Walker steps in my way. "I want you in there."

My head pulls back an inch. "Why?"

Walker gives me a look. "You know him."

He has a point. I'm the person most likely to get Abbott to talk.

I'm still struggling to reconcile the fact that the man I worked with every day for the last several years is the same man who pulled out a rifle at Silver Pines today.

I nod in agreement, and Walker hands me a file and a few papers I may need. Then the three of us move together.

Before I enter the interrogation room, Santigo places a hand on my shoulder. "You got this."

I give him a half smile, grateful for his confidence in me.

When he drops his hand, I pull my shoulders back and open the door.

Abbott sits with both hands cuffed to the table, his jacket folded over the back of his chair. Without the coat and knit cap on, he somehow looks younger.

His hands shake, and his knee bounces rapidly under the table.

He's probably having an adrenaline crash.

Crossing the room, I sit down in the chair across from him and set the file on the table. Abbott's eyes are glued to the metal around his wrists. I wait another minute before I jump right in.

"Why?"

Abbot's gaze finally lifts.

"Did you know that Silver Pines destroyed the habitat of hundreds of prairie dogs?"

I keep my expression neutral. "Is that what this is about?"

Abbott continues with his own line of questioning. "Do you know what animal relies on prairie dogs as their main food source?"

My head tilts to the side. "Are you talking about the black-footed ferret?"

"Yes." Abbott nods as he makes a gesture with his hands like he's finally being heard.

I blink once. "So, you went to Silver Pines tonight in hopes of…what?"

Abbott's tone is factual. "Spreading the word. If more people knew, we could save the ferrets."

He's completely convinced by his own unreasonable logic.

"And you planned on doing that with a loaded gun and a can full of gasoline?"

Abbott's eyes move to the corner of the table. "You can't make an omelet without cracking some eggs."

There's the drop of doubt I can exploit.

"I need you to hear me loud and clear." Resting my arms on the cold table, I lean forward. "The moment you bring violence into your cause, your validity and your credibility go out the window. You could've made a difference, but you chose to kill two—"

Abbott's eyes widen. "Kill? I didn't kill anyone."

"Forgive me if I don't take you at your word." I shrug. "You brought a rifle to a public place and aimed it at Neil Redford in the middle of a crowd. You fired the gun twice."

Abbott's forehead wrinkles in confusion.

"And then there's Derek Holt and Reverend Ricks—"

Abbott's back straightens. "Oh, God. You think *I'm* the Debt Collector?"

If surprise could be manufactured, I'd never seen anyone fake it this well.

I angle my head toward him, lifting my brows. "You were carrying around the essentials of a serial killer."

Abbott shakes his head fervently. "I didn't do that. It wasn't me."

His face is different from earlier when he *thought* he was telling the truth. Now he almost seems scared.

An image arrives without warning.

Blood and skin in Bear's teeth.

"Have you been bitten by a dog recently?"

Abbott's mouth pulls down into a frown. "What does that have to do with anything?"

"Have you?" I repeat.

"No." Abbott's answer drags out, ending on a high note like he's confused by my question.

I open the file and hand him the top paper. "This is a search warrant."

"For what?" Abbott takes the paper and reads through the detailed wording. "You need to look at my body."

"I need to check you for a dog bite," I clarify.

Abbott sighs, dropping the warrant on the table. "If that's what will make you believe me, fine."

Walker comes in with keys for the handcuffs and remains in the room as Abbott removes his clothes. It doesn't take long to search his skin.

When I come up empty, a part of me is relieved while the other part is heavy with disappointment.

"Satisfied?" Abbott snaps.

"You can put your clothes back on," I inform him. "I'll be right back."

In the hall, I meet Walker and Santiago.

"Just because he doesn't have Bear's bite mark doesn't mean he's not the Debt Collector," Walker reasons.

"But it's a fairly strong fact that could rule him out," Santiago debates.

Walker's right. One missing bite mark didn't erase everything Abbott had done.

But Santiago's right as well.

The outline we'd been building around the Debt Collector suddenly had a hole in it.

And no matter how many times I tried, Abbott no longer fit inside the frame.

"Something's wrong," I mutter.

Walker glances over. "What?"

I lean against the wall and rub a hand over my jaw. "We each took a theory, but I think we need to focus on the one that says Blake's stalker and the Debt Collector are the same person."

Neither of them says anything, so I continue.

"Think about it," I press. "Every victim somehow circles back to Blake. Derek. Manny. Now, Neil Redford was almost shot at Silver Pines. Blake gets followed. Someone breaks into her motel room. Someone sets her car on fire."

Santiago's brow furrows.

I look between the two of them. "What if we've been looking at this all wrong?"

Walker slowly straightens. "You think we should've assumed that the stalker and the Debt Collector are the same person from the beginning."

"I think everything keeps leading back to Blake."

The hallway falls quiet.

Walker stares past us, his mind working. "If that's true," he says slowly, "then Blake was never caught in the middle."

"She was always the center of it," Santiago finishes.

Santiago pulls out his phone. "I'm going to call Javier. He needs to know what's going on."

I'm more determined than ever to solve this, to find the person behind everything and put him in the ground.

Permanently.

CHAPTER 52

BLAKE

The logical side of my brain understands why they left me here.

There is absolutely no reason for me to be involved.

Unfortunately, the logical side isn't as loud as the other side. The louder side is pissed as hell, pacing the living room, and threatening mutiny.

The house feels too large when everyone else is gone. A fire crackles in the living room. A clock ticks somewhere behind me. Bear follows each lap I make past the windows, his nails clicking against the hardwood like he's counting how long it takes me to lose my mind.

Javier sits on the couch in the living room reading Levi's veterinary journal as if the entire world hasn't gone sideways. Every few minutes, I glance at him, hoping he'll suddenly be as antsy as I am and want to do something else.

He doesn't.

Apparently, Levi's academic journal on veterinary practices really is interesting like he claims.

"You're wearing a path in the floor."

I stop in my path. "Then at least he'll develop a hobby. Renovations."

Whipping out my phone, I tap on the most recently added contact and move to another room. It only rings a few times before the other end picks up.

"Hello," Ángel answers.

"Got room for company?"

Ángel answers immediately. "Always."

Bear grumbles at me as he watches me pace along the back window in the kitchen. "Plus one judgmental dog."

"The boys leave you behind?" Ángel assumes correctly.

"They left me under Javier's supervision like a suspicious package."

"I can hear you," Javier hollers.

I peer out the back window. "I'm going crazy in this house."

"I'll pull out the bourbon."

My shoulders relax at his answer.

"My kind of guy," I return, the smile on my face evident in my tone. "I'm coming on Shadow."

"I'll also get the stable ready."

"Thanks, Ángel."

"Any time, my dear."

I lower my phone and find Javier watching me over the top of Levi's journal.

"Ángel invited us over."

Javier doesn't look up from the journal. "Did he invite me?"

"He invited Bear. I assume you're included by association."

Javier gives me a look. "I don't know if going is the best idea."

Shoving my hands on my hips, I glare. "I'm letting you know, not because I need permission, but because I'd rather not sneak out." I throw on my winter gear and march out to the barn.

I'm entering the barn when I hear "Not without me!"

The smell of fresh-cut pine still lingers inside the new barn, but the last of the construction crew packed up two days ago. The scaffolding is gone. The sawhorses have disappeared. Even the muddy tire tracks left by their trucks have been swallowed beneath fresh snow.

Horses shifted contentedly behind polished pine doors, hay rustled beneath steady jaws, and warm golden light spilled across the aisle.

For weeks, the fire has been all I can see when I step through these doors.

Burned beams. Smoke. Ash.

Now it's just a barn again, exactly as it should be.

By the time I have Shadow saddled and ready to go, Javier is waiting for me on top of his own horse.

"It's been a long time since I raced someone like that," Javier admits. "Better luck next time."

I give Javier a side eye at the way he rubs salt into my wounds. "Why does that feel like a taunt?"

"I've been living the vaquero life since before you were born. I want you to feel like this is your home because Santi and those boys already do, but I never want you to show me up."

"You really care about them, don't you?"

"I've been loyal to this family since before Santiago was born. But if something were to happen to you while you're on my watch, I won't live long enough to worry about losing my job."

Shadow's ears flick lazily as she picks her way along the familiar trail. Fresh snow muffles every hoofbeat until it sounds as though we're floating instead of riding.

Javier rides beside me, every so often pointing toward something I've never noticed before.

A hawk's nest tucked into a cottonwood. Deer tracks crossing the creek. An old branding post that's probably older than both of us combined.

Maybe I've been too busy surviving to really see Falling Sky.

Or maybe I'm finally starting to belong here.

Determined not to be a thorn in Javier's side, or at least no more than I already have been, I keep my mouth shut when the falling snow makes me shiver.

It's my own damn fault for not wearing a thicker jacket.

Instead, I force my gaze over the landscape. I may have spent my childhood in Evergreen Falls, but I feel as if I'm seeing it for the first time.

Another snowflake lands on Shadow's mane as a deafening crack interrupts the stillness. The sound echoes through the trees, bouncing off the mountains until it seems to come from everywhere at once.

Shadow shies violently beneath me, and Javier's gelding rears.

"Javier?"

He doesn't answer. Instead, he slowly folds over the saddle horn.

My heart lurches into my throat. "Javier?"

He slides from the saddle and disappears into the snow with a heavy thud.

"No."

I don't remember hitting the ground. One second, I'm on Shadow, then the next I'm on my knees beside Javier, my gloves instantly turning slick with blood. "No, no, no..."

My hands shake as I press against his shoulder. "Javi, look at me."

His eyelids flutter.

He's alive. Thank God.

I yank my phone from my pocket.

No service.

I search for the smart thing to do when another sound reaches me.

An engine—deep and growing louder.

Relief floods my chest so fast it hurts.

Someone heard the shot.

I stagger to my feet, waving both arms. "Help!"

Headlights weave through the trees before a dark pickup bursts onto the path, tires crunching through fresh snow. The driver's door flies open, and a figure hops out.

Grant.

My shoulders drop a fraction, beyond grateful to see another human being.

"Grant!" I cry, running toward him before pointing back toward Javier. "Someone shot him. I don't have cell service."

Grant looks past me toward Javier lying in the snow. His face remains strangely calm. Then he sighs. "I'm sorry, Jelly Bean." He meets my eyes. "We have to leave him."

I stare. "What?"

"We're leaving."

"No!" I shake my head furiously. "We can help him!"

Grant takes one slow step closer. His voice never rises. "Not going to happen."

"No." I shake my head so hard my braid slaps against my coat. "No, we can get him into your truck. We just need to—"

His hand grips my wrist like a vice, a twinge of pain shooting up my arm.

"Grant, you're hurting me." I try to yank away. "Let go," I grunt.

His touch feels wrong. Cold. Possessive.

Slowly, I look up at him. "Grant..."

His jaw tightens. "You did what I asked before, Jelly Bean."

Confusion washes over me. "What are you talking about?"

"I told you to come back to Evergreen Falls."

Is he...No, not Grant. No way.

His smile is heartbreakingly gentle. "I really hope you'll listen to me this time, too."

My world tilts. "No..." I yank my wrist free and stumble backward toward Javier. "No!"

Grant sighs. "I was trying to do this the easy way."

Every instinct I have screams.

Run.

I turn, barely making it two steps before something crashes into me from behind and knocks the air from my lungs.

Strong arms wrap around my waist, wrenching me off my feet.

I scream. "Stop!"

He doesn't respond. He simply hauls me backward as though I weigh nothing.

I kick and thrash. My boots connect with his shin, and my elbow slams into his ribs.

He grunts, but his hold doesn't loosen.

"Don't make this harder than it has to be."

"I hate you!"

"I know."

He opens the door to the backseat of the truck and tosses me inside.

Bear growls, sprinting forward and snapping his teeth at Grant.

When Bear gets close, Grant pulls a baseball bat out from the floor by my feet and swings.

"No!"

Tears stream down my face.

Bear falls to the snow, whimpering.

"Son of a bitch!" I shout and lunge for Grant, ready to make him bleed.

Before I can reach him, the door slams shut and the locks click.

My stomach drops.

No, no, no.

I scramble for the handle, but my hands grasp at air.

He ripped out the door handle.

When he hops into the driver's seat, I pounce, but Grant is ready for me. He grips my hands and tugs, pulling me over the center console. Grants grips my hair and slams my head down onto the dashboard.

Pain rips through my skull.

My vision blurs, an abyss creeping in from the edges.

Unable to keep my eyes open any longer, darkness becomes my world.

The last thing I hear is Grant whispering into my ear, "I'm sorry I had to do this, but you need to know the truth."

CHAPTER 53

WALKER

The fluorescent lights of the sheriff's office give way to the biting Wyoming cold as Levi and I step outside through the back door.

Santiago stands outside the employee entrance with both hands shoved into the pockets of his Carhartt jacket. The floodlights wash the color from his face, leaving him looking almost ghostly against the snow.

The second he sees us, he shakes his head. "It's bad out front."

He's right.

We couldn't go out the front door because that's where the reporters are, the ones who were covering the grand opening. I'm sure many of them think they just got their career-making story with what happened today.

Abbott sits in a holding cell inside. The ski resort has been evacuated. The crisis should be over.

Instead, it feels like it's only beginning.

Abbott isn't the Debt Collector, but he isn't innocent either.

The distinction matters.

One man acted out of desperation.

The other meticulously plans.

I feel like I'm back at square one.

Levi leans against the wall next to Santiago, staring off into the trees. I don't need to ask to know what he's thinking. Abbott has been his vet tech—his friend–for years. Then the man walks into Silver Pines Resort with a rifle. He's lucky the first shot missed Neil or else he'd be dealing with a whole other shit storm.

My phone vibrates in my pocket, and part of me wishes I could throw it into the snow and forget it ever existed.

But I can't.

I answer the call without greeting.

"Walk," Jolene clips. Her tone is all business.

"We've got another one."

Everything inside me goes still. "Where?"

"Maintenance crew found a body at Silver Pines."

Thankfully, Santiago's car is parked here in the back, so we get to bypass all the camera crews. Ridge stays behind at the station with Abbott since Tessa is still at the hospital.

We speed through the streets, racing toward the mountain that looms ahead, its lights still glowing against the night sky. Families should've been laughing inside the hotel tonight. Instead, the parking lot is flooded with red and blue emergency lights.

The grand opening banner still hangs over the entrance.

WELCOME TO SILVER PINES

It almost feels like a cruel joke now.

Tad gives me a rundown as he walks us down the hall, letting me know they put out the fire before it spread beyond the body.

The smell reaches us before the body does.

Gasoline and burned flesh.

Santiago pinches the bridge of his nose as we duck beneath the crime scene tape. "I don't think I'll ever get used to that smell."

I clap him once on the shoulder. "Nothing wrong with that."

He nods.

"Just don't contaminate my crime scene."

Santiago's face wrinkles up. "No promises."

The body sits in the chair behind the desk, looking as if he were working. I doubt he expected someone to walk through the door.

The nameplate on the edge of the desk is in pristine condition.

Neil Redford

"Well, there's no need to wait and figure out who this is," Levi comments.

I nod. "We need to photograph everything."

Santiago exits the room and jogs to his truck to get the items we need.

Levi examines the body closer.

"Is there anything in his mouth?" I ask.

Levi forces the jaw open and angles his head to get a better look. "Not that I can see. If the killer stuffed something in there, it's too far down. Dr. Adler will have to be the one to get it."

"Maybe the name tag is our only clue," I theorize.

"More like a flashing neon sign," Levi comments.

Santiago returns, loaded down with supplies. The shrill ring of his phone cuts through the oppressive silence of Neil's office.

He barely glances at the screen before answering. *"Hola, Papí."*

I snag a camera and begin photographing the scene while Levi continues to examine the body.

Behind me, Santiago's boots stop moving. "What?"

Something in his voice makes me lower the camera.

He's staring straight ahead, every muscle in his body rigid. "When did she leave?"

My stomach tightens.

Levi looks up from where he's crouched.

Santiago's complexion drains of color. "She should've been there by now." He listens for another few seconds before pinching the bridge of his nose. "I'll call you right back."

The office suddenly feels too small.

"What happened?" I ask.

Santiago lowers the phone slowly. "Blake called Dad about an hour ago." His voice is strained, almost disbelieving. "She said she was coming over."

My pulse quickens. "And?"

"He waited for her." Santiago swallows. "She never showed."

Levi is already reaching for his own phone before I can say another word. He hits Javier's contact, placing the call on speaker.

The line rings.

Once.

Twice.

Three times.

"Hi, you've reached Javier Nolasco. Sorry—"

Levi hangs up and calls again.

Same result.

A knot forms in my chest.

Santiago's skin is now ghostly pale. "Javi always answers."

I radio Jolene and let her know where we're going. She assures me that she'll get the scene handled. I don't know if that means she's sending Ridge or something else. But I don't have time to clarify with her.

I turn toward Santiago. "Call your dad back. Tell him we're on our way."

Santiago doesn't move. His eyes meet mine. There's fear in them.

Real fear.

"Walker..." Santiago stumbles, unable to find the words.

He doesn't have to.

I already know.

Something is terribly wrong.

CHAPTER 54

SANTIAGO

The tires spit gravel and snow as Walker drives my truck, tearing down the county road toward Falling Sky.

No one speaks. There isn't anything to say.

Every possible outcome runs through my head, and somehow every single one ends with Blake.

Hurt. Alone. Afraid.

I squeeze my phone so tightly my knuckles ache. Javier still hasn't answered a single call. He always answers.

"When exactly did she leave?" Walker questions.

"My dad said she called about an hour ago," I answer.

Levi's fist pounds on the back of my seat. "She should've been there twenty minutes after she left."

Pulling into Falling Sky, Walker doesn't bother stopping at the house.

Walker steers off the ranch road and onto the narrow trail leading toward my dad's place. Tree branches scrape against the sides of the truck, and every passing second feels like another punch to the gut.

I lean forward in my seat, straining to see through the darkness.

"Come on," I whisper.

My dad's pickup sits about two miles down, hazard lights blinking against the darkness. He kneels on the ground beside a dark lump, his shoulders rigid. A flashlight lies next to him, shining light across the ground.

Walker slams the truck into park.

I'm out before the tires stop rolling. "Dad!"

My boots sink into the snow as I sprint toward him. The beam of my dad's flashlight bounces wildly between two bodies.

Javier.

And Bear.

"Pressure, *hijo*!" he barks before I even reach him. "Take over. I need to check the dog." His voice is steady only because he's forcing it to be.

I drop to my knees beside Javier, replacing my father's blood-soaked hands with my own. Warm blood immediately seeps through my gloves.

My stomach twists.

There's too much.

Levi crashes down beside us, already digging through the trauma kit he'd grabbed from the truck.

"Keep pressure right there," he orders me.

Walker is speaking into his radio before his knees even hit the snow. "Jo, I have an adult male with a gunshot wound to the shoulder located approximately two miles south of Falling Sky Ranch. I need EMS asap."

Static crackles.

"Copy, Walk. Ambulance is en route."

My father crawls the short distance to Bear.

The pitbull lies on his side, chest rising in shallow, uneven breaths. One eye is swollen nearly shut, and blood mats the fur around his head.

"*Pobrecito*..." my dad whispers, running a trembling hand over Bear's neck. Bear stirs, trying to sit up. "Easy, *mijo*. Easy."

Bear lets out the faintest whine.

My dad closes his eyes for half a second, swallowing hard. "He's alive," he says, though I can't tell whether he's reassuring himself or us.

Levi switches over to Bear. "Head trauma," he mutters. "Probably cracked ribs, too."

"I know," Dad replies quietly, stroking Bear's head. "I know, good boy."

I can't stop staring at Javier. His face has gone almost as white as the snow beneath him.

"Javi."

He doesn't stir.

I squeeze harder against the wound. "Come on, *viejo*."

His eyelids flutter. "Santi..."

"I'm here," I assure him.

His gaze drifts past me, searching the darkness. "Blake?"

The question punches the air from my lungs. "We're going to find her."

His lips part again. "I—it was..."

The words come out no louder than a breath, then his eyes slip closed.

"No." Panic surges through me. "Javi."

Levi catches my wrist. "Don't shake him."

"I can't lose him." My words catch in my throat.

"You haven't." Levi's voice remains unnervingly calm. "He's unconscious."

Buck, Javier's horse, grazes several yards away, reins dragging through untouched snow. Shadow moves along beside him.

No Blake.

My father's voice breaks the silence. "They fought."

We all turn toward him as he points to the snow a few feet away. A splintered baseball bat lies half buried beneath fresh powder. Nearby, Bear's paw prints overlap with deep boot tracks.

Blood stains both.

Walker crouches, studying the ground. "Bear went after him."

"He tried to protect her," Dad says softly.

My chest tightens.

Walker slowly stands. "The cameras."

Levi looks up from where he's bandaging Bear's head. "What cameras?"

"The trail cameras we installed after someone followed Blake."

Hope flares inside me for the first time since Dad called.

Maybe whoever did this made a mistake.

"Ángel." Walker looks at my dad. "Stay with Javier until EMS gets here."

"I wasn't planning on going anywhere." Dad gives one firm nod. "Javier took care of us for most of his life. This is the least I can do."

Walker looks to Levi and me. "Come on."

Levi hands the trauma kit to my dad and hops to his feet, following Walker to my truck.

I squeeze Javier's hand one last time. "You hold on, *viejo*."

He doesn't answer. I don't know if he hears me.

I can only pray he does.

At the house, the front door slams against the wall as we rush inside. Walker heads straight for the office while Levi and I follow close behind. Walker wakes the computer and opens the security program.

My pulse pounds loud enough to drown out everything else.

The loading screen feels endless.

"Hurry," I mutter.

A lifetime passes before the feed from the first camera appears.

Walker clicks the recording for camera one.

A timestamp glows in the corner, and Blake rides past on Shadow with Javier right beside her on Buck. Bear bounds happily through the snow, weaving between the horses.

All normal.

Walker drags the timeline forward, switching to camera two, further down the trail. Nothing but snow, trees, wind, and silence.

A minute later—Headlights. A dark pickup eases into frame.

Every muscle in my body locks.

Walker pauses the video.

Levi leans forward. "Back it up."

The truck slowly rolls through the frame again. The windshield reflects too much light.

No license plate. No driver.

Walker lets the recording continue. The pickup disappears deeper into the ranch.

Nobody speaks.

Then the truck returns, driving back the way it came.

But it's faster this time.

Much faster.

Walker immediately opens the ranch map mounted beside the monitor. He compares it with the camera locations. His finger traces one of the service roads.

"It never hit camera three," he informs us.

Levi steps closer. "So it turned off."

Walker nods. "It had to."

He follows the road with his finger until it ends.

We know where the road dead ends.

My mouth clamps shut as my pulse speeds.

Walker's finger stops at the dead end. "The cabin."

Not just any cabin.

Our cabin.

The place we'd spent years dragging monsters so they never hurt another soul.

Walker's phone buzzes against the desk, and he answers. "Walker Maddox."

Jolene's voice crackles through the speaker. "The state lab just called."

Walker straightens. "Go ahead."

"The DNA from the cigarette butts and dog bite came back."

None of us utters a word.

Sweat forms a rivulet across my forehead.

"They matched," Jolene announces.

"And?" Walker prompts.

My hands tremble.

"It belongs to Grant Calloway."

The room goes deathly still.

Levi closes his eyes, gripping the edge of the desk so hard that his knuckles turn white.

I feel like someone punched straight through my chest.

Grant.

The texts, the bodies, the stalking. Everything. It was all Grant.

But why is he targeting Blake?

Walker lowers the phone with agonizing slowness. His jaw clenches so tightly I think he might crack a tooth. "He planned this."

Neither Levi nor I disagrees.

Because he had.

Every fire. Every crime scene. Every step had led us here.

Walker grabs the truck keys. "He's waiting for us."

Levi moves to the gun cabinet along the back wall, removing guns and ammunition. He tosses me a Smith & Wesson and Walker a Sig Sauer, then we each get a box of bullets. We load our magazines and pack extra just in case.

Levi pulls a pump-action shotgun for himself, loads the shells into the magazine tube, and pulls back the action with a metallic click. Resting the barrel on his shoulder, Levi stomps back to the front door to leave. "Let's not keep our old friend waiting."

CHAPTER 55

BLAKE

Pain arrives before consciousness. It throbs behind my forehead in slow, relentless pulses, each one sharper than the last. Something warm slides down my temple, slipping across my cheek before dripping onto my shoulder.

Blood.

My stomach rolls.

The last thing I remember is Grant's truck. His hand wrapped around the back of my neck.

Then darkness.

I force my eyes open. Firelight flickers across rough-hewn log walls, stretching long shadows across a wide plank floor. Somewhere nearby, wood pops inside a stone fireplace, filling the room with the scent of burning pine.

My vision swims. Nothing looks familiar.

Where am I?

My tongue tastes like copper, and my wrists ache. My spine lets out a small shiver, my coat gone.

When I try to move, metal digs into my skin. Confused, I twist as far as the cuffs will allow. Both wrists are locked together around a thick cedar support post in the middle of the room.

Panic claws its way into my throat. "No..."

The movement sends another wave of dizziness crashing over me. I squeeze my eyes shut until the room steadies again.

Across from me, boots scrape against the wooden floors. Someone stirs the fire.

Grant.

He crouches beside the hearth with his back to me, using an iron poker to shift burning logs deeper into the flames. Sparks swirl up the chimney while orange light dances across the shoulders of his heavy coat.

Without turning around, he says over his shoulder, "Morning, Jelly Bean."

A shiver runs through me.

His voice is so normal.

Like, we're meeting for lunch instead of...*here*.

I swallow hard.

Grant rises to his feet and faces me. His eyes linger on the blood running down the side of my face. "You hit your head pretty good."

I narrow my eyes. "You slammed it into the dashboard."

He shrugs. "You wouldn't stop fighting."

"Fuck you." My cheeks flame.

The corner of his mouth twitches. "There's the Blake I remember."

I tug uselessly against the handcuffs. The steel bites into my wrists.

"You know," I mutter, "this would've been a lot easier if you'd just asked me to coffee."

Grant laughs. Actually laughs. "I missed your sense of humor."

"I can't say the same." My lips draw taut into a thin line.

Grant's smile fades, looking over my face.

"Why me?"

Grant studies the fire for a long moment before answering. "Because none of this works without you."

"I wasn't even here." My voice cracks with frustration. "I moved away. I had a happy life."

He nods like my words don't have a valid point. "I know."

I lean toward him, the handcuffs burrowing into my wrists. "Then why drag me back?"

"You're the missing piece."

I frown. "What?"

Grant finally looks me in the eyes. "They would've kept their mouths shut forever."

"Who?"

He smiles. "The three idiots who are coming to save you."

My heartbeat slows as a chill works its way down my spine.

He's right.

Walker. Levi. Santiago.

Grant folds his hands together. "They'd have carried every single one of their secrets to the grave."

"What does that have to do with me?"

He looks directly at me. "You're the only person whose opinion they care about."

The realization lands like a stone in my stomach.

He never wanted me.

He wants...*Them.*

"What did you do?" I spit out.

"I think telling you what I *didn't* do would take less time." He laughs at his own joke like it's the funniest thing he's ever heard.

I angle my head. "The Evergreen Gazette?"

"Walker was taking too long to figure it out. Dragging his feet as always." Grant rolls his eyes and mumbles, "Lazy ass." He takes a deep breath. "I handed him the answer on a silver platter, and he still couldn't figure it out."

My lips part as I blink.

He really has planned it all out.

Something catches my eye. A length of black iron rests across the glowing logs. Not a poker exactly. One end disappears into the flames, and the other...

Ends in a symbol.

Even from where I'm sitting, I recognize the shape of the molten metal. FS for Falling Sky—the ranch brand.

Ice floods my veins. "What are you doing with that?"

Grant's gaze follows mine. "Oh." His smile widens. "You noticed."

He turns slowly, taking his time as he reaches for the iron. The metal glows a deep orange. I can feel the heat radiating from the bright orange end from where I sit.

Instinctively, I press my back harder against the cedar post. "Grant..."

He walks toward me. "You know..." His voice is almost thoughtful. "I spent years watching those three dole this out to people they decided deserved it."

He crouches in front of me, lifting the hem of my shirt.

"I figured it was only fair."

My breathing quickens. "Fair?"

"You've chosen their side."

Planting my feet on the floor, I push back into the column as hard as I can, but no matter how hard I try, I can't get away.

"Wh—what're you—"

Grant cuts me off. "You still don't get it. I gave those guys every opportunity to collect the debts that were due. They didn't take care of it, so I had to step in. Derek Holt, Reverend Ricks, Neil Redford. Each of those men was corrupt. Hypocrites."

He's the Debt Collector.

Grant's jaw tightens. "So now..." He glances at the glowing iron, holding it in front of his face. "You get to carry their mark."

He lowers the hot end to my stomach and presses in.

Every other discomfort I'm feeling right now fades into the background. My scream claws and scrapes at my throat on its way out.

The agony.

The familiar smell.

My eyes lock with Grant's. They're nothing short of pure glee.

When it pulls the brand away, the pain doesn't leave. Acid wells up inside me, threatening to come out. It takes everything in me to swallow it down.

My nose drips as tears run down my face unobstructed.

Grant returns the poker to the fire as the sound of car doors slamming echoes through the thin walls.

"Ah. Here comes the cavalry now. Right on time."

The front door crashes inward hard enough to rattle the windows. A blast of freezing mountain air rushes through the cabin, carrying snow and the smell of pine with it.

Three figures fill the doorway—Walker, Levi, Santiago.

They each have their guns trained on Grant.

For one impossible heartbeat, the world goes completely still.

They're here.

Relief hits me hard, stealing my breath, then dread takes its place just as quickly.

No.

My pulse spikes. "Don't..." I whisper before I can stop myself.

Every ounce of fear I've seen them hide over the past few weeks crashes across all three of their faces.

Levi goes pale. Santiago's shoulders sag with visible relief before stiffening again. Walker doesn't blink. His entire focus stays locked on me.

"Baby Girl."

My throat tightens. "I'm okay," I lie.

Grant laughs. "Your parents taught you better than that, Blake." He levels a sneer toward my guys. "No, she isn't."

He presses the muzzle of the pistol that I didn't realize he had against the side of my head.

All three men freeze.

"There we are," Grant says pleasantly. "Now I have everyone's attention."

Santiago's eyes drop to my exposed stomach first.

The hem of my shirt still hangs twisted above the fresh burn.

The angry red skin is already swelling around the unmistakable Falling Sky brand.

His expression changes instantly. "No..."

It's barely more than a breath before Levi's gaze follows. Every bit of color drains from his face.

Walker looks last. His jaw locks. His eyes go flat.

I've never seen Walker look like this.

Not angry. Worse.

Controlled. Lethal.

Grant notices. "I thought she'd earned it."

Santiago takes one step. Walker throws an arm across his chest without looking away from Grant. "Not yet."

Grant grins. "Good."

He wants them angry.

Grant reaches into his coat. For a terrifying second, I think he's reaching for another weapon. Instead, he pulls out an envelope.

He tosses it across the floor, and photographs scatter over the wide pine boards. My brows crease as I sit up to get a better look at the images.

Blood, bodies, Walker, Levi, Santiago.

They're standing in this very cabin.

My stomach knots.

Grant gestures toward them. "Go ahead. Tell her."

No one moves.

"I said," His smile widens. "Tell her." The gun pushes harder into my temple.

Walker slowly lowers his weapon a few inches. "They're real. How did you get these?"

Grant lifts his brow. "How do you think?"

Walker's eyes squint as he pieces the puzzle together. "You set the garage fires."

"Ding! Ding! Ding!" Grant chuckles, putting on a show. "By George, I think he's got it." Grant pulls back on the hammer of his gun, returning his aim to my face. "Now the pictures. Tell her." The excitement on his face sends a shiver down my spine.

Walker swallows, his gaze connects with mine. "We've killed more people than just your father."

The thoughts swirling in my mind crash against each other as the room waits for my reaction. Even Grant waits, a wide smile splitting his face in two.

I look at the photographs again.

Then at Walker.

Then Levi.

And finally, Santiago.

One question slips out. "Were they hurting people?"

Walker answers first. "Yes."

"Murder? Rape? Child predators?" I question further.

Levi nods, and I look at Santiago.

"They would've kept doing it?"

His voice is rough. "If we didn't stop them."

I flinch involuntarily. The thought of these people still roaming free makes me sick to my stomach.

But they're not.

Because of *them*.

"Thank you," I say with a dip of my head.

Grant's smile falls from his face. "What?"

I narrow my eyes at Grant. "I thanked them," I answer him condescendingly.

Spittle flies from Grant's mouth. "They're murderers!"

"They're protectors." I tighten my jaw.

"They lied to you!" Grant argues back.

I keep my voice even. "They protected people."

Grant waves his arms wildly. "They're monsters!"

My eyes turn cold and proud. "They're *mine*."

Grant actually takes a step backward. It seems nothing about this is going according to plan.

"Now it's your turn, Grant." Walker's voice stays remarkably calm. "Tell her."

Grant shakes his head. "No."

Levi's top lip pulls up on one side. "You brought us here for the truth."

Grant's eyes narrow.

"Tell her why we stopped talking to you." Walker doesn't move. "You owe her that."

Grant laughs bitterly. "I don't owe anybody a damn thing."

Walker's voice booms, reverberating off of the worn walls. "You owe the little girl you abandoned."

The words land like a slap.

Grant's face twists, and he loses control. "Fine!" He shoves the barrel of his pistol into my face. "You want the truth?" He laughs again. "I knew."

Everything inside me stills, and I turn my head to look at him, his gun now trained on my forehead. "Knew what?"

He shrugs. "When you were little, I walked in one night."

I stop breathing.

"I saw enough."

Walker closes his eyes. Santiago's nostrils flare out. Levi's eyes glow with a deadly fire.

Grant keeps going. "I needed Landon. We were buying land together." He points toward the window. "That stupid fucking resort?"

My stomach drops. "Silver Pines?"

"That was our idea." His breathing grows heavier. "Landon had the connections, the financing, the bank."

Walker quietly finishes the sentence. "And you decided Blake wasn't worth losing the deal."

Grant doesn't deny it. "You don't throw away millions of dollars because a kid gets hurt."

"Is that why you killed Neil?" Levi questions.

"Neil, the reverend, Derek." Grant holds out his arm, gesturing to the cabin. "Right in this very room."

Walker blinks. "The cleaner smell."

"Bingo!" Grant smiles widely. "Man, you're on a roll."

My mind is still stuck on his earlier statement.

A kid gets hurt.

The room disappears.

I don't hear anyone breathing anymore.

"You knew," I breathe out, my eyes trained on the way the flames dance in the fireplace.

Grant shrugs. "Yeah, and I looked the other way."

"You knew," I repeat in a deeper tone.

"It wasn't my business," Grant snaps back.

My vision blurs.

My fingers brush against my back pocket.

The tiny handcuff key.

Ever since Walker made it a habit of handcuffing me, I made it a habit to carry this around.

My pulse steadies as something inside my mind shifts irrevocably.

He knew.

He knew I was suffering. He knew my father was disgusting.

And he did *nothing*.

He watched me in my pain so he could turn a profit.

Grant keeps talking, still trying to justify himself and pretending he isn't every bit the monster Landon was.

I slip the key into the lock and turn.

Grant never hears the tiny *click*.

CHAPTER 56

BLAKE

The cuffs loosen around my wrists.

"You knew," I accuse again.

Grant scoffs. "I did what I had to do."

"You're pathetic." Levi's words drip with a concentrated dose of hate as he takes a step forward.

Grant's gun swings to Levi. "Don't move!"

Levi freezes.

Walker slowly lifts one hand. "Easy, Grant."

"No!" Grant screams, the composure he'd worn all evening finally shattering. "No more talking!"

His chest rises and falls in frantic bursts as he throws his hands in the air. "You ruined everything!"

Walker keeps his voice low. "You did that yourself."

"I was supposed to have that land!" Grant spits. "That resort should've been mine!"

"It cost you your soul," Santiago seethes.

Grant laughs. "My soul?" His finger tightens on the trigger. "You three don't get to lecture me about souls."

He looks at me and repeats, "They're murderers."

My face flushes with rage. "They're better men than you'll ever be."

My words slap him in the face, and his expression twists. "You stupid bitch."

He raises his gun, aiming it at my men.

My men.

Everything slows.

Walker doesn't flinch. Levi shifts his weight. Santiago's finger lands on the trigger.

None of them moves because no one wants to be the reason Grant pulls the trigger.

I do.

My hands slip free from the cuffs, and without thinking, I launch myself at Grant, my shoulder slamming into his side.

The gun discharges.

The deafening crack echoes through the cabin. Wood explodes from the log wall.

"Blake!"

Grant and I fall into a tangled heap.

Walker is on Grant instantly. Levi yanks me back and then crashes into the fray, trying to wrench the pistol free. Santiago grabs Grant's wrist, and the gun clatters to the floor.

The four men slam into the stone hearth. The branding iron clatters from the fireplace.

A burning log rolls across the old wooden floor, and the dry wood floor smokes.

Grant drives an elbow into Walker's jaw. Walker grunts, and Levi loses his grip. Grant tears free.

His boot kicks the burning log farther into the room. Flames race across the wood, licking at the wall.

The cabin groans as smoke curls toward the ceiling.

"Santi!" Walker barks. "The fire!"

Santiago reaches for the extinguisher mounted beside the fireplace.

Grant dives for his gun.

"No!" Walker tackles him again.

The pistol skids further across the floor, sliding right to my feet.

Grant and I see it at the same time.

We both move.

My fingers close around it first, and I rise to my feet, hands trembling so violently I can barely hold the weight.

Grant freezes.

The only sound is the roar of the growing fire.

Walker slowly circles around Grant, coming to my side. Levi and Santiago do the same.

"Baby Girl, give me the gun."

I shake my head adamantly.

"Blake..." Grant stares down the barrel, his voice softening. "I didn't mean—"

"Don't." The single word comes out steady—far steadier than I feel.

Levi inches closer to my side. "Butterfly, you don't have to do this."

"*Mi Cielo*." Santiago slowly reaches toward the gun, his voice calm. "Come here."

"I do." I take a steadying breath, calming myself in the eye of the storm.

"You knew what Landon was doing to me." My voice goes eerily calm. "And you chose money."

Grant takes one cautious step toward me. "You're not like them."

I tighten my grip.

Grant moves forward another step.

The fire snaps loudly behind him, and a beam overhead creaks.

"You're a good person."

A bitter laugh escapes me, and the ceiling groans again. "You're wrong."

Grant's face falls.

"I *chose* them, remember?" The smile on my lips isn't one of joy. It's filled with unadulterated retribution.

With the gun in one hand, I lift the hem of my shirt with the other. "And now I carry their mark."

Grant's eyes widen as he lunges for me.

My finger wraps around the trigger and squeezes.

The bullet tears through Grant's shoulder, pushing him backward, right under the collapsing loft.

A massive timber crashes between us, and the entire cabin quakes.

Fire explodes upward.

Grant's screams drift above the wildly dancing embers.

He reaches through the flames. "Help me!"

Instinctively, I want to help, but then I see a little girl curled beneath the blankets, staring up at her starry sky and praying that someone would open the bedroom door.

Grant coughs violently. "Please!"

Walker reaches me first. He gently takes the gun from my hands. "Blake."

I don't answer.

My eyes never leave Grant. I watch as his skin bubbles and burns, as he suffers from his own torture.

The flames climb higher, and Levi wraps an arm around my shoulders. "We have to go."

I don't argue. I simply turn and let him lead me away.

The cold air hits me like a slap. I collapse to my knees in the snow. Someone wraps a blanket around my shoulders. Someone else cups my face, checking the cut on my head.

Levi.

Walker kneels in front of me, his hands searching my wrists, my face, my shoulders as though he needs to convince himself I'm whole.

Santiago carefully lifts the edge of my shirt. His eyes land on the brand, and his throat works. "I'm so sorry, *mi Cielo*."

He presses the gentlest kiss imaginable just above the swollen, raw skin.

Sirens echo through the mountains. Red and blue lights dance across the snow. Firefighters rush past us toward the cabin. Deputies that I don't recognize fan out around the property.

Someone calls my name, and I look up.

Ángel.

His clothes are streaked with dried blood as he clutches Javier's hat in one hand.

Santiago is on his feet before Ángel reaches us. "How is he?"

Ángel's eyes fill.

"Bear's okay," Ángel informs.

Relief washes over all of us.

Ángel's gaze drops. "But..." His voice breaks. "Javier didn't make it."

I'm unable to sit up any longer. Walker catches me as I slump forward.

Santiago doesn't cry immediately. He simply stares as if he didn't understand the words.

Then his knees buckle.

Levi catches him, pressing his head to Santiago's. I watch as his lips move, offering whispers of love and comfort.

I force myself to my feet, only achieving the movement with Walker's help. Stepping forward, I wrap my arms around Santiago. He turns in my arms and folds against me as Walker holds our combined weight.

Santiago's shoulders shake, allowing himself to grieve.

The four of us stand together beneath the falling snow while the cabin burns behind us.

The fire consumes the entire structure—the roof, the walls, the secrets, the lies, the pictures.

Everything Grant built his life around turns to ash.

I rest my hand on the skin above the Falling Sky brand on my stomach. It still hurts. Maybe it always will.

But as Walker covers my hand with his, Levi takes my other, and Santiago leans his forehead against mine...

I realize that Grant was wrong.

He didn't mark me as belonging to Falling Sky.

I already belonged.

Not to the ranch or the symbol.

I belong to a family that chooses me.

And I choose them back.

EPILOGUE

BLAKE, FOUR MONTHS LATER

The first thing people notice is the mountains, not my paintings.

The gallery overlooks the Tetons, and every few minutes, someone drifts toward the floor-to-ceiling windows, distracted by snow-covered peaks glowing beneath the late-afternoon sun.

I don't mind, though. Some things deserve to steal the spotlight.

Jackson Hole feels different than New York ever did.

Slower. Quieter.

People linger instead of rushing. They study brushstrokes. Ask about color palettes. Wonder aloud what inspired one piece over another before reaching for the little red sticker that marks another painting as sold.

The gallery owner warned me that this collection would resonate with people. I didn't believe her. Now nearly every placard wears a tiny red dot.

Every painting hanging in this gallery costs me something. Some demanded sleepless nights. Others took months before I could bring myself to touch the canvas. A few required tears I didn't realize I was still carrying.

Every single one holds a piece of the woman I used to be.

None of them are about survival anymore. They're about what I survived—what I lived.

I wrap both hands around a glass flute of champagne, more for something to do than because I actually want to drink it.

It's strange. For years, I painted because I didn't know how to survive without it. Now I paint because I'm finally learning how to live.

A familiar laugh echoes through the gallery. I'd recognize it anywhere.

"Sav?"

I turn just as Savannah barrels into me, nearly sending champagne over both of us.

"There she is!" she squeals, wrapping me in one of her trademark bone-crushing hugs.

I laugh harder than I have in weeks. "You flew all the way to Wyoming?"

She pulls back, feigning offense. "Please. Like I'd miss my best friend's gallery showing."

My chest warms. Behind her stand three men I've only met in person a couple of times.

Hunter gives me a small nod. "We figured she'd be unbearable if we let her come alone."

Rory grins. "She was unbearable anyway."

"I heard that," Savannah shoots over her shoulder.

Luke steps forward with an easy smile. "Congratulations, Blake."

"Thank you."

Savannah loops her arm through mine and immediately starts turning slow circles in the middle of the gallery. "I swear every time I look at one of your paintings, I want to cry."

"That's because you cry during dog food commercials," Rory deadpans.

"I have a tender heart," Savannah defends.

Luke snorts. "You cried because Hunter trimmed his beard."

Savannah wrinkles her nose. "It was a difficult transition."

Hunter sighs dramatically. "I live with this."

I laugh until my stomach hurts.

I catch Walker across the room speaking with the gallery owner. He hasn't turned off his sheriff's instincts just because we're an hour away from Evergreen Falls. His gaze still sweeps the room every few seconds.

Some habits never die.

Levi stands beside the refreshment table, explaining the difference between oil and acrylic paint to a couple who only asked him where the restroom was. He'd somehow turned a thirty-second conversation into a lecture about pigment quality.

I smile behind my hand.

Across the room, Santiago laughs as one of the older patrons shamelessly flirts with him.

He notices me watching and winks.

I shake my head.

The past few months have settled into something that feels remarkably ordinary. The best kind of ordinary.

At one point, I started browsing apartment listings, but the search didn't last long.

Somewhere between Walker making me a house key, Levi filling the pantry with my favorite snacks, and Santiago expanding his closet to fit more clothes for me, the decision had apparently already been made.

I wasn't a guest anymore. I'd simply been the last person to realize it.

Life on the ranch kept moving. It had to.

Jack stepped into Javier's boots without anyone asking him to. Not because he wanted the title. Because someone had to make sure the horses were fed before sunrise. Someone had to mend fences. Someone had to keep teaching the younger wranglers the way Javier once taught him.

A few weeks later, they hired another wrangler to help carry the workload. No one replaced Javier. They simply learned how to carry what he'd left behind.

Silver Pines never closed. For a while, everyone thought it might. Neil Redford's death nearly buried the resort before it truly had the chance to open.

Instead, the town refused to let another greedy man's choices define its future. New management stepped in. The employees kept their jobs. The slopes stayed open. Tourists filled the lifts every weekend.

Martha complains constantly about how busy the diner has become. I've never seen her happier.

Bear recovered exactly as everyone predicted. Levi insists it was excellent veterinary care. Walker claims Bear is simply too stubborn to die. Santiago says he's spoiled.

They're all right.

Bear spends most mornings asleep beneath my easel, snoring loud enough to shake the floorboards of my studio, or playing with Shadow.

"Congratulations." The gallery owner appears beside me with another red sticker in her hand. "That's the last one."

I blink. "The last one?"

She smiles. "You sold every painting."

Emotion catches in my throat.

Every painting.

Well...

Almost every painting.

My eyes drift toward the far wall. One painting still hangs beneath its spotlight. It doesn't have a price. Never did.

The gallery owner follows my gaze. "I've had several people ask about that one."

"I know."

"They were disappointed."

"I know," I repeat.

She smiles knowingly before slipping away to greet another guest.

I cross the room. The painting isn't the largest in the collection or even the most technically impressive.

It's simple.

Javier rides beside me beneath a pale Wyoming sky, the first snow of winter dusting the trail ahead. Shadow stretches her neck toward Buck while Javier turns slightly in the saddle, one weathered hand lifted in the middle of explaining something I probably wasn't listening to. He's smiling—not because he's posing, but because he's laughing at something I'd said.

The mountains rise behind us. The trail disappears into the pines.

Looking at it doesn't remind me of the day we lost him. It reminds me of every ordinary day before that.

The lessons. The teasing. The quiet rides. The way he looked at me like I was already family before I believed I was.

A small brass plaque hangs beneath the frame.

NOT FOR SALE

"I thought somebody would've talked you into selling it."

I smile before I even turn around.

"No amount of money is worth that painting."

Santiago steps beside me, his arm slipping around my shoulders.

His eyes linger on Javier's smile. "He would've complained the whole time you painted him."

A laugh escapes me.

Walker slips an arm around my waist. "No doubt about it."

Levi takes my hand.

The four of us stand together in comfortable silence.

"You know," I whisper, studying the painting, "I used to think art was where I hid."

Walker kisses the top of my head.

"But it became where I healed."

Levi squeezes my hand. "And now?"

I smile. "Now," My gaze drifts from Javier to the three men

standing beside me, "now I get to paint a future instead of running from the past."

Outside, the Tetons stand unchanged beneath a brilliant blue sky. Inside, laughter fills the gallery. For years, I believed surviving was the best I could hope for.

I was wrong.

I found a family—a home.

And somewhere between the ashes and the snow...

I finally found myself.

THE END

If you're not ready to leave this world, the universe continues...

The Devils of New York is a complete, three-book series set in the same universe.

Crime. Obsession. Chosen family.

The books must be read in order

Start with book one here:

FRACTURED FEAR

Turn the page for a preview of
Fractured Fear Chapter 1

FRACTURED FEAR

The Devils of New York
Book 1

CHAPTER 1

SPENCER

Footsteps echo down the hall and I force myself to think fast. I open the closet, the bathroom door, and curtains. Hopefully it'll make them think I searched the room and moved on.

Praying I fit, I lay flat on my stomach and squeeze under the wooden bed frame. My ass barely makes the cut, but now I'm tucked away with my head at the foot of the bed. Laying my cheek against the carpet so I can see in the two inches of space between the bed skirt and the floor, I cover my mouth with my hand and attempt to slow my rapid breathing. It seems impossible, but I have to try or they'll hear me. If they find me, who knows what will happen next.

I don't want to find out.

A pair of brown leather Oxfords come into view and stroll into the bedroom. The shoes pace about the room and stop right in front of my eyes. "Spencer, dear. Come out, come out wherever you are."

My phone alarm goes off and I jolt upright in bed. I'm covered in sweat. Again.

Shaking off my nightmare, I glare at my alarm.

What idiot thought waking up at 5 a.m. to go to the gym was a good idea?

Yeah, that was me.

I knew I would fall back asleep if I left my phone next to me on my nightstand, like usual, so I set it on my dresser on the other side of my room. Even though it feels like I just fell in bed five minutes ago, I realize I need to start crawling to my phone across the room to turn my alarm off and get my ass in gear.

Damn, Yesterday Spencer. She outsmarted Today Spencer.

After I make my way across my room, I stumble into the attached bathroom and catch my morning glow in the mirror. More like morning disaster. Rat's nest for hair and dark circles under my eyes. Definitely looks like I got five minutes of sleep. Constantly waking up from nightmares throughout the night will do that to a person.

I wash my face, brush my teeth, and throw on a pair of leggings and a sports bra. Yesterday Spencer set out today's clothes, so I'll let her slide with the phone on the dresser stunt.

Shoes on and hair up, I'm ready to go, and I can't think of any more excuses to delay the start to my day.

I put my headphones in, press play on my running playlist, and head out the door. I lock up behind me because this is New York, not the Houston suburb where I'm from. You don't leave your front door unlocked here like Mom always did growing up.

I head down the stairs, out the shared door that's wedged between my studio, Clay Creations, and the coffee shop, The Mudhouse. Warm humid air blankets me with a comforting familiarity.

Bringing my ankle to my ass with my opposite hand, I allow myself only a few minutes to stretch. If I go any longer, I'll fall back asleep right here on the sidewalk. There's an unknown substance a few feet away that made an appearance last week and has yet to wash away in the two rainy days we've had since then, but I would still curl up on my side and catch some Z's on the pavement.

Done stretching, I start off with a jog.

I used to run when I was younger. I was pulled aside in gym class in seventh grade and the cross country coach tried to convince me to join the team. But I was never a competitive person. I'm still not. Competing would have taken the joy out of running and it did. Mom made me join the cross country team the next day.

Now I run for myself again. I run because I want to, but also because I have to. I never want to feel stuck and helpless like I did that night.

As *Lion* by Saint Mesa blasts through my headphones, I turn left a few blocks down onto Ninth Ave. I don't like to take the same route every morning. I like to keep things interesting.

More like I don't want to make it easy for some psycho to snatch me up, I'm cautious like that.

My first week in New York, three years ago, there was a woman kidnapped and killed just three streets over from where I live. Her name was Natalie Cabrera. She was just living her life carefree and happy, but it was stolen from her. She was only twenty-four years old.

So here I am, like a crazy person, running at 5:30 in the morning on my way to the gym. Just like I have done almost every day for the last two and a half years. I used to go at night, but my trainer told me that wasn't the best idea and that women are more likely to be abducted at night. Thus the masochistic ritual of early morning workouts began.

Adjusting to my new life was ... well, an adjustment. Busy sidewalks, jam-packed streets, pushy street peddlers, the smell of urine and decay, an alternating chorus of "get out of my way" and cat-calls being hurled in my direction every few minutes.

My mind wanders back to my first moments in New York, like the first time I was using the subway and someone asked me if I wanted to see snow. My social anxiety shoved me out of the driver's seat and responded, "No, thank you" to the man with greasy hair who reeked of cigarette smoke. I stared across to the other window the rest of the ride. I convinced myself that if I didn't make eye contact, he wouldn't ask me again. He didn't.

Then I went home and searched on the internet what "snow" could mean. Cocaine. It means cocaine.

There was another time when I decided to brave Times Square to go to the M&M store. I saw a man in a brown robe walk across the street. He then began to untie the knot at his waist, and I was too shocked to look away. It's like when you know a car accident is about to happen and no matter how much your mind screams at you to avert your gaze, you can't. That was me. Thankfully for the sake of my eyes and memory, an officer was right there and stopped the man before he could *disrobe* himself.

And then there was the time I decided to explore Chinatown. I wanted to see if the knock-off purses were actually as great as everyone says. Newsflash! They weren't. I was approached by strange men with Bluetooth earpieces on every corner, asking if I wanted to buy everything from Gucci to Prada. I said no every time. I wasn't going to be that girl that disappeared into a back room and never came out.

Running in the morning means less people out and about. Plus, there's something peaceful about being awake before everyone else when the sun is rising. Less noise, and no one to tell you that you didn't make his over easy eggs the way he likes. Just peace.

My mind wanders as I continue my run. Unfortunately, my mind has a mind of its own and goes down the path of last night's dreams. It's a scene that has played out many times in my mind. I lived it and my mind won't let me forget what happened the night before I left.

I wasn't supposed to see, and I wish I never did, but I can't take back what happened. I can wish on all the stars in the sky and not a damn thing will change.

I never should have agreed to go on that first date with him. I was only seventeen when I met my ex. He was twenty-seven. My mom was so excited when I bumped into him at my first art show. A gallery in town was accepting small artists' work and somehow a few of my pots and sculptures were chosen. He was charming and attentive, he asked thoughtful questions, and seemed genuinely interested in my work.

Just the thought of that night has me steaming with anger. Anger with him for lying. Anger with myself for falling for his act.

He knew exactly how to build me up only to tear me down himself a few hours later. He was an expert at it.

He broke me down lie by lie with each strategic word. Then he rebuilt me so many times that eventually there was nothing of me left. I was the doll he wanted, the perfect image of an obedient little servant, and I stayed through all of it. I never once tried to leave, I didn't even threaten it.

I shake my head to give myself a reset. I can't remain a passenger on this thought train, it'll send me into a panic. That's not something I want to do today. Instead, I focus on putting one foot in front of the other and lengthening my stride. I embrace the burn in my legs and the sting in my lungs. The pain brings me back to the present rather than letting me journey through my upsetting past.

As I arrive at Joey's Gym I try and fail to take deep breaths, relieved I don't have to battle my own brain anymore. This place has been a sanctuary since the first time I walked through the doors. As I walk inside, my mind is cleared of the fog that is always present after a nightmare.

Here no one looks down their nose at me. Here I am powerful. Here I am in control.

"You look like shit," a gravelly voice says to my right.

I look and see sweet old Joey standing behind the front desk. The white-haired man always says that. It's like his way of saying "Good morning, beautiful. Aren't you just a glorious ray of sunshine on this otherwise dreary morning?"

Ha. Yeah, the charming lightweight champion from 1979 would never let those words leave his mouth.

The first time I met him, he came off as harsh, but he quickly changed his tune.

"What do you want?" he asks gruffly when I approach the front desk. There's that New York charisma.

"Umm, I saw in the window that you offer self-defense classes." I say without looking him in the eye, keeping my gaze cemented on the floor.

"Hey." His voice grows soft.

I glance up and see that look in his eyes. Pity. I hate pity. I don't need to be pitied. "I just need classes," I say in an attempt to sound firm. "If you don't have any open spots. Just let me know and I'll be on my way." My tone gets stronger as I speak each word.

He returns to his brash self but still not as rough as when I walked in. "I got a spot for you. No need to get your panties in a twist."

And that was that. I signed up for classes and now he trains me one on one. Every morning he tells me I look like shit and I respond with…

"And you look like a shriveled up dick."

It's our way to check in with each other. If he ever greeted me differently, I'd be worried he finally lost his mind and succumbed to old age.

"Get some water and go stretch. You'll be no good if your muscles lock up ten seconds in."

I walk over to the dinged up fountain attached to the wall, take a sip then stretch on the mats. As much as I love to hit inanimate objects, stretching also calms my mind. I get to focus on breathing, holding my form and nothing else. There's no room for anything else in my brain when I feel the pull of my muscles.

Once I'm all stretched out and ready to go again, Joey sets a grueling pace. Burpees, jump rope, back squats, and leg lifts. He says we're not getting in the ring today because I went too hard yesterday, but we both know it's because he can see the shadows under my eyes, so today is just strength training. Weights mixed with cardio. Basically death.

He's never asked why I'm here and I've never told. But he knows. He knows when to push and when to back off. I've cried during workouts a few times. Usually after a terrible nightmare while I'm at the punching bag.

One day in particular was especially difficult. In my dreams, I had relived the worst part of my last night in Texas, and I couldn't shake my body's natural responses. Joey made me stop sparring when my tears blurred my vision and involuntary bursts of noise started to escape my throat. He pulled me into his office, sat me on the couch, and didn't say a word. I wailed from the agony I felt. Not only did my ex break my body that night, but he also broke my heart.

Joey sat next to me and pulled me into his arms as my tears puddled onto his shirt.

"It'll be okay. It's just for now. This pain isn't forever."

"But it hurts so bad." I expressed through the haze of relived trauma.

"I know, kid. I know." He didn't let go until the sobs had subsided. Then he called a cab and took me to The Mudhouse. When we got there, we sat for hours, conversing over cups of lukewarm coffee.

Not once did Joey ask what had happened or what I had been through, that's not him.

Now when those memories haunt me into the light of day, I go straight to the punching bag. As I pound the leather with my wrapped fists I imagine what I should have or could have done differently that night. I imagine punching *him* in the face. I imagine running sooner than I did.

I can't change it now, but I can prepare. I can train. I can continue to be stronger than the fear I'm fracturing one punch at a time.

ALSO BY IVY KING

The Devils of New York

Fractured Fear

Tainted Truth

Veiled Vengeance

Standalones

Dark Whispers

Silence in the Snow

Broken by the Covenant - releases 2026

ABOUT THE AUTHOR

Ivy King is a why-choose dark romance author who lives in the mountains of Idaho with her book husband, four wild kids, and cuddly pitbull. When Ivy isn't writing smut, you can find her tending to her emotional support houseplants, wrapped in a fluffy blanket and reading romance novels, doom scrolling on her phone, or watching true crime.

ACKNOWLEDGMENTS

My Soul Sisters,
You know who you are, and I want you to know that your love and kindness are healing me one interaction at a time. I love that we can talk about anything from motherhood to politics to tarot cards and astrology. You two are my rock and my safe space. I know I can always come to you with anything. I can't put into words how much I love you. XOXO

To the Fucker Who Put Me Through Hell,
I'm still not ready to talk about you. Even after writing this book, I still can't. Fuck you for that.

Made in the USA
Coppell, TX
27 July 2026

85085255R00256